FOREVER RED

A Novel in Three Parts

R. F. Cutler

ISBN: 1501073613
ISBN 13: 9781501073618
Library of Congress Control Number: 2014915983
CreateSpace Independent Publishing Platform
North Charleston, South Carolina

Dedication

This book is dedicated to my best friend, cheerleader, lover and wife Cindy. Always in my corner preparing me for the next round of knock downs.

I couldn't have completed this book without the expertise of Deb Handel and the encouragement of Dave and Lovera, Ben and Dar, Rex and Shari, Karen, Mike and daughter-in-law, Laura. You too Amanda Bowman Thanks guys!

My love to my boys, Thaddeus, Layton and my Savior Jesus Christ.

To all the Billie Magics out there that have captivated some young man's heart. Also my dear, late friend Jack. I'll never forget

R.F. Cutler

Disclaimer:

This book is fictitious. Every name in this story does not portray anyone living or dead.

Cover design and section divider design by Debra Handel

Handel-Design.com

PART ONE

FOREVER RED

PART ONE

THE DEATH

There he stood looking out at the New York skyline, his back to his three member staff. His black Armani suit cut to fit his body as perfectly as if it had been poured around him. His shoes were black and never seemed to have a scuff or a mark, like black stainless steel. From their seated vantage point he appeared to be a giant, but his six three frame did seem bigger than life. When he turned, the look on his face told them this was going to be bad. His lips were closed but the muscles in his jaw rippled as if chewing a piece of beef jerky. Nothing had been said for over a minute but seemed a lifetime to the three. His dark hair looked as though it was radiating the light streaming into the thirty-sixth floor large picture window. Wisps of grey around his ears gave him away as about forty. His white tie had one single red stripe circling the top like a candy cane, and holding it to his shirt was his gold tie bar embedded with diamonds. Before a word was uttered, both hands slid into his pockets as to see if he could pull something out that would make them feel even worse. His eyes appeared like blue steel as he removed his glasses. He squinted slightly like Superman intending to burn a hole in something with his laser vision.

"Where in the hell are your brains?" Richard yelled, not looking for an answer.

Richard V. Barr, Jr. was the CEO of Aurora Planning, LLC. His father in law, Robert Miller, was the founder and still came in the city for coffee and conversation with "the guys", a group of business owners all in their seventies and early eighties. Bob was not involved in the day to day operations, and trusted Richard to run the company as he saw fit. The office didn't see Bob around much these days.

Richard had no compassion for the hundreds of people he had fired or just eliminated their jobs. He was all about making money, and a lot of it! The last company he purchased was a family-owned business that made trash containers. The father and son business had been their pride and joy for the past forty-eight years, but they were in over their heads to the bank. Richard sent his team to sell off assets and fire sixty-three employees. They pleaded with Richard, but never returned their calls. A month later the son sent Richard an obituary and a nasty note about how his father had committed suicide. Yolanda, Richard's secretary, wanted to know if they should send flowers. Richard told her it wasn't necessary because he was old anyway. Richard had taken his company from $1.5 million to over $200 million in just twenty years. If a company could be purchased, Richard bought and dismantled it in the time it would take most people to ride the subway to the Cloisters.

"You guys really let me down! Richard said with conviction. We had them by the balls, and you let it slip away with not even a goodbye. What went wrong with the foreclosure we had it court?" Before one word was uttered, there was a knock at the door, it slowly opened. Richard's secretary was standing with a small piece of paper held tightly in her hands. "I told you never to interrupt me when I'm in here with these idiots!" he yelled.

She said, "I think maybe you should see this."

He just stood and looked at her with disgust. "Yolanda, you've worked with me for over ten years and you still don't get it." "Give it here!" He opened it, looked out the window, and said "Shit! All of you get out of my sight!"

As soon as they left the room collectively, his team wanted to know the contents. "Yolanda, what was the note?"

"His father died back in Indiana"

"We never heard him mention any family he had living in Indiana or even that he had a family."

"I've been here for ten years, and have never heard Indiana mentioned either," Yolanda said "I guess it isn't too important to him."

The door suddenly opened, "Yolanda, call Cal and have him bring the car around!" he yelled. Within ten minutes the black limo pulled to the back entrance of the Feinman Building and Cal jumped out to open the door.

"Where to Mr. Barr?" Cal asked.

"Run me home."

"Do you want to go by the club?"

"I said home, or doesn't that compute in your little brain?" The glass went up in the divider so all conversation ended as it always did. Cal looked in the rear mirror, and *thought how could all that money and looks end up in one person? It's just not right.*

***

Richard's first call was to Gas City, Indiana. "Mom, it's me. What happened to Dad?" he asked.

"Oh, honey, he has been under the weather but wouldn't go to Dr. Ben," she said. "Tim found him in the barn today next to the old milker. We rushed him to the hospital in Evansville, but they said he passed away about two hours before your brother found him. Dr. Ben said it was probably his heart and that he will sign the death certificate tomorrow. I called Sissy at the shop, but she just cried and hung up the phone. She is coming over in about an hour. Tim and Pamela Sue are here and Pastor Roger is coming over in the morning. Probably services Saturday at the church. It's just happening so fast. Can't really believe how today started. We've been married for over fifty-one years."

"But Mom, how are you?" Richard asked.

"Ricky, my mind is going in all directions and I love that you called right away," as his voice flooded her with so many memories. "You know he absolutely adored you."

"I know, Mom. I'll call Anne at her office and Eric's school as soon as I hang up."

"Shelby, Hofer and Friedman" the receptionist answered.

"I would like to speak to Anne Barr," Richard said abruptly.

"I'm sorry, but she is in Federal Court today. Would you like her voicemail?" The receptionist answered as if she had much more important things to do.

"No, I'll call her on her cell." he shot back.

"All phones are banned from court," she replied. He never let her finish before he clicked her off.

"Lincoln Àcademy, may I help you?" the operator said in a nice friendly voice.

"I would like to speak to the guidance office." Richard said.

"One moment please."

"Guidance office."

"This is Richard Barr. I would like speak to my son Eric!"

"I'm sorry, but his father called him in sick today"

"Who do you think I just said I was?" Richard said with disgust.

Long pause, "Oh."

Another quick hang up. This really did seem like a long drive home. As Cal pulled into the drive, Richard noticed a red Volvo parked next to the six car garage. "Cal, pull around back." He jumped from the car, and went into the kitchen. Beer bottles, an empty vodka bottle, ash trays with cigarettes, and roaches piled high. The basement door was ajar, and heavy metal music was banging away in the theater room. "Eric, I know you're down there, so come up!" Richard shouted with distrust.

"Ok, Ok. Just give me a minute," Eric said in a raspy voice

"I said now!" Richard went up the stairs and waited. After about ten minutes passed, Eric, Julie, Tony, and Kandy came stumbling up.

"Sorry, Mr. Barr." Julie said. The three left, with Eric looking like a contestant from a survival show.

"Go take a shower, I need your full attention!" Richard said rudely.

Eric's only comment was "Shit!"

Richard picked up what he could but ignored some nasty floor stains from God knows what, because the maid would be there in the morning to do her thing.

About two hours later Anne pulled into the drive in her yellow Porsche with the top down. Her short, light auburn hair circled her beautiful chiseled face. She looked as though she had just come from one of the islands, ready for a great dinner and relaxation. She pulled in the garage and grabbed her briefcase as she swung her long tan legs out of the low-riding car.

"What are you doing home so early, and what is that smell?" she asked.

"Let me get Eric and maybe we can find out what happened." Richard said, as she grabbed a wine glass from the marble island that sat in the middle of the kitchen. For not knowing, or even wanting to know how to cook, the kitchen was a chef's wet dream. It had the best of everything and much more. She poured her wine in the glass and noticed Richard had a Scotch and water in his hand.

"I didn't think you would be home so early either. Thought you might be banging that new law intern you've been talking about," he said sarcastically.

"Lucky for you he was sick today, or I'd be in his pants in a heartbeat"

"I don't give a damn what or to whom you do anything with."

"I feel the same, Honey. You're such a devoted husband and dedicated pipe layer to whoever needs your services." she said sharply

"Here comes the kid"

"You guys just bite me!" He yelled back. You both are a couple of losers and never give me any freedom or let me just chill with my friends. Most of my friends have their own space and unlimited time to just hang".

"What's this all about?" she asked.

"Apparently our POW here had some friends over and were engaging in some adult pleasures like beer, vodka, grass, and probably unprotected sex."

"Eric, is this true?"

"Like I said, you two are losers."

"For seventeen you sure have a lot of knowledge of this whole world and just where we seem to fit in." Richard said. "This will be the third school in three years and next year you can sign up for the Army. Won't that be fun? Since I have my loving family around me, I want to tell you both that my dad died today in Indiana, and the funeral will probably be Saturday. I'm leaving tomorrow and would like to have you go with me."

Eric said, "No way! I'm not going to Mayberry and see all the hillbillies that belong to our family. Count me out!"

"Rick, I have the forgery case in Federal Court in two weeks. I don't think I can go either, sorry."

"I'm going back to Indiana, no matter what," and went to his room to pack.

As he was filling his suitcase, his mind drifted back to his mom and dad. They had supported him in everything he had tried to do. His dad knew that Richard's heart was not the farm. His father helped him financially and his letters of encouragement came at a time when he really needed them. As he looked around his bedroom, he noticed there were no reminders of his former life. Indiana or Gas City were not to be found in anything he had, and he felt a little sad that he never kept anything from his past. It had been several years since he had been back and was looking forward to seeing his family. He hoped that someday Eric could meet his Indiana family and see that they weren't the hillbillies he imagined.

The Beauty Shop, Gas City, Indiana

The yellow and red sign never did hang quite straight. At least once a week someone would say, "It's just a little off."

Sarah Barr never took it personally anyway; she would just nod and say, "You're right." Sarah had just turned 40, and except for her flaming red hair, she was a not a "looker" to the guys. She was on the plump size and never wore much makeup except for an occasional wedding or the 4-H Banquet held in the fall. Her clothes were plain and drab but she usually wore a brightly colored smock in the shop. Her shop was in her home which stood at the corner of Elm and Indiana Streets. It was a modest yellow home with the beauty shop up front and living quarters in the back. She had a large basement where she kept all her beauty supplies and extra crafts she sold. Sarah's Charm and Chatter had a nice ring to it for a beauty shop, but everyone called her "Sissy." Her son, Todd lived with her and would bring her supplies as she needed them. He was 25 and mentally challenged but was her "right hand man." Everyone loved Todd and he loved them back. She became pregnant at 14 and everyone said it was Pastor Jones's son, Taylor, because they moved to another church soon after Sissy and Taylor had gone to the Gas City High School Prom together. She seemed content with her little shop and steady customers where she shared all the local gossip with the girls.

When the call came she was just finishing up Mrs. Gourley's hair, and the sobbing began. "Mom, I'll be over soon as my next appointment is done. I love you, goodbye." The really deep sick feeling started. While waiting for Libby Shepard, she went in the back and vomited twice. Only maybe one or two other times in her whole life had she felt like this, and it was years ago.

"Mom, wants the matter?" Todd asked.

"Grandpa died this morning"

"Wow, are going to have lunch at Grandma's house? I want pancakes!"

"We'll see. Here comes Mrs. Shepard. Go get me some more auburn tint honey."

"Ok Mom, coming right up" and down the basement he flew.

"Hi, Mrs. Shepard." Sissy said fighting back the tears.

"I heard about your Dad. Everyone has said what a wonderful man he was. Since we are new to town, we didn't really know your dad very well. I know he supported the church for many years and in many capacities. I think Roger is meeting with your mom shortly about services and a church dinner."

Sissy quickly changed the subject, "What about changing the color today with a nice auburn rinse?"

"That sounds good but not too much color. I like a subtle look."

Libby Shepard never wore a dress or skirt that was not above three to four inches from the floor. She wore no jewelry except for her wedding band but occasionally some red lipstick, and her husband preferred her bare arms not to show.

Sissy could see Todd watching a cowboy movie from her vantage point. He loved horses, cowboys, Indians, and his imaginary best friend, NeeNee. "Honey, turn it down a little. The shooting is too much for mom right now."

"Ok Mom," never looking up with his head still glued to the small flat screen.

"So, do you like our little town so far?"

"Very much. We really feel God's presence here. Pastor Roger and I came from Iowa with a desire to really build up the church. Your father and mother helped us move in, and your mother made us dinner for the first two weeks we were here. She is an amazing cook! We also would like to introduce some new music with drums and guitars for the morning worship service. We hired Pastor Ken as our worship leader and youth pastor; he is such a dedicated young man. He has a wonderful voice and now leads the choir. I'm also a member," she said with great pride.

"That sounds wonderful; maybe Todd and I will come back to church again. I was wounded by the church a long time ago, so I didn't feel that Todd or I would fit in. I do miss the singing. We are going to my mom's when we finish here to see if she needs anything. My brother Tim and his wife Pamela Sue live on the farm next to my parent's farm, and I know they will be a great support to her, Sissy said. My brother never left Gas City and he worked alongside my dad his whole life. I have another brother, Rick, who lives in New York City and is very successful. He never comes back here and rarely calls, but mom said he will come back for the funeral. It's probably been eight or nine years since he has been back, but it will be good to see him. Almost done. Let me just brush it through after I remove the towel, and you can be on your way."

"Oh, my gosh! What happened?" Mrs. Shepard shrieked.

"Looks like I put too much auburn in the rinse." Sissy said softly

"Auburn? It looks fire engine red!" he said sharply.

"It'll look softer if you wash it tonight with a small amount of vinegar."

Todd looked away from the western. "Wow! Her hair looks like yours, Mommy."

Sissy hated to say anything but, "That's twenty today"

"I hope this will come out before choir practice tomorrow night," Mrs. Shepard replied back rudely.

"Me too," as Libby Shepard ran to her car with a towel pulled around her head. Come on Todd, let's go to Grandma's, she's expecting us, and she'll fix you something to eat." as she put the closed sign in the door.

The Trip to Indiana

Richard came out of his bedroom and looked down the hall at Anne's bedroom to see if any light was coming under her door. Looked pretty dark, he thought. They've had separate bedrooms for almost eight years and rarely would enter each other's space. It was sacred. Eric slept in the basement surrounded by all his gadgets and electronics. They seldom entertained, even though the house was set up for massive parties and gatherings. Richard came down to put coffee on, but there was a pot already warming.

Anne came in from the back yard. "I'm going, and I'm making Eric go, but I had to bribe him with some rock band tickets in the front row section."

"I'm not making any of you go! Is that understood?"

"We know. I'm almost packed, and even Eric is already moving down there. I hate to think what these tickets will set me back."

Richard went to the garage in disbelief. He couldn't imagine why the family would go back to Gas City with him. The big black Mercedes 500 SL hummed as he turned the key. A road trip- this could be good or really, really bad, he thought. New York traffic leaving the city wasn't too bad at 6:00 AM. , but look at all those suckers coming into work, trying to squeeze into the Holland Tunnel, he thought. Anne set right to work on her laptop and Eric to his earphones. This could be a pleasant trip.

Richard's mind traveled back to Gas City High School where he led them to the state baseball championship, then on to Indiana University, receiving a full ride baseball scholarship. In his junior and senior years, IU won the Big Ten Baseball Championship and he was nominated for All American honors. He majored in business and went to Columbia University in New York to get an MBA, and here he met a young woman in her first year of law school. He was totally smitten. Anne Miller came from a very wealthy and influential New York family. She grew up with every opportunity a young women could have and more. She introduced him to all the right people, and he seemed to fit right in. He met her parents at their summer home in upstate New York, and he loved the life style: maids, a driver, three gardeners and the like. All he had to do was to ask, and it was given. He could even tell the cook what he wanted for dinner and there it was. No menu. Just ask.

Her father's partner had passed away soon after they were married, and he was asked to join the firm. He jumped at the chance, and now he was the captain of the ship. His dealings were never on the up and up, but he got the job done and made plenty of money along the way. He had forty-six people under him and not one would make a move without his approval; he liked that power.

He looked at his son in the rearview mirror to see his head moving up and down to some horrible rock music. Eric had always been a problem. When he came from the womb, he was defiant and even refused to be breast fed. Not much had changed in seventeen years. He had been caught with drugs and spent six months on home arrest. What a joke that was! They were afraid to leave him at home alone, never knowing what might happen when they were at work. He pulled a knife on a guy at a nightclub and was arrested for that; again not much came of it. He had talked about suicide before, but never seemed to dwell on it. Oh well, it was his life, Richard thought. Eric never followed through with anything, and even taking his life would probably be botched up. Rick remembered one summer Eric got into sailing, but when the season ended, so did his enthusiasm. Eric's girlfriend, Kandy also had been busted for drugs and loved rock concerts more than anything on the planet. They knew she was his source, and her brother was a known dealer. She would call night and day and usually seemed high on something. Richard and Anne tried to separate them but that just brought them closer together. Eric had been to the farm once when he was about eight and complained about the smell the whole time. Richard was sure that this would be about the same scenario as before. Richard didn't think that Eric would even remember his grandmother, and so far this had been a quiet trip.

The miles added up, and in southern Ohio just before they crossed into Indiana he stopped, and said, "This may be one of our last stops, so if you need a break, here it is." Richard had let Eric drive about two hundred miles but he just couldn't close his eyes to get any rest. Anne and Eric went into the huge truck stop in Tell City, and they were amazed. Everything under the sun was there. Western clothes, cowboy hats, country and western CDs, food, portable refrigerators you could plug into your cigarette lighter, and anything you could ask for labeled, "'We love Ohio." When they came out, Richard was talking to some old guy that had a small car lot next to the gas pumps.

"Hey buddy, want to trade that car of yours for a great looking pickup truck I got over here?" He asked.

"Not today."

"I even have a matching one for the little lady. Yours is black, and I have a nice red one for her. What do you think?"

"Not in my life time, old timer," he said sarcastically

Back in the car, Eric said, "Dad, they have everything in there except a perfume counter, lots of shit" Things were starting to look familiar as they crossed into Indiana. It's been such a long time since he was home, and the guilt was starting to build in his stomach. He would talk to his dad about once a month, and the conversation always ended up being about crop prices or the cattle sales. He was not interested in either one, and his dad probably sensed it. It will be good to see his brother, Tim, and sister-in-law, Pamela Sue, again.

Pamela Sue worked on the farm, and pretty much everything they ate came from their garden or butchering shed. She was one good cook! Pamela Sue had a huge heart and would do anything for a person in need; she was seldom seen without an apron around her pudgy middle. His brother was his height but had a little pooch of a stomach. He was blonde like their mother and very handsome. He seldom wore anything except jeans or Carhartts, and his powerful hands were like dried leather. One time when they were having a cookout on the farm, he reached in the fire and picked up the hot coals with his bare hands to move them around before he put the pork on the grill. He went to Purdue University for one year but came back to the farm to do what he really loved. He met Pamela Sue in high school, and they never dated anyone else their whole lives. Tim said she proposed to him and gave him a ring before he had a single thought of marriage.

Their two children, Moses and Rahab, worked on the family farm. Rahab was becoming a great cook like her mother, and Pamela Sue said she had a sweet voice and had starred in many school plays. Moses was tall and blond like his father and worked the farm every waking moment. 4-H was a big part of the kids' lives, especially around Lincoln Co. Fair time. They lived at the fair grounds for a week and even slept with their animals like most of the other 4-Hers. Rick thought he probably wouldn't recognize them now. One more turn on 600 East and they will be able to see the old white farm house. There it was! Caught in a time warp, nothing seemed different at all. The whites where hanging on a clothes line connected to the back door. His mother turned to see who was coming, and her smile seemed to out shine the brilliant sun that was beating down on the white sheets and pillow cases hanging like banners on the Fourth of July. Richard's guilt suddenly disappeared. He thought things were going to be alright.

Mabel's Restaurant, Gas City, Indiana

All the buzz was about Richard Barr's funeral. The restaurant was called Mabel's, but Mabel died six years before, and Yvonne took it over as she had cooked there for over twelve years. Now the unofficial name was "Mom's". Yvonne looked after each person that came through her doors, so they just called it "Moms".

"Don't forget your umbrella. Better get gas today; I heard it's going up two cents tomorrow, or where are your gloves?" Yvonne would say to the group of farmers who were sitting at the large round table. The usual response was, "Ok Mom", in unison. She could dish out whatever they would throw at her and then some. If you wanted to discuss anything of importance, you would need to go to "Moms" early each morning.

The diner wasn't much to look at, but it was homey and had a nice feminine touch to it. The entrance leaked a little when it rained hard, so Mom put a bucket by the drip, and the bucket had a sign that read H20. There also was a sign as you came in that said "Wipe your feet or leave your boots." Below the sign was a long tray where the farmers could place their boots if they had been working in the fields. All the tables had red and white checkered tablecloths with little wooden outhouses in the middle holding the salt and pepper shakers. The chalkboard above the kitchen announced the specials of the day and Mom would put a person's birthday below the specials and give them a free slice of pie of their choice. The kitchen was so efficient that Chris, the cook, could talk to the patrons and never look down to find something he needed. The kitchen had a backdoor that opened to the alley, and when Chris would hear the familiar knock; three raps a pause then one more, he would put four complete meals outback for the Hay Family. Everyone in town knew that the Hays were down on their luck, as the expression goes. They also knew Larry Hay always seemed to be out of work or between jobs, but it never kept him from having a few drinks with the boys each day at Harry's Pub. Mom and Chris knew at least the three little Hay children had a warm meal in their stomachs when Stormy Hay would wait each day to get the food for her children in the alley behind Mom's.

The blunt of most jokes around the big table were about the funeral director, Bill Sales. "Here he comes," they would say "looking for business," or "Where's your shovel?" and many more like those. Bill was a likable guy, and as soon as he sat down, the conversation centered about the big funeral for Richard, Sr. "Where's the funeral going to be?" they asked.

Bill took a sip of coffee and grabbed a slice of wheat toast from Carl Jackson's plate. "It's going to be at the Faith Baptist Church on Saturday at 11:00 AM. There'll be visitation at the funeral home Friday evening until 9:00 PM. We're expecting a huge crowd at both locations. He was loved by everyone he ever met." Bill said. They all nodded in unison. Richard Barr had been a part of the group for many years and no one sat in Richard's usual spot today. Every man at the table was a good friend of his and a few good stories were told by the guys.

If a stranger would have walked in Moms and looked at the big round table, they would have seen fifteen men dressed in overalls and work boots and one guy with a dark blue suit with a beautiful white carnation in his lapel and thought "He doesn't fit here." The conversation soon went back to grain prices and how many acres the Johnson boys were trying to buy. Business as usual, at Mom's.

THE FARM

The Mercedes door opened. Eric was the first to get out. "Phew! It stinks out here" Eric said in disgust.

Mary Barr said quickly "Country air. It'll grow on you. Now give me a hug before I throw you in with the pigs." Her white hair was thick and combed back into a simple bun. She wore a gingham apron with a soft blue dress that almost touched the ground. Her face was tan, and her hands were so wrinkled that it appeared she was wearing soft leather gloves. She hugged the grandson she never really knew, very tightly, as to say, "I may never see you again, but you're flesh of my flesh" The trunk popped open and Rick and Anne exited the car, at the same time. Mary rushed to Anne and said "Thank you for coming. This means the world to me" and another big hug followed. "Ricky, you look so much like your dad when I first met him," Mary said softly. She kissed him on the lips and held him tightly. Welcome home, son."

The house smelled like fresh baked bread and was warm and very comfortable. "You two can have your old bedroom. I pushed the two twin beds together in the middle of the room, so there should be plenty of room to move around in there." Rick and Anne just looked at each other with no expression on either face. "Eric, you can bunk in Tim's old room because I turned Sissy's room into a sewing area for my little projects. When you all come back down, I have some food fixed for ya."

When Rick walked the stairs to his old room, his mind was flooded with memories. The house smelled the same, like old leather and fresh peeled apples. He opened the door, and it was as if he had just left a week ago. Trophies, ribbons, photos, and his old 4-H Jacket hanging probably right where he left it twenty-three years before when he went to IU and the jacket even smelled the same. The room was about one third of Anne's dressing room back in New York and looked like an antique store exhibit. She put her hands on her hips and looked around with a disgusted expression.

"Sorry," he said it'll only be for five days."

She looked at him "I guess this will half to do, since the closest motel is thirty three miles from here," and began to unpack. Anne wasn't sure how she could cope with the circumstances because even the one bathroom was down the hall.

Eric turned left at the top of the stairs and went to Tim's old room. "Oh my gosh!" he exclaimed to himself. The walls were covered with cowboy pictures, 4-H Ribbons, and a saddle in the corner draped over a small wooden saw horse. Next to the bed was a record player with a pile of 45's. Eric looked at the vinyl records, and felt he had gone back in time, putting one on the spindle. The first song was some old guy singing about his wife and his dog leaving him. On the dresser was a picture of two boys standing next to a very large horse, one blond, one dark haired. It must be my dad and Tim, as he pondered the old black and white photo. They looked pretty buffed for a couple of farm boys, he thought to himself. For some reason Eric felt very comfortable in the small room. The only electronics were a record player and a cowboy riding a horse clock on the dresser. The old room smelled like old wood and leather, but Eric really liked the feel of the room.

Eric went down to the kitchen and noticed it was full of food. "All the neighbors and church ladies sent food, so you won't go hungry in the next few days," his grandmother said. Sit down and I'll fix you a snack, looking into his eyes for some recognition. Here's a piece of cherry pie with homemade ice cream."

"What does homemade ice cream mean?" he asked.

"Pamela Sue made some this morning in her kitchen and it's fresh."

Man he thought, Ben and Jerry need to talk to Pamela Sue; it was something he had never experienced before. It seemed to melt on his tongue with all kinds of flavors hitting his brain at the same time. The cherry pie complemented the ice cream with a blast of ripe cherries and a heavy lard crust. "Thanks Grandma, this is awesome!"

"Eric, just call me Dommy. I would like that. "My grandma was Dommy, and it's very comforting to hear it again."

"Ok, Dommy."

Rick and Anne came down to the kitchen and sat at the small table. "Dad you got to try the cherry pie and ice cream." Eric exclaimed.

"Maybe later. Where are Tim and Pamela Sue?"

"They'll be over later. How about some good old fashioned food?" Mary asked.

"You've got to try the ice cream!" Eric exclaimed.

"Ok, Mom a small piece, and let Anne try that banana cream pie for starters."

"Wow! Anne blurted out. Where did you get that recipe for the pie?"

"Old family secret. We import the bananas from Brazil to start with." she said as Anne gave her a puzzled look with her big brown eyes. "Just kidding; I'll give you the recipe before you go back."

Just then Tim came bounding in the back door. "Hey, bro." he said with great enthusiasm. "What's new in the big city?" Tim was very handsome, and his thick long blond hair hung almost to his shoulders. His face was tan and the stomach looked like it had put away a few of Pamela Sue's dinners and homemade ice cream.

"You know, in New York you could do that hair into a pony tail and fit right in." Rick said with a big smile.

"I've been telling him for three weeks to cut the hair," Pamela Sue said standing behind her husband with everyone not even knowing she was in the room. She stood five three if that and had a beautiful smile as she pushed Tim aside. She too was a little round, but her face radiated health and a love for living. "Let me see, can this be Eric? We can sure see what family tree you fell from." As she laughed.

Mary said, "Sit down, you two, and have some pie."

Rick rushed over and embraced his brother. He extended his arm to include Pamela Sue, "I really do miss you guys. We need to gather more often." Rick said with little tear in his eye. This surprised Eric because he had never seen his father get emotional about anything in his seventeen long years. "Where are your kids?"

Pamela Sue answered, "Moses is at the farm store, and Rahab is decorating with her Spanish Class at the high school and making scenery for the school community play. You'll see them tonight. We're having a cookout at the farm for our family." Pamela Sue walked over and put her arms around Anne who was sitting at the kitchen table. Anne thought Pamela Sue smelled like a combination of ginger snaps and burning leaves, and her mind flew back to her

Girl Challenger days around the camp fires in Vermont. "We are also glad to have you in our family," and kissed Anne on the cheek.

As Mary was dishing up some ice cream; she couldn't help but notice her two sons embracing each other. This was more than she ever hoped for. As young boys they had a strong bond and would defend the other in any circumstance. To see them together again, even though it was the death of their father that brought them here- it was ok.

Pastor Roger's Home

Libby Shepard came running in the house sobbing. "What's the matter, honey?" Roger asked.

"I'm done in this town. I'll never be able to leave the house again," she said between her sobs and hiccups. She took off her towel to reveal the most brilliant red hair her husband and children had ever seen.

"Wow, Mom!" Her daughter exclaimed.

"Where's the vinegar?" she yelled as she ran into the kitchen.

"Libby, it's going to be all right." Roger tried to assure her as she darted up the stairs to the bathroom.

By the time Roger came up she had taken off her blouse in front of the mirror and was reading the label on the vinegar bottle. "Come here," he said gently. She turned to face him as he pushed the bathroom door closed. He kissed her tear streaked cheek and lips. He slowly reached around and unfastened her bra. He picked her up and pushed open the bathroom door with his foot and carried her to their bedroom next door. He softly laid her on the bed, undressed her and himself. Her crying had stopped ten minutes before when he gently cradled her in his arms. She now laid on the bed, naked and in complete wonder. He slowly brought his body on hers. The next thirty-five minutes were spent in each other's arms: wet, unscheduled sex in the middle of the day; "it was magical" she thought.

He raised up on one arm and looked her in the eyes, "Please don't wash too much red out, I like it a lot." For the past twenty-three years of their marriage she had never felt this passion between them.

She got out of bed, again looked at her hair and naked body in the mirror as she ran a soft brush through the bright red plumage and whispered to herself, "I just had an affair with my husband."

Tim and Pamela Sue's Farm

Mary said, "We can all walk to Tim's if everyone carries their load. It's only about a half mile, and it's a beautiful night."

"Dad, can we take the car?" Eric asked as they were leaving Dommy's house.

"Let's just see if you can keep up with your grandmother."

"Very funny."

As they walked, the air was filled with all kinds of noises. The dirt road made a funny pattern as their shoes left behind their footprints of all different sizes. The stars were out, and the half moon was brilliant. Eric didn't like the unknown darkness and stayed close to his dad but not too close for him to notice. As they approached Tim's house, they could see the bonfire glowing in the back. All the farm cats scattered as they walked up except for Korven; he was too fat and lazy to move.

"Hi, Uncle Rick." Moses and Rahab yelled out.

"Hey Kids. "This is your cousin, Eric."

"Welcome to Indiana!" Moses yelled again. Moses was also tall with blond hair. His skin was dark from the sun and he wore blue jeans and plaid shirt to fit the expectation Eric had about his country cousins. Rahab was plain like her mom, no makeup, but she had thick brown hair pulled back by a rubber band. She was wearing denim capris pants, white blouse with a 4H emblem on the collar and brown leather cowboy boots. She was little plump and ordinary but grabbed a cinder block like it was nothing and carried it to the fire.

Tim said, "Sit. The meal will be around the fire tonight." I asked Sissy to come over, but she is really under the weather."

"I hope she'll be better by the funeral on Saturday," Pamela Sue said.

Eric looked in amazement. Steaks, chicken, baked beans, corn on the cob, potatoes, corn bread, all cooked on that fire in front of him. The adults poured wine from an old glass jug, and the kids drank lemonade infused with some kind of fruit that Eric loved. What a feast! Everyone talked and laughed all at the same time. His cousin Moses ate like there was no tomorrow and had a complete second helping of everything that was passed.

After the huge delicious meal, Pamela Sue said, "Why don't you kids show Eric around the farm." Eric thought this will be a treat; maybe they have a trained chicken that can play the piano. They walked around the back of the barn into a small door. They went in first and he followed to see a huge room with a large loft above. There were bales of hay stacked to the roof on one side and all kinds of ropes and pulleys on the other. A loud banging noise came from a stall across from them and Eric could see a mule kicking the sides with all his might. Moses and Rahab never looked over.

Moses walked over, brushed aside some loose hay, and lifted an old floor board. He reached far down and retrieved a large glass jug and carefully set it down. It looked very clear and unthreatening. Moses said, "Try our local soda pop, but just a small swig."

Eric put it to his lips and took very little. As he handed it back to Moses, his mouth, tongue, and throat were on fire. "Shit! What is that?"

"This is our answer to a local microbrewer." He answered back. "Mr. Hanson makes it for the locals and all we have to do is clean out the jug and get a refill for $5.00. Moses pulled out some cigarettes and handed one to Eric. "This will help." Rahab didn't take a drink but pulled out her own smokes and sat back on a bale of hay. The kids talked about music and the new talent show on television and how it wasn't fair that the guy with the Vietnam Tee shirt got eliminated in the third round. The jug got passed around again and Eric thought maybe his cousins weren't too bad after all.

As the adults sat around the fire, Tim said, "We will help mom with the farm and check on her daily.

Anne spoke up, "If you need money or if we can help hire workers, all you have to do is call."

Mary said, "I'm still sitting here you know. I will be just fine. I don't need your help, and the nursing home is just up the road if it comes to that. I love you guys but let me grieve for your dad and give me some space, Ok? The funeral will be hard, so I may need to lean on all of you if that's all right. Just give me your shoulders and not your pity."

Rick threw his last beer can in the fire, and said, "I love you Tim and Pam, and I know that you'll be that rock that dad once was. Also we're just a phone call away. I'm just so sorry I haven't been here for all of you. Honey, let's go back to mom's, I'm starting to really fade."

Tim said," I'll round up the kids, they're probably admiring Rahab's prize goat."

Sissy's Beauty Shop

It was getting late, and Sissy just finished cleaning the brushes and combs. She sat in the beauty chair and looked into the large wall mirror behind her station. Her fears again were welling up in her chest, and she ran to the bathroom just in time to empty her stomach. The terror was real and also the nightmares. Sissy was so happy to have Todd in her home because she knew Todd would never let anything happen to his mother. She had no desire to date or see a man but always told her customers that the right man hadn't shown up yet. Sissy loved to talk about male movie stars and heartthrobs, but deep down, she could care less.

"Todd come up to bed." She yelled down the basement.

"I'll be up in a minute; NeeNee is reading me a cowboy story."

"Todd, I'm getting tired and we both need to go to bed."

"All right mom, two minutes."

Sissy washed her face and put on her nightgown. Todd went directly to his room and started getting ready for bed.

"Give me a kiss, and I'll fix you biscuits and gravy for breakfast. By the way, what story did NeeNee read to you?"

"It was about Roy Rogers and his horse Trigger. Roy had a girlfriend and her name was Dale."

"I don't remember having a book on Roy Rogers."

Frustrated he said, "Mom, I told you its NeeNee's book and he is reading to me"

"Ok honey goodnight." She walked to her room puzzled, because this wasn't the first time Todd told her of many facts that his friend had shared. One time, Todd stated to her that Mrs. Howard wouldn't make her appointment that day, because she would be in an accident. Five minutes later Mr. Howard called Sissy to say his wife had wrecked the car; she was alright and would reschedule next week. When Sissy confronted Todd; he said NeeNee told him and went back to watching his western.

Sissy's room was next to Todd's, and she always left the hall light on. Each time she entered her room, she looked under the bed, double locked the door and pulled her handgun from under the mattress. Her demons were real, and her only hope was to fall asleep quickly.

Back to Mom's House

As they walked down the dirt road, it was pitch black. They all walked close together, except Eric was weaving back and forth. "Stop clowning around." Rick said. Mary thought that this was a wonderful evening having her two boys back together and sharing some old stories. Rick, too, felt a peace that he had not experienced for such a long time. Even Anne felt good. The food was great, and the four glasses of Pamela Sue's homemade strawberry wine made her feel light and carefree. No thoughts of Federal Court or even the young intern she had been sleeping with. They could see the soft glow from the front porch light that Mary had left on- almost home.

As they walked into the house, Mary said, "I'll wash those clothes for you in the morning if you leave them outside your door in the hamper. We all smell like we've been sitting in the campfire. Now, up the stairs with all of you and get some rest. Mary said in a firm voice, Big day tomorrow," as she slipped into her bedroom.

Eric went right to his room still weaving as he climbed the stairs and thought maybe he'd try a couple more 45's before sleep. Rick and Anne went into their room and closed the door. They both just stared at the two twin beds pushed together in the middle of the room.

"Whew," Anne said as she took off her sweater. "This does smell like smoke."

"Give me your clothes, Rick said, I'll put them in the hamper." They both undressed facing away from each other. She looked around at him and noticed his bare bottom which was firm and tight from all those hours at the health club. He too looked around and saw her nice firm breasts and the gentle curve of her golden tan back. Their eyes met. They both laughed out loud. "How old are we?"

"I guess sixteen again," she replied as they both smiled at each other. She slipped her warm nightgown on and he went down the hall to the bathroom carrying all the smelly clothes. He brushed his teeth and above the mirror was his old sheriff's badge hanging on the wall from his dentist from forty years ago. "Nice clean teeth" it read. He thought probably his mom had never thrown anything away. As he came down the hall, Anne came from their room, and both made some weird eye contact as they passed each other. She too saw the badge above the mirror and had to grin.

He got into bed, and the old feather mattress seemed to engulf him. Anne came into the room, and she too was surrounded by her mattress. She started to giggle, and Rick also started to really laugh. "Just like the Ritz," he said laughingly.

"I was thinking the Plaza." She said giggling. They both started an uncontrollable laugh. "Stop it! I'm going to pee the bed."

Still smiling, she slowly rolled over on top of him in a very gentle movement. She could feel his hardness through her nightgown as she looked directly into his dark brown eyes. Nothing was said but their breathing became heavier. Her lips slowly came down upon his as the smell of burnt wood, wine and Chanel flooded his brain. She pulled her nightgown up, still keeping their lips pressed together. He reached down, and his shorts were quickly thrown onto the floor. Her legs parted and he slipped into her wetness. Both let out a slow moan. She moved her body up and down as they looked into each other's eyes. What was going on? They both thought. Not a single word was uttered, and the movements continued. Again she pressed her lips, on his and again they both repeated a gentle moan. He pulled her nightgown off and also threw it on the floor next to the bed. He cupped her breasts, and she arched her back to receive the full stroke of his hands. He wrapped his arms around her as they both climaxed together. She went limp on top of him as he kissed her neck and ran his fingers through her light brown hair.

"Wow!" He exclaimed. She rolled off him and he looked at her body lying next to him. The little cowboy hat night light gave her a glow that made her look like a delicate piece of china.

"Rick," she said in a soft loving voice, we've got to keep this together."

Rick counted back in his mind; it must have been five years since he made love to his wife. This was good, really good, and off to sleep they went.

AURORA, LLC, NEW YORK CITY

As James walked into the large glass entrance on the Thirty-six floor of the Feiman Building, he expected to see no one. I mean it's only 7:00 A.M. he thought. The receptionist was there at the front desk, and all thirty- one clerks were at their computers. Richard wasn't there and wouldn't be for another four days, but his presence still seemed to linger over the office. His personal secretary, Yolanda, came out of her office and greeted him with a hot cup of coffee. James was one of the three negotiation buyers that had their butts chewed out just three days before. He told Yolanda to gather the employees and have them meet in the board room. Ten minutes later they crowded in.

"What's this all about?" some asked.

James said, "What are we going to do for Richard's dad? Do we want to send flowers or a donation or what?" he continued.

Someone from the back of room said, "Let's all go to lunch and have drinks on the company." Everyone laughed.

"The obituary from the newspaper requested donations to their local 4H Club. I'll pass the hat and you do whatever you feel." James said. "Make yourselves comfortable because I put together a ten minute Power Point presentation last night, and you might find this interesting."

The opening picture was a young man standing next to a large cow holding a blue ribbon. "Yes everyone, Richard was a farmer." James exclaimed. Isn't it amazing what you can find in Cyber Space?" The other pictures flashed up on the screen, and the giggles and laughs began to grow. Richard wearing his Gas City High School letter jacket with a big rocket across the front. The caption read, "Rocketeer of the Month." More baseball pictures, a prom picture with his hair slicked back and his date looking off to her right like she saw something better to do. There was a photo of him holding a chicken by the neck standing in front of his farm house. The last picture James had photoshopped Richard's and Yolanda's heads on the famous picture of a guy and his wife with a pitchfork entitled "American Gothic" by Grant Wood. It brought down the house, except for Yolanda's expression. "One more piece of trivia," James said. "Gas City has a huge population of 1306 people, and it's way closer to Kentucky than Indianapolis like we first thought. Matter of fact, almost into Kentucky." Now let's count the donations."

"MOM'S DINER" AT 6:00 AM

As usual the big round table in the corner was filled with farmers and the local Farm Bureau Insurance agent, Lester. "Here he comes," they all said as Bill Sales came through the door wearing his black suit and white tea rose in his right lapel. "Heard yer having a scratch and dent sale on some caskets this week," someone remarked. "This guy will be the last guy to let you down," another said among the laughs. He sat down again being way over dressed for that table. He grabbed a piece of toast from Lester's plate and took a sip cup of coffee. All that kidding was the way he started each day at Mom's Diner.

Bill told the guys that Mary wanted them to be pall bearers at the funeral and carry the casket at the cemetery. Every man raised his hand to be included. Bill said that Steve Watson from the V.F.W. was going to try and play taps at the cemetery but wasn't sure he could get through it for his good friend Richard, Sr.

Eldon Smith told the table he saw Rick Barr come through town in a big Mercedes but wasn't sure of the model. The guys then talked about the time Rick pitched a no hitter against New Durham High School in the playoffs. New Durham was ranked third in the state and only managed to get two runners on base. Bob Magic hit a triple in the 6th inning to put the game away for good. What a game they all thought!

Bill knew this was the funeral of the year for him. Not only will the whole town show up, but also representatives from the Indiana State Fair Association and the Indiana State Livestock Association. It was rumored that the governor might be there along with the secretary of state. Now we're talking real celebrities he thought. Everything had to be just perfect.

"Pastor Shepard called me today for some stories about Richard since the minister is new in town. I gave him your phone numbers, so you might be getting a call tonight." Bill said.

"I'll tell him some stuff, but he better not expect me to stand up there." Lester said

Mom came over to see if anyone needed a warm up. "You guys put on some nice clothes before you all go the funeral home and church," she said with authority. And if any of you ever want hot coffee in this place again, you best not wear those darn farmer boots to the funeral."

They all looked down and said, "Yes, Mom."

Dad and Mom's Farm

It wasn't quite 6:00 A.M., and Eric awoke to smell bacon and bread baking down stairs. He looked at his parent's room, and no one seemed to be stirring as he walked past their door.

"Hi, Dommy."

"Good morning, Eric" as she rushed over and planted a big kiss on his forehead.

"It smells really good!" he exclaimed.

"How about some pancakes, bacon, and fresh baked bread with honey?"

"It sounds great, but I'm not allowed to have stuff like that. Our cook only gives me yogurt and whole grain cereal."

"Bull crap! I make the best pancakes that ever existed. Now sit down! If you like them, I'll tell you two secrets that make them the best. I've never told a single soul, and I know you won't repeat it." She said with a grin. A stack of six cakes and a slice of bacon were placed in front of him. The pancakes were small around but stacked high.

"Dommy, I can't eat this many."

"Eat what you can, Eric," she said with her back turned to him.

"I didn't know bacon could be this thick," he said as he looked down at one half inch slab. Man! These pancakes are unbelievable! He thought. The syrup and butter sure seemed to compliment her masterpiece.

"You're grandfather once had thirty- eight pancakes and still has the family record," she said with a smile.

"Dommy, can I have another stack and some more warm syrup?"

Upstairs Rick sat on the edge of the bed and looked at his watch. What! Eight o'clock he thought; I haven't slept like that for years. Anne was fast asleep almost completely engulfed in her feather mattress. He slipped his pajama bottoms on and walked down the hall to the bathroom. As he went past Eric's door, he thought to himself that kid won't be up until noon. On his way back to the bedroom, he smelled something wonderful coming from the kitchen. He walked in, and Anne was sitting up on the side of her little bed.

"Good morning," she said with a great big smile. Come over here," she whispered. He walked to her bed and stood in front of her. "I want to say good morning to my little Rick and tell him thank you." She pulled him close as he stood in front of her. She gently lowered his pajama bottoms to his ankles and stroked him softly. She guided him into her warm, moist mouth, and he moaned very quietly. Rick ran his fingers through her soft brown hair and helped guide the rhythm he needed. The slow movement of her head and hands brought him to the grand finale at the fireworks show. She looked up at him, his eyes were still closed. In a minute he came back to reality, opened his eyes, and slowly bent down and kissed her full on the lips.

"Someday I may call for a similar favor, she said in cooing voice. Now, let's go down and have breakfast, jumping out of bed, I'm famished."

SISSY'S BEAUTY SHOP

It was early, and Tim pushed open the front door of the shop even though it said closed. "Hey, Sis!" he yelled.

"We're down in the basement. Be right up!" she yelled back. Todd and Sissy came up the stairs, and gave her brother a huge hug.

"Hi, Uncle Tim." Todd said with a big smile.

"Hi, cowboy," he shot back. "Who are you today?" Tim asked, as he noticed a pair of cap guns strapped around Todd's waist and a white cowboy hat perched upon his head.

"I'm the Lone Ranger, but I can't find my mask. Maybe NeeNee took it."

"Todd, go back down to the basement and look real hard," his mother said and off he went.

"Pamela Sue thinks I need a trim," as he eased into her beauty chair.

"You do. You know I won't be at the funeral home or church, as she grabbed her scissors from the drawer. I've closed the shop for three more days, and I won't go out until the funeral is over."

"Everyone knows you're real sick and won't bother you until this is all over." He said.

"I finally quit vomiting, but I can't eat anything except toast."

"Pamela Sue and I will bring over some food from the funeral dinner for you and Todd. My wife is insisting. Do you want me to take Todd to the funeral?" he asked.

"No, I want my man here with me. There you go. Now you look like a human being," she laughed. He got up and held his sister for a long time. She began to cry loudly, and he stroked her hair.

"You'll get through this," Tim said and handed her a tissue that was next to her brushes. Just then Todd came running up the stairs,

"I found my mask!" he exclaimed.

Tim said, "Great, but where's Tonto?" as he kissed his sister on the cheek. Todd looked at his mother with a puzzled look.

"Thanks a lot, Tim," she said sarcastically.

Sales and Son Funeral Home

It was an old Victorian home one block from the main street if you can call it that now. Most shops had closed and everyone shopped in

Evansville which was thirty-three miles to the west. The funeral home needed some paint but was well maintained by Bill Sales and his son, Wyatt. Wyatt was still in high school but wanted to get his funeral director's license as soon as he graduated. The funeral chapels were downstairs-Bill and family lived upstairs.

"Wyatt," his dad said, "I need you to wash the cars before Mr. Barr's funeral tomorrow," as his son was putting on his tie. Remember the funeral for Harriett Parson? She had fourteen children, fifty-seven grandchildren, and eighty-nine Gt. Grandchildren; I think we'll have a bigger crowd than Harriett's." They were expecting an over flow crowd today and were busy getting flowers set up as Angie, the florist, was coming in the back door.

"I have the casket spray, Bill" she said, "where do you want it?"

"Just place it there for now," he said not looking up. When he did look up he noticed the spray had not a single flower in it. There were corn stalks, wheat, cucumbers, radishes, green peppers and big bunch of tomatoes in the middle. He thought to himself now that's a fitting casket spray for a farmer. Bill noticed a small spot on Richard Barr's tie and sent Wyatt for the spot remover. It probably came from some of Mary's wonderful chicken gravy that she was so well known for. All Bill could think of, as he looked into the casket, was Gas City had lost its most revered citizen.

Back At The Farm

Richard and Anne came down the back stairs directly into the kitchen. It was almost 9:00 AM. "Good morning," they said together. Eric was finishing his third stack of six pancakes.

"Dad, Grandpa has the family record for most pancakes, and I'm just finishing on number eighteen. I think I'll break that record someday."

Richard and Anne sat at the table, and his mother came between them and put her arms around both their necks and said, "You'll never know how much this means to me that you are both here" with a small tear coming down her cheek.

"Hey, you two!" Eric yelled, "What was the deal with all the laughing and moving the furniture last night in your bedroom?"

They both blushed like a couple of teenagers. "Your mother and I thought of a real funny joke last night and couldn't quit laughing."

"What was it?" Eric shot back.

There was a long pause, more blushing and Anne said, "I can't remember it, can you Rick?"

"Right, Mom."

Richard quickly followed up with. "Eighteen pancakes. That's great!"

Anne took her first bite of a pancake and thought this is the lightest thing I've ever eaten. "Eric, I do think you might break the record someday." she said with a smile. Dommy's pancakes were legendary and kept their secret close to her vest.

Rick's memory exploded with thoughts of Tim, Sissy, and he sitting around that very table eating, laughing and getting ready to do the chores. They were good memories but seemed so long ago. Anne and Eric would never understand the Barr Family dynamics but then again, Rick seemed a little fuzzy himself.

"Rick, will you go in town and pickup my dress shoes at Jim's Shoe Repair?"

"Sure, mom. Whatever you need just ask; also may I have another stack of pancakes?"

Sarah's Charm and Chatter

Rick pulled up to his sister's shop, and everything seemed dark inside. Todd said, "Mom, someone's coming up the walk."

She looked out and saw Rick coming up the stairs and thought how much he looked like their dad.

"Open the door for him; I'm going to put on a bathrobe."

Todd opened the door even before Rick could knock. "Hi I'm Todd. Have you seen Tonto?"

Rick stepped in the small cluttered shop and said, "I'm your uncle Rick. Is your mom here?"

Sissy came out wearing an old brown bathrobe and worn yellow slippers. "Hi Rick, she said with a smile. Don't get too close. I think I have the flu"

He still rushed over to her and gave her a big brother hug. "I won't stay long. You probably need your rest. I can't believe how big Todd has gotten"

"Yep, he's five ten and eats like horse."

"What's with the Tonto questions?"

"Oh, your brother came for a haircut today and mentioned something about Tonto since Todd is the Lone Ranger, and now he's full of questions. I told him I will be Tonto, but he said I'm a girl, so I have to be Tonto's wife. He really is good company for me and a great help around the shop."

"Are you seeing anybody?"

She answered back, "No, I've been too busy with the shop and all."

"Come on sis, you need to mingle with adults and get out of here."

"Rick, you don't get it. I'm happy here and need no one to preach to me," she said with conviction.

"I'm sorry, just trying to help. Can you at least make the visitation for dad tonight at the funeral home?"

"I'll see, but this bug has a tight hold on me, and I don't want it to spread through the family.

"Well, if you or Todd needs a ride, please call the farm, and Anne and I will pick you up."

"I'll keep it in mind, but how are Anne and Eric?"

"They're good. I shouldn't say that; Eric is a monster, and we have no control over him. He's been in a lot of trouble and his girlfriend is a drug dealer. Anne had to bribe him to come back for Dad's funeral, so what does that tell you? He'll probably end up dead on some New York City Street or in prison for a long time. I'm sorry to unload on you; I know you are grieving too, and not feeling well to boot."

"Rick, thank you for sharing; I miss the three of us running around the farm with Mom chasing us with the garden hose. Great memories Rick."

He gave her another big hug and kissed her on the forehead. "I have to run; Mom wants me to pick up a pair of shoes for her at the shoe repair. I'll stop back with Anne and Eric soon. You won't recognize Eric. He's getting tall like me. "Bye Todd," he said, but the Lone Ranger was too connected to the western he was watching to notice his uncle leaving.

TIM AND PAMELA SUE'S FARM

Pamela Sue was the commanding officer of the farm. She had two big picnic baskets of food sitting out to take to the funeral home for family snacks. Her idea of a snack was fried chicken, potato salad, a vegetable platter, a German chocolate cake, cupcakes, and a dish of mints. She hoped this would keep her family from going hungry the next few hours. She had all the clothes laid out for her family and had even shined Tim's dress shoes. Moses was missing a button on his coat, and Pamela Sue had it replaced in less than a minute. She loved her family and would do anything for them.

Getting dressed, she looked in the mirror and thought how plain she was compared to Tim's good-looks. She combed her hair and put in a pair of earrings her mother had left her. A little lipstick might help she thought. She turned to come out of the bathroom, and Tim was standing there in his western jacket, black dress pants, newly shined shoes, and he looked so handsome she thought. He came up to her and kissed her and said how much he loved her and appreciated all she does for the family. A warm feeling came over Pamela Sue and put her small hand in his. She now knew how Cinderella must have felt and off to the funeral home they all went, not in a gold chariot pulled by six white horses, but a silver dual wheel Ford pickup truck.

Sales and Son Funeral Home

"Dad, here comes the Barr Family." Wyatt said with excitement.

Bill Sales straightened his tie and bared his smile in the mirror to make sure the pulled pork sandwich he had for lunch wasn't stuck to his front teeth. "Hi, Mary, Our whole town loved Richard and he will be missed" he said in a soft voice.

"Thank you, she said with a smile. Well at least there will be one less person at Mom's who won't be poking fun at you." They both had a good laugh with that remark. Can we see Dad now before the others come?"

"Come this way, and Wyatt will open the doors for you," He said quietly.

The big French doors opened, and Mary felt a little faint. She grabbed Tim and Rick's arms at the same time. The room was filled with flowers and the smell was almost overwhelming. There were pictures everywhere but the one she noticed was their wedding picture at the head of the casket. They looked so young and naive. She too felt the spray of vegetables and wheat on the casket fit him to a tee.

Mary sat in a chair at the head of the casket, and her boys flanked her on both sides along with the grandchildren. Comment upon compliment flooded the families' heads. Everyone who was anyone was at the funeral home that afternoon. Even Rick's old prom date came up and kissed him on the cheek. He didn't recognize her until she brought up that magical evening together. Anne looked over and almost burst out laughing. She had on a red and white polka dot dress and with her size, it that made her look like she was wearing a small circus tent. Rick looked over at Anne, but he couldn't tell if she was crying or laughing in her handkerchief.

Most of Rick's old friends and high school buddies said, "We've got to get together sometime" and Rick thought to himself for what?

Eric had been standing by the casket for a long time. He excused himself and walked outside to the back of the funeral home and sat on the steps. The street lights were on and there was a pleasant glow from Sales and Son neon sign. He reached in his leather jacket for a cigarette and had just put it into his mouth when he heard

"Got another smoke there, buddy?"

He turned to see a beautiful girl wearing a denim jacket and a plaid skirt that came to her knees. Her long blond hair hung straight down from tan face. She wore no makeup except a soft pink lipstick. She sat next to him and put out her hand. He couldn't take his eyes off her as he reached in his pocket for a cigarette.

"I'm Beverly," putting out her hand again and crossing her long legs clad in pink and brown cowboy boots. He was trying to gather his thoughts as she said, "Did you know Mr. Barr?"

Finally Eric said something. "I'm Eric, and he was my grandfather."

"Oh, you're the ones from New York; my dad played baseball with your dad in high school when they won the state championship."

"Do you still live around here?" he asked

"What does it look like? No, we live in Hollywood but come back to visit the local hillbillies when we get depressed," she said back sarcastically. "Your grandfather helped me and many others with our 4H programs; if it wasn't for him, I couldn't have gone to Indianapolis for the 4H barrel riding competition. I won state last year," she said boldly.

Eric thought to himself, I'm not going to ask her what barrel riding is, and he still couldn't quit staring at her. "What kind of music do you like?"

"I like the oldies," she replied as she took a long draw on her cigarette.

"Me too. Mega Death, Scorpions, and Zeppelin are my favorites."

"Well, mine are Porter Wagoner, Hank Williams, Jr. and Patsy Cline."

Again he thought to himself, I have no idea who these people or groups are, and I'm not going to ask that either. "What do you do for excitement around here?" still trying to make small talk.

"Oh, we like to count the number of cars that cross Main Street on any single night," she said mockingly.

He could see he was getting nowhere. He stood to stretch his legs and kept looking at her as she sat smoking the cigarette. She flipped the cigarette toward the funeral sign and stood to go. He was right in front of her, and this she didn't like. She grabbed him by the throat and his left arm, put her leg behind his and down he went in the grass. Instinctively he reached into his leather coat and grabbed his switch blade. Swish. It came out. She kicked his hand, and the knife went flying into the grass. She reached behind her back under the denim coat brought out a long shinny Bowie knife. For a moment he didn't know what happened. He looked up at her. Her beautiful blond hair glistened in the street light; her knife reflected the neon sign which made it look about a foot long. She now stood over him with a smile. He couldn't help looking up her dress to see pink cotton panties. His heart was going to explode.

"Like what you see?" she asked. She then sat on his chest, pinning his arms to the ground, and to this he didn't mind a bit. She looked at him for a moment, stuck her knife in the grass by his head and lowered her lips to his. "You're kind of cute," as she pressed her lips to his. Her hair covered his head; her wet lips tasted like a fresh Georgia peach along with a hint of tobacco. Her hair smelled like fresh vanilla and sandalwood and he knew from this point on, his life would never be the same again.

The kiss only lasted for a few seconds but to him it was an eternity. She sat up and said with a smile, "You can call me Billie, and I'll call you an old Indian name, "Little Blade." She jumped up to the beeping horn of an old pickup truck. "That's Dar; she's my ride" as he looked over at a cute short haired brunette waving at him. Billie ran to the truck as Eric turned on his side in the grass. She looked back at him one more time as she jumped in the truck that was playing some old country song. As the truck turned the corner he noticed the back window had a pink stenciled sign that read "*Silly boys, trucks are for girls.*"

BACK TO THE FARM

Everyone was exhausted as they left the funeral home. "Do Pamela Sue and you want to come over to the house for a slice of pie?" Mary asked.

"No, Mom, but thanks. We all need to get some sleep, and the kids need to do a couple of chores before we all bed down." He kissed his mother and Pamela Sue, Moses and Rahab all gave her a hug before climbing into the truck. Rick took the family back to the farm with no one saying much. They all came in the kitchen and their shoes were abandoned at the back door.

Anne said, "My feet are killing me," as she walked up the back stairs to their bedroom.

"Goodnight, Mom, Rick and Anne said. We love you." Just Eric remained in the kitchen with his grandmother.

"Eric, want some ice cream?"

"Thanks Dommy, I would." She scooped two bowls full and put fresh strawberries and chocolate syrup in front of him.

"Say Eric, how did you get grass stains on the back of your pants at the funeral home?"

"I must have sat down in the grass." he responded, thinking back of how he was pinned to the lawn of Sales and Son Funeral Home with a knife to his throat by a tall blond cowgirl. What a night!

"Dommy, do you know a girl named Billie that came to the funeral home tonight?"

"Yes, that's Bob Magic's daughter. They live on a farm about two miles east of here by the old fairgrounds. Bob and your dad were best friends in high school and never did anything without the other. Why do you ask?"

"Just curious, I'm going to bed too, Dommy, love you." As he ascended the stairs he thought Billie Magic. What a perfect name.

Saturday Morning Funeral Day at Mom's Diner

Only about half the usual guys were sitting around the big table. Mom came over to give the seven farmers and one insurance agent a warm up in their coffee cups. "I guess most of the guys are doing chores so they can be at Richard's funeral at the church, she remarked. I'll be closing the diner at 10:00 this morning to go to the service and the cemetery and reopen after the church dinner. So drink up boys."

"Oh, that reminds me, I have to pick up three pies at home for the church luncheon today," Lester said. "I better be going, or I may be sleeping outside tonight"

"Don't forget you guys," Mom said, "wipe your feet before you go into the church. God knows you're always tracking something in here, and don't forget to take an umbrella. It's supposed to rain."

"Yes, Mom," they all said. At that they all got up and headed for the door knowing it might be standing room only at the Faith Baptist Church today.

Mary Barr Farm

Mary was up at 4:00 A.M. and sat on the edge of her bed in a soft white nightgown that Richard had given her at Christmas. She looked over at Richard's side of the bed and sighed. She knew his side would never be slept in again by any man, and she was all right with that. Her spirit was heavy today and she felt no motivation whatsoever. Her closet was filled with nice clothes, but nothing looked appropriate for the funeral at the church. Richard's favorite dress was a dazzling pink, but would she dare wear it to the Faith Baptist Church? She looked again, but nothing struck her eye. She had black, dark brown and navy dresses: They just weren't what she wanted. Pink it is. She slowly dressed and walked into the kitchen. Food didn't sound good today, so she had a bacon, lettuce, and tomato sandwich for breakfast; this was her favorite.

"Hi, Dommy, Eric said what are you having for breakfast?"

"A BLT. Want one?"

"Sure, and maybe some strawberry ice cream for my breakfast desert."

"You know kid; I'm going to have the same. For a New York boy, you are adventuresome, I like that."

"Dommy, what do we do at the church today?"

"Just nod our heads when anyone says how great a guy your grandfather was. I would like for you and Moses to help carry the casket to the grave."

"Are you going to be all right living here by yourself?"

"I was raised to be independent, and I too was a free spirit. Maybe someday I will tell you a big secret, and you can judge for yourself."

"I'm going to get another scoop of strawberry. Want some?"

"Sure, Eric, what the hell; it's going to be a long day sitting in the church. What do you think of my dress? Is it a little over the top?"

"Dommy, you look hot!"

"That's all I wanted to hear. Your grandfather used the same words; now I feel real good about my choice."

Rick and Anne came down to the kitchen. Eric and Dommy were just finishing up their second bowl of ice cream. "Well, I like your nourishing breakfast you two are wolfing down." Rick said.

"Dad, how about a BLT and ice cream?"

"That doesn't sound too bad. What do you think Anne?"

"I think, I'll finish my BLT off with a slice of banana cream pie, especially since we're eating so healthy today." Anne said with a smile.

"Mom, I like your dress." Rick said.

"Eric and I decided that black and navy just wouldn't cut it, but I'm sure the ladies from Faith Baptist will put my outfit at the top of the gossip list."

Faith Baptist Church

It was 10:00 AM. Bill and Wyatt Sales had the casket and the flowers down front by the altar. Pastor Roger Shepard came out from the back and looked things over which met to his approval. "Bill, if you need anything I'll be back in my study," Roger said.

"The family will be here soon, so we'll be in the back of the church." Bill popped a breath mint, and handed one to Wyatt. "Remember, whatever the family needs for closure today. We need to be there for them."

The big oak doors opened. Mary Barr, her children, grandchildren, and her husband's brother, Clyde, from up north in Indiana entered. There was a peaceful silence in the church that morning. The Barr Family came down front and stared at the casket and flowers as they sat in the front pews. The only person missing was Sissy. Tim had stopped by the shop to see if she was better but he found her in bed and Todd was watching his usual Westerns he reported. Soon it was a steady flow of friends coming in and passing by the casket. Rick's old prom date came by and kissed him on the cheek again. Anne immediately grabbed her handkerchief and put it to her face to conceal her smile and giggles. Today she was wearing a lime green long dress that made her look like a giant cucumber. Rick just rolled his eyes. Eric kept looking around for his "Magic Girl" but couldn't find her and felt something empty inside.

The old organ came to life and everyone recognized "The Old Rugged Cross" which was played by Pastor Ken, the associate pastor. More hymns were played softly as people found their seats. Mary thought, as she looked at her watch, that she must keep herself together for this. The choir came out from the left side of the altar, and the Pastor from the right side. He looked around and not a seat was empty and about forty people were standing in the back. The choir stood until he nodded to them to be seated. His eyes caught his wife's flaming red hair, and as he nodded, he winked at her. This made her feel very special. After he winked, Libby looked around in amazement. From her vantage point she counted, one, two, three, more red hairdos like hers. She wondered if all three went to Sissy Barr's shop, and one lady sitting in the second row tipped her head at Libby as to say "Girl, you're among friends, welcome to the club." Libby sat up a little straighter and thought she should get a pair of red pumps the next time she goes to Evansville, grinning to herself

Pastor Roger opened with a prayer and read the obituary. "Richard Barr was a man of God; he was devoted to his church, his community, and his family. I'm not going to go on and on about Richard and make this a long service since everyone here knew him better than I." The service lasted two hours. "Amazing Grace" and "In the Garden" were sung by Pastor Ken and the choir.

The president of the Gas City Lions Club spoke first, telling the crowd how Richard helped sponsor the eyeglass drive for needy families in third world countries. Richard flipped hamburgers at the annual volunteer banquet and helped build the Lions club float for the 4th of July Parade for the past ten years. Richard put flags on the veteran's graves on Memorial Day, and at this the president got choked up and sat down.

Next the president of Indiana Farm Bureau told of Richard's dedication to Indiana farming by sponsoring Farm Day at all the local schools and rebuilding an old combine that now sat at the Indianapolis Museum.

The Lincoln Co. Fair Board president spoke of how Richard helped rebuild the grandstands that burned to the ground six years ago in July. At every Lincoln Co. Fair, Richard donated his time to demonstrate horseshoeing and thrashing. Richard spent every waking hour at the fairgrounds during fair week.

The 4-H Board vice president spoke of the youth activities Richard was involved in, like the Barr Family Scholarship and his donation of the hay and straw for the children's animals. His closing comment was that he loved the children and promoted family farm activities. He ended with Richard being a true American.

Everyone could tell that Tim Watson was really nervous when he stepped up to the podium. Tim was only sixteen, and his face was flushed before he uttered a single word. He spoke about Future Farmers of American and Richard's involvement. He told the people of the wonderful bus trip to Idaho last year and how much they learned. The kids helped build a Native American Youth Center with

Mr. Barr's help. "Mr. Barr drove the bus and paid for all the group's meals." he told them as he wiped his forehead with his sleeve and hurriedly sat down.

Finally the Gas City Volunteer Fire Chief stood. He told of all the pork chop dinners and fundraisers Richard had worked on. He mentioned that everyone would remember the time Richard saved all the horses and cattle from the Yoder's barn fire twelve years ago. This truly made him a hero. He concluded with, "Our Fire Truck will lead the procession to the cemetery," sticking his chest out another couple of inches. The pastor concluded with a prayer and Bill Sales ushered the people by the casket again.

Eric's heart picked up a couple of beats as he saw Billie Magic come by the casket. She took a step toward him and whispered, "Hey Little Blade, call me tomorrow." Even from where she stood he could smell her vanilla-sandalwood scented hair, and she was still wearing that pale pink lipstick.

Only the family remained by the casket. Mary stepped up and took off her husband's tie. She reached into her purse and pulled out a pair of needle nose pliers and gently placed them in his hands. "Now," she said, "you look more comfortable and you'll always have your favorite tool. Who knows, God might need some repairs done up there. Goodbye, Honey, I'll see you soon," and kissed him on the forehead. The rest of the family stepped up and either patted his hand or kissed him.

Bill and Wyatt stepped in and said, "We're ready to go to the cemetery now." And sure enough, there was the Volunteer Fire Truck with about fifty small American flags draped on it. It just started to sprinkle as they left the church, and Mary thought how appropriate. We need the rain.

Oak Grove Cemetery was five miles out in the country. As they pulled in, it looked like every other headstone said "Barr" on it. Six generations of Barr's were buried there, and they still had enough room for another six. When they got out of the cars, Richard's brother, Clyde, walked over to where his wife was buried and his name was there on the headstone just waiting for his date of death.

He too missed his beloved Josie. Standing 25 yards from the casket, Steve Watson played "Taps" with tears streaming down his cheeks onto his old Korean uniform. Next, Hugh Jackson played "Amazing Grace" on his bagpipes. It didn't take long for the crowd to realize he hadn't practiced in a long time and at least half of them wondered if he was wearing underwear beneath his old baggy kilt.

The pastor had spoken only ten minutes as the rain began to fall. "One more thing," he said, "come on back to the church for lunch; the ladies made enough for Patton's Third Army." Everyone got back in their cars and each car slowly pulled out. No one noticed the lone figure in the camouflage parka still standing by themself at the edge of the woods.

FAITH BAPTIST CHURCH BASEMENT

Lots and lots of food. Pretty much the same words: "He was a great man", "He'll surely be missed," and the best one, "God only takes the best".

Mary was wearing down, and Pamela Sue could tell. "Let me take you home to take off those horrible shoes," she said. Mary liked Pamela Sue because she would always share her thoughts. Tim was lucky to have her, Mary thought, but he also knew his place in the whole scheme of things.

Eric was stuffed. He walked over to his cousin Moses who was having his third piece of pie. "Say, do you know Billie Magic?"

Without looking up Moses said, "Who doesn't?" Moses just finished the pie and was going back to the desert table again.

Eric wasn't sure how to take his answer. His fifteen year old cousin, Rahab, was walking up the stairs to the parking lot for a smoke, and he followed. Eric sat next to her as she lit up a cigarette and handed him one. "I was just wondering," he asked, do you know Billie Magic?"

"She's very popular at school and not afraid to give her opinion. I think she's going to IU in the fall when she graduates, to study Law.

Most guys don't stand a chance with her; she has strong moral principles and will not compromise. Why do you ask? Do you like her?"

"Nah, but she seems like a nice girl" he told her thinking to himself that he'd rip out his heart and give to her on a silver platter if she asked. Then he thought, I've only known her for a day, been knocked to the ground, got one kiss on the lawn of a funeral home, and a knife pulled on me. I must be crazy!

TOUR OF GAS CITY

Moses came up from the church basement and complained about how full he was. "Come on, cousin, I'll give you a tour of the town," Moses said patting his stomach. Moses lit up a cigarette and off they went. He pointed out what businesses used to be here and there, instead of what businesses still remained. They walked by the gas station, and Moses said he had to get more smokes. Eric walked in and in the corner were two ice cream tables and chairs. He looked into the cooler, and the sign said "Five Great Flavors Today." He saw vanilla, chocolate, strawberry, Calvert, and Wolf. Three of the five he easily recognized. Moses walked over, and Eric asked what Calvert and Wolf flavors were. He told Eric that the two flavors were named after Gas City's most famous citizen, Calvert Wolf. He explained that he was a famous artist, and Gas City was his home. He told Eric the house was just up the block and is now a museum.

"Let's go." Eric said. It was a huge Victorian home that had been completely restored. Moses asked if he would like a quick tour, and they went in.

Eric thought the house was magnificent. The curator knew Moses and let the boys come in at no charge. Moses said he used to date her daughter. Each room was filled with the artist's work, and one room was his studio. The canvases, brushes, and paints were the exact way the artist had left them sixty years ago. Even his coffee cup had a plastic see through top so you could see his coffee that was still in the cup. The curator said he had died in this room and nothing had been moved for the last sixty years. She also explained there were coffee cups in every room because he had a caffeine addition.

The last room they went in was huge. It must have been the parlor and had bay windows on both sides of the room. There was only one enormous painting in the room and a guard sitting at a small desk in the corner glaring at the boys. It was a painting of a nude woman sitting on a chair looking out of the one bay windows. Eric was completely taken in by the painting. The woman's skin was flawless, but she had no face. The title was "Unfinished Nude". As Eric looked at the painting, he noticed there was a small mirror to her left that reflected her torso and arm. In her hand she was holding a locket, but it was barely visible to the viewer. The locket appeared to have a small horse on the front, but it could have been a unicorn and seemed to wrap around the model's fingers. The curator said the artist was working on this piece when he died. She told them the model had never been found, but everyone thought she was a young local girl. They were told after he died, the painting had an estimated value of five million dollars. She also told them every painting he had done was valued over half a million dollars, and his work was hanging in most major galleries of the world.

As the boys were leaving she explained that the artist never had any family, and he left his estate to the city with the stipulation that the nude was never to be removed. She told the boys that many universities send students to view his work, and this was Gas City's most prized possession. Eric wondered why the artist was going to finish the face last because it looked as though the painting was complete. She told them that it was rumored the artist had an obsession for the local girl, and he didn't want to expose her face to the world until the very end.

The boys left and Eric told Moses, "That's the most beautiful painting I've ever seen."

Moses said, "The two ice creams, Calvert and Wolf flavors are both coffee flavored, but the Wolf flavor has chocolate infused since

Calvert Wolf was a coffee freak. The other weird thing is our grandmother, Dommy, was rumored to have been his model." Eric just laughed, but he saw Moses was serious. "Think about it. She would have been seventeen when Calvert died. She also lived in town not two blocks away from his house."

"Has she ever mentioned it, or told anyone she wasn't his model?"

"She won't talk about it, and just laughs when asked," Moses said. As they walked back to the church, Eric thought, that nude woman couldn't be my Dommy.

Sissy's Beauty Shop

As promised, Rick brought two heaping plates of food from the church dinner, and Anne carried a basket of dinner rolls and four deserts. Todd saw them coming up the walk. "Mom, that guy is coming back"

She quickly looked out the window and threw on her bathrobe and slippers. "Let them in, honey."

Again before Rick reached the door, it flew open with Todd standing there wearing a thin black blanket around his shoulders and sun glasses. "Come on in." Rick and Anne took the food directly to the kitchen and put in on the counter.

"Where's your Mom? Rick asked.

"She's in the bathroom," pulling down his sun glasses a little.

"Hi, Sis," giving her another big brother hug. You remember my wife, Anne, don't you?"

"It's been a long time, but yes and please be seated" she said just above a whisper.

"We brought food from the church dinner and everyone was asking about you." Anne said.

"Thank you for food, and I'm just now starting to feel better." Todd went running by them and down the basement stairs.

"What happened to the Lone Ranger?" Rick asked.

"Today he's a secret agent and his hideout is in the basement." "He won't let me down there because I might be a spy", and with that, they all chuckled.

Anne looked around the small shop with outdated equipment and a worn out beauty chair. The hair dryers were put together with electrical tape and the beauty poster next to the mirror was from the seventies. There were birdhouses and ceramic crafts on a dusty shelf for sale. Her appointments were written on a chalkboard that probably came from some old grade school that had been torn down. Anne thought; who would come here for a hair treatment?

"We're leaving day after tomorrow," Anne said, "and we'd like to get together with you before we go"

"I'll call the farm tomorrow and let you know if I'm up to it. Thanks again for the food," also in a whisper as they were leaving the shop.

Getting in the car Anne remarked, "Funny she never asked about the funeral."

Sales and Son Funeral Home

Bill and his son Wyatt pulled the cars in the garage and walked into the funeral home. His twelve year old daughter, Susan, was running the vacuum cleaner and told her dad he had a couple of messages. He couldn't help thinking how much she looked like her mom. It wasn't easy raising two children on his own but he felt he had really tried. Wyatt ran upstairs and turned on the television and yelled at his dad that the Cubs were playing Cincinnati at five. He and Wyatt were big Chicago Cubs fans as was Bill's father before him. Wyatt changed into shorts and a Cub's jersey, and his dad did likewise. They walked downstairs to see if Susan needed help. They straightened the chairs; put the flower stands away, and all three headed up to the apartment.

Susan came in and her boys were sprawled on the couch. They now had their Cub's hats on and were yelling at some umpire. She told them she was going to fix pasta and wanted to know if a salad and garlic bread were in order. Even though they had just had a huge church funeral dinner, they both said

"Yes."

As Susan walked from the TV room he felt sorry for the responsibility he had put on his daughter. Even her name Susan wasn't a good choice because the kids called her "Soupy" at school and Soupy Sales will probably always stick. The Cubs lost, but dinner was perfect.

He told the kids he needed to rest and went into his bedroom as they remained watching a reality show. He put his Cub's hat on his dresser next the picture of his wife Ellie and him. The picture was his favorite of them together; they were at Wrigley Field watching the Cub's, and both were caught smiling at each other. She looked so beautiful and happy, and it was such a great memory. After Susan was born, Ellie became depressed and unresponsive. She would do the shopping at 1:00 AM so as not to see anyone. She didn't want to leave home and stayed in her room for hours. He tried to get help and the medication would sometimes perk her up, but that was rare. She took her life seven years ago this May. He had done many funerals for lots of people, but this one seemed like yesterday. He lit the small candle next to her picture, as he had done every day for past seven years, and told her, "Goodnight Ellie."

BACK TO THE FARM

It was early evening as Mary, Rick, Anne, and Eric stumbled into the house. Mary said, "I'm bushed, I'm going to lie down for a while, and later on I'll fix something light for dinner."

"Mom, don't even think about it. We'll manage not to starve to death."

"I have to work on my computer for that federal court case coming up next week," as Anne started up stairs, "and Rick, I need to talk to you when you come up."

"Eric, what are you doing now?" Rick asked.

"I want to have a bonfire tonight, and I'll get all the wood together for out back."

"Be careful, Son, some of the chickens have teeth."

"Boy, Dad, I didn't realize how funny you really are." he said with a smirk.

Rick went up the back stairs to his old room and flopped on his little feather mattress.

"Rick, Anne said in a quiet voice, remember yesterday morning I mentioned that I might need something from you like you received from me?" He nodded. "Well now's the time" as she slipped her dress over her head and gently lowered her blue silk panties.

"Let's try to make less noise" he said with a grin that filled his whole face.

They hadn't touched each other for several years and now all of a sudden they both had a craving to satisfy one another. As they climbed into their little beds, each wondered what had happened. A desire just welled up in them, and they both had a longing to touch and taste each other. Just maybe, they had fallen in love again!

***

It was dark, and Eric's bonfire was great. Everyone pulled up a lawn chair, and Mary came out with Graham crackers, marshmallows, and Hersey Bars on a big plate. "I think smores are on the menu tonight. It was a wonderful day and a great tribute to Richard. So many people truly loved your dad," Mary told them as she looked over at Rick. Just then Tim, Pamela Sue, and Rahab walked up to the fire. They pulled up chairs and joined the group.

Rick said, "I want you all to come out and see us in New York this summer. The trip is on us, we have lots of bedrooms, and we'll show you the sites."

"We can do it after we plant and before the county fair. Maybe early August."

Rahab said with excitement, "I really want to go."

Tim looked at Eric, "Did your dad ever tell you the story of Albert Harris?" and before Eric could respond.

Rahab said "Dad, don't!"

"I'm just curious if the Barr family story has been passed on." Eric shook his head no. Tim moved his chair a little closer to the fire and started talking in almost a whisper. "Before our grandfather bought his farm it used to be a Boy Scout Camp. The main building was just over there, as he pointed to the barn. Every summer the scouts would come here from all over Indiana and Kentucky. The camp director's name was Doc, and he had been here many years. In 1937 there was a camper named Albert Harris, and he was kind of a loner. The story we heard was that he always kept to himself. One night in early summer, about this time of year, he disappeared from camp. The camp counselors, scouts, and Doc looked everywhere for him, and his parents offered a reward for his return. The whole summer was spent looking for Albert. They never found him.

The next summer some scouts were sitting around the campfire and a scout saw a dirty little boy in his uniform walk past the campfire at the edge of the woods. He never thought much of it until he told his counselor who told Doc. The search started again. No Albert. But at night they could hear someone call the name "Doc" from deep in the woods. The next summer three scouts saw him, again very dirty, wearing his scout hat and avoiding the other campers. This went on for many years and many scouts and counselors heard him call the name "Doc." By this time he had a beard and long hair. His parents died many years ago, but the reward still remains and is now worth many thousands of dollars. The fire was very low, and Tim's voice was just above a whisper. He said very slowly, "If any of you ever hear him call the name…just then, behind Eric, Moses hit a big metal pot with a hammer and yelled "Doc" at the top of his lungs. Eric and Anne jumped straight out of their chairs and ran to the other side of the fire holding on to each other. The rest of the family started laughing uncontrollably. "Well, Tim said I guess the Barr family does know the story after all."

The fire died down and so did the conversation. Even after the story, they all looked at the fire with a feeling of peace. Only a few dead marshmallows remained in the fire as they slowly walked from the glowing embers. "Goodnight everyone" they all said together.

Eric said, "Goodnight Albert," and the porch light went out.

Sunday Morning

That familiar smell was coming from the kitchen. Eric looked over at the small cowboy clock on the dresser. Eric thought to himself six o'clock. You've got to be kidding. Down the back stairs he went, "Hi, Dommy."

"Did you sleep well?" she asked.

"I did until those two roosters started in at four-thirty this morning." I always thought they crow at daylight."

"I think there's a competition between the guys. They're always stealing hens from the other. Now, what do you want for breakfast? I do have fried mush you might like."

"Sure, why not? Do you have some of that thick bacon left?"

"Coming right up, Little Blade" she said with a smile. "I heard what Billie called you in the church and I don't want to know where the name came from. It's ok Eric, I'm the only one that heard her, and it's our secret."

Rick and Anne came down as Eric was finishing his third helping of mush. "Mom, how did you sleep?"

"Believe it or not I passed out last night. My feet were throbbing and my calves were killing me, but when I did get to sleep, it was all night. I'm not going to church today; I just don't have it in me."

"Do you think all the saints will cut you some slack?" Anne asked

"I still can't get over Libby Shepard's hair. She was even wearing some dangly earrings at the funeral; totally out of her character."

"Well, Anne and I fell asleep as soon as our heads hit the pillows."

"What dad, no jokes or loud laughing last night?"

"Like I said Eric, right to sleep."

"Dad, can I borrow the car today?"

"Where are you going?"

"Oh I don't know, just drive around"

Mary said, "You can use grandpa's old truck if you like. He would like another generation of Barr's using it."

"Is it Ok, Dad?"

"Sure, just don't get lost."

"Honey, the keys are in it," his grandmother said. Out the door he flew. Now he thought; how I can get to the Billie's house without asking anybody for directions? The old truck sat high with the oversize tires on it. There was a shotgun hanging in the back window and he almost felt invincible as the truck fired up with a big roar; an adventure awaited!

FAITH BAPTIST CHURCH

The 10:00 o'clock worship service was set to begin. The choir was in the back room going over a couple of hymns. Pastor Ken was leading the choir and told them they were getting new choir robes in two weeks. He told them it took three months to decide on the colors and what was being shipped was it. He would not reveal the colors and assured them that God would be pleased. The only comment from the back was "It better not be green!" Pastor Ken had gotten emails, notes, phone calls and a German chocolate cake on what each member thought the colors should be. He thought to himself that God surely must have a good sense of humor because his was just about gone.

Pastor Roger talked about the mission they supported in Haiti and the children would be passing among the congregation with small buckets for change. He announced the Ladies Aid Circle carry in potluck dinner would feature a dynamic Christian speaker on Wednesday. He reminded the ladies to pick up their pots, pans, and dishes in the lost and found or they would be donated to the Salvation Army. Roger spoke of the youth group's trip to Colorado, and they would be showing slides of the Native American Mission School they painted. He paused for a few minutes until Pepper Hudson took her screaming three year old son, Jackie, his diaper bag and two stuffed animals out the back door.

His sermon today was on sacrifice and told of John the Baptist giving up everything and living only for the Lord. In his sermon, he mentioned Richard Barr, Sr. and what he had done for the church and community. His comment was, "Richard set a high standard we all should model." People across the church nodded, each with a memory of Richard Barr. The choir stood to sing "How Great Thou Art," and Pastor Roger noticed his little redhead, second row up on the end, wearing her brand new red pumps and probably little else beneath the black choir robe. She winked at him this time, and he couldn't wait to get home, because the kids were away at Bible camp.

THE MAGIC FARM

The white fence wasn't hard to spot. The big sign by the road said "Magic" and had a large horse holding a magic wand. "Oh my gosh! He uttered to himself, there she is." His hands were sweaty, and his heart was racing as he pulled up by the barn.

She rode her horse over to the fence and said, "Hey, Little Blade." He got out of the truck walked over to the fence, and climbed on top. Billie had on tight jeans, plaid shirt, and a Pacer's baseball cap. He noticed the same brunette girl that picked up Billie at the funeral home was riding around the inside oval. So what brings you to the Magic Farm?"

"Just riding around and noticed the sign."

"Yeah, right!" she came back with. "We're training a new horse, and you're welcome to watch." He saw her go full gallop then stop, then back again over and over. She and the horse seemed to be one. Whatever he did, she seemed to match it with her body. Many a time she would pull on the reins hard to let him know who's boss.

Her father walked over to the fence where Eric was sitting. "You're Rick's boy, aren't ya?" he asked

"Yes, I am."

"I saw you at the funeral for your grandpa. You look a lot like your dad when I knew him. He too is a wonderful man and saved my life once", as he headed for the barn. "Ask you dad about it sometime."

"I will, Mr. Magic"

Billie and her friend Dar finished riding and tied the horses by the water trough. The girls walked over to the bales of hay, beating their pants with their hats to get off any unwanted dust and sat down. "Come on over," Billie said.

From behind the bales, Darlene produced a clear bottle of their local soda pop. Dar was a cute brunette with short, almost boyish hair. Her eyes were large like big brown almonds. She wore tight blue jeans with a large horseshoe belt buckle, bright yellow very tight tee shirt and old worn tan cowboy boots. Eric remembered that stuff all right. "Have a taste," Dar said.

He did, but a real small one this time, letting the clear liquid slowly warm his mouth and throat. After two small gulps he felt pretty bold, "Say, do you want to come to New York City? We have plenty of room, and I can show you all the hot spots."

There was a minute pause as she looked all around the farm. "No thanks, I have everything I've ever wanted right here." She got up and walked over to Eric, put her hands behind his head and kissed him on the cheek. Today her skin smelled liked lilac and vanilla, and her lips were so soft. She then whispered in a low and sultry voice, "You are darn cute!" gently kissed him on the lips, jumped over the fence, onto the horse, and around they went.

Dar got up, took one more swig, and said "Don't give up on that one. She's a keeper, just needs a little training."

On the truck ride back, he replayed Dar's words over and over. Eric dated many girls and had sex with most of them. This girl was completely different than anyone he had ever met. He was completely under her power, and he had no idea why. He couldn't sleep, and his mind seemed to have lost the off switch because all he wanted was Billie. He just kept thinking. I got to get a grip here!

Gas City Band Concert

It was a beautiful Sunday afternoon. After leaving Billie's Farm, Eric drove downtown to try the Calvert or Wolf flavored ice cream. He pulled the pickup in front of the small convenience store and noticed his cousin Rahab sitting on a blanket listening to music coming from the small bandstand in the park. There were about fifty older people and two younger couples sitting on lawn chairs.

He walked over "What's going on?"

"The first Sunday of each summer month the city band puts on a free concert."

Eric looked puzzled, "Why are you listening to old show tunes with some big band thrown in?"

"It's not the music Eric, but the drummer."

Eric looked at the skinny- pimply faced boy pounding out the beats and wondered why the kid would play with fourteen members of the city band having an average age of about seventy.

"His name is Terry, and he's kind of my boyfriend. They couldn't find a drummer because Mel Johnson, the old drummer, died this winter. He was eighty-six, and his granddaughter told me they buried him with a snare drum and six sets of drum sticks. Isn't that wild? I guess Terry was their only option, but he gets $45.00 for the two hours he plays, and after the concert he's taking me to drag races in Mill Creek. Eric, don't say anything to my parents. They'll kill me if they know I'm with Terry."

"I won't even mention I saw you. Hey, what flavor of ice cream should I try the Calvert or the Wolf?"

"Don't buy either on. They both taste like crap. Stick with strawberry."

Mary's Farm

Eric pulled into Dommy's farm; his parents and his grandmother were sitting on lawn chairs facing County Road 600 E.

"Where have you been?" Rick asked.

"Just driving around and got some ice cream uptown. What have you been doing all day?"

"We've been reminiscing about your grandfather and your dad growing up in this small town. Gas City probably seems very backward and unexciting compared to New York City."

Anne said, "Quite the contrary, we have met so many nice, genuine people here. I've noticed that what you see is what you get in Gas City."

"Dommy, I like the kids here, and no one seems to want to outdo the other."

"Oh there's plenty of competition here; we just go about showing it in different ways. I heard Alice Cummings say yesterday at the funeral dinner that she liked my dress, but apparently I didn't have many other choices in my closet. Got to love her."

"Well, Rick's old prom date, I think it was Janet, asked how much a face lift costs in New York," Anne said with a smile," I could take that at least three different ways. I was so tempted to ask her where she bought her clothes because Barnum and Bailey do travel the Midwest."

"That's why you are such a good lawyer, Honey."

"Let's go inside and see how many leftovers we can get into. I'm getting hungry, and I'll call Sissy and Todd and see if they want to join us," Mary said.

"Dad, when we get back, I want you to tell the Albert Harris story, and I'll scare the hell out of my friends."

"I like that idea; let's practice on Hazel the housekeeper, and maybe your mom can help with the surprise."

"Dad, can we stay a couple more days?"

"No, we have to get back to work and your mom has that court case, but why do you ask?

"I like it here a little and have met a couple of nice kids."

"We have to leave early in the morning."

GOING BACK TO NEW YORK.

The roosters were at it again. Yep, 4:30 the cowboy clock said. Eric knew they were leaving at 6:00 A.M. and he was mostly packed. He came down to the kitchen, and his grandma had her back to him and was attending to something in the oven.

"Hi, Dommy." She turned, and tears were streaming down her cheeks. "What's the matter?" he asked as he put his arm around her waist.

"Everything. Your grandpa leaving me; you all going back to New York and those two roosters," she said with a smile. They both had a good laugh at that. "Sit down Eric. I have a breakfast casserole coming out of the oven right now."

"Dommy, can I come back this summer when the fair is on?"

"Of course you can. This is your second home I would love to have you stay here."

Rick and Anne came down the stairs with their bags. "Eric," Anne said, "Please put these in the car for us."

"Mom, I really want you to come out to New York with Tim and Pamela Sue in August," Rick said.

She came back with, "Honey, I'll think about it. Let's leave it at that. I made you some French toast, and I've packed some goodies for the trip home."

"Sissy never called us back, so I'm assuming she's still sick." Anne said.

"Tim and I will go over to the shop and check on her in a little while. I can't even begin to tell you what it meant to have all of you here with me. This week has really been rough for me, but you were there when I really needed someone to smooth out the trouble spots. Eric, I can't tell you how much I will miss our little talks in the early mornings. Thanks again, and have a safe trip back. By the way, if you would like a barn cat or a rooster to take back to New York, I have a couple in mind," she said with a big grin.

***

"OK, Mom, my stomach is full, and so is the tank. We'll be on our way. No cats or birds but thanks for thinking of us." Hugs and kisses followed, and Mary walked them to the car and continued to wave until she appeared like a dot in his rear view mirror.

"Dad," Eric said, "can I come back this summer to stay with Grandma and go to the Lincoln Co. Fair?"

Rick seemed startled. "Wait a minute! You want to come back to Gas City, Indiana, stay on a farm, go to a 4-H Co. Fair with smelly animals; eat elephant ears, and hangout with the local farm kids? Is that what you just asked? You were going to Cape Cod and to sailing school this summer. What happened with that?"

"You're right about one thing; I do want to hang with the local farm kids," he said with a smile as his mind drifted off to a certain cowgirl.

The car stopped again at the Tell City Truck Stop, and Rick got out to fill the car. "Dad that old guy over there is waving at you."

"He's the guy that owns that little car lot and wants to trade my car for a truck. He is a funny man." Eric and his mother went into the truck stop to use the bathroom. Eric still couldn't believe how much crap this place sold. Right on top of the CD pile was Hank Williams, Jr.'s Greatest Hits. For 99 cents he'd check him out. Back in the car and on their way.

"What did you buy in there?" his dad asked.

"Just a CD."

"Please don't play that heavy metal in the car."

"It's not that. It's Hank Williams Jr."

"Eric, what happened to you in the last six days?" his mom asked.

"Not sure," as he slid the CD into his laptop.

EARLY AT MOM'S DINER

The usual chatter came from the round table in the corner. The guys were working out the final plans to go to Bill Daniel's farm and help him out. Mom came over to warm the coffees. Everyone got a warmer except Marvin.

"Hey!" Marvin said "Where's mine?"

Mom said, "I told you not to wear those boots to the funeral, didn't I?"

"I couldn't find my shoes."

"Your bare feet would've looked better. Go get your own coffee."

"Yes, Mom." he said sheepishly, and all the guys went "OOOOOO" in unison.

Mom brought over an empty cup and set it at the place that Richard normally called his and filled it to the top. "There," she said "This is for Richard today."

Bill Sales got praises, not put downs as he took a piece of toast from Marvin's plate.

"You did a great job for Richard's funeral," they all said. "A fitting end to a well lived life."

Lester remarked, "Bill, no matter what you do for my funeral, and that includes anything, please don't have Hugh Jackson play his bagpipes. It sounded like half a dozen cats fighting over a piece of fish. Everything else was perfect, but what's with the pastor's wife's hair? Whoa!"

AURORA PLANNING LLC

Cal dropped Richard off at the back door of the Feinman Building. No words were exchanged. He took the service elevator to the thirty-sixth floor, stepped off, with Yolanda at her desk. "How did it go?" She asked.

"I'll tell you later. Call the three stooges in the board room ASAP."

Linda, David, and James walked together down the hall looking at each other not saying a word. James hoped nobody told Richard about the Power Point he showed at Richard's expense. Oh, well, he thought, I should be able to find some kind of work. This is a big city.

"Sit down." Richard commanded. They opened their lap tops and just stared at the screens. "James and Linda, I need you both to go to Kansas City, Missouri, in the morning to close the American Rubber Plant deal. After the papers are signed, you will fire the 168 employees on the spot. You then will post a notice hiring them back at half their current salaries. If they don't bite on that, they're gone for good. Any questions?" he asked.

James asked, "I thought that deal was a no go."

"I closed it yesterday from Indiana when you assholes were in your nice warm beds. You guys don't know jack shit! Now get going! Oh, by the way, thank all the staff for the contribution in my father's name. We have enough money to put up a building at the fairgrounds in his honor."

As the three left the board room, they all remarked, "This was his first thank you to us in seven years. He must be mellowing."

Sarah's Charm and Chatter

Tim and his mother walked in the shop even though the closed sign hung in the door. Sissy was standing at her station cleaning out her brushes. "Hi, Honey," Mary said. Sissy ran to her mother and gave her a long affectionate hug. "How are you feeling?"

"The vomiting and diarrhea stopped on Saturday, the day of the funeral. I'm feeling much better. There was loud music coming from the basement and Sissy said, "If Todd asks if you are a spy, please tell him no. You see, he's a secret agent, and it'll make things go much smoother around here."

Mary laid a picnic basket on the kitchen table and told her there were lots and lots of leftovers from the funeral dinner. Mary told

Sissy all about the funeral and the many friends that had come. Everyone wanted to know how Sissy was feeling.

Tim told his mom he had to go to the hardware store since they were in town, so they got ready to leave as Todd came running up the stairs wearing a blanket cape and sun glasses and in a loud voice said "Are you people spies?"

"No," they both responded in loud voices.

"That's good." And back down the basement he flew.

They all laughed, and as they opened the door to the shop, there stood Libby Shepard, and she immediately stepped in. Sissy realized that the vinegar hadn't done very much on the brilliant red and she knew she was in for a long tongue lashing.

With a deep sigh, Sissy said "Yes?" Libby reached in her purse pulled out two twenty dollar bills, placed them in her hand and, sauntered out the door. Not a word was spoken as Sissy looked at the money in utter amazement and Libby just drove away.

THE DANIEL FARM, GAS CITY, INDIANA

Bill Daniel was a hard worker and wonderful provider for his family of eight, but bad luck fell upon the farm. His barn was struck by lightning and burned to the ground in a matter of two hours. He lost his tractor and several cows, but today over forty men gathered to have a barn raising. There were eighteen Amish men and boys, and they set to work on the framing. The rest of men were busy preparing the foundation. It was hot, but the women put up a tent and provided fresh lemonade and cold water for the men. You could hear saws roaring and hammers striking their targets all over the structure, and the fresh smell of new lumber and sawdust filled the air. At noon, the women called the men over for a fine luncheon with homemade pies, cakes, and Patsy Yoder's famous fried chicken.

At 7:00 P.M. the structure was completely framed in, and tomorrow the men would finish the job. Bill and Jill Daniel, along with their six children waved goodbye and just stared at the beautiful barn as the men and women left in trucks and horse-drawn buggies. The neat thing was they never asked for help; their friends just showed up. Jill broke down in tears, and her family surrounded her with a family hug and many kisses.

The Barr Home in New York

It had been almost two months since the funeral. Things were back to the Barr Family normal. Eric was mouthy as ever. He had been late to school eleven times, and they found pot in this coat. His girlfriend, Kandy, wasn't hanging around much anymore, but she called all the time and told Eric she could get some "good stuff," but rarely did Eric answer her calls or emails. Most of his calls were back to Gas City, Indiana, but Billie wasn't much of a conversationalist. Most of her comments were to the point, but she did remind him of the big week at the 4-H fairgrounds, and he so wanted to be with her.

Anne won the federal forgery case and celebrated by taking her intern to the Bahamas for a long weekend. She was moving up in the law firm and soon would be a full partner. She came home late most evenings and rarely had contact with Richard except an occasional meal or a hello in the hall. Their marriage was back to the old ways and both seemed all right with that.

Richard was making a lot of money and putting many families on the street. He closed three more deals and personally fired seven of his office staff. They were all petrified of him and never knew what kind of mood he would be in as he stepped from the elevator each day. He was staying at his girlfriend's apartment two nights a week. The family rarely spoke, but they got along. In two weeks, Tim and his family were coming to New York. Rick's comment to his family was, "What are we going to do with them?"

Mom's Diner at 6:30 AM

Today sixteen guys were sitting at their usual round table. The Lincoln County Fair was rapidly approaching, and most talk was about the cattle auction and the tractor exhibit. Jenny, the waitress, came over to give the guys a warmer up. "Where's Mom?" Lester asked.

"She isn't feeling very good today and is home in bed. I think she is depressed. You know, she is behind on the mortgage and she may lose the diner to the bank. Remember, you never heard it from me."

"How much does she owe?" "Can you tell us that?"

"Hold on, let me get Chris. I think he knows more." Chris was the cook and was Jenny' husband. He came from kitchen wiping his hands on his apron.

"Chris, what's the deal with Mom?" someone asked.

Chris pulled up a chair next to Bill Sales and told them what he knew. "Mom told Jenny and me that she only had two months to pay up the mortgage and back interest or the credit union would foreclose. "She has tried to get more people in, like having fish dinners on Fridays and the steak fest on Saturdays. She said it has helped some, but not nearly enough. She also hasn't much money for advertising, except word of mouth," Chris said. He got up and headed back to the kitchen. "This has been her life and her love for the past twelve years ever since her son died in the swimming accident." The guys all looked at each other and knew they could help. There were quiet whispers going around the table and they all agreed to meet at the credit union as soon as it opened at 9:00 AM.

***

When the manager, James Shellabarger arrived at 8:50 A.M., the credit union parking lot was full of pickup trucks. He thought he must have forgotten about a meeting, but for the life of him couldn't remember which one. As he got out of his car, the men exited their trucks.

"Jimmy," Lester called," we need to talk."

Realizing his office was way too small; he moved the group down the hall to the meeting room. He still had a puzzled look as they all tried to find seat. "Ok, gentlemen, what's this all about?"

Carl Jackson started, "We heard you have the mortgage on Mom's diner, and we want to know the particulars."

"I can't give you any information. It's protected by law."

Lester spoke next, "We are here to help Mom and not to spread rumors."

"I absolutely will not tell you anything."

"Jimmy, remember the time you crapped your pants at the little league game in Union Mills and I took you to the bathroom and cleaned your ass, bought you a new pair of pants, and no one was the wiser?" Lester asked among the chuckles in the room.

"You guys, I can't do it!" he said firmly.

"Ok then," Carl said, "each one of us has an account here. Two of these men are on your advisory board; one of these guys has the insurance on the building, and if I can speak for the rest, we all want to pull our money out of your credit union today." All the men started to get up.

"Whoa! Whoa! I know I can get into a lot of trouble telling you anything, but I can't afford to lose my sixteen biggest accounts either. I'll be right back with the file." He left the room, and they all gave each other fist pumps and big smiles. He came back in, sat down and opened the file. "She owes $4,000.00 in back payments and another $28,000 on the building."

"That's all?" Carl asked

"That's it in a nutshell, gentlemen."

Marvin reached into his bib overalls, retrieved his checkbook and looked around the table. Each man nodded but no words were spoken. He wrote a check for $32,000 knowing each man would pay his share. He handed the check to James, and said "Jimmy, make the deed out to Mom but tell no one about this."

They all got up to leave each shaking James's hand. Carl said, "We weren't going to pull our money out but you just needed an excuse to satisfy a bunch of dirty farmers."

"By the way," Marvin said, "we never knew you crapped you pants, and if the deed isn't delivered tomorrow that story will circulate all over town."

"Have a great day," they all said. In the parking lot they came up with a plan to surprise Mom. The day after tomorrow was the date they set, and Carl headed to his workshop.

MOM'S DINER TWO DAYS LATER

The guys were sitting around the table grinning. It was like Christmas morning, and they couldn't wait to open presents under the tree. Mom came out to warm the coffees, and the guys just stared at her. In the middle of the table was a wooden model of Mom's Diner with the same matching colors and sign painted on the little building. She looked and said "This is beautiful, but what was it?

Carl picked it up and handed it to Mom. "Open it."

She lifted the top off and inside was a paper rolled up tied with a ribbon. She put the little diner down and opened the paper. The deed read Yvonne Clarkson owner of 115 Main Street, Gas City, Indiana. "What is this?" she asked.

Marvin replied, "It's your diner now."

She burst into tears and ran into the kitchen to show Jenny and Chris. She went out the back door into the alley and held the deed to the sky and shouted "Thank you, God, for putting those guys into my life. I'm not sure what angels are supposed to look like, but just maybe they do wear overalls." Returning to the table, Mom kissed each man on his forehead, because she just couldn't talk. Lester told her the Saturday, after the fair, the guys were coming over and paint the diner so she would need to pick out a color. They would also be putting a new roof over the entrance, and Bill was donating a new sign with bright colors and a catchy logo. As each man left the diner, she didn't notice any halos, but some awfully big hearts stuffed into old work clothes and one dark blue suit.

Gas City Family Arrive

It was August 14th, and a big silver dual tire Dodge truck pulled into Rick and Anne's driveway. Moses said, "Holy crap! I didn't know we were visiting royalty."

Rahab exclaimed, "Look they have a pool with a slide and high dive."

"After you kids quit drooling, help unload the truck." The truck pulled around back of the house by the garage. There was a small door next to six car garage, and it was open. "Ok, kids, we have a lot to unload," Tim said.

Just then, a pleasant looking woman came out to greet them. "I know who you are, and the family is expecting you." she said. If you have things to bring in, I'll open this garage door. By the way, I'm Hazel, the housekeeper. Welcome."

Tim started handing things from the back of the truck. Two bushel baskets of Indiana sweet corn, four cases of an Indiana beer, two large coolers on wheels, and medium size cooler that said "Danger" on it.

"Your brother and sister-in-law are in the city and probably won't be home for about three hours. If you have something you need to keep cool, bring it in the kitchen. You may put the cooled items in the refrigerator over there." Pamela Sue walked over to where Hazel had pointed but couldn't find the refrigerator. "I'm sorry," Hazel said, "just push the yellow button." Pamela Sue pushed the button, the oak paneling slid open, and behind it was a large glass door that also opened. Pamela Sue stepped in the room and looked at all the food on shelves, neatly arranged. It was bigger than her bedroom. She was completely speechless, so she placed her food on the shelves and stepped out. The glass door closed, and the oak paneling slid back to conceal its contents. Hazel said, "The freezer is next to it. Push that other yellow button." Same thing happened; paneling opened, glass door opened, and she stepped into the room that was the freezer.

This time she did say, "Wow!"

"When you're ready, I'll show you the bedrooms."

Pamela Sue couldn't wait. Tim and his family each had one suitcase, and they carried them up the long, winding stairs. Moses said with a big grin, "Too bad you don't have and elevator."

Hazel replied "We do." Tim and Pamela Sue's room faced the front of the house which had a large fountain by the driveway.

Moses's and Rehab's rooms faced the pool, tennis court, and some kind of outdoor bowling alley.

Rahab said, "I could get use to this," and jumped on the canopy bed.

"When you get settled in, come on down. I've fixed some finger sandwiches and snacks. You can eat out by the pool if you like."

Moses said with a big laugh, "I've had pig's knuckles before but never a finger sandwich."

As they were coming down the stairs, Pamela Sue said, "I want to go back in the refrigerator again." Tim just shook his head.

They went on an expedition, exploring the house and yard. Pamela Sue just loved to push buttons. Tim told her she might push something she might regret. In the library she pushed a red button and a wall rotated to reveal a full bar with glass mirror. In the living room she pushed a blue button, and the three fireplaces started at once. In the study she pushed a brown button to reveal a huge aquarium hidden behind a very large photo of a tranquil beach scene. Still, her favorite was the refrigerator.

They sat by the pool and had beer, wine, lemonade, and snacks. "Sit down with us." Tim said to Hazel.

"I have too many things to do." She did stand and talk for a while. "My family is originally from Denmark," she said with pride. My father started a company that dried oak leaves and made them into Christmas wreaths. He was very successful but died young. My mother, brother, and I tried to keep the business going but had no knowledge of sales, so the business failed. My mother passed away last year, and my brother lives in California. I heard you're from Indiana. I've never been to the Midwest, but Eric says it's cool. I have to get dinner started, but if you need anything, just ask," she said with a nice smile.

Anne was the first home. The garage door opened and the yellow Porsche glided into its bay. She came through the kitchen and noticed the silver pickup truck in the back. "Where are they?"

"By the pool Mrs. Barr."

Anne dropped her briefcase by the door and walked out on the terrace. "Welcome," she said with a big smile. They all got up and hugged her. She kicked off her shoes and plopped down on a patio chair. Her glass of wine arrived instantly. "How was the trip?" she asked stretching her long legs like cat getting up from a nap.

"Very uneventful, but we brought fresh picked corn, steaks, and a ham from Indiana. Would you like to have a cook out some night this week?

"That sounds fabulous. Let's make it Friday night"

Moses asked, "Where's Eric?"

"Oh, he's serving a detention at school," she said with a sigh. He'll be home in about an hour. I'm going to change, and I'll be down in a minute," as she headed for the stairs. "Help yourself to whatever you want."

Pamela Sue looked over at Tim and said "I need something from the refrigerator." Tim looked at the kids, and they all shook their heads.

Cal dropped Richard in the back of the house. He too noticed the big silver pickup truck. As he walked into the kitchen no words were uttered, but Hazel handed him his glass of 30 year old scotch. "They're by the pool," she said.

Richard walked out, hugged the four and too plopped down into a patio chair. He raised his glass and said "Welcome to New York. I knew Sissy and Mom wouldn't come out."

"Mom doesn't want to leave the farm and Sissy's life is the beauty shop. Sissy says thanks again for the money you gave her. She was completely taken back by your gift and bought a new stylist chair and two new hairdryers. She's in pig heaven, and they started the 4H building at the fairgrounds last week in Dad's honor. It will be fantastic," Tim said.

Eric walked in and asked "What's the word from Indiana?"

"Not much happens in Gas City," Moses said with a sigh.

"Don't say that. Your bull, Caesar, is up for the grand champion steer this year at the fair," Pamela Sue said with pride

"Like I said, nothing much happens."

They had dinner in the dining room. Hazel served a Danish dish that looked like a hamburger but was much better. Smothered in gravy, with new potatoes and red cabbage, the Gas City clan had no complaints and even asked for seconds.

Anne said, "Tim and Pamela Sue want to have a cookout this Friday, and they brought a bunch of good food from Indiana, including sweet corn they just picked."

"It sounds good to me, but I will be running a little late on Friday. Go ahead and get the party started. I'm looking forward to Indiana sweet corn on the grill," Rick said.

It was getting late, and Tim told them he needed sleep. He excused himself and called for Pamela Sue. She said she had to get one more thing from the refrigerator, and she'd be up.

Kansas City, Missouri

"I have the maps, and the cooler is filled. The three guns are in the trunk under a blanket and all we have to do is fill up the car," Larry said, I even know what the house looks like."

His friend asked, "How long will it take to get to the bastard's house?"

"I figure two days tops. New York City isn't that far away." They threw their empty beer cans in the street and jumped into the car for a road trip. As the car back out of Larry's driveway, one couldn't help but notice the license plate with the logo "The Show Me State". Larry thought to himself, he's going to pay!

MOM'S DINER.

Marvin got up to fill his coffee cup. "Ok, Mom" he said, "If I promise never to wear the boots to any social function again, will you please serve me coffee?" The whole group turned to look at Mom for an answer. She stood looking at Marvin and noticed he had his feet up on the empty chair exposing a brand new pair of black wing tips. He had the biggest grin they had ever seen on him. She couldn't help but smile and poured him his warmer up.

"They look very nice, but with those dirty bib overalls, they just don't seem to fit," and gave him a big wink. "The rest of you could take some lessons from Marvin, here," she said as she turned to leave.

"Yes, Mom," they said in unison. Just then Bill Sales walked in and the comments began. "We heard your hearse died on the way to the cemetery," someone said, and "Bill, are you sure you bury six feet deep?" Bill smiled, sat on a seat next to Lester, and grabbed a piece of toast from Marvin's plate.

Bill looked over and noticed Marvin's shoes "Nice! Are those for your funeral?" The whole table laughed out loud and Bill thought maybe he should dish some out on these guys once in a while.

Mom filled their cups, put the coffee pot down and sat in the corner. She just stared at her boys. Even though she was only forty-three she knew her calling was to watch over these men. Seeking her approval, they would show her a dress they bought for their wife, or a piece of jewelry for a special occasion or ask where to take their wife out to dinner in Evansville. They knew she would be brutally honest and tell them the truth. Many a dress was returned, thanks to Mom's opinion. She even was asked in private one time about a sex toy their wife might like. That's where she drew the line. She had no opinion on that subject.

Rick and Anne's Home

Tim was up first. He walked down stairs to the kitchen, looked at the hidden refrigerator, and shook his head. He stared at the tall chrome coffee maker and couldn't see how it even opened. All of a sudden it started brewing coffee and in less than a minute, it was brewed and hot, just waiting for his cup. I like this gadget he thought. The coffee was awesome and filled the whole kitchen with a wonderful aroma. Tim walked outside and noticed six men working on the lawn and bushes. They were oh so quiet, he thought. One man had on a plaid shirt, so Tim walked over to him. "What time do you guys start? Tim asked.

"We start at 5:30 AM and are done by 9:00 AM" the Hispanic man said.

"That's what time we start on the farm. My name is Tim, and this is my brother's house. We are here on a visit. By the way, do you need a hand with that large branch?" Tim asked, "I have a chain and wench in my truck over there"

"My name is Victor Mendez. This is my lawn business, and these amigos are my crew" he said with great pride. We are all family and do every house in this neighborhood, and yes that wench will work just fine. Thanks."

Tim put his coffee cup down and pulled the truck over to the branch. The wench did its work, lifted the branch and placed it put it into Victor's truck. Tim said "Your crew is so quiet, that I didn't even know you were here."

Victor said, "The people in this neighborhood don't want to see or hear us, and that's ok with me."

Everyone was stirring now. Hazel had a nice breakfast waiting on the patio, bagels, fruit, cereal, and three kinds of juices. What a glorious morning. They talked about the trip into the city. Rick told them he would meet up with them at noon and gave them an itinerary. Anne said she had the day off and would be their guide. Wherever they wanted to go, she'd be with them. Rahab wanted to go to the Statue of Liberty, and Moses wanted to see the 911 spot. Rick asked Anne if she wanted their driver to take them in or ride the subway.

Both kids yelled, "The subway!"

Off they went into the city that could either lift you or crush you. The subway was crowded, and both Tim and Moses got up to let two ladies sit. They got some strange stares for that move, and Anne just smiled. People were staring at Tim like he was some kind of cowboy or part of an advertising stunt. He had on newer but worn jeans, a big silver belt buckle with a bull on it, brown worn cowboy boots, red plaid shirt with silver tips on the lapels, a brown and black cowboy hat with his thick long blond hair hanging almost to his shoulders, a three day growth on his tanned face, and all that on a 6'3" frame. Anne thought no wonder everyone is looking at him. He's way too handsome and has not a clue why the women are looking at him like they are. One girl asked Tim if she could have her picture taken with him. Her girlfriend pulled out her cell phone, and it's now probably on her Facebook Wall Anne thought.

Rick met them at Rockefeller Center, and they ate lunch outside by the skaters. "What did you kids see?" Rick asked. They started talking a mile a minute, sharing every detail of their day. Rick just kept smiling as they went on and on.

Anne said, "The biggest hit has been your brother. People are stopping him and asking him about Texas. Isn't that a hoot?" Just then two very attractive ladies came to the table and asked Tim for a picture with them. "See," Anne said with a big smile. Pamela Sue just looked over and thought, what's the big deal?

"Tim", Richard said, "do you want to see my office? It's not far from here." They all walked down Fifth Avenue to the Feinman Building. When the elevator doors opened, they were met by Yolanda, as she had an important message for Richard. "Show them to my office." Richard said.

The receptionist took them down the hall past the large room with thirty computers and thirty secretaries. They all stopped. After the receptionist seated them in Richard's office she came back by the large room. The buzz around the room, was, who is that guy? And did you see that tight butt? And somebody said "I'd like to have his baby."

Yolanda told them to be quiet, he was Richard's brother from Indiana. Yolanda said, "I wonder if he's married, as if that would even make a difference with you girls," trying to hide a little smile. As she left the room, "You better stay away from that Marlboro Man," she added.

Arriving back at the house, everyone was bushed. Hazel had a pork chop dinner with all the trimmings waiting for them, and after dinner they went out on the terrace. Eric had the cousins come downstairs to his room. Speakers, posters, flat screens and a large pool table made up his bedroom.

"Hey, you guys, have you seen that girl Billie?" he asked, trying not to be too obvious.

Rahab said, "Moses, I told you he had the hots for her."

"I just think she's kind of cute," Eric shot back.

Moses said, "Yup, we just saw her three days ago. She was swimming naked in our pond."

Eric sat straight up with his eyes as big as Texas. "Really?"

"No, not really, but you're right Sis. He's a goner." Moses said with a laugh.

"My summer school is over next week, and I'm coming to Indiana for the fair."

"Why don't you ride back with us, and we'll try and accidently have you two meet somewhere."

"You'd do that for me?

"Sure! You're family, and we only have one other cousin, and he's a secret agent," Moses said as they all laughed.

***

The next morning Tim was the first one up again. He bolted down the stairs into the kitchen and right up to the coffee maker; instantly it started to brew. He thought to himself, I got to get one of these. He walked outside with his coffee cup in hand and there was Victor and his crew. "Good morning Victor." Tim said in a quiet voice.

"Buena's Dias, Senor Tim."

"Say, we are having a cookout here tonight. Would you and your family like to join us?"

"Are you sure it's all right? We've never met your brother before."

"I'm sure he won't mind."

Victor said proudly, "My wife makes the best salsa and guacamole in the world. We'll bring a bunch for everyone."

"Great! See you tonight about six." and Tim walked into the kitchen to check out the coffee maker again.

Everyone sat around the breakfast table and talked about the day before and the expedition into the city.

Rahab said with great excitement, "Uncle Rick, we saw Tom Hanks walking his dog right along the street, and he spoke to me."

Anne said, "It's true, he was in SoHo walking along Broome Street, and Rahab didn't bother him except to say good morning and he said it back to her."

"Nobody in Gas City will ever believe me anyway."

Rick told Tim when he got into the city; Cal would bring the car back to take him shopping for the cookout that night. Tim thought that would be good as he hadn't seen any grocery stores within five miles of Rick's home. Tim also forgot to mention he had invited seven Hispanic gardeners and their families for the evening.

Cal pulled up in the big black limo, and Tim came out holding Pamela Sue's list. Cal opened the back door for Tim, but Tim closed it and jumped into the seat next to Cal. "We seem too far away from each other to talk," Tim said and stuck out his hand "Hi, I'm Tim."

Cal thought to himself these two can't be brothers. "Where to?"

"My brother said that Whole Foods would be good for our cookout tonight."

"What kind of food is on your list?" Cal asked.

"Chicken, ribs, potatoes, vegetables."

"I got a way better suggestion." Cal said with a smile, "Harlem."

"Let's go."

The limo pulled up in front of Leroy's. It appeared to be a small butcher shop with an old blue sign that had faded over many years of weather and soot. The e in the sign was almost gone, and from a distance it appeared to read L roy's. As they walked in everybody behind the meat counter came around and hugged Cal.

Leroy said, "Who's the cowboy?"

"He's Richard's brother and I told him I would bring him to the best meat market in the city."

"You've come to the right place, Tex." Leroy said. "Now what's on your list?" The two big boxes they carried out were filled with chicken breasts and wings and the other with baby back ribs. On the way back, Cal and Tim really bonded as brothers, but they were probably the most unlikely pair in all of New York: black, white, city and country.

They talked about their wives and families. Tim said "My wife makes the best chicken barbeque sauce that ever existed."

Cal countered, "My wife, Lizzy, makes the best barbeque ribs sauce in the City of New York."

"It's settled," Tim responded "You and your family are coming to the cookout."

Tim arrived home with the food, and the kitchen was a mad house. Pamela Sue was the general in charge, and everyone was taking orders. Pamela Sue's barbeque sauce was slow cooking on the stove, and boy did it smell good Hazel thought. Rahab was in the dining room making invitations. When Tim was gone, Pamela Sue said "What's a cookout without at least fifty people?" Rahab took old brown paper grocery sacks, burned the edges like a pirate map and wrote. "Come over to the Barr's. We're cookin out and six is the hour"

Moses thought it didn't look too fancy, but at least it's to the point. Tim walked outside, and Victor had come back to pick up his clippers. "My brother has a big grill out back, but it won't handle sixty people. You mind helping me dig a fire pit over by the Bocce court?"

"I can do better that." He got on his cell phone and said something in Spanish "It's all taken care of Senor Tim. We'll line it with stone and brick and put a wire mesh over the top for grilling." Victor said with pride. " My amigos are on their way."

Rahab and Moses went from door to door distributing the invitations. One lady told them there were no solicitations permitted in the neighborhood. "It's not," Rahad said, "It's a cookout."

Lizzy came over with a large iron pot of something. She said as she entered the kitchen "I'm Cal's wife Lizzy, and I have some great barbeque rib sauce."

"I'm Pamela Sue, and I heard about our husband's bragging on us. I don't know about you, but those boys will not be disappointed," she said with a shout.

Lizzy walked over and gave her a fist pump. "Let's shift this party into high gear!"

Hazel was cleaning the Indiana sweet corn and putting aluminum foil around the potatoes. She stopped and looked at all the activity and said, "We all could open one fine restaurant if we chose." All the ladies nodded without looking up from their masterpieces.

Victor's crew dug a pit and lined it with brick and fieldstones. Tim thought it looked absolutely perfect. They put some old wood stumps around the fire for people to sit and put their drinks on. Victor told the guys to hurry home and get cleaned up for the party. He also reminded his brother-in- law to bring his accordion and guitar. Victor told Tim that the music he can play is fantastic, and his wife can sing anything thrown at her. Off the guys went, and Victor left to get his good tequila. Moses and Rahab lined the patio with festive multicolored lights and streamers. Tim looked around and thought how much his brother will be surprised.

Richard looked at his watch and thought he could be home by 7:00 PM. Anne too was looking at her watch as she called home. "Hello partner." Someone said on the other end.

"Is this the Barr residence?"

"This Pamela Sue, can I help you?"

"It didn't sound like you, and what's the noise in the background?"

"Oh were just playing Santana in the kitchen" she said with a laugh.

"Can I pickup something for the cookout tonight?"

"No, but I hope we have enough parking. Goodbye" Pamela Sue said. As Anne folded her cell phone she thought to herself "parking?"

At six people started to arrive. The terrace had tables lined all around the pool. People came in ties, long dresses, jeans, shorts, tank tops, and just about everything in between. At first it seemed kind of sterile, soft talking with everyone wondering at how they could fit into this crazy mix. The guacamole and salsa were a hit, along with a tub of margaritas Victor brought. There was Gumball Head Beer from Indiana, and the cooler marked "Danger" was sitting all by itself but having frequent visitors. Some asked what was in the danger cooler. The standard answer was Gas City Soda Pop. Tim put chicken, ribs, corn, potatoes and some black Angus steaks on the grill, and as the smell descended upon the crowd, the oohs and aahs were heard everywhere. The party was now in full swing.

Anne tried to pull into the driveway but it was full of cars. What's going on he thought? Walking around back, she was stunned. She only knew about six people of the sixty there. A short Hispanic man ran up to her and said, "Buenos noches," and handed her a margarita.

In amazement she stumbled into her own yard and Hazel ran up to her and said "Mrs. Barr, you got to try the guacamole and salsa." As in a trance she walked over to the serving table and noticed a big pit had been dug in her yard and fire was breathing on the huge array of food. The margarita was awesome! She had another, kicked off her shoes and tried to figure the whole thing out. Pamela Sue handed her a shot of Gas City Soda Pop and down it went.

"I hope you're not mad," Pamela Sue said, "We invited a few neighbors."

The warming effect of the margaritas, Gas City Soda Pop, and the fantastic smells from the pit only made her think she had arrived in Heaven. "I love it! I just hope Rick feels the same way."

The black limo pulled up to the house, and all Richard could see was a billowing cloud of smoke coming from his back yard and about thirty cars parked every which way. He thought the pool house was on fire. He jumped out and ran to the back yard. He looked like he had been struck by lightning. The same short Hispanic man ran up to him with a margarita and said, "Buenos noches." Rick scanned the crowd and saw Anne sitting in a lawn chair laughing loudly. He walked over and noticed she had salsa all down the front of her silk business suit.

"Hi honey. You'll love the margaritas, and be a dear and get me another." The margaritas and the smells lulled him in a mellow mood as he walked over to his brother who busy tending the grill.

"Hey, bro" Tim said "This is one hell of a cookout!"

Richard finally uttered his first words. "I'm not even going to ask how you built a fire pit here and invited God knows how many people since I left for work this morning."

"The food is coming off now. Then I'll introduce you around."

Richard met his neighbor, Harry, who lived directly behind him. He was the President of New York University. He also was introduced to his yard man, Victor, his wife Ruthie, and their daughter Starr who was an orthopedic surgeon at John Hopkins. He met Cal's wife Lizzy and their son, Sean, who had a full ride scholarship to New York Academy of Art and had some of his art work hanging at the Art Institute in Chicago. The list went on and on. He was introduced to neighbors he never knew existed. It was almost midnight, and people were dragging home. All the comments were, "The best party we've ever been to, and I hope you do this again soon."

Even his neighbor Harry said. "Last Saturday I had dinner with Donald Trump at his home, and your food beat his hands down, and why don't we cut a hole in our fence so we can see each other once in a while?"

Tim was sitting by the fire and invited his older brother to sit with him. As the brothers scanned the yard, it looked like the remnants of an old college party. They both started laughing out loud. The fire was dimming and everyone was in bed. Tim said "Rick, I need to tell you something, and you're not going to like it."

NEW YORK STATE LINE

The 86 Dodge Charger crossed into New York State. Larry and his buddy picked up another six pack, snacks, and gas. "We should be there at 5:00 AM, and I have a plan." Larry said. "The picture off the internet shows a large glass window next to the front door. I'm sure he has an alarm, but if we break the glass, he will run to the front stairs and, we shoot him on the staircase."

His buddy asked, "What if his wife or kid comes out?"

"Let's kill them all," and they got back into the car. His anger was burning his insides like an acid attack, but he knew it would be over in a few hours.

THE TRUTH

Both brothers scanned the fire without saying a word. Tim said in a quiet voice, "I know how much you loved our dad as everyone back home did." He then hesitated for a couple of minutes. "Rick, truth is; he was a liar and a child molester." Rick thought there was going to be a punch line and looked over at Tim with a big smile. Tim had his head down and was poking at the fire.

"What do you mean?" still looking for some facial expression.

"The bottom line is," again another long pause. Tim looked up at his brother and said, "He raped our sister, and Todd his is son."

Rick's mind was trying to make some sense of the boulder that had just been dropped on him. "What?"

"What I'm telling you, no one knows except Sissy. When we were young, I caught dad going into her room many times late at night. He always said Sissy was having a bad dream, but I knew better. When Sissy became pregnant, she told dad she wanted to keep the baby or she would tell everyone what had happened. Sissy cried a lot, confided in me, and made me promise never to tell anyone what he had done. When our minister's son dated Sissy a little, Dad blamed the pregnancy on him and the pastor left town. He even got the church council to write a scathing letter to the Bishop. "My God Rick!" "She was only fourteen!"

Rick still could not wrap around his brain this story. "Does Mom know?" he asked.

"No, nothing has ever been mentioned; she devoted her life to that man. Why do you think Sissy was never around at Dad's funeral? She never asked anything about it and wouldn't let Todd near the funeral home or church. She was sick all right and the vomiting was for real. The only good thing Dad did for Sissy was to set up a trust for Todd. Remember that tool box dad had in the barn? He always kept it locked because he had his best tools in it. That too was a lie. Underneath the tray of his good tools was a pile of child porn. It was sick stuff, and I feel ill when I think about it. I discovered it a year ago when I was looking for a wrench. When I found Dad in the barn that day, he had been masturbating to that sick pile of crap. He had a heart attack while living this secret life. It serves him right! I positioned him by the old milker, like he had been working on it, and then I burned the pile of garbage even before the ambulance arrived. I even covered for him at his death"

"How is Sissy in all of this?" Rick asked, still in total disbelief.

"Not real sure. Pamela Sue has been going over to see her more often, but even she doesn't know the circumstances. The fair is next week, and we'll make sure she gets out and enjoys herself."

Rick never saw this coming. His mind was still blurry, and the margaritas probably added to it. "Now I understand why Sissy never really dated and was so shy around boys as we were growing up. It all makes some sense now. You don't think Sissy would take her life, do you?'

"I don't think so; she loves Todd too much and has been his caregiver since he was born."

Rick stood and looked at the fire one more time and said, "I need to go to bed, but I do appreciate your honesty." He gave his brother a long, strong hug and turned toward the house realizing there wouldn't much sleep tonight. He felt ill but thought a good night sleep would help, and in the morning it could turn out to be only a dream.

The Confrontation

Larry was pumped. This was third time he had circled the block. "You know what to do. I'm going to park the car at this house next to his. The bushes will hide us, and the car, as we go up the driveway. I want the pistol, and one shotgun, and you can have the automatic rifle," Larry said. "The masks are in the trunk by the guns, but let's put them on just before we reach the house. "There is no one up," he said as he looked at his watch that read 5:15 AM. Slowly Larry pulled the car in front of the neighbor's house. They each loaded the guns and slipped the masks in their pockets. Very quietly they started up the Barr driveway not realizing that seven sets of eyes were following their every movement.

All of a sudden they heard "Obtenerlos," and seven small Hispanic men were all over them. They were pushed to the ground, and long pieces of twine were wrapped around their feet and hands. "Podermos matarlos" was uttered. Victor walked over to them lying face down on the cement and said,

"My brother wants to know if we should kill you. You could disappear in the next five minutes and never be heard from again. What is your business here?" Victor asked. They said nothing still feeling stunned from the attack. "I'm sure you're not hunting squirrels." Some Spanish was being spoken and finally Victor said to the men, "I'm a little hung over, so we are not going to kill you but call the police instead."

Three police cars arrived, and they knocked on Richard's door. Richard looked out and thought someone had called the police from last night's party, and they just arrived. The Sergeant had him walk out to the police car where they were handcuffed, and asked if he knew them. He said he had never seen the men before in his life.

The officer said, "One of the guys is talking and I guess you own a factory in Kansas City where they lost their jobs. They said they came here to scare you." The Sergeant told Richard if his lawn crew hadn't been there, he probably would be dead.

Victor walked over to Richard, and now the whole family was standing in the yard. With a big grin Victor said to the Sergeant, "These are my Amigos, and we took care of the problem."

Hazel piped up, "Let's all go in, and I'll fix a big breakfast for everyone." Victor and his crew laid down their clippers and rakes and followed Hazel into the kitchen. Richard thought this has been the craziest twelve hours of his life and slowly followed the group inside.

Heading Back to Indiana

The truck was loaded; everyone was exchanging hugs, kisses, and fist pumps. "Sunday will be a good traffic day to head home brother." Rick said. Tim motioned and the two walked around to the back of house.

"I'll miss you Rick," Tim said with tears streaming down his face. "I feel so much better telling you what I've been carrying for last thirty years. You'll never know," as the sobs began. Rick too was tearing up, and they embraced for a long time. "Rick, I know you'll be in my corner if I ever need to talk or cry. It means the world to me," Tim said again blowing his nose on his plaid handkerchief. Rick was speechless and slowly walked back with his brother to the truck. Moses, Rahab, and Eric were in the back seat of the truck already listening to music.

Anne said, "Take good care of Eric for us, and for life of me I cannot understand why he wants to go to a county fair in Indiana."

Mom's Diner

All the talk today was about the fair. The sun was barely up, but all the farmers at the round table were talking about the farm exhibits. The guys were taking bets on whose old tractor would win first prize.

All the men knew that if a guy could win first prize for the best tractor, he had just reached the pinnacle of achievements. This was the Oscar for the best of the best and second place never really mattered. Everyone there had a tractor except Bill Sales and the Farm Bureau agent, Lester. Last year, Marvin had the old Rumely Oil Pull that won, but this year the rumor was that the Anderson brothers had a tractor they had been working on all winter and had kept the information a secret. Since Marvin had bragging rights for a year now, they all thought it should be their turn to boast a little. Plus they all thought that Marvin was over the top with his tractor stories and wearing the blue ribbon to the diner. Mom came over and told the boys she would give the winner free breakfast for a week and that included the steak and eggs which was the most expensive item on the menu. With this new information, she had just upped the ante, and the competition would really be fierce.

The 4-H kids worked all year for this week, and they too were so excited. Not only could they win a blue ribbon and a small amount of cash, but at the end of the week the votes were tallied for the 4-H Member of the Year. With this honor went a $10,000 check for their future schooling. There also was the animal auction where the kids could sell their chickens, goats, ducks, and livestock for a good amount of money. Four years ago, Butch Vanes sold a gallon of milk from his dairy cow for $2,800.00, and everyone thinks that record won't be broken for a long time.

"Ok guys, I'm heading out," Lester said.

"Me too. I have to set up the Democratic and Republican tents, and that's always fun because they all want me to wear a campaign button," Marvin said laughing.

Mary Barr Farm

Tim and Pamela Sue dropped Eric off in the barnyard by the back door. Dommy came running out, and threw her arms around Eric. Tim saw Eric was now in good hands and drove off.

"Good to have you back, Eric."

"I'm really glad to be here, too."

"Come on in, and I'll try and manage to find something to eat."

"Sounds good; I'm a little hungry."

He came into the kitchen; the smells, creaky chairs, and the old wooden table made him smile. His home in New York just didn't have the same warmth and satisfaction as this old place.

"I'll run my stuff up to Tim's room and be right down."

He went up the old familiar squeaky stairway to his old bedroom, and right there next to the little feather bed was the record player and a stack of 45's. Eric put on a Patsy Cline record. Billie loved Patsy, and so Eric played it through a couple of times, just in case Billie would bring up her name or the song. He laid back on the small feather bed and stared at the ceiling thinking about Billie. He wondered if the spark was still there and what he could say to break the ice. He knew nothing about horses, farming, or anything to do with country living. He realized he could never bluff Billie. He was going to try and be himself.

Eric and his grandmother had a wonderful talk. She was so genuine and told Eric about his father and growing up in Gas City. She told him, even as a young boy, his father was driven and she knew his place was not on the farm or Gas City. When Rick left the farm, things became different. Tim was now the center of attraction and Richard, Sr. never got over Rick leaving.

"Eric, I know the reason you came back, and I'm so happy you came to see me, but don't let Billie Magic get away. Now up to bed with you, the fair starts early tomorrow."

Lincoln County Fair

The two rooster's alarm clock went off as usual, but for some reason Eric didn't seem to mind. Eric's grandmother fed him a big pancake breakfast, but he didn't come close to his grandfather's record of thirty-eight. She asked him if he had ever been to a county fair before. He told her no, but he had been to Six Flags Great America in New Jersey. She just laughed and told him he would be in for a big surprise today. She said he could have the truck all week for going to the fair or for just driving around. He kissed her and walked out the back door having no strategy as he drove to the fair. He knew his cousins were there, and would take him under their wings. It was a warm August morning, the windows down in the truck, and Eric was listening to Hank Williams, Jr. As he pulled in the parking lot the smell of food and animals descended upon him, and for some reason he felt quite at home. The Ferris Wheel, Tilt A Whirl, and many more rides were going full blast. There were a lot of screams and yells as the rides spun around and around. He headed toward the livestock area and thought to himself that the new jeans, boots, and plaid shirt he was wearing should easily blend in with the 4-Hers.

He saw Moses first, and then his eye caught Billie brushing down a large pale white horse while eating something he had never seen before. He continued to walk toward Moses. "Hey, cousin!" Eric yelled.

"Come on in I'll be showing my steer in a few minutes, and we can walk over to the arena together. Here, help me brush him down again. I'm almost finished." He handed Eric a large bristle brush, and as Eric was brushing the very large animal, he looked over at Billie who was looking back at him. She smiled and mouthed the words, "Hi, Little Blade." He smiled back and held up one finger as to say, "I'll be back shortly." She nodded and kept brushing the horse.

"Here," Moses said and handed him the leather strap that was tied to the bull's neck. You lead him over." Eric pulled on the strap and the bull never moved an inch. He pulled harder and still the bull seemed very content just to stand there. Moses started laughing out loud. "Sorry cousin, just having some fun with you. If you want him to move, you need to call his name out loud. Just say, "Caesar, move." Eric thought this won't work.

Eric said, "Caesar move," and the eighteen hundred pound steer slowly followed Eric's lead. Eric felt pretty important as he walked past the other exhibits. Caesar followed Eric all the way to the large arena. He then handed Moses the strap and sat down on the bleachers and looked into the large ring filled with animals. He wasn't sure what would happen next. Two judges came out and looked Caesar all over. They lifted his leg and looked in his mouth like he was getting his yearly physical. They then went over to a table in the corner and presented a very large trophy with a steer on top to Moses. Moses was grinning ear to ear as the crowd of over four hundred stood, applauded, and whistled. He carried the trophy like he had just won an Olympic Gold Medal. He looked over at his dad and nodded with a tear coming down his cheek.

Eric walked back to the horse stall, and Billie was sitting on a bale of hay with her friend Dar. Both girls had on a pair of short shorts, white tee shirts and cowboy boots. Eric thought they looked really hot. "Hi, Eric," they both said.

"What, no nickname today?"

"Naw, we're done with that," Billie said with a smile. "If you can brush and lead Caesar like you did, then the nickname doesn't fit anymore. We're real happy for Moses. He raised Caesar from a calf and nursed him back to health several times over past few years."

"What are you two eating?" Eric asked.

Dar said, "I'm eating a deep fried stick of butter and Billie is eating a deep fried Twinkie. You got to try these."

"I will put them on my to do list," Eric said as they all laughed.

"We are both riding after lunch, so stick around and watch us," Billie said. As Eric was thinking of a way to win her over, she walked up to him and just stared. "You look like a Hoosier now, with the jeans and the shirt, but there's just something missing," as Dar nodded. "I know!" Billie exclaimed and threw a large handful of horse manure on this shirt and pants. "There, much better." and the two ran off.

Eric sat by the corral and watched as horse, upon horse was paraded around the large oval ring. When Billie came out, he just about died. She was dressed all in white, with a white cowboy hat trimmed in silver. She had on eye shadow, lipstick, rouge, and her hair was braided and held back with a large silver barrette. Eric thought she was the most beautiful thing he had ever seen. His heart was racing as Billie walked around the corral giving him a wink as she passed him. The girls mounted their horses and one by one rode around barrels that were at each end of the circle. He never looked at the others, but when Billie rode, his heart was in sync with each stride of her horse. She looked like a white apparition as she flew past him. All the girls finished and were waiting for the judge's decision. "Beverly Magic" was announced, and she rode her pale white horse to the middle of the circle. The people erupted in a loud applause and yells. The judges handed her the trophy, and she took a victory lap and rode right up to Eric, jumped off, kissed him on the lips in front of six hundred people, jumped back on her horse, and rode toward the stables. Eric thought, this was only the third kiss, but the best. Her lips tasted like sweat, vanilla, and peaches. Damn her, he thought, as he walked toward the stables.

SARAH'S CHARM AND CHATTER

Tim and Pamela Sue were tooting their horn in front of the shop, and Sissy was in the basement preparing for her big event. She thought I just can't keep going on with the demon living inside me. She put just the right chemicals in the trunk knowing her pain would be over soon. She locked the trunk, and put the key around her neck. She fluffed up her hair and called for Todd.

"We have to go Honey, Tim and Pamela Sue are here to take us to the fair." Todd was ecstatic; the noises, the smells and of course the cowboy shooting gallery. Tim gave Sissy twenty dollars for Todd's chance to win the large black stuffed horse. Todd kept shooting and shooting but never seemed to hit the bull's eye. Sissy reached into her pocket and pulled out another ten dollars. The young carnival worker looked at her and told her he had to reload Todd's gun. He stepped in back for just a second and handed Todd a different gun.

The very next shot Todd hit the Bull's eye. The lights and bells went off like a Vegas jackpot.

The young worker said, "Great job!" and handed Todd the large black horse. She had never seen Todd so happy. He just beamed.

He winked at Sissy, and she said "You'll never know what you just did."

Todd rode every ride at the fair but wouldn't let anyone hold his prize possession. Tim joined them and they walked to the 4-H exhibit hall. There was every kind of homemade craft under the sun, from photography exhibits to homemade jams and jellies. Pamela Sue had blue ribbons on just about every food item she submitted. Sissy casually walked over to the quilting exhibit and slowly glanced down at her two quilts. She got a blue and a red ribbon for her entries; her insides started doing jumping jacks, but on the outside she seemed calm and uninterested. There was going to be a demolition derby, but Todd was already bouncing off the wall from his prize and the all the sugar he consumed. The two left the fair, arm in arm, both feeling like winners.

Lincoln County Fair Stables

It was late, and the 4H kids were slowing down. Eric sat on a bale of hay and watched, as Billie brushed her horse. She threw a blanket on him and closed the pen. "Want to walk around? She asked. He put out his hand, and she responded. They walked for several minutes without saying a word. "Eric, I really like you, but I will not have sex with you. I'm waiting for the right guy, and you may be him, but for now I have to follow my heart." She turned and passionately kissed him.

He held her tight and thought if the world comes to an end right now, It'll be just fine.

"I sleep on a bed of hay in the stables with my horses and you're welcome to join the group if you like." He thought, well this will be a first, but then he told her he wanted a deep fried Twinkie. They both laughed and walked toward the horse barn. The bed of hay was huge and as far as he could see, there were 4-Hers everywhere. As they curled up together sharing a blanket, he thought, she's worth waiting for. He loved the closeness and her smell was driving him crazy, but he closed his eyes. Sleep finally found him amid the animal noises and snores from the 4-Hers.

New York City, New York

Cal pulled the limo in front of Richard's house, and out he came looking like the fashion plate that Cal had come to expect. Cal started driving and the glass divider lowered.

"Your wife's barbeque rib sauce was fantastic! Also your son is a handsome young man and a very good artist to boot. I went on line and saw some of his work; he is very gifted. Thanks again for running my brother around and for coming to the cookout. We had a blast." Cal nodded as the glass went back in place and Cal thought, wow, a compliment from Richard Barr!

As Richard stepped from the elevator, Yolanda handed him a cup of coffee. She followed him into his office and said that Linda and David were back from Kansas City, and their report was on his desk. Richard's mind was not on the report or even the business today; he couldn't quit thinking about his father and Sissy. How could he have missed all the signs, he thought? He saw them interact every day for years, and nothing seemed to be amiss. And what a secret his sister carried in her heart for all this time. He couldn't understand how she could get up each morning and not think about the past. All she had to do was look at Todd to be reminded of what had happened to her.

Across town Anne was sitting in her spacious, beautifully decorated office going over papers she needed for court that day when her young intern quietly stepped in and kissed her on the neck.

"What in the hell do you think you are doing?" she asked sharply. His face got bright red and he started to say

"But I thought," and she cut him off immediately.

"You don't think! Never, never, do that again! I'm not here to date you or mother you. It's only sex and it's on my terms. Also, don't put flowers on my desk again. I know it's you, but I don't need this shit." He lowered his head and opened her door to leave as she said, "Don't forget to have the Parkinson file on my desk by four."

Mom's Diner

All the talk around the table today was about the fair. Most of the men had been at the fairgrounds helping set up tents and assisting the 4H kids with their animals. The Lincoln County Fair was the social event of the year to these farmers and pretty much everyone in town. Two churches had food tents and the 4H exhibits were a product of many months of work by the kids. The exhibit hall was set up for the local merchants to promote their products or services. There were free rulers, pens, fly swatters and this year Mr. Foster, from Foster's Hardware, gave away a bag of assorted nails and screws. This proved to be a big hit with the locals. Two guys got up to leave because one was judging chickens and the other hogs. They both felt pretty important as they sauntered out the door. As they were leaving, Bill Sales entered, plopped down, and grabbed a piece of toast from Lester's plate.

"Hey, don't you ever buy toast?" Lester asked.

"Why should I with all the grief you guys give me. It's just a way to pay you all back." Bill said with a smile. "Thanks to you jokesters I eat and drink here for nothing."

They all agreed that this was the best Lincoln County Fair ever, but they had been saying that for the last 27 years. Bill noticed Rev. Shepard and his wife sitting in a booth by the window. Her red hair sure set her apart from the rest of the gals in the restaurant. All the round table guys watched as they walked out.

"Man!" Lester said. "Is it me or have her dresses gotten shorter?" Just then Mom hit him in the back of the head with a menu.

"You boys better watch those eyes in your heads!" she exclaimed. They all nodded, "Yes, Mom."

THE FAIR

All the kids were stirring now. Animal preparation was first on their lists. They fed, washed, and brushed them, and some even used hair dryers and mousse. Eric couldn't get over the care and attention these animals got. He kind of compared it to his dad's 63 Corvette. That car had never seen even one raindrop in all these years. Billie and a bunch of other kids and he walked over to the church tent for a great country breakfast. In New York City the meal would have cost at least forty dollars. Here it cost $3.85, and there was no tipping. The day before Eric left for Indiana, he had a bagel and a latte for $14.60. They continued to the arena and the livestock auction was going full bore. He saw Moses sitting across the arena, waiting for his turn to sell Caesar. He waved at Moses and the kids told him not to do that unless he was going to buy the cow in front of him, as they all laughed. The auctioneers were Amish, and Eric couldn't understand a single word they were saying. When the gavel came down, whoever had his hand up last, bought the animal. It happened very fast and Eric sat with his hands in his lap after that.

Sleeping on hay, shoveling manure, and eating deep fried Twinkies was a whole new experience for Eric, and he loved it. All the kids treated him with respect, and they knew he could carry his load. Eric was sitting on a bale of hay and about thirty 4Hers came to Eric and presented him with his own 4-H jacket. Billie apologized for throwing manure on him but told him it was a rite of passage. Every moment with Billie had been a slice of heaven for Eric. The kids were loading up their animals and stacking the hay bales for the trip home. The week was coming to an end; the tents were being taken down; and the rides packed for another county fair somewhere. The week seemed to go very quickly. Billie kissed him as Darlene loaded the horse trailer.

"Eric Barr, thank you for a great week, and damn you're cute!" kissed him once more, jumped into the truck and waved at Eric as the truck and trailer pulled away. Eric climbed into his grandpa's truck shaking his head and drove away still wearing the green and white 4H jacket.

Dommy's Farm

Eric woke on Sunday and felt a little depressed. His grandmother asked him "Why so sad?" He told her about his feelings for Billie and she comforted him with a large slice of apple pie and ice cream. She noticed his 4H jacket, and he told her how he received it from the kids. She told him the 4Hs stand for head, heart, hands, and health. The white stands for purity and high ideals and the green for springtime, life, youth and growth.

"Never take it lightly, Eric." After he finished the pie he sat back and stared at the jacket draped over the kitchen chair. "Say," she said, "You need to go to her house and tell Billie just how you really feel about her. Don't hesitate; you may never have this chance again."

He jumped in his grandpa's truck and drove to the Magic Farm. Billie's dad was just coming out of the barn as Eric pulled in. "Hi, Mr. Magic," he shouted, Is Billie home?"

"No, she left this morning for her grandmother's in Ohio." Eric's heart was ready to explode. She never said goodbye. She just left. They spent almost a week together and shared everything. Now this. Eric started back toward the truck feeling like he had just been kicked in the groin. "Hold on, Eric," Mr. Magic said, "She left you a box." He walked back into the barn and retrieved a small cardboard box. Eric accepted it as it were a pirate's treasure. "By the way, she's not good with goodbyes."

Eric put the box in the truck and sped off. He drove to Sales and Son Funeral Home and walked behind the building where he received his first kiss. He sat on the grass and opened the box. There was a little wood frame with a picture of them sitting together with an old blanket wrapped around them watching the closing fireworks display. The color from the rockets made them both look angelic. The note attached read, "You do light me up. Love, Billie."

Eric just laid back on the grass and yelled, "Yes!"

Eric got back into the truck and drove straight back to the Magic Farm. Before he got out, he put his switch blade knife into the little box that Billie had given him. He wrote, "Me too," and tied it with a string from his grandpa's truck.

Bob Magic saw him pull up and came over to the truck. "Back again?"

"Will you give this to Billie for me when she gets home?"

"Sure. Be glad to."

"Mr. Magic, my dad won't tell me how he saved your life. Will you?"

"Come over here son, and I'll tell the true story of your dad's sacrifice."

The two sat on a bale of hay and faced each other. "When we were in high school, we both dated different girls. Our school rivalry was Mill Creek High School. Your dad and I went to a dance there with six other guys from Gas City. We danced with many girls, and were having a good time. When we left the school, there were twelve guys waiting for us. We knew that at least two of them had knives. The pushing started, and we could see that the person they really wanted was me. Apparently I had slow danced with the wrong girl and probably had my hands on her. The guys told us we could all leave if we left now, except for me. Six of the guys left, and your dad stood with me. He picked up a stick, and we stood back to back. His only comment was, "This could be bad." They came at us from all directions, and I was stabbed twice, once in the stomach and once in the leg. Your dad was stabbed in his back twice. We really took a beating, but we got our licks in too."

"On the way home, your dad drove and I was trying to keep us from bleeding to death. He drove us to Union Mills Hospital, and walked in looking like we had had just driven over a thousand foot cliff. We worked on our stories and told the police we fell off a roof.

No one bought the story, but we stood firm. See, I had a full ride track scholarship to Purdue, and your dad in baseball to Indiana University. I lost my scholarship due to my leg injury, and if your dad had been stabbed in his arm, he too would have never gone to Indiana University. He risked it all for me. Even your grandparents never knew the truth. Your dad had a chance to run like the rest but he stayed with me, and it's too bad we don't keep in touch," as a tear trickled down his cheek. "You know when I first bought the farm, I needed money for equipment, and the bank wouldn't lend me anything. A mysterious donor sent ten thousand dollars to the bank, and only thing I found out is that it came from New York. I called him, but he denied it. See Eric, my life was saved by your father." Bob Magic hugged Eric and walked into the barn wiping his eyes saying, "I will give this to Billie for you"

New York City, New York

Richard told Yolanda he was leaving early. It had been a good week; they purchased a company in Milwaukee and were now in the process of dismantling it. Somehow he was not satisfied. Not only the days but also the nights were plaguing his mind with his father and sister. He blamed himself for not seeing the tragedy. Cal dropped him off in the front of his house.

"You won't need to pick me up tomorrow," he said and slowly walked to the back yard. He loosened his tie and sat looking at the only fire pit in the neighborhood. He thought back to the wild and crazy barbeque which still seemed to be the topic on everyone's lips.

Hazel came out when she saw him sitting there. "You're home early today. Can I get you something?"

"Yes, he said, "please get me one of those Indiana beers in the frig, and get one for yourself." Bewildered she walked in the kitchen and retrieved two cold beers. "Sit down," he said, lifted his beer toward hers, and said "Skol" and she returned the "Skol" to him. He kicked off his shoes, and she did likewise. "Tell me," he said, "What's Denmark like?"

It had been a long time since she had been there, but she shared her childhood memories like it was yesterday. He got up, walked in the kitchen and returned with two more beers. By now Hazel felt very relaxed, told him she liked his family very much, and they were so kind when she had nothing. He nodded as she shared more stories of Copenhagen. Now she was very relaxed having put down her third beer. She told him that Anne and Eric loved him very much; she could see it in their eyes and actions. "Your family may not tell each other, but there is a strong bond there," she said. Richard sat taking in the warm sunlight and Hazel's words, like a soft spring rain coming upon him.

He walked back inside and came out a few minutes later with two more beers. "Oh, Mr. Barr, I can't. I have dinner to fix."

He responded with "We'll order out" and handed her a small piece of paper.

"What's this?"

"It's a trip to Denmark," he said with a smile. She unfolded it, and it was a check for ten thousand dollars. She just stared in unbelief. She immediately started to cry. "We'll have none of that at the Barr Home. You may leave anytime you wish, but I expect at least one post card" He handed her his handkerchief, and said "Skol" She lifted her beer and thought, prayers can be answered.

"I'll order a pizza. What do you like on it?" he asked and walked in the kitchen to get the phone.

Anne's Office in Manhattan

She stared out the window and thought back to Gas City. When Eric came home he was all talk for three days. The people were nice, but there was nothing to do except farm and go to the diner. If she lived there, her size four figure would become a fourteen.

She looked down again at the file on her desk. She was going to prosecute a former Federal judge tomorrow and had all his corrupt dealings on tape. This case had kept her up at night for the last two weeks. There was a secret offer from his attorney to look the other way, with the promise that good things would come her way when a Federal judgeship came available. This guy was connected, and the offer was valid. She knew what was right, but the job offer would set her up for life. The judgeship would open up financial and political avenues she could only dream about. Anne kicked off her high heels and put her feet on the desk. She looked out the window and could see the Statue of Liberty as she looked across the water. Anne thought maybe Miss Liberty could send a clear answer. The file just stared back at her as it was closed and put into her briefcase. Oh well, she needed to either take the intern to a hotel or go to the lobby bar for a drink. Anne put her shoes back on and walked to the door and thought, of the two; Jack Daniels was a lot less complicated.

BARR HOME NEW YORK

Richard, Hazel, and Eric finished off the pizza and walked out on the terrace. Richard and Eric sat down and Hazel started to wipe down the chairs. "Sit down." Richard commanded. "You're on vacation so live it up."

She walked back into her room and came out with a Danish bottle of Akvavit, "OK," Hazel said "If I'm on vacation, then the three of us will have a toast to my new adventure." They all raised their shot glasses and said, "Skol" "Mr. Barr, I just called my brother in California, and he's going to meet me in Copenhagen. We haven't seen each other for ten years." And she started to tear up again.

"I said none of that at the Barr House, but we're very happy for you. I'm going to retire early tonight," Richard said and started to get up. Hazel rushed over and kissed him on the cheek, and yes the tears were flowing like Niagara Falls.

It was late when Richard heard Anne come up the stairs and walk down the hall to her bedroom and close the door. This had been the usual routine for the last eight years. He wondered if she had a tough day, but dismissed the thought and went back to his computer. Anne wanted to tell her husband about her day but thought he won't care anyway. She turned off her light and couldn't sleep. Richard turned off his light and couldn't sleep. Eric turned off his light and couldn't sleep. Hazel left her light on and stared at the check. She knew for sure she would not sleep one wink tonight.

It was 4:15 AM. Richard got up and knew what would have to happen. He put some clothes in a duffel bag and walked down to the kitchen. As soon as he walked past the coffee marker it started and brewed him a hot pot of coffee. He filled a thermos with the coffee and unplugged the coffee maker. He put it under his arm and walked to the garage. He threw his duffel bag in the trunk and set the coffee maker in the back seat. He walked back in and printed something on his computer. He put the note on the counter and quietly started the car and pulled out. He never looked back at the house; the memories just weren't there anymore.

The Barr Farm

Mary got up with the rooster's call as usual. She walked into the kitchen, but it seemed so empty and lonely. She made a cup of coffee and sat at the table thinking about all the years she fixed her husband and children countless meals. The laughter and the stories were more numerous than the sands. Eric had been such a joy to her; she knew if Billie was around, he would be back. For some reason today she seemed a little disturbed. She couldn't describe her feelings but knew something was going to happen. She was taking Sissy and Todd to the diner at 8:00 A.M. and still had plenty of chores to do. Ok, she thought, it's just another day, so shut down the brain and get working. But even when she walked out back by the clothes line, it seemed as if there was a different smell in the air.

She finished all the chores and took a long bath. She put her dress on and combed her hair back into the tight bun she usually wore. She took her jewelry box down from the closet shelf, sat on the bed, and opened it. There it was, right on top: her most prized possession, the unicorn embossed locket. She hadn't worn it for sixty years and thought maybe today is the day. She put on a simple pair of earrings and a bracelet that Tim and Pamela Sue gave her for her seventh birthday. She put the necklace on and something came over her as if she was having a panic attack.

Her thoughts went back sixty years to a seventeen year old blond girl who was smart, beautiful, and deceptive. Her memory was still great, and each small detail was burned into her brain. As she touched the locket, her head was flooded with remembrances. The first time she took off her clothes for Calvert Wolf she felt very alone and vulnerable. The artist assured her and complemented her on her form and gracefulness. No man had ever spoken to in such language before. He handed her the locket so she would have something to hang on to and feel in her hand. This seemed to reassure her.

When she got home from school, she told her mother she was babysitting for the Curry twins and out the door she would go, down the alley and in the back door of the Wolf home. He always had a glass of milk and some sort of snack for her. She first would walk into the large parlor and see her form beginning to take shape on canvas. She then would go into the small library and disrobe and walk past him into the parlor and pick up the locket. Her large, red stuffed chair was positioned by the right bay window. They would have small talk about her school and activities but rarely talked about him. Sometimes he would come over and comb her hair, resting his fingers on her beautiful neck, to make sure each hair was the same as the last sitting, and sometimes his hand would brush her nipple. She didn't mind his gentle touch. He also had the very familiar scent of Old Spice and cherry pipe tobacco.

One day, after almost two months, he told her of his life as an orphan. He ended up in Gas City to live with his Aunt Ruth in the very same house. She sent him to study art in Austria and Germany. He mainly studied landscapes, but he preferred the human body.

He told her he had many models from all over Europe, but she was the best he had ever seen, and she blushed. He paid her well, and she bought a new car with her earnings. Her mother just thought the Curry family was very generous because those twins were a handful.

The day he died was like all the rest. She disrobed in the small library, walked over, picked up the unicorn necklace and sat in the red chair. He told her the painting would be done soon, and all he had to do was to paint her face. He asked her if she would mind that Gas City and the world would be looking at her nude body. She told him that it would be an honor for her face to be on the canvas. He came over and kissed her on her cheek and she blushed. Twenty minutes later he slumped to the floor. She didn't know what to do. She hurriedly got dressed and grabbed the locket and ran down the alley. She called the volunteer fire department to report that Mr. Wolf was in his home not feeling well. That was the last time she was in the house or saw the painting. She took the locket off and put it back in the jewelry box and thought "Today isn't the day to wear it, maybe tomorrow."

Barr Home in New York

When Anne got up, her only thoughts were centered on the court case today. The complications just kept replaying in her head, so the quality of sleep was nil. She came downstairs and the coffee maker was gone. Maybe Richard took it to have it repaired she thought. Hazel was up and had the breakfast all laid out for the Barr Family. Hazel was so excited, she could hardly contain herself. She explained what Richard had done for her, and the tears started in again. Anne thought Richard was very generous and congratulated Hazel on her trip. Anne looked in the garage and Richard's car was gone. Her only thought was he took it into the city for a change of pace. Anne finished breakfast and went upstairs to get her briefcase and touch up her hair. She looked into Richard's bedroom and nothing seemed out of place. She came down, and Eric was eating his food.

Hazel told her that when she got up the coffee maker was missing, and there was a note on the counter. She handed it to Anne, and in big bold letters it read "GONE". Eric said he knew nothing about the note, so she placed it in her bag and headed to court.

Tim and Pamela Sue's Farm

Pamela Sue was washing the dishes, and she could see Tim and Moses wrestling in the yard. Moses had his father pinned to the ground and both were laughing out loud. They loved each other and this was how they showed it. After dinner they would go to the barn to finish the chores and usually a comment would start like "Hey old man, try and keep up with me" or "You punk kids don't know what work is all about," and the wrestling or a basketball game would ensue. This would go on until there was a victor or an excuse like "I think my back is out." They came it filthy dirty, dropped their clothes in the mud room and headed upstairs in their undershorts laughing all way. Pamela Sue loved the relationship her boys had.

Her parents had very little, and her father farmed for the Scholl Family. He was only thirty-three when he was killed on a corn picker. The Scholls let her mother and three children live at the farm for two years. Her mother was killed the following spring in car accident. Pamela Sue lived with her grandmother and helped raise the two younger children. She learned to cook, sew, and just about everything else. She worked the fields from dawn to dusk, came home and helped fix the evening meal with her grandmother. She had little time for a social life, and every penny she made went into the cookie jar in her grandmother's kitchen.

She met Tim at a 4H Club meeting, and knew he was going to be hers. He was tall handsome and loved to work his dad's farm. He never noticed Pamela Sue until she helped him bale hay in the fall that year and worked right alongside of him on the hay truck. When they finished they sat on the truck and drank Cokes. She leaned over and kissed him, and that was all he needed for the fall of Rome. She asked him to every dance, and he accepted gladly. The only run-in she ever had was with Lovera Ann Mosley. Pamela Sue caught her kissing Tim behind the grandstands at the Gas City High School Stadium but that relationship only lasted as long as it took for Pamela Sue to knock out Lovera Ann's front tooth and blacken her eye.

Her life had been hard, but if asked, she would disagree. The love she had for Tim was immeasurable, and she knew he felt the same. She had to remind him of every anniversary, birthday and special event, but she knew he would come through in the end with some surprise. The worst present was the table saw for their fifteenth anniversary. The saw went back, and she still wears the small gold cross as its replacement. When she gets into bed each night, she always prays a prayer of thanks for all the blessing that God has given her and kisses Tim on his cheek

Crossing into Indiana

Richard pulled into the large Tell City Truck Stop and started to fill the tank. He looked over at the old man that had tried to trade cars with him. The old guy walked over and asked again, "Buddy, are you ready to trade with me today?" Richard just laughed and glanced over at his small lot. "I just got a newer Dodge truck with only eight thousand miles on it." For some reason Richard walked over to the tiny lot.

"How much?"

"I'll take your car and give you ten thousand." Richard wasn't sure what came over him, but he stuck out his hand and made the deal. Richard paid over a hundred thousand for his Mercedes and traded it for a pickup truck. He still felt real good about it, and the old man felt really, really great about the deal. Richard put the coffee pot and his duffel bag in the truck, and off he went. The old guy couldn't wait to use his phone.

"Honey, I just made the best car deal I've ever made. I'm coming home and take you to the finest steak place in Southern Indiana."

Federal Court House, Brooklyn, New York

Anne pulled into the underground parking garage and her Porsche glided into her reserved spot. The judge's attorney was standing waiting for her. As she got out of the car the attorney said "I hope you made the right decision on that subject we talked about."

She grabbed her briefcase and turned to him with a big smile and said "Yes, I have made the right decision and thanks for asking." They walked up to court together making small talk about the great weather. There was another case in court before them, so they waited in the conference room. The former judge came in with his other three attorneys and nodded to Anne as if to say "Thanks, I owe you." She only made brief eye contact, but she did smile back at him. Anne thought if she knew how to pray, this might be great time to unleash a big one.

The case lasted all day. Many witnesses and testimonies were heard on behalf of the former judge. It was 4:00 PM, and she made her closing statement to the Special Federal judge on the bench and closed her briefcase.

The judge then said, "I find the defendant guilty on all counts. Sentencing will be October 15th." And with that the gavel fell. The officers came over and handcuffed the former judge and lead him away.

His attorney came over and said to Anne "You just cooked your goose, lady!" and stormed out. As she took the elevator to the garage she knew she had done the right thing but for some reason her decision just didn't feel like it. I need a Jack Daniels she thought as she headed for home.

Tim and Pamela Sue's Farm

Tim was walking out of the barn and didn't know whose truck was pulling in the drive. Rick jumped out and walked over to his brother. Tim said, "What's up, brother?" and embraced him.

"I need your help; I want you to go for a drive with me."

Tim jumped in the truck and asked, "Are we going to New York? Because if we are, I better tell Pamela Sue I won't be home for dinner."

"I'll have you back in thirty minutes". Rick pulled out of the driveway and turned left, went a quarter of a mile and turned left again. They pulled up in front of a big for sale sign. Rick jumped out and Tim followed. "This is it!" Rick exclaimed

"This is what?"

"I bought this place, and I need you to help knock down the sign."

"I know this may seem like a dumb question, but why did you buy this place?"

Rick responded with, "This is my new home."

Tim was still trying to sort all this out as they pushed over the large wooden sign. They got back in the truck. "I've left New York, and I bought this online from the Ault Family. It has twelve hundred acres and a remodeled farm house. Our properties joined each other and you've always said you would like to have more ground. There is even a low area for cranberries."

"Where's Anne?" Tim asked.

"She'll stay in New York with Eric; their roots are from there. By the way, look in the back seat."

"Oh my gosh the coffee maker!" Tim exclaimed

"It's yours brother, a gift from New York. Let's take it to your house and I'll set it up for you."

When they arrived back at Tim's farm, Pamela Sue was baking some pies. Rick told her the whole story and said they would be neighbors. She told him to sit and put a big piece of cherry pie in front of him.

She said, "Let me see your hands." He held them out and she shook her head and told him that he better take a picture of his hands because they won't look like this is a few weeks.

Anne and Eric's Home, New York City

Anne got home and was completely spent. She barely had enough strength to get out of her car and get into the house. Hazel met her with a glass of wine and told Anne she was just finishing up her packing. She would leave on Monday and be back in three weeks. Anne asked if Richard was home, and the response was no. Eric came up from the basement, and she asked if he had heard from his dad. Eric thought he was still at the office, and Anne thought probably at some secretary's house.

Anne and Eric had a quiet dinner together. Eric was going to a club in the city, and Anne went straight to her room. She watched television until her eyes couldn't say open any longer. She drifted off to sleep thinking how close and intimate she and Rick had gotten in Indiana. The little feather mattress and his room surrounded in 4H ribbons and pictures was still a vivid memory. Crazy thoughts she told herself, and pulled the covers over her head and tried to erase the whole day that was still plaguing her mind.

Mom's Diner

Tim and Rick walked into the diner and sat at the round table with the usual guys. "Well, well," was the response. "The Barr boys are joining the low lifes at out humble table."

"Knock it off you guys. My brother Rick bought the old Ault Farm and is going to stay a little while."

"We all loved your dad, and he was a straight up guy, so we'll give you the same respect." Lester said.

"Thanks," Rick answered "I'll try not to be a pest to you guys."

"How've you been feeling, Rick?" someone asked, "because here comes Bill Sales." And everyone one laughed.

"By the way," Marvin said, "Watch your toast; it seems to disappear when Bill is around;" again the laughter.

Rick's usual breakfast was with bank presidents or CEO's of any number of businesses, but today the venue was good. No one tried to outdo the other, and every one of the men asked if they could help him or lend him some equipment. He liked that and his breakfast only cost him $4.53 for the special. Rick liked the men, and he could see right from the start, that these were real caring people. Mom asked Tim and Rick as they left, if they would mind if she named a dish on the menu after their dad and they both said, "No, thanks," simultaneously.

ANNE AND ERIC'S HOME, NEW YORK CITY

It had been three days and nobody had heard from Richard. Anne came home and was getting something from her purse. There it was, the note "Done". Anne called Rick's office, and Yolanda said they had not heard from him. She called the club to see if he had been in to work out, and the response was no. She had a feeling and called Tim and Pamela Sue's house. Pamela Sue answered and after about two minutes of chatter, Anne asked if Rick was there. Pamela Sue handed the phone to Tim. He told her Rick was there, and he bought the farm next to his. Tim wanted to know if he needed to relay a message to his brother. She told him it wasn't necessary but she would stay in touch. She put the phone down and poured another glass of wine.

She walked up to Rick's bedroom and sat on his bed. Anne looked at the walls with all the fine art and remembered back to his old bedroom with cowboys, his letter jacket and blue ribbons pinned everywhere. She could even remember the smell of old wood and leather. She closed her eyes, laid back on his bed, and gently put her fingers into her blue silk panties. Anne continued touching her vagina until she realized she needed a nice warm bath. In the bath water she slowly caressed herself until she reached an orgasm. It was wonderful; the wine, warm water and lavender scented bath oil was exactly what she needed.

Tomorrow she would have to call her parents first thing in the morning. She knew they could give her advice on what to do next. She put on her warm cotton pajamas and slipped into deep sleep thinking back to the intimate touch they shared in the little bedroom decorated by a teenage farm boy.

MARY BARR'S FARM

Tim called his brother and asked him if he had time to go their mom's house and move some things for her. Rick arrived, and Tim was sitting at the kitchen table eating a pork barbeque sandwich his mother had just made. She told Rick to sit and eat. He pulled up a chair and dug in to a delicious lean piece of pork that Pamela Sue had just butchered.

"The church is having a garage sale and if you boys don't mind, would you please take those two green chairs, sofa, and old lamps to the church for me? It's all down the basement." They finished their food but turned down the lemon custard pie she had just baked.

The boys felt like they were in some haunted movie plot because the entire basement had only two light bulbs, and it was damp and eerie down there. When they were young, it was the last place they wanted to be. They hauled the furniture up and put them in Tim's truck. They went down one more time to turn off the lights, and Rick noticed his dad's old Army trunk in the corner.

"Look, it's dad's army trunk from Korea," Rick said. It had a lock on it, but it wasn't locked. The boys opened it, and it was full of his metals and letter's from their mom to him. Something was wrapped in tissue paper and was stuck in the corner of the trunk. Tim opened it, gasped out loud, and dropped it back in the trunk. He immediately stepped back like he had seen a ghost.

"What is it?" Rick asked. Both boys were now standing about four feet back staring at the beat-up old trunk.

"You look!" Tim said.

Slowly Rick walked over having no idea what he might find. He opened the paper and shouted, "Shit!"

Tim now came up behind him and they both looked in utter amazement. It was an old Boy Scout Hat, and in the lining was written A. Harris. The hat was very dirty, and with it was a newspaper article about a missing Boy Scout, dated 1937.

Rick exclaimed, "I thought this whole Albert Harris story was a family joke and campfire tale!"

"Me too."

They read the old, yellowed article from the Evansville Gazette. The article mentioned Albert Harris just disappeared from the camp and how desperate his parents were to find him. They apparently were a very well to do family from Evansville, and Albert was their only child. It stated that a bank held the reward for the return of the missing boy. Rick got out his cell phone and called the First National Bank of Evansville. He told the manager that he was a writer and would like some information on the Albert Harris reward account. It took almost fifteen minutes and the manager came back on and talked to Rick as he nodded his head. Rick hung up the phone and looked at his brother.

"There's $860,000 in the account." They both stared at the hat again and gently placed it back in the truck.

BROOME STREET CAFÉ, SOHO, NEW YORK

Robert and Marge Miller where very wealthy people, but you wouldn't know it. They took the subway into the city and enjoyed being around all different types of people. When Anne arrived, they were already in the cafe and trying to decide what to eat without spending a small fortune. They both got up and hugged Anne and sat down again.

"Your father can't decide between the waffles or the bagel surprise." "What do you think dear?" Marge asked.

"For the money, Dad, the bagel surprise is the best. I've had it, and it's all homemade." Anne thought to herself for almost eighty years old, those two are sharp.

"Honey, what's on your mind?" her mother asked.

"Rick has left me, and I don't know what to do." She said with tears trickling down her cheek.

"Do you love him?" her dad asked.

"I do, but we have drifted so far apart. We have nothing in common."

Her father looked over at his wife with a smile and said, "Should I tell her?"

"Why not?" was her mother's response. Just then the waitress came to take the order, and her father ordered the waffles because he felt like waffles.

Her father told Anne that he and her mother had something to tell.

"Twenty years ago I had been having an affair with my secretary but denied it to the end. I moved out of the house and moved in with this young lady. This lasted for about three days and your mother came to the apartment and pulled the fire alarm in the hallway. This was early in the morning and people were scrambling for the fire exits, and your mother stood in front of the apartment with an extinguisher. As we opened the door, she gave us a blast of water that almost knocked us over. She came into the apartment and said she was a fireman, and was here to put out a fire. We were soaked. I looked at my secretary and then at your mother; there was no comparison. We left hand in hand as the real firemen were descending the stairs. Not only did she put one fire out, but started another right here," and he touched his heart.

"Our advice honey." "Go start that fire that has been smoldering for a long time". Marge said. "We'll watch Eric. He can stay with us."

"I don't think I can live in Indiana, but I'll at least visit him. You two have been wonderful." Anne got up to leave.

Her father said, "I think I have one regret though; I should have gotten the bagel surprise, it was cheaper."

RICK'S NEW FARM, GAS CITY, INDIANA

The sun was coming up and Rick thought he had slept very well for being in a strange bed that the previous owners left. The Ault Family was so excited to sell the farm that they left many items for Rick to enjoy. They left an old vacuum cleaner that looked like an old moped with very small wheels and a huge headlight. The plaid couch, matching drapes, and lamp were a nice touch if you lived in the 1950's. The one slice toaster and bright yellow blender fit the décor perfectly. At least the yellow stove and blue refrigerator worked. By the front door was a BB gun with a note attached that read "For the squirrels." And he thought sooner or later he would find out what that meant.

He pulled a stuffed chair onto the porch, put his feet on the railing, and drank a good strong cup of coffee. On the porch was an old radio from probably the 70's sitting on a card table. He pushed the power button, and instantly an old country song started to play. Since he had no television, this might be his entertainment for a while. He looked around at all the trees and open ground. The small apple and pear orchards were loaded with fruit and smelled fresh and wonderful today. He apparently had inherited two old cats because they came up on the porch and sat on either side of him. They surveyed the farm along with him. For right now he named them Dick and Jane; it seemed appropriate. He slipped into the overalls, and out to the field not really knowing what he might find.

Rick told himself, he could do a solid hour on the Stairmaster and lift weights at his club but digging holes for a fence was about going to kill him. Every muscle in his arms ached and throbbed. A truck pulled up, and Bob Magic jumped out. "I heard you came back. I guess we just can't keep the farm out of the boy, now can we?"

Rick smiled and walked over to the fence. "It's good to see you, Bob. I hope you're not asking me to go to a dance tonight I might be a little tired in case a fight should break out," he said with a big smile. Rick put out his hand across the fence, and Bob responded with his.

"I have an auger on my tractor, and I'll be right back with it." Bob said. "It'll take us no time at all to put this fence up. Whatever you need from me, all you have to do is call. I'll never be able to pay you back for what you did for me. By the way, I told your son the story of how you saved my life back in high school. The only part I left out was that your beating was worse than mine, and you almost died yourself." Again Bob put out his hand and told Rick he'd be back in twenty minutes with the tractor.

ANNE AND ERIC'S HOME, NEW YORK CITY

Anne came home with a new hope in her heart, but thought to herself, how am I going to break this to Eric? He will be crushed and probably never talk to me again. She called Eric up from the basement to sit on the patio with her. "Eric, she said I don't know how to tell you this, but your father has moved back to Gas City and bought a farm. I don't know if this is permanent, but I need to be with him." Eric said nothing but just stared at his mother with a blank look on his face. "I'm going to leave in the morning and I talked to your grandparents. You can stay with them." Now Eric looked agitated. She continued, "I called my office and I told them I'm taking a sabbatical and will call them at a later time. I'm sorry, Honey."

Eric jumped to his feet and said, "Bullshit! I'm not going to stay at your parents. I'm going with you. I love Gas City, and I love Billie Magic. I can get into Indiana University this fall, and their business school is next to none." He now was smiling. "Mom, I know this is going to be a huge adjustment for us all, but the Barr's are for it." He hugged her. "Just think, you can be the only attorney in town and there is circuit court judgeship opening this fall. I just hope Dad hasn't bought a rooster."

Laughing out loud, "Me too!" she exclaimed. "Now let's get packing and try and start a new life for ourselves,"

"You know, he said, our ancestors did it with mules and wagons; I guess we can do it in a Porsche."

SARAH'S CHARM AND CHATTER

Sissy thought today is the day. She fed Todd a big breakfast, but the idea of food almost made her sick. Todd was watching some Western, and she slipped down the basement. She took the key from around her neck and opened the small black trunk. She checked the chemicals again and knew the combination would work. As Sissy closed the trunk she began to cry. She knew it would be over soon and finally she would have peace. Sissy carried the trunk up stairs and put in in her old car. She got a kite, a soccer ball, and a butterfly net for Todd. This will keep him busy until someone arrives she thought. She called her mother and told her that she was a wonderful mom and that she could always count on her for whatever she needed growing up on the farm. She talked for thirty minutes, and almost everything said was about her mother's love for Todd and her. When Sissy hung up, Mary thought, How odd, but she must be missing her father.

She made one more phone call, then said, "Ok, Todd, let's go."

"Mom, where are we going?" "Can we get pancakes today?"

"Not today Todd. We're going to the cemetery to visit your grandpa's grave." She said in a low voice. It was a beautiful day. The sun was shining through the autumn trees, but Sissy never noticed. Her heart was racing now and hands were oh, so sweaty. She turned on 600 East, and in the corner was an arrow pointing to Oak Grove Cemetery. She now could see the cemetery in the distance and knew right where the grave was located. "I can do this," she said as the tears welled up in her eyes.

MOM'S DINER

Mom looked around the diner and thought those guys really did come through. They painted the diner white, and the bottom half was a light red. It certainly stood out and looked so fresh and new. Bill put up a new sign that read "Mom's" in large, bold print with "Home

Cookin" below it. It gave the old diner a kick in the pants, and everyone couldn't help but notice it from three blocks away. The guys fixed the roof over the entrance so there would be no more leaks. Tidy Tucker graded the parking lot and put in bright yellow parking bumpers. Lester built a cedar planter, and planted a variety of beautiful perennial flowers. Harry bought a new music receiver so Mom could play her Johnny Cash songs for the patrons. Mom bought new red and white shirts for her staff, and even Chris, the cook, had a new red and white apron with his name in the right hand corner. He loved that. In honor of the guy's remodeling job; Mom added two new items to the menu, "round table hash brown potatoes" was the first. She told them it was the usual hash browns, but she added bologna to it. It actually was ham. The other was the "farmer's special" that would change every day as her mood moved her. They all loved the recognition.

The guys were sitting at the round table, but the conversation was not about cattle or corn prices today. All the attention was on Tidy Tucker. Tidy's real name was Terrance, but he inherited the title "Tidy" in grade school, and it stuck all these years. He was meticulous when it came to keeping things in order. His desk in school never had a thing out of place, and even his pencils were arranged according to size. He lived on a small farm by the old fair grounds that had belonged to his parents. They had both passed away, and he had never lived anywhere except the farm. Every item on the farm had a place. All his tools were hung in the shed and barn with a silhouette drawn around them to show the place where they would need to be replaced after use. The front yard of the farm house was mowed so well that it looked like a small golf course; even his eating utensils and coffee cup had a specific place at the round table.

He was sixty, and never married and was the quietest of all the guys around the table. He was a good listener and if asked a question, he would say back, "But how do you feel?" As far as he could remember, he had never won anything in his life. But today was different. He had won the best antique tractor prize at the fair. He competed against sixty-eight other fine entries, and as promised, Mom gave him a free breakfast for a week. Today he was eating steak and eggs and all the guys were praising him. His trophy was in the diner window, as requested by Mom, and every once in while he would glance over at its place of prominence. All the men around the table had put their tractors up for judging, but they were happy for Tidy. His tractor had belonged to his father and was in perfect shape. It was a 1922 International "816". He took better care of it than most people their own health. Tidy even had the original tires hanging in the barn. He had never entered before, but the offer of a free breakfast was too much for him to pass up.

One time some of the guys thought about sneaking into his shed and rearranging his tools, but Carl thought he might have a stroke. Tidy finished his free breakfast and sat back in his chair with great satisfaction. He hoped Mom would leave the trophy there for a long time so he could see it every morning he came in. Tidy had taken care of his elderly parents at the farm and had little social life. He did think one time that Sissy Barr was cute, but there was a twenty year difference in age, and he also heard she was kind of messy; that wouldn't do.

Crossing Into Indiana

Anne pulled in at the Tell City Truck Stop. She was getting gas and Eric went in to look around.

Eric came out and exclaimed "Look! It's dad's Mercedes!" She looked over and sure enough, there it was all shined up with the little old guy sitting in his folding chair.

She walked over. "Did my husband trade you for his Mercedes?"

The old guy said, "He sure did and what a beauty"

"What kind of deal would you give me for the white pickup truck?" she said. He looked over at the Porsche and thought Lightning can't strike twice, can it? There wasn't much haggling, and in twenty minutes Eric was driving the new white truck as Anne was looking in the mirror at her new white cowboy hat and turquois earrings and necklace.

The old man was on the phone. "Put your best dress on, Honey, I'm taking you to a play and that lobster place in Evansville tonight. Man, have I been blessed!" and hung up the phone.

Oak Grove Cemetery

Rick was working on his porch, and his cell phone rang. "Rick, I'll be there in five minutes; Sissy called and is going to take her life!" Tim yelled. Rick was waiting by the road as Tim came flying up. Rick jumped in and off they went. "Sissy called a few minutes ago, and she is going to the cemetery to end it!" he exclaimed. "I never told her you knew, but now I probably should have so we could have done some kind of intervention"

Rick said, "I knew she couldn't keep all this inside forever."

"I called the volunteer fire department, but they won't be here for thirty minutes."

They could see her car parked at the bottom of the hill by their father's grave. Todd was running up and down the hill with the butterfly net. They ran up the hill and saw Sissy slumped over their father's grave covered in blood. Rick rolled her over, and she exclaimed "It's done!" Her dress, her face, and hands were all red.

"What's done?" Tim yelled

"This," and they looked at their father's grave. Every single blade of grass was stained a brilliant red. She had red dye all over herself, and she began to sob. Rick and Tim also started to sob. They held each other very tightly for the longest time. Sissy said, "I can go on now; I've been released" They all looked at the grave and continued to hug each other and cry as a lone figure in the camouflage parka stepped quietly into the woods.

Todd ran by with the butterfly net and yelled "Can we get pancakes now?"

Not The End!

PART TWO SEEKING ALBERT HARRIS

PART TWO

Richard Barr, Jr.'s Farm: Surprise Visit

Richard looked at his hands; his sister-in-law, Pamela Sue was right. It had only been a little over a week; the fingers were cracked, bleeding and sore. In the last twenty-three years, Richard had never so much as picked up a rake or taken out the trash. There were plenty of people to do this for him in New York, but in Indiana he was on his own. The late August sun was starting to set below the apple and pear orchards when a white pickup truck pulled slowly down the lane to his farm house. He didn't recognize the truck, and neither did the two cats sitting next to him. Dick and Jane were now a part of his farm family, and boy could they catch mice and chipmunks! The truck pulled up by the porch, and Rick was speechless. The passenger door opened, Anne jumped from the truck. Next his son, Eric, exited the driver's door.

"I like what you've done to the place," She said with a smile.

Still in utter amazement, "What are you doing here?"

"Well, Dad, Mom and I thought you might need some extra help on the farm. We assume you forgot everything about farming, so here we are to help you do whatever you do."

"Are you staying here or just dropping by?"

"I know this may sound really crazy, but we are here to live with you." Anne said

"What about your career in New York? You are so close to becoming a full partner in the firm."

"Eric and I will take one day at a time. We don't know what to expect or experience but are here for now, and we'll try and make the best of things."

"Eric, what about you getting into New York University?"

"Dad, I checked on line and I've enrolled in Indiana University. My classes start next month."

"You know, I'm not real sure of my future either. I'm trying to deal with some demons and thought that Gas City would be a good escape. When the time comes, I will share with you both about my move and the Barr family itself, but for right now, please let me work through this pain."

"Fair enough," Anne said, "now where do we sleep, and do you have any furniture?"

"You'll love the furnishings here. The Ault family left us a lot of great stuff which pretty much all came from the 50' and 60's. A great deal of plaid and you'll love the lime green shag carpeting in the living room. Come on in, and I'll give you the grand tour."

They both ran up to Rick and hugged him. Anne gave him a passionate kiss and ran her fingers through his dark hair. "We know this isn't going to be easy, but like Eric said, the Barrs can do anything."

Tim and Pamela Sue's Farm

Tim came into the kitchen holding a plaid handkerchief over his nose with Moses right behind him laughing all the way into the house. "Ok, you two, what happened?" Pamela Sue asked trying not to laugh.

"I bet Dad I could beat him in basketball and even spotted him ten points. Well, I made up the ten points in about three minutes, and he jumped on my back. My elbow went back and caught him right on the nose. Serves him right." Moses said with a laugh.

"Come here honey, let's look at the nose," she said with a big grin on her face. This hadn't been the first time the two came in after chores bleeding or limping. Pamela Sue knew this was the bond between father and son, and it was strong. They would wrestle, play basketball, or just trip the other to get things going. They loved the other so much, and both looked forward every night to some kind of competition. "It's not bleeding much. Go put some ice on it to keep the swelling down, and by the way, you two get out of those dirty clothes."

"You made two illegal baskets and stepped out of bounds," Tim said with a smile, holding the ice pack on his nose.

"Get out of here Dad! Admit it; you just can't keep up with a fine player like myself. The best thing now would be a nice black eye to go along with the nose." They were standing in their undershorts; Tim threw his ice pack at Moses and chased him up the stairs. Pamela Sue picked up the dirty, sweaty clothes and smiled. Moses would graduate high school next year, and all this would change. He would be off to Purdue University, and Tim would lose his best friend.

Rahab came downstairs and walked directly into the laundry room located next to the mud room. "Mom, those two are wrestling in your bedroom and are making a lot of noise; I'm trying to finish my book and report."

"It's ok, dear. Bring your book down, and we'll sit on the porch together. I love you, honey, but Moses and your Dad need this time together. It took me a long time to realize this is how they show love to each other."

"Mom, I just don't get it; they're punching each other and Dad has a bloody nose."

"Tell me about your book and why you are so intrigued with the vampires."

Mary Barr's Farm

Once again Mary fixed a meal just for herself. The house seems so big and empty since her husband, Richard, passed away four months before. She had plenty of memories, but none could hold her in their arms or listen to her cries. Richard would snore so loud, she would go to the small sewing room and sleep. Now she wished for just one loud snore or to hear him flush the toilet late at night. She had only loved one other man in her seventy-nine years, and he too passed away. He was forty-eight years older, but she still remembered his gentle touch and the smell of Old Spice aftershave and cherry pipe tobacco.

Many people had sent cards, notes, food, and promises of getting together; that well had already dried up. Now she had only herself, and she was angry. How could he have left her the way he did. She had no warning. Went to the barn like he had done so many times before. He never came out. He didn't tell her goodbye or how much he loved her. She marched upstairs, threw his toothbrush and shaver in the trash, put on his old plaid work shirt and slipped beneath the covers. She hoped that sleep would find her quickly.

Richard Barr's Farm

"Come on in to our new home," Richard said with a smile.

Anne and Eric walked in the old farm house and said nothing. They looked at the plaid drapes with matching chair and lamp, green shag carpeting, the dining room table with six mixed matched chairs, blue refrigerator, yellow stove, and a plaque hanging in the kitchen that read "Bless This Humble Home". Anne started to laugh and Eric went ballistic.

"How much did you pay for this place?" Anne asked as she sat in the plaid overstuffed chair.

"Dad, we thought you were a great businessman and could make great deals on anything," Eric said still laughing out loud.

"Think this is something, just wait until I get out the vacuum cleaner. It's self-propelled, has a headlight, seat, and you can ride it around the living room, cleaning the shag carpet as you go." Richard said, now laughing. All three laughed until there was nothing left.

"Don't forget, the bedrooms are upstairs, and you're in for a real treat." Just then, the cats walked in the house each carrying a mouse. "Oh, yeah! Here come our local exterminators, let me introduce you to Dick and Jane."

They walked upstairs; on the landing was a large painting of Jesus holding a lamb. Anne knew the art work in the New York home was valued at over a million dollars, and these pieces could probably fetch thirty bucks on a good day. The master bedroom had a king size bed with leopard print bedspread and matching leopard print drapes. In the corner was an orange chair with donkey stenciled pillow. There were two large red and orange throw rugs dotted with several white and yellow stains. The large green dresser was apparently held together with several layers of duct tape. On the wall facing the bed was a picture of a cow, appearing to be taking a crap.

Anne said, "No! Take that down!" Rick thought to himself, well, that wasn't too bad.

Eric's room had a double bed with a pink pony stenciled on the throw. He immediately took it off and threw it on the floor. "No way, Dad!" was his comment. Rick was surprised that his son left the picture of the girl riding a white horse through a meadow. Eric's dresser had little ponies painted on each drawer but Eric decided to leave them for now. His room did have a nice view of the barn and corral. He noticed a rooster strut into the barn and thought, he'd better be mute or he will be dead. Dick and Jane jumped up on Eric's bed and just looked at him for some direction. "Well you guys, I've never had a pet before, so this will be a new experience for us all." "Do you two like roosters?" The cats just looked at him. Me neither. We'll get along just fine." It was getting stuffy, so Eric turned on the window fan, and nothing happed. Dick and Jane curled up together at the foot of this bed like some kind of ritual, and off to sleep they went. At least Eric was pretty sure there would be no mice or chipmunks in his room tonight.

Sarah's Charm and Chatter

"Todd, what are you doing down there?," yelling down the basement, "come on up to bed." Sissy said

"I'll be up in a minute, NeeNee are I just finishing up a game of dice"

NeeNee was Todd's imaginary friend. Todd would play with NeeNee for hours and this had been going on for many years. Todd didn't socialize with many people, but NeeNee had been his life-long friend since he was probably four. Sissy let the situation go on even though Todd was now twenty five, but NeeNee kept Todd busy when she was running the beauty shop. Todd told his mother that NeeNee loved cowboys and Indians as much he did, and NeeNee had once ridden a horse. Sissy thought there were so many strange happenings since NeeNee had arrived. Several times when Todd was an infant, she would hear Todd's baby bottle hit the floor, and she would get up to retrieve it. Todd would have it back in his mouth. Other times Todd would leave his room with toys scattered, and she would return to arrange them. They were all back in their original place. He just told her that NeeNee didn't like things messy. Sissy knew there was no NeeNee, but if Todd wanted him as a friend, why not?

She tucked Todd in bed, and he always said his prayers. Todd thanked God for his mother, cowboys, Indians, horses, and lastly NeeNee and NeeNee's sister. She kissed Todd and asked why NeeNee wouldn't come and see her. His response was that he didn't like big people and turned over. Sissy had so much to process since her father, Richard Barr, Sr., had passed away four months ago. Her father had raped her at age fourteen, but the healing was coming. She knew it. She now could sleep through the night; it had only taken her twenty-six years. She knew for sure he would not sneak into her bedroom. Now the nights were awesome, but she still left the hall light on and double locked her bedroom door.

RICHARD AND ANNE'S FARM

Richard helped carry the suitcases up to the bedrooms. Anne and Eric didn't bring much because they weren't sure what to expect, and their expectations were correct. The one bathroom had a tub/shower combination with a yellow sunflower shower curtain and matching towels. Anne opened the medicine cabinet to put in her toothbrush and cologne, and there was Rick's shaver, toothbrush and his cologne. In New York they had separate bathrooms, bedrooms, and medicine cabinets. They hadn't shared a bathroom since the days at New York University after they were first married. Those days seemed simple, Anne thought, but as she looked around, it was back to simple with capital S. As she looked in the mirror, Anne noticed a forty-two year old woman looking back at her thinking, what have you done?

Rick came into the bedroom and turned on the window fan. "The AC isn't working today," he said with a grin. "Oh that's right. We don't have air conditioning. It hasn't been too bad up here; there is usually a southern breeze that keeps it cool. We have a choice: either underwear or nothing at all."

Anne gave him a funny look and said, "Is this all planned out?"

"Yep, just trying to get my bride of twenty three years naked. What do think?"

"It's ok by me, but Rick, you have to get rid of that leopard print blanket. It reminds me of some old black and white movie with a bad ending."

They both laughed, and he immediately threw the blanket out the window.

"That was a little dramatic, don't you think?"

"Come here," Rick said and he gently lead her to the king size bed, minus the leopard blanket.

Both put their hands on each other and quietly sat on the edge of the bed looking at each other's body. The bed let out a half a dozen squeaks as they laid back. They started to laugh and knew this love session was going to be a real challenge.

Mom's Diner

It was 5:45 A.M., and the round table of farmers and local guys was nearly full. Tidy Tucker just couldn't help looking over at his tractor trophy in Mom's window. He was never one to brag, but boy did he love to come into Mom's each day and check out his prize! He competed against the best old tractors in Lincoln County and beat them all hands down. The trophy represented the only award and probably any public recognition Tidy had ever experienced in his sixty-one years in Gas City, Indiana. He just broke the world's record for being the proudest man on the planet.

Rick, Tim, and Eric walked in the diner. "Here come the Barr brothers with another Barr," someone said, and everyone turned to see them approach the table.

"This is my son, Eric. He'll be staying here with me on the old Ault Farm."

"We know all about Eric," Lester said, "He was here for the county fair and slept on the pile of hay with Billie Magic. You two make a nice couple, and we all got to see the 4H jacket the kids gave to you; trust me, they wouldn't have done that except to say you have been accepted into their group."

Eric blushed and sat next to his dad.

"Nice trophy," Rick said.

"Yeah, I kind of like it," Tidy said trying not to be too boastful.

"How's the farm coming along?" Bill asked.

"There is more work than I ever expected. The Ault's left me with a big project, and it's hard to find a place to begin or end," Rick said.

"Remember back in 1969 when Jimmy Ault was killed in Vietnam? That seemed to be the beginning of their downfall, Marvin said. They didn't associate with many people and within four years the farm ground was rented out. Alice Ault passed away two years later and Bill Ault went into a nursing home in Evansville about three years after her death. Their daughter Cathy has rented the property all this time and now she has been diagnosed with ALS. I believe she still lives in Orlando with her daughter, Jinni."

"That's where I had to send the check for the purchase." Rick said.

"If you need help, all you have to do is ask any one of us," Harry Carter said. "You know the Amish carpenters are the best anywhere, and remolding or building is their specialty."

Mom came to the table and took the orders. Everyone got the special, meatloaf, smothered in gravy, fried potatoes, toast and coffee. Bill Sales just had coffee and was looking to take something from the other's plates.

Mom looked at Eric and with a big smile said, "I've heard about you and Billie Magic."

Eric thought to himself that apparently the whole town was in on their relationship. He will try and be as tight lipped as ever, but this might prove to be a challenge.

On the way back to the farm, Rick asked Eric about Billie. This was the first he had heard about it, but the town sure had the inside scoop. He told his father of their relationship, and she was going to Indiana University in the fall to study law. He said Billie was a very determined young woman, had very high moral standards, and had never tried drugs. Rick already liked her and he hadn't even met her. He told his father he was in love with Billie and he thought she felt the same about him. Rick thought back of how her father, Bob Magic, and he were best friends, and now his son was in love with his best friend's daughter. Rick could tell Eric had surrendered his heart to this girl. Maybe this move to Gas City was what they all needed.

Back To Richard and Anne's Farm.

Rick and Eric arrived back at their farm, and Anne was sitting in the large overstuffed chair on the front porch. She had her bare feet on the railing, holding a cup of coffee, and Dick and Jane were sitting on each side of her. Anne saw the boys exit the truck, talking mile a minute; this was a rarity for her husband and son. Usually the conversations were limited to one or two words and occasionally a sentence. Rick softly punched Eric in the arm, and Eric walked around the truck and got in the driver's seat. He drove down the lane and tooted the horn as he approached county road 700E. Rick walked up the porch and sat on the railing facing his wife. She was wearing a soft, blue sundress hiked above her knees and a pink baseball cap.

"Where is he off to?" Anne asked

"He's going over to Billie Magic's Farm. I just found out at breakfast today he liked her, and they spent a week together at the Lincoln Co. Fair. The whole town knows. Did you know about this or did he tell of you of his love for this girl?"

"Rick, this is the main reason he came back to Gas City and is going to Indiana University this fall. He truly loves her, and I've never seen him so happy. She has only let him kiss her a few times, and that's the line she draws in the sand. He's ok with this. She told him she was still a virgin and will only give herself to the man she loves and trusts. She has strong values and principles; I wish I could say the same of our son. I truly think this girl can turn Eric around and give him some purpose to his life. This sure is refreshing compared to the girls Eric has slept with, especially Kandy, back in New York."

Rick started rubbing Anne's beautiful, slender, tan feet she had resting on the porch railing. "Speaking of loose women," he said as he ran his hand up her long tan leg. She lifted her toes toward Rick and he softly put her toes in his mouth and ran his tongue between them. The taste was salty but wonderful in his mouth. She lifted her other foot and he again licked and caressed her feet to the sounds of Anne's sighs. She gently parted her legs and he noticed she wasn't wearing underwear. He tenderly touched her vagina and clitoris as she let a quiet moan from her throat. She now was wet and took a hold of his hand and pressed it tightly to her love triangle, helping guide his fingers to the spot. He stood and kissed her passionately on her lips, never taking his hand from beneath her dress. His gentle strokes and her quiet moans continued. She reached up and touched the hardness through his jeans; he too moaned. "Let's go upstairs and make music together on that old squeaky bed," he said with a smile, as he led her up the stairs. Dick and Jane just looked up from their positions on the porch and watched as their new owners went into the house, until they sighted a mouse on the corner of the porch. The hunt was on!

BILLIE'S FARM

Eric pulled into the farm lane and up to the barn. He saw no one around and walked into the barn. Billie had her back to Eric and was putting some kind of oil on a saddle. She was wearing white tennis shoes, white short shorts and a pink tight Tee shirt with a stencil of a carrot on the back. She turned to see him, and from twenty yards away they both ran to each other like some movie moment. His heart was ready to explode and her blonde hair was flying back as she ran. The embrace was awesome! She smelled like a fresh, mowed lawn with a hint of lavender perfume. Her soft pink lips touched his and an electric charge shot through them both.

"Wow!" Eric exclaimed.

"Double Wow!" Billie shouted. " I really missed you, Eric Barr, but for the life of me, I still can't figure out why. From our first kiss on the lawn of Sales and Son Funeral Home, you've opened up a new chapter in my heart."

"Maybe it was the knife you put to my throat; did you ever think about that?"

"It wasn't the knife, but you do have the distinction of being the only boy I ever pulled a knife on at a funeral home. What do you think of that?"

"I'm so glad to be in that exclusive category. I have missed you a bunch too but you have haven't emailed me very often."

"I'm not into social networking; I'm into face to face meetings, and sharing a kiss and a warm embrace like this," kissing him again, throwing her arms around his neck.

He knew he had to control himself because her breasts were pushing tightly on his chest and she wasn't wearing a bra. He would have had a leg amputated if she would just take off her shirt right now. Get a grip, he thought.

"We heard you and your mom moved back to the old Ault farm to be with your dad. Is it true you are going to Indiana University this fall?"

"Come on, let's sit on the hay, and I'll explain it all to you." She released her hold around his neck and sat down next to him. He was glad in a way that she let go of him because he was certain she felt the bulge through his jeans. "We moved back to support my dad, and even my mom is trying to fit in. She wasn't sure how to turn the stove on, but now that's a distant memory. Most of our meals consist of anything she can fry on the stove, but Pamela Sue has also kept us fed the last couple days. My dad came back here because he has a family secret that has apparently been plaguing him for some time. He told us when he was ready; he would share it with my mom and me. It must be very important to him to leave New York and his company on the spur of a moment, and yes I have enrolled at IU this fall and will study international business." Eric couldn't help staring at Billie as she intently listened to him with her big, beautiful blue eyes. Her skin was flawless as he touched her tan, muscular arm. She responded with a hand running through his dark hair. Eric wasn't sure what second base was, but he was ready to take their relationship to the next level.

"I'm glad you came back," she said with a smile. A bunch of 4H kids have been asking about you; you've made quite an impression on the group. We're having the annual banquet in two weeks, and I would love to have you be my date."

"I don't know, I have so much to do, and your friend Lucy with all the sheep has already asked me. She emailed me and I told her she was hot; I'm thinking Lucy right now," he said with a grin.

Billie pushed him down on the hay and straddled him, pinning him to the ground. "You know Eric Barr, if you want to see what Billie Magic is capable of, just keep it up," planting another soft kiss on his lips. "If you mention Lucy again," reaching behind her back pulling out her long Bowie knife, "you might be missing an ear or two."

He looked at her tight tee shirt and straining breasts beneath and knew the bulge was back. "I was just kidding, and I hope you knew I was"

"I did, Lucy is going to the banquet with Teddy because he loves sheep nearly as much."

"My best friend, Tony from New York, may come out to see me in couple of weeks. Do you think Dar would go out with him? He's never been out of New York City, and Gas City will be a brand new experience for him along with a nice country girl like Dar. We all think his dad is in the Mafia because when we ask Tony what his dad, Anthony, Sr., does, he just says, "dry cleaning." They live in a mansion in Sheepshead Bay, New York, and I want him to experience Indiana. He's a cool guy."

"Dar just broke up with her boyfriend, Tony, so this will be good, another Tony in her life. Maybe he'll be here for the banquet, and we can double date. By the way, I've seen the swelling in your pants; you don't have to be embarrassed around me. I get it. Let's go inside, and I'll make lemonade." grabbing his hand as she helped him up from the hay.

Eric thought, well, the bulge secret is out of the way and boy, she is brutally honest, and into the house he went.

SISSY'S BEAUTY SHOP

Sissy was just finishing up Harriet Carter's hair when Todd came running up the stairs. "Mom, I want a cat," Todd said with great enthusiasm.

"Honey, we'll talk about this later after I finish here."

"But Mom, NeeNee thinks it will be a nice friend for me."

"Todd we'll talk about his later, now please, bring me some cream rinse from the basement."

"Ok Mom, I'll be right up."

"Who is NeeNee?" Harriet asked

"Oh, it's Todd's imaginary friend and this isn't the first time NeeNee hasn't told Todd he needed something. NeeNee told him Todd needed a dog, a horse, strawberry ice cream, a flat screen television, a trip to Disney World, and God knows what else. So far I've taken him to Disney, and he has his own television. NeeNee always seems to come up with some great ideas for Todd. Would you like any color today?"

"No, thank you, just a cut and curl. Pastor Roger's wife sure talks up your shop. She now is known for her flaming red hair and sassy new look. When they first came to the church, she rarely left the house or even made eye contact. Now she is the president of the ladies guild and started a bowling team called the Red Strikers. All the ladies have bright red hair except Marge Harding, but apparently she is wavering."

"Libby sent all the ladies to me for the color; at first they weren't too sure about taking the leap, but now the Red Strikers have evolved. I guess they all went to Evansville and spent the night last week and when I asked them what they did, the old saying was repeated: "What happened in Evansville; stays in Evansville." Libby came over last Friday and brought some great wine; we sat in the yard and talked about our town and the church. She said that this is the first time in her life she has an identity of her own. She was known as the pastor's wife at the last four churches they attended. Her father was domineering as she grew up he demanded her full obedience. She could never make a move or get his approval on anything she ever attempted. Now at forty-three she has evolved. Libby told me that her husband absolutely loves her hair and he can't keep his hands off her." Sissy said with a smile.

"I heard those ministers can be pretty horny." Harriet said with laugh.

"I don't know about that. Remember old Rev. Fleming? I just can't picture him in bed with anyone, especially his wife, Ruth, she would never let an ankle show beneath her long dresses. Ruth always got her hair done on Thursdays and would refer to her husband as Rev. Fleming. They did have a daughter, so apparently something happened between the sheets," Sissy said as they both started laughing out loud.

"Good point, Sissy, but now I have a mental picture of Ruth Fleming taking off her clothes in front of the pastor, showing off her tattoos with his name inked on her butt," Harriet said between the laughs

"Or the other cheek might say "Jesus Saves" boy, we are bad, aren't we?" Sissy laughed.

Todd came running up the stairs and wanted to go to his grandmother's house. "Soon as I finish with Mrs. Carter, we'll go." Sissy took the towel from Harriet's hair. "I wish you wouldn't have planted that picture of Ruth Fleming in my head. I'm going to be laughing all night."

"Goodbye Sissy, Goodbye Todd, and say hi to NeeNee for me," Harriet said as she left the shop."

"I will, Mrs. Carter!" Todd shouted back.

Tim and Pamela Sue's Farm

Anne Barr pulled into the barn yard of Tim and Pamela Sue's farm. She carefully stepped from the truck because cats running all over. Pamela Sue came from the back porch wearing her traditional plaid apron. "Hi, Anne, what brings you to our place?"

"Can we talk?" Anne asked

"Sure, come on in the kitchen, I have a roast to bring out." Pamela Sue gave Anne a big bear hug and kissed her on the cheek. "Sit down; would you like some pie or a warm pork sandwich?"

"I would love some, thank you."

Pamela Sue turned her short, stocky body toward the stove. "Now what's on your mind?"

Anne started to tear up. "I don't know if I can make it here. I haven't a clue how to cook, clean, wash, iron, or change the sheets. Rick and Eric have been very kind and helpful, but I've never done a single one of these tasks in my life. I grew up with maids, cooks, and gardeners. I just won't fit in here, and I know it. The house is a pit and there is no air conditioning. There is not one stick of furniture that matches and the cats keep bringing in dead mice and placing them at my feet. I plugged in the hairdryer today. It blew a fuse, and half the power went out in the house."

"I always find that some good food will give you a new perspective on things." Pamela Sue handed her a warm barbeque pork sandwich, a slice of banana cream pie, and pulled a chair up to the kitchen table. "You know, I too feel inadequate many times. I don't know how to set a table, and I'm not sure where the fork, knife, and spoon are supposed to go. I grew up learning all these tasks you mentioned but I don't know how to put clothes or jewelry together. I learned how to sew, cook, and clean since I was a little girl. I helped raise two younger brothers after our mother passed away. I would work in the fields all day and would come home and help my grandmother cook and sew, but I never learned the social graces. When we go a restaurant, I just look at the table next to us to see how they eat and what fork they use." Pamela Sue was now tearing up as she spoke.

"I never realized we were so much alike because I thought you were never intimated by anything. We both married Barr brothers and we certainly know what that means." Anne said with a smile.

Pamela Sue cut herself a piece of banana cream pie and looked intently at Anne. "I'm going to be very honest with you. I can teach you all these skills, but this will never be your heartbeat. You will never, never enjoy doing these chores. This is not what makes up Anne Barr. I do have a solution for you; call Hazel your housekeeper in New York, fly her here for a while. She can stay in the extra bedroom next to the kitchen and do what she does best. Also Tim and I know all the Amish builders; your house can be remodeled practically overnight, unless you want to keep the green shag carpet, plaid drapes, and matching couch." Pamela Sue said with a grin.

Anne looked up from her pie like she'd been struck by lightning. "You're absolutely right!" she said with a smile. She jumped up from her chair and threw her arms around Pamela Sue. "I think this food does give me a better outlook on things. By the way, will you cut me another slice of the banana cream pie?"

"Let's go sit on the porch; I have some strawberry wine in the basement I've aged for about six months. It's time to break the seal and celebrate. I'm really glad you came back to be with Rick; he's missed you a ton."

MARY BARR'S FARM

Mary Barr was just finishing up the last minute details for her family cookout tonight. She would have her children, their spouses, and all the grandchildren; boy was she excited! She needed something like this to build her spirits. It was nearly six o'clock, and the long table was set for a family feast. The old harvest table was stored in the barn, and six generations of Barrs had eaten from it. In the top corner of the table was carved the initials "J.B 1868". No one in the family knew who J.B was, but they were all sure in had to be a Barr. The table sat about fifteen feet from the fire where all the food was to be cooked. Even the old silverware and glasses came from grandma Barr's home. Mary had placed fresh flowers and a small candle by each place setting.

Mary could hear Tim, Pamela Sue, Moses, and Rahab coming down the lane laughing loudly. "Hi, Dommy," Moses and Rahab said as they ran to their grandmother.

"Hey kids! Moses, will you start the fire and Rahab, will you help me bring out the food?"

"Hi, Mom," as Tim approached her and threw his long powerful arms around his mother. "Thanks for having us, and what can I do?"

" Please put the food on the fire when your brother and sister arrive."

Just then Sissy and Todd pulled up the drive in her old Chevy. Todd jumped out almost before the car stopped. "Hi, Dommy," and ran to his grandmother.

"I swear, Todd, you've grown another foot."

"Dommy, can I have a cat?"

Mary looked at his mother with raised eyebrows. "I'll tell you about it later," Sissy said with a sigh.

"Well, Todd, we'll see; I certainly have plenty to choose from," as she put her arm around her grandson.

The big white truck pulled up, and Rick, Anne, and Eric got out. Tim sought Rick out and gave him a strong brotherly hug. "Here we are again, eating with the Barr's." Rick said with a smile.

"If eating ever becomes an Olympic sport, our family will definitely take home the gold." Moses said with a laugh.

"And Moses, you'll be our team captain," Rahab said back with a smile.

The fire was hot and ready for the onslaught of food. Mary had marinated chicken breasts and started bringing out casseroles by the arm full. The chicken and corn cooking on the fire made everyone feel hungry. The seats and benches were quickly filled, as everyone waited for the food to come off the grill. Pamela Sue said grace, and the plates were filled to over flowing. So much laughter and the new adventures at Rick and Anne's farm house. Everyone loved the stories of the two cats bringing in their catch and the green shag carpeting was also a great laugh. Eric shared about Billie, and Todd brought up again about a cat. Sissy told everyone that NeeNee wanted Todd to have a cat, and if Todd wanted one, he could have his pick. Todd jumped up to find his favorite.

The chairs were now moved around the campfire, and Rick had an announcement to make. Rick went into the house, down the basement and fetched a small package rapped in tissue. He put it on his lap and then stood. "Remember the story of Albert Harris?" Rick asked.

Everyone let out a moan. "Uncle Tim, you scared the crap out of me when you told the story," Eric said as everyone laughed.

"Guess what? It's not a campfire story; it's real!" Rick exclaimed.

"You're not going to pull that one on us again." Rahab said.

"That story has been told for years and years and now we have another wrinkle to it. Is that what you're saying, Uncle Rick?" Moses asked.

Tim stood by Rick and said, "What he told you is true. Show them."

Rick carefully unwrapped the tissue, and held up an old Boy Scout hat in the air.

"You two should go on television. You'd make a great comedy team" Rahab said in disgust.

"Hold on everyone. Just hear me out." Rick said. "Tim and I were moving some furniture from the house for a church rummage sale, and we found dad's old army trunk in the basement. We opened it, and this was sitting off in the corner. There was a newspaper article stuffed into the hat. It's dated 1937 from the Evansville Herald and talks about a missing boy scout named Albert Harris." Now everyone leaned forward to hear the story. Rick carefully showed everyone the hat with the initials A. Harris sewn into the lining.

"Rick and I were in complete shock, so he called the bank in Evansville that offered a reward. Take a guess what it's worth."

Anne said, "A thousand dollars."

"Not even close Tim said, It's worth $860,000."

"Get out of here!" Rahab yelled. "When you guys put together a story, it's a whopper."

"I know this is hard to swallow, but the whole story is true. All we have to do is either prove Albert Harris is dead or still alive somewhere, and the money is ours."

"He would be eighty three or four by now." Anne said. "He could be living."

Up until now Sissy hadn't said a word. "Let's find him and split the money."

There was total silence except for Todd running around the farm yard trying to catch a cat. Everyone just looked at each other after Sissy's statement.

"I think we can do it." Anne said "I have access to the best private investigator in New York City and everyone at this table has the local connections. What do you think?" More silence and looks around the table.

"Shit, dad, if we get the money, we can get new carpet and air conditioning," Eric said with a laugh.

Sissy said, "I'm in; who else?"

Mary stood and put her out stretched arm toward the others. Everyone followed and laid their hands upon the other. "I feel like a quarterback in a huddle waiting for the big play surrounded by my teammates. Let's do it!" Mary said in a firm voice.

"This could be fun," Moses said with a smile.

"Ok, but we can't mention this to anyone. Why don't we gather at the beauty shop a week from tonight and see what each of us has come up with. I have a large extra room in the basement and we can set it up as an investigation room like they have on television," Sissy suggested.

"All right, one week from now at 7:00 P.M. Rick said, but not a word to anyone."

Just then, Todd came running up to the fire with a large yellow cat in his arms. "I'm going to call him mustard." Everyone howled.

Back to Rick and Anne's

"Is this the big secret you came back to Gas City for?" Anne asked.

"No, Tim and I just happened to stumble on the hat two weeks ago and didn't know what to do."

"I'm sure there will be many blind alleys, but with this investigator and my knowledge of the information highway, we may get lucky. I'm going downtown tomorrow and get a small office where I can have electronic access and a desk. Oh, by the way, I'm having Hazel come from New York for a while to help organize the house and cook for us." Anne said as she walked upstairs

"Praise God! This has been your greatest decision since you came." Rick said with a grin.

"I also hired the Yoder Family builders and they'll start on Monday. Pamela Sue told me these Amish guys are true craftsmen, and they work ten hours a day. You know Rick we really could make this place a go. I'm really happy to be here, and Eric is ecstatic. We only have a few more nights without air conditioning and the old squeaky bed; let's go up and give it another test drive," as she extended her hand to her handsome husband.

"If anyone can find Albert, it's you. You are in your element and are very good at what you do, I guess the best. I also know your oral skills are phenomenal, so how about a nice blow job."

She blushed and said "Thanks for the vote of confidence, and with that, I'll give you the finest, slowest, stroking that ever existed. I'll caress your balls as I lick little Rick up and down and you'll beg me to finish you off. This one may be the one etched in your memory forever." as she closed their bedroom door.

"I've never heard you talk like this. What has gotten into you? I'm really turned on and my mind is already recording everything you've said."

"Just sit back partner; you're in for a real rodeo," she said in a cooing voice, and put on her white cowboy hat. She lowered his pants, and he was at full attention. He sat on the bed, and she knelt before him, parted his legs and just smiled at the husband of her youth.

Eric could hear his parent's squeaky bed and hoped they were just changing the sheets.

Mom's Diner

Tim and Rick pulled into to Mom's. Rick said, "Don't forget, not a word about what we talked about last night. Maybe we can ask some questions without being too obvious. Most of these guys were raised around here and must have some knowledge of Albert Harris."

"Hey guys, Tim said, "What's new in the lives of the most prominent, good looking men in Gas City?"

"What have you been smoking, Tim?" Lester asked with a grin.

"Tim and I will have the special," Rick said.

The talk was pretty much the same: cattle prices, rain, no rain, and baseball. As if the kidding wasn't enough for Bill Sales the funeral director, he was die hard Chicago Cubs fan. It was mid fall and the Cubs were in next to last place.

"There's always next year you know," Bill said, and with that someone threw a piece of toast at him.

"That was a good accurate throw; maybe the Cubs can use another starter," Marvin said.

"My son asked me about a rumor of a scout that disappeared from Gas City many years ago. I think it might have been close to my father's farm." Tim said casually like he really wasn't looking for a response.

"Yeah, I think he disappeared in the 1930's. Some people say it was a made up story just to close the camp. Two days after his disappearance, another scout drowned in the pond next to the mess hall." Tidy said.

"My father told me the same story and the police and a private investigator were all over town asking questions," Lester said. "I think your grandfather tore the old buildings down when he bought the camp grounds from the scouts. Here again, that was over seventy years ago; who knows."

"There is one guy that might know something. Old Mr. Galey claims to have known the Boy Scout, and his bunk was right above the missing scout's. He's told the story at least a thousand times, but the story has changed half the time," Harold said.

"Where is Mr. Galey now?" Rick asked.

"I think he's at Shady Grove in the extended care unit. My mother was there for six months and Mr. Galey would come into her room and talk about the scout camp over and over. She passed a year ago and Mr. Galey could have passed away, too." Marvin said.

The conversation went back to grain prices and the possibility of rain. Tim and Rick finished their breakfast and said goodbye to the guys, knowing they were leaving the diner with more information than before.

"What do you think? After chores, let's go to Shady Grove and talk to an old Boy Scout," Tim said

"Come by the farm about 1:00 P.M., and I'll be ready with a tape recorder," Rick said with a smile.

"I just hope the old guy is still alive." Tim said, shaking his head.

ALEXANDRIA, VIRGINIA

There was a faint rapping at the office door. "Come in," was the voice beyond the door.

"Sir we might have a slight problem," said the clean cut, middle-aged man.

"Close the door and sit."

"The Evansville bank called the other day, and someone was inquiring about the Albert Harris Trust. He identified himself as a reporter and only wanted to know the amount."

With a deep frown on his face, the older man looked across the desk at the younger man. "Keep me informed if there are any other inquiries. If they continue, you know what has to be done."

"I do, Sir. So far it's been smooth sailing, but if the waters become choppy, their little boat will have go down."

"I trust you can handle any problem that may arrive."

DOWNTOWN GAS CITY, INDIANA

Anne Barr had plenty of empty buildings to choose from. She walked down the street and found what appeared to have been an old barber shop or real estate office. She called the number on the sign in the window and the man said he could be there in fifteen minutes. An old truck pulled up and a sixtyish man got out and walked right up to Anne.

Anne put out her hand. "I'm Anne Barr."

"I know who you are. You're Rick's wife from New York and you two bought the old Ault farm. I met your son, Eric, at the Lincoln Co. Fair last month. Billie Magic and he make a nice couple. By the way, I'm Ted Taylor and this is my old office."

Anne thought that the introduction went well, since he just told her everything she needed to know about herself and family. She wondered if Ted knew about the blow job she gave Rick last night, but she wasn't going there. "How much for the space?" she asked.

"Let me find the keys, and I'll show you what I have." He held the door for her as she walked in first.

He couldn't help looking at her slim figure in the tight jeans and light cotton tee shirt. She had on a baseball cap with her hair pulled back into a ponytail, and boy, did she smell good!

"This used to a barber shop and then a small insurance office. In the next room is a desk and beyond that a small bathroom. There is a window air conditioner, and it works really well for the whole office. I was thinking $125.00 a month."

"Is that for the utilities?" Anne asked.

"Ok, I'll take $110.00 and pay the utilities-will that work for you?"

"You got yourself a deal. When can I move in?"

"Today if you like, and I'll haul the old barber chair out if you want."

"No just leave it for now," she said. She wrote Ted a check for $660.00. "I'll pay for the first six months and you can just mail me a receipt."

He looked at the check and said, "Wow, thank you for paying ahead. I know this will be a good business relationship," thinking to himself that he would like to take it a step further with Anne Barr. He handed her the keys and shook her hand.

She threw the old canvas tarp off the barber chair and sat down to survey her office. She couldn't help but laugh $110.00 a month. Her office in New York was $13,000.00 a month and, even though she had a window that faced the Statue of Liberty, she now had a dirty window that faced Jim's Shoe Repair and Vacuum Cleaner Shop. She swiveled the chair to face the ten foot long mirror on the east wall. She figured at least if a hair was out of place, it would be recognized immediately. This barber chair was fun. She just kept spinning around in circles. Except for sex, this might be a great stress reliever, she thought.

Shady Grove Nursing Home

Tim and Rick pulled into the parking lot, and looked at the old building. They were both very familiar with this old place; it was the former Gas City High School, with a lot of memories for these boys, both good and bad. The old school section wasn't being used, but the addition, probably from the seventies, was now a nursing facility. Tim had told his brother on the way in that he had called and Mr. Galey was still living at Shady Grove.

"Hi, we're here to see Mr. Galey," Rick said.

The young nurse told them he was in room 112 just down the hall. As they walked away, she couldn't help thinking, for a couple of older guys, they're hot.

"Mr. Galey?" Tim asked.

The old gentleman turned his wheelchair away from the window and faced the two brothers. "Are we related?" Mr. Galey asked in a quiet voice.

"No, I'm Rick Barr and this is my brother Tim. We would like to ask you a couple of questions if you feel up to it."

"Are you boys related to Isaac and Richard Barr?"

"We are. Isaac was our grandfather and Richard was our dad. Our father passed away just a few months ago," Tim said.

"I knew both your grandfather and dad. Fine men."

"Do you remember Albert Harris?" Rick asked.

"Do I ever! Albert and I were in the same cabin when he disappeared." Mr. Galey's eyes were now bright and attentive.

"Can you give us some details about Albert?" Rick asked

"I have forgotten many things in my life, but I remember 1937 like it was yesterday."

Rick and Tim both smiled at each other. This could be a big break in the missing scout case as Rick started the recorder.

"It was a hot June day when we arrived at Camp Blackhawk. I was the resident scout for our cabin because this was my fifth year, and I was three years older than the others. Doc, the camp director, and I got along great. Doc was about fifty at the time and had run the camp for over twenty-five years. Doc's life and passion was Camp Blackhawk. Doc, six other counselors, and I would have staff meetings each morning before the campers would wake up. I noticed that Tuesday morning Albert Harris wasn't in his bunk, so I assumed he was in the latrine. When I came back from our meeting, Albert still wasn't there, but his bed was disheveled. I asked the other boys if they had seen Albert, but no one saw him leave the cabin."

"When did you realize Albert was missing?" Tim asked.

"Almost immediately; I ran to get Doc and the search started. We searched all that day and Doc called the local sheriff to assist. I think Doc called Albert's parents in Evansville in the early evening, and they arrived in an hour. The sheriff called the local farmers and hunters to help because they knew the area like the back of their hand. This went on for two full days, and then we were hit with another tragedy." Mr. Galey seemed to get chocked up and asked for some water.

"What else happened?" Rick asked.

"On the morning of the third day, Doc found the body of Jacob Brown lying face down in the small pond we used for swimming. The pond was only six feet deep at the most. The coroner came out and told Doc it was an accidental drowning, but I had my doubts."

"Why do you say that? Tim asked

"Jacob Brown picked on Albert without ceasing. He would pull Albert's pants down in front of all the guys or take his food and smash it in his face in the mess hall. I would get so mad at Jacob, because Albert never did a thing to provoke him. After the drowning, Doc sent everyone home and cancelled camp for the rest of the summer. I stayed on to help look for Albert and be a rock for Doc because he was devastated. I stayed until the middle of August, but we never found a single clue."

"Why do you think it was strange that Jacob drowned? Do you have suspicions there was foul play?" Rick asked.

"Nothing concrete; it just seemed funny that two scouts went missing or died from my cabin. There were twelve other cabins, and mine took the brunt of the criticism. I answered so many questions from everyone, but no one blamed me. The responsibility fell on Doc's shoulders."

"What happened the next year?" Tim asked.

"It opened as normal, but Doc wasn't the same. They filled in the pond and tore down Albert's cabin. There were rumors that other scouts heard Albert calling Doc's name in the middle of the night, but I never heard a thing. Not many scouts came that year, so the camp closed in 1939."

"What's Doc's real name?" Tim asked

"Jim Clark from Lexington, Kentucky. He got out of scouting right after the camp closed and passed many years ago. We kept in touch until his death in 1945. That's it boys; I'm getting tired and snack time is in fifteen minutes."

"If you think of anything that might be of interest to the story, please call us. Here is my phone on the farm," Tim said.

"Why are you boys so interested in Albert Harris?"

"We're writing an article for the scouting magazine," Rick said.

"Good luck boys; I'll stay in touch," as he wheeled down to the cafeteria.

As they walked toward the truck, Tim nodded to Rick, "We've got a start."

Rick and Anne's Farm

Anne arrived home to find four black buggies and an old station wagon parked in her barnyard.

A tall man with greying beard walked over and put out his hand. “I’m Isaac Yoder and we’re here to look over the project. My four sons and two grandsons are taking measurements of your home. We have not been inside and were waiting for you to come home.”

“You could have called my cell phone, and I would have come quicker.”

“We don’t have telephones. The number you called and left a message for us went to a phone booth on the road by our home. We check it three or four times a day in case of a death in our family or an important message, like yourself.”

“Please come in, and look at the inside,” she said. Anne tried not to stare, but he had on a dark grey wool shirt, black pants, brown work boots, black suspenders, and a light tan straw hat. All the men were dressed the same, except for the two grandsons; they wore jeans and tee shirts with a peace symbol and Jimi Hendricks respectively.

Mr. Yoder talked with his sons, reached into his shirt pocket and produced a small tablet of paper and a pencil. He said something that she didn’t recognize. It appeared to be German. He wrote on the paper, folded it, and handed it to Anne.

“This is our price; please look it over call the phone number you have and leave a message. The price includes everything we do, including materials. We usually start at 6:00 AM and finish at 5:00 P.M. We bring our own food, and we will not work on Sunday for any reason. Thank you for considering us. All the men tipped their hats as they got into the buggies and Mr. Yoder in the station wagon. His grandson drove the car, and she was sure the young man felt pretty important driving an automobile.

She unfolded the paper Mr. Yoder gave her and was astonished. She slipped the paper into her back pocket and would show Rick when he arrived home.

TIM AND PAMELA SUE'S FARM

"You kids better practice. You only have a week!" Pamela Sue yelled.

"We've got it down. Don't sweat it mom!" Rahab yelled back.

"I can't believe you talked me into this stupid play," Moses said.

"I didn't talk you into anything. You get to dance and hold Lynn Loucks, big boy. That's the only reason you're doing this. She doesn't even like you. Why keep trying with her?"

"Someday she will see the real me, and I'll have to fight her off," Moses said with a grin

"Yeah, right!"

"Come down to dinner you two; it's hot." Pamela Sue yelled up the stairs.

They sat around the dining room table. Each place setting had fresh flowers and nice cloth napkins.

"What's the occasion?" Tim asked.

"Just wanted to make it nice for a change," Pamela Sue said with great pride.

"We haven't eaten in here since Thanksgiving." Moses said with a hint of sarcasm.

"Just enjoy and don't complain, or you'll be fixing your own meals."

"Sorry, Mom. It does look nice."

"Rick and I met with Mr. Galey today at the nursing home about Albert Harris."

"What happened?" Rahab asked

"He was a counselor in Albert's cabin and knew him well. He also told us another scout died three days after Albert disappeared. Rick tape recorded him and will put all Mr. Galey's memories on the computer and print it out for our meeting next week."

"Cool, this is really becoming a mystery," Moses said.

"The kids at school knew nothing, and everyone thinks the story was made up."

"Don't be too obvious when you ask people," Tim said, "We want to keep this in our family."

"Hey Dad, let's go out back, and I'll show you how to throw horseshoes." as he threw the napkin on the table.

"I was pitching shoes with your grandfather before you were a thought in my mind. I know I can take you, so you better be prepared for some serious crying. I'll take out a box of tissues just in case you need to wipe your eyes," Tim said with a grin.

Moses punched his father as he walked by his chair. "Come on old man."

Tim got up from the table and walked over to Pamela Sue. "Great dinner Honey, I loved the flowers and the napkins," and kissed her on the forehead.

Oh, my gosh!, she thought. He noticed. Pamela Sue had a warm feeling inside, and she started thinking of something special for tomorrow's dinner. "You two better not come in bloody from the horseshoe pitching," knowing full well it will probably end up a wrestling match.

"Mom, do you want to hear my song for the play next Friday?" Rahab asked

"Sure do. Let's just clear the table, and I'll come up to your bedroom." Pamela Sue thought "The Music Man" would be a tough play for high school kids to pull off, but Rahab was so excited to have the part of Marian.

Anne's New Office in Gas City

The barber chair stayed right where it was. She could sit in the chair and look out on Main Street and collect her thoughts on Albert Harris. Spinning around and looking in the long mirror was also fun. She now sat at her desk in the back office and opened her laptop computer. She emailed her law intern in New York and asked for some assistance. She asked him to gather all information from the Evansville Herald from 1937-1940 in reference to Albert Harris. Dale Galloway was only twenty-eight years old, but he was a whiz at getting information off the internet and social networks. She never explained why she needed the articles and was sure he wouldn't ask. She then called Harvey Adams in New York.

"Hi, Harvey, it's Anne."

"The rumor in the city is you have become a farmer in Indiana," He said with a chuckle.

"I'm here with my husband, Rick, and we are taking one day at a time."

"So why the call?" he asked

"I need for you to do a job for me. It involves a missing person and you're the best."

"Thanks for the complement, but when did this person come up missing? He asked.

"June of 1937."

"What? I thought you said 1937. We must have a bad connection."

"No, it is 1937, and we don't have much to go on."

"I've heard of a cold case before, but this one's in the freezer," he said with a laugh.

"I know it's a long shot, but I have Dale getting all the Indiana newspaper articles and sheriff's reports together this week. I will email everything as I get it."

"Just out of curiosity, how old would this missing person be?"

"We think about eighty-three or four," she said.

"Oh just a kid. Well that makes things easier. All I have to do is go to every nursing home in Indiana and call out his name. Piece of cake."

"Very funny, but will you do this for me?"

"Of course I will. You helped launch my career when I retired from the FBI. You have always been a friend and I'll stay in touch when I receive the info from you. By the way, have you learned how to plow a field or milk a cow?" he said with a big laugh.

"Harvey, you might be surprised what Anne Barr has learned since moving to Indiana. Talk to you soon."

Just then Rick walked in. "Hi, Honey," and sat in the barber chair. "This is cool," he said as he spun around and around. Did this come with the office, or are you going to start cutting hair on the side? Nice mirror, too. I guess your makeup will never be out of sorts with this thing looking at your every movement."

"I want to show you the estimate Mr. Yoder gave me for the remolding," as she reached inside her purse and handed the small folded paper to Rick.

"This can't be the right price. Rick said He didn't list the materials."

"Oh, but he did. That includes everything, and he and his sons can start on Monday. Can you believe it's only $8310.00 total?"

Rick said, "Call him right now before he changes his mind. Remember we had your bathroom remolded in New York, and it cost us $12,000. These guys are doing the whole house for so much less."

"I will as soon as I bring you up to date. I contacted Harvey in New York, and he'll take on the case. He's never had a missing person going back seventy-three years and thought this will be tough nut to crack. I think he will help because we have a long history of working together," she said.

"Did you contact your intern?" he asked

"I emailed him today to gather all the newspaper and police info he could get his hands on. He's very good at gathering data."

"He's also good at screwing my wife." Rick said sarcastically.

"Rick, that's over!" she said firmly.

"I'll have admit; we've had some great sex this last week and a half. It only took us eight years to discover the intimacy we both knew was there."

"Rick, don't give me grief about sleeping with someone else. You've screwed just about every one of your secretaries and some probably twice. You never even so much as kissed me, let alone touched me in eight years. I didn't think you knew I existed," she said with tears in her eyes.

"Ok. Bury the hatchet," he said as he jumped from the barber chair. He came over and gently put his arms around her and kissed her softly on the lips. "Maybe we can do it in the barber chair."

"I knew there was a reason to keep the chair," she said with a smile.

Tim and Pamela Sue's Farm

"Hurry up, you two," Pamela Sue said at the bottom of the stairs.

"We're coming Mom!" Her kids yelled back.

Tim came down the stairs all dressed up in his black slacks and tan leather sport coat. "Whew, Honey, you look great," Pamela Sue said.

"You're looking pretty hot yourself," Tim said as she twirled around in front to him.

"I bought a new dress and shoes especially for the play tonight. It wasn't too expensive, and I'm glad you like it."

"You are pretty in anything you wear or don't wear, especially your birthday suit," he said with a smile.

Pamela Sue blushed and put her short chubby arms around Tim's waist. "Oh, by the way, a nurse from Shady Grove called the house this afternoon and said Mr. Galey remembered something very important about Albert Harris."

"After the play tonight, Rick and I can stop at the nursing home and see what he wants. Rick is picking up Mom and I think Sissy and Todd will be there. Hurry up kids."

Gas City High School

When Rick, Anne, Eric, and Rick's mother arrived, the school parking lot was almost full. "What time was the play supposed to start?" Anne asked

"Tim told me 7:00 PM, but it's only 6:10 P.M." Rick answered back.

"This is a big deal in Gas City," Mary said, "all the locals come out for plays because we don't have any live theater except for the high school. The kids do a great job. The music director is young and full of energy. Don't worry, Tim and Pamela Sue came early to save us all seats down front."

As the four walked into the school, Rick had no remembrances. This was a new school since he graduated, since Gas City had consolidated with Mill Creek School. To the right of the large trophy case were pictures of former athletes and sport teams.

"Look Dad!" Eric exclaimed, "It's you." Sure enough a six foot black and white photo of Rick holding a baseball like he was getting ready to pitch. Underneath the photo was his high school pitching record and ERA. The plaque read "Most Valuable Player Indiana State High School Baseball Association." There was also a picture of the Gas City State Championship Team and Bob Magic was standing next to his dad. "Wow, Dad! I'm impressed."

Anne looked at the photo and took Rick's hand, and whispered, "I can't believe I've slept with an MVP."

He whispered back, "You even played with his balls," and both laughed quietly.

They found their seats down front where Pamela Sue was jumping up and down waving her arms.

Rick and Anne opened their programs and noticed Rahab had the lead as Marian. Anne turned to Pamela Sue and told her how excited she was for her. They both just giggled.

Tim leaned over and said Mr. Galey wanted to tell them something important about Albert Harris. They both agreed to go to Shady Grove after the play. Rick and Anne knew this was probably going to be a bad rendition of "The Music Man." They had seen it on Broadway twice and one time Dick Van Dyke played the role of Harold Hill. Oh well, they were there to support their niece.

The curtain opened and the scenery wasn't bad. The music was recorded, and the kids sang along to the melodies. Their voices were good, but when Rahab sang "Good Night My Someone," there wasn't a dry eye in the auditorium. Her thick brown hair was curled and she wore a soft yellow dress with cute yellow shoes. She sat looking out an open widow with the moon light streaming onto her face; she looked beautiful. Her voice was sweet and tender and when she finished, applause erupted and everyone jumped to their feet. Rick and Anne looked at each other. They had never seen people just keep clapping during a song in the middle of a play. When the part came for "Seventy Six Trombones" again everyone jumped to their feet and clapped. The kids made cardboard trombones and painted them silver and during the song, seventy-six cardboard trombones were lowered from the ceiling above the audience. What a great touch, Rick thought. There were only fifteen cast members, but boy did they put on a show. When the curtain came down, everyone stood, applauded, and whistled. Rahab came out to take her bow, and a young man ran out and handed her a bouquet of red roses. More flowers were thrown on stage and Anne got a tear in her eye. Of course Pamela Sue was bawling like a baby.

"I got to tell you, Honey, I've never seen such passion put into a play in my entire life," Rick said, "and they're not making a penny for it."

The audience was clearing out slowly and Rahab came out from the back holding her bouquet of red roses. Pamela Sue gave her daughter a big hug as she continued to cry.

"You were awesome!" Eric exclaimed.

"Thanks, but I'm pissed. Rahab said, the guy that played the male lead of Harold Hill is Jimmy Cross. When he gave me a kiss in the last scene, his breath was horrible. He told me he had just finished a plate of fish tacos before the performance. We have another play tomorrow, and if his breath is even half way bad, I told him I'd kick him in the balls."

Anne said with a smile "I wonder if Dick Van Dyke was ever threatened by his leading lady.

Tim said "Rahab you were great, I'm so proud of you and your mother will tell you the same, once she quits crying. Rick let's go to Shady Grove and see Mr. Galey."

Shady Grove Nursing Home

Rick and Tim arrived and walked straight to Mr. Galey's room. He wasn't in the room, but they found an aide at the end of the hall. Tim asked, "Where's Mr. Galey?"

"He passed away about two hours ago," she said.

"What?" Rick said, "He just called late this afternoon and wanted to tell us something. How did he die?"

"He must of had a heart attack or something, because we found him in his bed when we were doing the rounds."

"Had he been sick?" Tim asked.

"No, he came down to the cafeteria this morning for breakfast and never complained of anything."

"Where's his body? Rick asked

"Bill Sales picked him up an hour ago," she said, "and I called his nephew in Iowa. He'll be here sometime tomorrow."

Stunned, Rick and Tim walked to the parking lot. "I can't believe it," Rick said.

"It just doesn't make sense." "Let's try and connect with the nephew while he's in town. Maybe he knows something about Albert."

Alexandria, Virginia; The Next Day

There was a quiet rapping at the large oak door. "Come in, the voice said. Please sit."

The middle aged man sat and faced his mentor.

"I received your encrypted email last night just before I went to bed. I trust things went well in Indiana." the older man said.

"It did. I was only in town for two hours, just enough time to take care of a small problem at a nursing home and catch the end of a high school play."

"What did you see?"

"The Music Man," "and the local kids did a great job. I also scoped out the Barr family and for right now, we're all right. I'm leaving in the morning for New York City to look into a potential problem."

"Good!" the older man exclaimed. He reached into his desk and handed the younger man a playing card. This will help."

ANNE'S GAS CITY OFFICE

The coffee pot finished brewing, and Anne walked into the front room to retrieve a hot cup. She walked to the back office and turned on her computer. Her intern, Dale, sent her over a hundred articles and police reports. She knew she had to read each one and decide where this would lead her. At the end of his email, he wrote that he missed and wanted her. She wrote back a thank you and told him to get a girlfriend.

Each article gave some insight into Albert's family life. He had come from a very wealthy family in Evansville, Indiana, and was an only child. One article told of how he was a gifted pianist at the age of nine. The original reward was $50,000 and in 1937, that was a fortune; now $860,000 was a fortune to most people. She decided to call the trust department to see about the terms of the reward.

"First National Bank of Evansville. May I help you?" The receptionist said.

"I would like to speak to someone in the trust department."

'Please hold"

"Trust Department," an older man said.

"My name is Anne Barr, and I would like some information on a trust you are holding in escrow."

"What would the trust be listed under?"

"The name is Albert Harris."

"Please hold and I'll connect you with our senior trust officer Mr. Gable."

"This is Mr. Gable. How may I assist you?"

"My name is Anne Barr, and I am writing an article for the Boy Scouts of America Journal. I need the particulars on an Albert Harris Trust, dating back to 1937."

"I will be happy to send this to you. Please give me your mailing and email addresses. A copy will be sent right out. Good luck on your article and, if I can be of any further help, please feel free to call on me."

Just then an old farmer walked in. "Are you Mrs. Barr?" he asked

"Yes I am. How can I help you?"

"I need your advice; I'm George Little, and I bought a cow from Fred Jackson. The cow died just after he delivered it, and I want my money back. I know you are a lawyer from New York, so I need for you to tell me how to do this."

"I'm not real sure about Indiana laws but I can look up the statues for you on line. Did you have a contract?" She asked

"Yes, when I handed him a check, and we shook hands, that was our contract?"

"Stop back tomorrow and maybe I will have some information for you"

"Great! See you later, by the way, I was a good friend of you father-in-law, Richard."

She thought, this is all I need, giving out free legal advice to the Gas City locals.

Rick and Anne's Farm

When Anne arrived home, she couldn't believe her eyes. There were bearded men everywhere. Four black buggies and the old station wagon were all lined up in a row in the barn yard. She could hear hammers and saws, pounding, and zipping at a mighty pace. Sitting on the porch was Hazel, her housekeeper from New York. She looked really tired and only had a single suitcase.

"Hi, Mrs. Barr," Hazel said.

"You're a sight for sore eyes," and Anne gave Hazel a warm Indiana hug.

"It's a long trip by bus from New York City, but I made it, and what are all the bearded men doing to your house?" Hazel asked.

"We are completely remolding the old farm house to make it livable. Come on in, and I'll show you your bedroom."

"Wow, Mrs. Barr, I see what you mean. The green shag carpet and plaid chairs and drapes are somewhat out dated."

"Somewhat? This place is directly from the 60's," Anne said with a smile. "I know it's not much to look at now, but give this place two weeks, and it will be a palace."

Hazel's bedroom was large and comfortable. There was a bathroom just next to her room with an old claw foot bathtub. Hazel grew up with one of these and a good soaking was just what she needed. Dick and Jane walked into her bedroom and placed two dead mice at the foot of her bed.

"They like you; you'll fit in here nicely," Anne said with a smile.

Hazel opened her suitcase and took out a photo of her brother and her in Copenhagen. She took the old faded picture of a sunset off her wall and hung the picture of the two, and she couldn't wait to tell the Barr family of her trip to Denmark and seeing her brother after ten long years.

Eric pulled up in the truck, and Billie was so close to him, they appeared to be Siamese twins. The Yoder family never looked up from their jobs and the hammering continued uninterrupted. Hazel walked onto the porch as Eric and Billie came up the stairs holding hands.

"Well, well, Mr. Eric, you're looking good," Hazel said. She gave Eric a big hug and looked over at Billie.

"Hazel, this is Billie."

"I figured as much. You two do make a nice couple."

"We want to hear all about Denmark sometime."

"I can't wait to share my trip with your whole family. I just made some ice tea. Would you kids like some?"

"Sure, I just have to text Tony in New York, and I'll be right in." Eric said.

Anne's Office, Gas City

There were a few things that started to trigger Anne's investigative mind, and she just had to go back to her office. She called Rick and told him to meet her as soon as possible. He told her he was on his way and that he and Tim were to meet Mr. Galey's nephew at 4:00 PM at the funeral home. When he walked in Anne was sitting in her back office with a desk piled high with papers. He sat opposite Anne and took out his tape recorder.

"Seems as though the Albert Harris file has exploded with information," Rick said.

"It sure has, and wait till I read you this fax I just received from the First National Bank of Evansville. The trust for finding Albert was set up in 1937 and will be paid to anyone who finds him alive or that can prove he is dead. Get this: besides the $860,000 in cash there is also a mansion involved and a trust to keep the property up, and it's over $1,000,000. Albert's parents lived in the house and their thought, according to the trust, was if Albert was found alive he would have a house to come back to. I looked online, and the City of Evansville is now using the house for government offices and is paying a lease amount to the trust. This pushes the stakes even higher."

"I can't believe that no one in all these years, hasn't found him dead or alive," Rick said. "Let's take a trip to Evansville tomorrow to see the house and get a copy of Albert's birth certificate. I might even buy you a nice lunch at a real restaurant, and you could shop for some clothes."

"I like that offer; I really do need some new shoes beside the cowboy boots I wear pretty much every day. I sent the Boy Scout hat to the forensic lab in New York, and if there is any DNA of any kind, they can find it. They are the best, and I told them I needed it ASAP, and hopefully I will have an answer in three days." She grabbed Rick's hand, "Let's go home and see what Hazel has cooked for us I'm starving."

Billie Magic's Farm

Billie and Eric were sitting on a bale of hay holding hands and Bob Magic walked passed them into the barn. Just as he was entering he said, "Eric, you take good care of my Billie"

"I will sir, you have nothing to worry about."

"When does your friend Tony get here?" Billie asked.

"In two days and have you asked Dar if she would go out with him?"

"She told me it's a definite yes, and we are doing a double date for the 4H banquet."

"What are we supposed to wear to this?"

"It's dressy, but some just wear nice jeans and a coat. I'm wearing a new blue dress and light blue heels. Don't forget, this is the social event of the year and there will be at least fifteen hundred people."

"You always look great! You know, when we first met and you pulled a knife on me, I looked up your dress as you stood over me, and I'll never forget the pink cotton panties."

"I stood over you for a reason; if you hadn't looked up, I was just going to assume you were gay and that would be the end of that," she said with a laugh. "Besides, most of the time we're together you have the chronic bulge in your pants. I may have to do something about that someday soon."

Rick and Anne's Farm

Eric arrived home, and the buggies and lone rusty station wagon were just pulling out. The men tipped their hats toward Eric, and he couldn't help thinking these men were such gentlemen. In New York, the workers would probably give him the finger. The house smelled wonderful, and Erick knew Hazel was definitely back.

"Come on in and sit. We're just about ready to eat," Hazel said.

Hazel cooked a pot roast in the old yellow stove, and everyone knew she hadn't lost her touch since her trip to Denmark. Anne felt so good to have a nice meal in her new home. The Amish workers were like ants; they had already torn the back porch off and started putting up the solarium. Hazel was also glad to be back with her adopted family. She had a purpose, and now in Indiana, the Barr Family really seemed to love and complement each other. What a transition! She thought.

After dinner Rick and Eric walked outside to look at the construction. Not knowing anything about building, it looked great to them. They walked into the barn, and it was filled with junk. Rick told his son he would get a large dumpster, and start pitching. Eric noticed a pile of loose hay in the corner, but below the stack he saw a tire.

"Dad, what's that?"

"I don't know. Probably and old rusted out planter or tractor."

They both started clearing off the pile and saw it was a car with cover over it. They removed everything off the cover and pealed back the tarp.

"Oh, my gosh!" Eric shouted. They both stood looking at a 1969 Camaro Z28 convertible. It was black with a dark green interior. Except for the rotted tires, it appeared perfect. Rick slowly opened the driver's door and looked inside. The mice had eaten some small parts of the seats, but that was it.

"Check this out," Rick said. "The odometer only shows 1683 miles; this is like brand new. We've found a real treasure; this baby is worth a small fortune."

Eric sat in the driver's seat and wondered what kind of story this car could tell. Around the rear view mirror was hanging a bottle opener, and below that an old faded picture of a young girl.

"I'll bet it was the young Ault boy's car," Rick said. "He died 1969 in Vietnam, and the locals said the parents never got over their loss. The kid was probably the last to drive it, and I want you to be the next Eric. Take real good care of this baby and it's yours."

Eric threw his arms around his dad, "Thanks, Dad."

Rick tried to remember the last time his son had hugged him. His mind couldn't remember back that far, but he would never forget this one. "I'll call a garage tomorrow and have it towed into Evansville. Let's see how much it will cost to bring it back to original"

"Dad, you're awesome!"

SISSY'S BEAUTY SHOP

Todd came running up the basement stairs wearing a black cape and his Lone Ranger mask as Mrs. Herald was leaving the shop. "Mom, I have something important to tell you."

"All right Honey, but why don't you watch a cowboy movie until Mrs. Cannon comes out of the hair dryer. I'll come down stairs as soon as I finish her up," Sissy said.

"Ok, Mom," and down the basement he flew.

"I heard your sister-in-law is opening up a law office across from Jim's Shoe Repair Shop," Carol Cannon said.

"No, she's just renting an office to catch up on all the things she had doing when leaving New York."

"Well, George Little told everyone at the diner she got all his money back from the dead cow he bought from Fred Jackson, thanks to Anne. I think I'll stop and see her about my ex-husband, Harold. He's behind on my house payment, and he keeps calling me for sex," Carol said with a frown.

"Do you give him sex?"

"Yeah, but not all the time. He usually calls at night, but the positive side is, his love making only lasts about three minutes," she said with a laugh.

"Maybe you should charge him for the visits, and this way make the payments."

"You know, I think you're right," as Carol walked out the door with a big smile on her face.

Sissy walked down the basement and Todd was watching a western. "Now, what's so important?"

"I heard Uncle Tim and you talking about finding Albert Harris. NeeNee can help you find him because he knew Albert a long time ago."

"Thank you, Todd; if we need NeeNee's help I'll let you know."

"Ok, Mom," turning his head toward the television.

Sissy walked up the stairs, and Libby Shepard was standing there in flaming red hair for her Tuesday appointment.

Rick and Anne's Farm

It was noon, and the Yoder Family was sitting eating lunch around a long table they had brought. The Amish wives always came about his time with a meal for their husbands and sons. Today was fried chicken, baked potatoes, green beans, and some kind of vanilla pudding. The men all talked very quietly in almost hushed voices. Eric was sitting on the front porch, and a black limousine pulled into the barn yard.

His friend Tony jumped out. "Hey Eric."

"Don't you think your entrance is a little dramatic?"

"I flew into Indianapolis and my dad arranged for a car to bring me here. This wasn't my choice." It did look strange, a limousine, a rusted out station wagon, and four black buggies.

Tony grabbed his suitcase and walked into the house. "Hi, Tony," Hazel said.

"How long have you been here?" Tony asked.

"Just a few days, but I really like it. The pace is so laid back compared to New York; you'll see for yourself."

Eric and Tony went up to Eric's room, and Tony fell onto his bed. "I like the pink ponies on your dresser," Tony said laughing.

"We are slowly fixing the house up, and all those Amish guys down there are completely remolding everything."

"I thought maybe you just placed them there for my arrival, to make me feel like this is real country living. Do you think I can have my picture taken with them?" Tony asked.

"I don't know if Amish are OK with that, but let's ask."

"I want to send a photo from my phone to my mom and Louisa, because they won't believe me if I don't."

The men were just finishing up their lunch, and Eric asked them about a picture. They didn't care; they even put a straw hat on Tony for the picture.

Eric took Tony on a mini tour of the farm and told Tony about finding the old car in the barn. He also told Tony about fixing him up with Dar and going to the 4H Banquet. Tony just rolled his eyes and thought his best friend had lost it.

Anne's Office Gas City

Anne was just getting ready to leave the office, and her cell phone rang; she recognized the number from her office in New York.

"Anne, this is Robert. Can you talk?

"Sure what's up?

"I have some very bad news for you: Dale, your intern, was found dead this morning in his apartment. It appears to be a drug overdose and he must have died last night."

"That can't be!" she said in utter amazement, "he doesn't do drugs. He's totally into fitness."

"The medical examiner told me there were drugs and paraphernalia everywhere in his apartment. They are doing an autopsy in the morning, and this should reveal the cause of death. I'm really sorry to tell you this; I know you two were close."

"I just can't comprehend his death. I've known him for almost two years and had been to his apartment numerous times and never once did I see anything that revealed grass or drugs of any nature," Anne said. Please keep me informed Robert."

"I will, and when the funeral arrangements are made, I'll email you the times. Again, sorry."

She hung up the phone in total disbelief. She quickly realized that Mr. Galey died unexpectedly three days ago and now Dale. She felt it probably wasn't related, but she had to call Harvey Adams. She told Harvey about the two deaths and her concern for his safety. He just laughed and told her that nobody would hurt an old investigator over a missing person going back seventy-three years. The lab report was to be finished tomorrow, and he would send her the report on any DNA or blood, if there was any to be found on the old Boy Scout cap.

Rick and Anne's Farm

"Wow!" Tony exclaimed, "That was a great dinner."

"So, Tony, what do you think of Indiana?" Rick asked.

"Well, when I arrived there were six bearded men dressed in black and two teenage boys wearing AC/DC tee shirts sitting around a long table by the barn eating friend chicken and two women dressed in black waiting on them. There were four black buggies and black horses tied next to the barn. If that wasn't enough, I walked up to Eric's bedroom, and a large yellow cat dropped a dead mouse at my feet. All in all I guess it's been pretty good, and the only horse I've ever seen was in Central Park with a cop riding him. I can't wait until tomorrow."

Everyone laughed out loud, and Eric motioned Tony to come outside. "We're going to Billie's farm tonight, and I will introduce you to Dar, but maybe you should change your clothes. Slacks, sport coat, and a white shirt just may not fit in." Eric said with a grin.

The boys got into Eric's grandfather's old truck and headed toward Billie's. "Man, Eric, you sure are hooked on Billie Magic. I've never heard you talk about anyone like this before. By the way, your old girlfriend, Kandy, got busted again and will probably do time." Tony looked over his shoulder, "I can't believe you have a shotgun hanging in the back window. This would come in real handy in New York."

They pulled up the lane toward the barn; Billie and Dar were both riding around the corral.

"Which one is mine?" Tony asked

"The brunette is Dar."

"Holy shit, she's beautiful!" Tony exclaimed.

"Told ya."

The girls rode up to the fence as the boys got out of the truck.

"Hey, New Yorkers!" Billie yelled

Tony couldn't quit staring at Dar. In his mind he was prepared to go out with a toothless, two hundred and fifty pound sloppy farm girl. She was just the opposite; cute, tiny, muscular and with large breasts. She was wearing tight shorts and a yellow tee shirt with an image of Marilyn Monroe stenciled down the front. She threw her black cowboy hat over the fence and Tony noticed her short brown hair blowing softly in the breeze, like a pixie.

The girls tied up the horses and jumped over the fence. Billie immediately threw her arms around Eric's neck and kissed him on the lips. The four walked over to the bales of hay stacked next to the barn and sat.

"This is my best friend, Darlene, but you can call her Dar." Billie said.

"This is my best friend Anthony, but you can call him Tony" Eric said.

"This is my best friend Beverly, but you can call her Billie." Dar said.

"This is my best friend Eric and I guess you can just call him Eric." Tony said with a laugh.

Billie reached behind a bale of hay and produced a jug of water, or so Tony thought. "Would anyone like some Gas City Soda Pop?" Billie asked

"I know Tony would," Eric said with a smile.

They handed the bottle to Tony, "Better go easy on this stuff." Dar said.

"Wow! What was that?" Tony exclaimed.

"Like I said, Tony, a little goes a long way." Dar said with a grin.

Rick and Anne's Farm

Rick and Anne sat on their front porch and watched as the sun set behind the apple orchard. The evening was beautiful and Dick and Jane lay next to them taking a little nap.

"Rick, I received disturbing news today. My intern, Dale, was found dead this morning in his apartment from an apparent drug overdose."

"What? Didn't you just talk to him three days ago? Rick asked.

"Yes, and I never knew him to take any type of drugs. This whole thing doesn't make sense, and also Mr. Galey's dying so suddenly in the nursing home. Do you think any of this can be related?"

"I doubt there is any correlation between the two. Why would anyone want to harm these people on a case that goes back over seventy years? Tim and I talked to Mr. Galey's nephew today but he couldn't shed any light on Albert Harris. He told us his uncle would talk about the disappearance over and over again, but never had any clues on how or why it happened."

"I called Harvey in New York today and told him what happened and that I was concerned for his safety," Anne said. "He just laughed and told me not to worry about him and that the lab report on the hat would be done probably tomorrow. I have a bad feeling about this, but I don't know why."

"We haven't told anyone what we are doing; how can anything be traced to us? Let's go to Evansville tomorrow and look at the mansion and see what we're dealing with. I want a copy of his birth certificate and a look into his parent's past a little," Rick said with a frown.

"We're supposed to meet at Sissy's day after tomorrow and maybe we all can add something to this mystery. I've put every newspaper article in order and we should take this step by step to keep the hows and whens in some kind of timeline. I hope the DNA results will give us something to sink our teeth into."

"Don't forget, Saturday is the 4H banquet, and every generation will be there. My whole youth was spent thinking about the banquet and who I could make out with in the cloak room. Some years were way better than others, but this year I want to take you behind the coats and folding chairs to my secret hideout. Just maybe I'll get lucky again this year." Rick said with a big smile.

"Buster, I can almost guarantee you'll score this year, and I'll help you forget about all the others."

Billie's Farm

The kids were now laughing at just about everything because the soda pop had a nice warming effect on the group. Billie sat very close to Eric and Dar sat across from Tony. Dar patted the bale of hay with her hand and told Tony the hay was getting cold. He quickly moved next to her. His head was spinning not only from the alcohol but from Dar's beautiful skin and smell. He knew she wasn't wearing a bra and her short shorts revealed her tan muscular legs encased in pink cowboy boots.

"Will you be my date for the banquet?" Dar, asked Tony.

"I would love to go with you, but what should I wear and expect at this banquet?"

"Wear anything you like. There will be a band and dancing along with the 4H awards and scholarships. I think you'll especially like the hog wrestling," Dar said with a smile.

"Dar!" Billie yelled.

"Just kidding about the hog; I wanted to see your reaction, and my statement didn't seem to faze you."

"Growing up in New York City, I've seen and experienced a lot, but hog wrestling would be a new chapter for my diary," Tony said with a laugh.

"Let's go," Eric said, "We have a bunch of stuff to do tomorrow, and the first thing is to get you some new clothes for the farm and banquet."

Billie pressed her whole body against Eric, and gave him a long wet kiss. Tony just stood there feeling very awkward, but Dar came over and put the same movement on Tony. His legs went limp and he wasn't sure if he was still standing when the kiss ended.

"See you guys tomorrow." Eric said as the boys headed toward the truck.

"Holy shit Eric! What in the hell just happened?"

"You've just had your first encounter with an Indiana girl, and apparently it went well."

"Those two girls are hottest things on the planet. Why didn't you invite me earlier?"

"What about Louisa back in New York?"

"I've kissed Louisa more than a thousand times, but the one tonight made my legs go numb. I'm not kidding Eric; I thought I was going to faint. Her boobs pressed against me and that smell of lilac she was wearing put me in a trance. I'm going to ask her to marry me," Tony said with a laugh.

"Don't you think just maybe you're jumping ahead a little too quickly?"

"I don't know Eric, but I do want you to help me pick out some clothes that will make her fall all over me."

"Fair enough. I've just the outfit for you and I'll help turn you into a lady killer."

"I only want to attract one lady now, and her name is Darlene."

Tim and Pamela Sue's Farm

Tim and Moses came in the back door, and this time Moses had a bloody nose. "Ok, you two, what happened?" Pamela Sue asked.

"Dad elbowed me when we were playing badminton. I was standing at the net waiting for my shot, and he punched me through the net."

"I did not punch you; my arm was just getting ready to hit it back," Tim said with a smile.

"I swear you two! Is there any sport you guys attempt that isn't a contact sport?" she said with disgust. Now go get out of those dirty clothes, and I'll get some ice for the nose."

Rahab came into the laundry room as Pamela Sue was loading the washer. "Mom, why do you put up with all their child's play?"

"I told you, Honey. It's their way of showing love, and besides Moses will be gone next year and your father will be alone. He also loves you very much; he just shows it in a different way. Remember Saturday after your play, your dad came up to you and put his arm around you and said how proud he was of you? And then the young stage hand presented you with two dozen red roses. Your father bought the flowers and had the young man give them to you on stage. It was all his idea, and I promised him I wouldn't say anything to you."

"Really?" Rahab said in amazement. "I thought dad was only into Moses, and my life came a distant second."

"Well, since we're on the subject, remember last year when you received the scholarship for the acting and voice lessons in Evansville? You didn't get the scholarship; your father paid for all of it because he knew it meant so much to you. Honey, don't ever think you're a distant second; he absolutely adores you."

Rahab was now tearing up. "I never knew."

"I don't think you'll ever get a bloody nose from your father, but he carries you around in that big bleeding heart of his." Pamela Sue said with a smile.

"Mom, can we have some ice cream and sit on the porch? I just want to celebrate with you." as she put her arms around her mother.

"Strawberry, chocolate, or butter pecan?" her mother asked

"I'm thinking this has to be a chocolate night," Rahab said with grin.

MOM'S DINER

It was 5:30 A.M., and there were only two days until the 4H Banquet. All the farmers were talking about the event and each wouldn't miss it unless the Apocalypse just happened to fall on Saturday. The guys were taking bets on which 4Her would receive the all-round best

4H youngster of the year. Both Johnson boys and Moses Barr were mentioned, but Hank Hoover seemed to be their first choice.

"What time you are guys going to be there?" Tidy Tucker asked. "And will somebody save me a seat at a table up front?"

"Cheryl and I are on the activities committee, so we'll get there early and save you a seat. By the way Tidy, are you bringing a date this year, so should I save two seats for you?" Marvin asked.

"I don't think I'll have a date this year, so one seat is enough," Tidy said blushing.

Everyone knew Tidy had never brought a date in the fifty-three years the banquet had been in existence.

Larry said, "My sister is in town, and I can fix you up with her."

"No, I think I'll go as a long wolf this year." At that every guy, including Mom started to laugh uncontrollably. Now Tidy really blushed after he realized at what he just said.

"You guys better get dressed up for this, and don't forget to buy flowers for your wives. This is a big deal to them, and most of the time you tightwads won't open up the wallets unless it's for seed or a tractor," Mom said.

All the guys looked down at their coffee cups and said, "Yes, Mom."

Rick and Anne's Farm

It was nearly 6:00 A.M., and Tony sat straight up in his little inflatable bed. He looked over, Dick and Jane were sound asleep on his pillow; he threw back the sheets to see if they deposited a dead mouse or chipmunk by his feet. He felt so much better not finding any such prize in his bed.

"Did you sleep all right?" Eric asked.

"I must have; I didn't notice the two cats until about ten minutes ago."

"We're going over to my grandmother's house when we get up for a great country breakfast. You won't believe the pancakes and bacon. Her food is legendary, and the record for most pancakes is thirty-eight."

The boys came out the back door of the old farm house, and all the Amish men were busy hammering and sawing. Even though it was only 6:30 AM, Tony felt invigorated. The men stopped for a minute and waved at Eric and Tony. The boys jumped into the old truck and headed to the Mary Barr Farm. Tony asked Eric to drive by Dar's farm just to see where she lived. After the detour they pulled into Mary's barn yard. Eric noticed Moses's truck by the house as they walked into the kitchen. Moses was eating a big pile of French toast and looked up at his cousin.

"This is my best friend, Tony, from New York, and this is my grandmother, Dommy, and my cousin Moses," Eric said.

"It's nice to have you here in Indiana," Dommy said.

Moses stood and put out his hand, "Glad you're here."

Tony noticed that Moses was tall and very strong as he pulled up a chair to the kitchen table, and he loved the smells and the warmth of the small kitchen.

"What will it be boys?" Dommy asked.

"I've been bragging up your pancakes forever, so bring them on."

She started Eric and Tony with a stack of six. They devoured them in a heartbeat. She just kept serving, and they kept eating.

"Man, Dommy, these are incredible, and the bacon is unbelievable!" Tony exclaimed.

Eric finished with twenty-six, and Tony ate twenty-three.

"I don't think I can move." Tony said.

"I got to admit, for a city boy you really packed them away," Moses said.

"Tony is going to the banquet with Dar Moore," Eric said.

"Nice choice; I can already tell you're moving up in the world" Moses said with a grin. "I have to set up tables for the banquet, and if you want I'll save us all seats near the front."

"Sounds great. We'll see you Saturday, cousin."

"Can I get you boys anything else? I still have some batter left."

They both just groaned. "Those were the best pancakes I've ever had," Tony said.

"Glad you both liked them, and I will see you two at the banquet; also Darlene doesn't like roses. I hope that little bit of information might help you."

"Thanks, Dommy, it will."

Evansville, Indiana

Rick and Anne pulled up to 1010 Indiana Avenue, and their jaws dropped. "This is Albert's old house?" Anne asked.

"I guess so. There has to be at least eight bedrooms," Rick said. "Let's go in a check it out; it is a public building you know."

They walked through the large oak doors into the marble entrance way. A huge crystal chandelier hung above their heads, marble and oak everywhere. There was a directory just in front of the long winding staircase, and it appeared there were three city offices in the house. They turned left to the city clerk's office to get a birth certificate for Albert. In back of the small desk where the young clerk sat, was a ten foot marble fireplace.

"May I help you?" said the perky clerk.

"Yes we need to pick up a birth certificate from 1928," Rick said.

"Do you know what month?"

"I think June 10th was his birth."

"What is the name?"

"His name is Albert Harris."

She gave him a funny look. "Did you know this is his original home?"

"No, we didn't." Anne said trying not to let the cat out of the bag.

"Well, his bedroom is at the top of the stairs but has been locked for over seventy years. Everyone that works here is dying to see the inside. The trust officer at First National has the only key, and supposedly he has never been in there either. Kind of a cool mystery, isn't it?"

"It sounds fascinating," Rick said.

"Here you go. That will be $12.00."

"Thanks for your help."

"Before you two go, check out the gardens in the back. The locals use it as kind of a small park."

They walked to the back of the house, and the ponds and flowers were breathtaking. There was a plaque next to the coy pond that read "Albert, we miss you. Come home, son, we'll be waiting."

As Rick and Anne got into the car, Anne said, "This place is unbelievable, and just think the family set aside a fortune to take care of it until Albert comes home."

"Or we can prove he's dead," Rick said. "Let's get lunch, and look the certificate over."

They went to a nice bistro two blocks from the Harris Mansion, and Rick opened the birth certificate and nothing seemed amiss. His father was Arthur F. Harris, and his mother Wava Otis Harris. From the newspaper notices that Dale had sent from New York, it stated Arthur was a railroad builder throughout the Midwest. He sold his company to Union Pacific for $12,000,000 in 1929, the beginning of the stock market crash. They were very wealthy, and his mother was related to the Otis Elevator Company. There were no other children, and Arthur had only one brother. The parents didn't care about the expense of finding their son; they just wanted him back at any cost. One old article mentioned four private detectives working on the case around the clock, but none seemed to find many clues.

"Do you want something nice for the dance tomorrow?" Rick asked

"I would like that, but what does one wear in the cloak room for a make out session?"

"I'm thinking about something denim and very short."

"Should I go commando?"

"I didn't think underwear was even an option," Rick said with a laugh. "Let's go shopping."

Rick and Anne's Farm

Eric and Tony were sitting on the front porch tired from a half day of shopping. "Do you think Dar will really like my new outfit?" Tony asked.

"She'll love it. Just be careful you don't come on too strong; don't forget these girls all carry big knives."

Just then Billie and Dar pulled into the barnyard. "You boys new in town?" Dar asked. "Oh, that's right. You really are new in town," and the two girls started to laugh.

"We're going to the ice-cream shop and wanted to know if you would like to join us? We heard they just added a new flavor, so that brings it up to five." Billie said with a smile.

"Let's go, but who's driving?"

"Dar is; she's the designated driver tonight just in case we over dose on vanilla," Billie said with a laugh.

All four piled into the pickup truck with Billie sitting on Eric's lap and Tony pressed tightly to Dar. They arrived at the gas station, and sure enough there was a new flavor. The five were Calvert, Wolf, vanilla, butter pecan and strawberry. Tony just looked in amazement at the Calvert and Wolf flavors.

"Don't ask, just try the Calvert. It tastes like coffee with a hint of chocolate. We'll explain the flavors to you on the way to the park," Eric said.

The four arrived at the park and sat in the swings. "The two flavors were named after a famous artist that lived here. His home is about four blocks from here, and maybe Eric will take you; it's full of naked women." Dar said.

"That's my kind of art. By the way are your parents going to the banquet? I'd like to meet them." Tony said.

"My parents and especially my dad are really down right now," Dar said. "I know they haven't considered the banquet."

"What's the matter?" Tony asked.

"About four months ago my parents were involved in an auto accident in Indianapolis. They backed into a car and the man claims he was injured. It was only a fender bender. The couple got a hot shot attorney from Cincinnati, and now claim he is losing his sight. He is unable to work or sleep, or so he says. My dad's attorney found out this isn't his first time at suing, but has done this act many times, over the last ten years, and believe it not, the attorney is his brother-in-law." Dar started to cry. "We may lose our farm."

Tony put his arm around Dar "My dad has cousins living in Cincinnati and maybe he can help; what are your parent's names?"

"Their names are Bill and Barb Moore, but it's too late for that now; they are going to court in one week, but thanks for the gesture."

"I hate to change the subject, but Eric and I bought new outfits today, and I have a feeling you two won't be able to keep your hands off us at the banquet." Tony said with a smile.

"Well, Dar and I also have new clothes, and we're thinking all the guys will be hitting on us, so you two better stay real close if you know what's good for you." Billie said with a laugh.

Billie and Dar each gave the two boys a soft gentle kiss and headed for the truck.

"I do like the Calvert ice cream, Tony said, "and I want to see this famous artist before I go."

The girls drove back to Eric's house and had a nice passionate goodbye for each.

Tony said as the boys found the stuffed chairs on the porch, "Is Billie really good in the sack?"

"I wouldn't know; I've only kissed her and, that's it."

"Yeah right!"

"I'm completely serious; I haven't even touched her. I totally respect her boundaries and morals, but it hasn't been easy. I want her in the worst way; there are some nights I think I'm going to just die."

"What are my chances with, Dar? Do you think she'll put out for me?"

"I can't help you there, but I do know she likes you a lot. Billie told me tonight that she had never met anybody like you. Dar truly has the hots for you, but go slow. These Indiana girls have a different set of standards."

"What does that mean?

"Here again, I'm not real sure, but these girls are definitely worth waiting for. You know, Tony, they are the brass ring on the Merry Go Round, and I hope we don't miss our chance to grab it."

"Well, truthfully, I have never met anyone that has come close to Darlene Moore. The trouble is, I want more; get it more?" Tony said with a smile.

"Come on; let's go to bed before you come up with something as dumb as your last statement."

"I'll be up in a minute. I told my dad I would call him and let him know his little boy is safe and sound in the corn fields of Indiana."

Mom's Diner 5:30 AM

"Well, you guys, tonight's the night," Bill Sales said as he sipped his coffee.

"I wonder how many reservations there are?" Marvin asked.

"Last year there were fourteen hundred and eleven, and I think just maybe we'll surpass that." Bud said. "It seems like many more people have called."

"I hope they didn't ask Wonder Boys Band again this year. What a terrible embarrassment that turned out to be. They were pretty good until about 10:30 P.M., and the booze caught up with the Wonders. Remember when Doug Wonder fell off the stage, and they took him to the hospital?" Bill said.

"That was almost as bad as Dick Wonder pulling his pecker out when they sang YMCA." Marvin said with a laugh.

Now the whole table was laughing, and Bill remarked, "And he had nothing too important to show either."

"I'm darn sure the Wonder Boys won't be asked to ever do anything musically again," Mom said as she filled the coffee cups.

"I do know the Raging Rounder's square dance group will be back again this year. They were very popular with the older set and you won't see a single pecker among that group." Marvin said.

"This year there will be valet parking as you arrive. The Watson brothers volunteered and for only fifty cents, they'll park your car and retrieve it when the party's over," Bill said.

"I think Gas City has now officially jumped into the 21st Century." Tidy said. "Just think, valet parking."

RICK AND ANNE'S FARM

The whole family was up, and Hazel had just put breakfast on the table. She fixed a large platter of scramble eggs, biscuits and gravy, and fresh watermelon from the garden. She was really getting into this farm menu. In New York she only fixed whole grain, no salt, sugar, carbs, or flavor for the Barr Family. Now she had free rein to fix whatever she chose.

"Hazel, are you going to the banquet tonight?" Anne asked.

"No, it doesn't even sound fun."

"This will be our first banquet, and we want you to go with us. Apparently this is the biggest thing that ever happens in Gas City, and you can get to know some town's people. Oh, I forgot, there is one at this table that has experienced the banquet and he's sitting right there." Anne said as she looked at Rick.

"Dad, what was it like when you went?"

Anne quickly interrupted, "He won't know; your father spent most of the evening in the cloak room," as she started to laugh.

"Your mother has a warped sense of humor."

"Hazel, I have a nice red summer dress you can wear, and I'll call Sissy and see if she can get you in to do your hair. It's settled." Anne said.

"I heard you boys have dates tonight." Rick said.

"I'm taking Billie, and Tony is going with Dar Moore. We bought Tony some great clothes for the banquet; I think he'll make a big splash."

"I still can't get over you two falling for Indiana 4-H girls." Rick said as he shook his head. "They are cute girls, but don't forget, they carry knives."

SISSY'S BEAUTY SHOP

There were cars everywhere as Hazel pulled up to the little shop housed in a small yellow home. Hazel stepped into the door and there were conversations flying in every part of the shop.

"Just grab a chair; I'll be with you in a minute."

Most of the conversations were about the outfits, makeup, jewelry and shoes to be worn at the 4-H banquet. Hazel also heard about a husband who just got caught cheating and two more that might be next on the list. In the thirty minutes she sat there, she had the scoop on just about every marriage, affair, and face lift that happened in Gas City. Hazel liked this place and some of the ladies even asked her opinion on what shoes would work, or would she keep a husband that slept with the cook at the truck stop?

"Come on over, Hazel, Sissy said. "Sorry about the wait but today is crazy. What are you thinking about your hair?"

"You know, I've had the same dirty blonde hair my whole life. If you have time, give me some suggestions."

"Want people to sit up and take notice?"

"Sure why not."

"I'm thinking platinum blonde," Sissy said.

"Let's do it! It worked for Marilyn Monroe, why not Hazel Henry?"

"I like the way you think. The Gas City 4-H Banquet will never be the same when Hazel Henry walks in." "You have my guarantee on that."

Hazel was now so excited about a total transformation; she thought she might pee her pants.

42nd Street, New York City

Harvey was sitting watching the Mets when there was a knock at his apartment door. He looked through the peep hole and saw a Catholic priest standing there. He opened the door and a middle aged priest stood there with a small leather bound note pad.

"Can I help you?" Harvey asked.

"I'm very sorry to bother you, but Anne Barr thought you might want this information I have on Albert Harris. If this isn't a good time, I can come back."

"No, come on in I'm just watching the Mets get clobbered by the Yankees."

"Please sit. Anne never told me you were coming or that there were new clues."

"The information I have might prove to be very helpful for you."

He opened his note pad and slowly turned it toward Harvey. Harvey had to squint, as the writing was very small.

"I have a magnifying glass that might help," the priest said.

He reached into his robe and handed the glass to Harvey as he stepped behind him. Harvey never saw the small metal club hit him in the back of his head. He instantly fell forward on the coffee table. He never moved a muscle.

The priest pulled out his cell phone. "You can come up now," he said in a soft voice.

Gas City Conservation Club

It was 6:00 P.M., and every seat was taken. The old club resembled Mari Gras on steroids. Streamers, balloons, flashing lights, and a twenty-five foot bar; Billie and Dar were sitting looking for their dates.

Hazel was sitting with Anne, Rick, Pamela Sue, and Tim. The four of them couldn't quit staring at Hazel. Her hair was platinum;

she wore a bright red dress, red high heels, and the brightest red lipstick that Avon sells. Marilyn Monroe would be jealous.

"I can't get over the change." Anne said in disbelief. "You look fabulous!"

"I thought; what the hell! I'm forty-eight, single, with no man on the horizon, living in Gas City, Indiana, and had always admired Marilyn Monroe. What do you guys think of that?"

"We're happy for you, and if you slowly turn around there are about eight guys checking you out," Rick said.

Winking, Anne immediately said, "This could be a good night, but don't forget to be home by midnight."

The 50/50 raffle started, and people were lining up at the buffet table like this was their last meal. Mel Roberts was playing his accordion doing his interpretation on some 80's tunes. Just then someone put a dollar in his glass of beer thinking it was a tip jar. He wasn't happy.

"Where are those guys?" Dar asked.

"Oh, probably waiting for a grand entrance," Billie sighed.

Just then the boys walked in.

"Get a load of those guys," Moses said as the girls turned.

Eric was dressed like Johnny Cash, completely in black with a guitar hung over his shoulder, and Tony was a mirror image of Elvis. He too had a guitar hung over his white jump suit.

"Oh my gosh!" the girls said in unison. "We didn't realize we're dining with stars tonight," as the boys made their way toward the table.

"Well, you two are right; you both made quite a splash with this crowd," Dar said with a big smile.

"Thank you, thank you very much," Tony said in his Elvis voice as he took off a blue scarf and tied it around Dar's neck.

"Johnny and Elvis have been resurrected again. Halleluiah! Praise God!" Billie said.

Just then twelve year old Amber Collins ran up to the table and wanted a picture taken with the guys. She thanked them and kissed both on their cheeks.

"See, there are people here that appreciate real talent," Eric said. "You girls better keep an eye on us; Tony and I might be in real demand tonight."

"Let's go get in line for food. Hanging around superstars makes one mighty hungry," as Dar grabbed Tony's hand.

"You boys look great! Dar and I were just having some fun." as Billie kissed Johnny Cash on the lips.

As Eric and Billie were walking back to their table, he noticed his parents, Tim, Pamela Sue, his grandmother, and some stranger eating their dinner.

"Hi, folks."

"Well, well, Johnny Cash; we hope Elvis and you will grace us with a tune later on," Rick said.

"Not sure dad. We are already in demand; I'll have to confer with the King."

The blonde at the table turned to face Eric. She looked so familiar but Eric couldn't quite place her.

"You got to be kidding!" Eric exclaimed. "Hazel, you're hot!"

"You know Eric, I feel hot tonight, and that was a nice compliment coming from Johnny Cash."

The Raging Rounder's Square Dance club put on quite a demonstration. When they concluded, they asked for volunteers to come up and learn some steps. Immediately Billie and Dar grabbed the boys and pulled them up front. The music started, Elvis and Johnny were completely lost. Swing your partner, Dos Sa Do, Allemande left, and Promenade were words that the boys had never heard. The two couples were laughing so hard, they had to sit down.

"That went well," Eric said still laughing.

The dancers found their seats and the master of ceremonies, Marvin Gorman pulled a chair to the center of the room and cleared his throat. "We certainly all know what is next."

The crowd yelled in unison, "Sailor Skafish"

A middle aged man, wearing a sailor's cap, walked to the middle of the room carrying a small trunk. He sat down, smiled, and then opened the trunk.

The crowd yelled, "Peter and Patsy!", and at that he put two ventriloquist dummies on his lap. The dummies were dressed like farm kids with matching cowboy outfits and boots. Peter and Patsy talked to each other and told jokes from the sixties and seventies. Eric and Tony were laughing so hard their sides hurt, and tears were running down Tony's face as the girls just looked at them. The show lasted twenty minutes and was the funniest experience of Eric and Tony's lives.

Eric finally composed himself and asked why they called him Sailor.

Dar said in a disgusted voice, "Because he always wears a sailor's cap, but his real name is Leonard."

"Doesn't anyone here see his lips are moving? I mean really moving; like he's talking? He isn't a ventriloquist," Eric said whipping his eyes.

"Why don't you boys make yourselves useful? Go get us something to drink?" Billie said with a sigh.

Tony came back from the bar with four Cokes, and Eric put some Gas City Soda Pop in each. Eric had cut out a small hole in his guitar and slid a flask of the good stuff inside. Billie and Dar just shook their heads. As the band was setting up, Marvin told the crowd to hush for a minute. He stepped out onto the dance floor with a microphone in his left hand and a beer in the right. He thanked all the volunteers and the Cater Aid catering service for a fine meal and Sailor for again a great show and tradition for the banquet. Someone from the back of the room thanked him for not having the Wonder Boys Band this year; the crowd erupted in shouts and whistles. Marvin gave a short history of Gas City 4-H and listed all the past presidents. Marvin's wife slowly came out of the crowd with an envelope in her hand.

"We all know what this is," Marvin said as Cheryl handed him the sealed letter. I have in my hand a $10,000 scholarship for the 4-H Member of the Year. Every 4-H member had a vote along with the board of directors, and this represents the highest honor any 4-H member can receive." Now the crowd was hushed as Marvin tried to open the envelope without having to put down his beer. Every eye was trained on Marvin as he kept fiddling.

"The winner is Beverly Magic."

Billie was stunned along with half the crowd as Eric turned and gave her a kiss on the cheek.

"Well, come on up and get the check." Marvin said spilling some beer on his shoes.

As in a trance she slowly walked onto the dance floor as the crowd rose to their feet among the yells and whistles. Marvin handed her the mike. She looked over at her dad and smiled as Bob Magic ran to his daughter's side and completely engulfed her in his large arms.

"Way to go baby."

"I don't where to start. I love 4-H, and it has given me a purpose and a safe home. I know my mother is looking down right now with a great big smile. I love you mom, and I will do my best to represent the State of Indiana in the National Barrel Riding Championships in Tulsa. I'll try and bring the trophy to Gas City," as she started to cry.

Now the crowd started to chant, "Billie, Billie."

Billie sat in complete amazement as people came up to the table, hugged her, and patted her on the back. A tall skinny guy with a crew cut came over and tried to kiss her on the lips, but she just turned her head. Eric didn't like that, but Moses told him the guy was Billie's old boyfriend, and that relationship was over.

ALEXANDRIA, VIRGINIA

The two men sat across the large desk from each other.

"How were things in New York?" the older gentleman asked.

"It went very well. I think all the holes have now been plugged, and I can't see the investigation going much further. The Boy Scout hat is still a small issue, but I have someone on the inside, and that should be resolved in the next couple of days."

"Are you going back to Gas City or Evansville in the near future?"

"There shouldn't be any reason for me to go, but if my sources call me, I can be there in a matter of a few hours. Anne Barr has an inquisitive mind, and if I need to take someone out, it will probably be her. Eric Barr's friend from New York is visiting Gas City, and his friend's father is Anthony Becko, but the two boys are just pals, and Tony will be going home in a few days."

"Who's Anthony Becko?

"You know, he's the crime lord they call Bentley. He's connected to Washington and the federal justice system, but again, this is small potatoes so there won't any involvement from him."

'I'm leaving for Rome in the morning, but keep me informed on any new developments," the older man said as he stood to leave.

"Have a safe trip, Father."

GAS CITY CONSERVATION CLUB

The band started to play, and two men rushed over to Hazel to ask for her hand. She looked at both and picked the taller, dark-haired gentleman. She danced three dances, and sat down with Rick and Anne, but that only lasted for a minute until another guy came over to dance. She slow danced with him, but one man never took his eyes off of Hazel every time she stepped onto the dance floor. Hazel loved this attention; plus she couldn't remember having so much fun. Finally he decided to make his move. It took every fiber in his body to stand and walk over to Hazel. He stood next to the table but not a word came out.

"Hello, Tidy" Rick said.

Tidy swallowed hard and said, "Hi Rick, great party," never taking his eyes off of Hazel.

Tidy reached way down inside his soul. "Would you like to dance?"

Hazel smiled, "Sure."

Rick's table grinned. They had never seen Tidy dance in the fifty-three year history of the banquet. Anne thought they made a nice couple, but Rick reminded her that, as far as they knew, Tidy had never been on a date in the sixty years of his life. Rick quietly whispered to Anne about the cloak room. He stood and took her hand as they sauntered casually toward the back.

As the last song ended, the lead guitarist walked to the microphone. "We have a special request tonight; I would like Johnny Cash and Elvis to please come forward. Two young ladies have asked you to sing "Love Me Tender" and go into "A Boy Named Sue." As Eric and Tony stood, they glared at Billie and Dar.

"No, boys, come right up on stage. We'll be your back up band."

The band started to play "Love Me Tender" and both boys looked at each other and grinned. "Let's do It, Tony"

Surprisingly, the two boys were pretty good, and even they were amazed at their performance. People stood and clapped as they gave each other a high five. They came back to the table and the only thing the girls could do was shake their heads.

"I'll be damned!" Dar exclaimed. "We thought you two would fall completely on your faces."

Eric reached into his guitar and pulled out the Gas City Soda Pop. "We had help" as he held up the bottle. Maybe we should take this gig on the road," as he looked over at Tony.

"Your heads are awfully big; I hope you'll be able to get your shirts off tonight," Billie said.

Tim and Pamela Sue walked by the table and patted both boys on the back. "You boys were good. Pamela Sue said. How about "Jail House Rock?"

"No, our dates are in need of our services, but thanks for the complement," Eric said.

The evening was wonderful. Couples danced, ate, talked, and made the trip to the bar several times. Anne now understood why everyone talked about the banquet six months before. Every generation of Gas City was represented, and each had their own little groups and friends to be with. Tony met a bunch of 4-Hers, and they all seemed to jell. Most kids just called him Elvis from New York, and he liked that.

"Well, that was interesting." Anne said as she and Rick exited the cloak room.

"For some reason, I remember it being much larger and I wonder when they started storing the Christmas decorations in the cloak room."

"How's this memory going to play back in your mind?" she asked

"It was good and so were you, but I have a terrible crick in my neck."

"Poor baby, when we get home I'll nurse you back to a full recovery."

It was midnight and people were starting to leave. Hazel and Tidy were completely engrossed in each other. Rick pointed to Tidy's table; Hazel and he were holding hands. Anne shook her head in disbelief as Hazel kissed Tidy on his cheek. The band members came over to Eric and Tony's table to thank them for their songs and get a photo of the group. Billie and Dar just couldn't believe how the boys performed.

The evening was beautiful as Eric, Billie, Dar, and Tony left hand in hand. There was a full moon and the evening air was crisp and fragrant. The four stood next to Dar's truck and soaked in the whole evening through their minds and pores.

"What a great night!" Tony exclaimed. "I've been to a lot of functions, but this one takes the cake. I have never sung publicly before, let alone dress like Elvis, and people were asking me for my autograph. My only problem was to either sign it Elvis or Tony Becko, and most of the time I signed Elvis. Your town is great, and so are the people." as he put his arm around Dar.

"You know, Tony Becko, I like you a bunch. I too had a great time tonight and you have been a breath of fresh air to Darlene Moore. Thank you," as she pressed her body to his. She kissed him with such passion his knees started to buckle again.

Eric and Billie were on the other side of the truck kissing and lightly touching each other. They both desired the other, but it was all right for now to stop. Eric knew when the time was right, they would have the best, intimate sexual experience imaginable. Billie knew the same. She wanted to help Eric with his desires, but couldn't cross that line quite yet. The mutual respect was glorious, and each wanted the same thing, but knew that now was not the time.

The girls got into the truck and blew kisses to Johnny and Elvis. The two friends watched as their heartbeats drove away in a 1984 Ford pickup. Tony turned to Eric, "Shall we go back inside to see if there are any groupies left?"

"Nah, let's go home and see if Hazel has any pot roast left."

"Sounds good. You know, after an evening of entertaining the locals, food will be great."

Faith Baptist Church

Pastor Roger Shepard was warned there wouldn't be many people in church today, and the advice was right. The music director, Ken, had only half the choir and even the organist didn't show up. Pastor Roger was dying to preach on the non-committed Christians that could stay out late for the 4-H banquet but not get up for church. Roger's wife, Libby, told him not to go there. The two of them were at the banquet, but left at 10:00 P.M., and when Roger looked around, the bar was three deep waiting for drinks.

"I'm glad to see you all in church today." He started, "You know the path to heaven is narrow and the path to hell is wide." Libby gave him a frown and narrowed her eyes toward her husband. "But today I will speak on Christ feeding the five thousand," and her frown turned into a smile.

There weren't enough men to collect the offering, so Roger stepped down and helped pass the plate. The service ended with the hymn, "Blessed Assurance," and the congregation started to file out. Roger and Libby stood at the back entrance and shook each hand as they left. Mrs. Wheeland took Roger's hand firmly and asked what if the people Christ was feeding didn't like fish or bread because she hates fish and bread has too many carbs. He had no immediate answer but would look into the matter.

RICK AND ANNE'S FARM.

It was going on 9:30 A.M., and Hazel was busy making scrambled eggs and sausage. Anne was the first one to come downstairs "Well, you sure were a hit last night."

"In all my years on this planet, I danced more than I ever have. I had such a great time and thank you for encouraging me to go. I still can't believe my hair is a platinum blonde, and when I woke up, I ran to the mirror just to see if the whole thing was a dream."

Rick now joined them in the kitchen. "There she is; the bell of the ball. I think you were the most popular woman there."

"I'm going on a picnic at noon with Terrance," Hazel said beaming.

"Who's Terrance?"

"You know, Tidy Tucker, but I like to call him Terrance."

"Tidy and you; I mean Terrance, seemed to really hit it off last night," Rick said.

"I've never had a man talk to me like he did, and want to know about my life. He asked me all about my Danish heritage and my trip to Copenhagen. He has never been to Europe, and we decided last night; we are going to take a trip together to Denmark and Sweden."

"What! You've only known him for twelve hours!" Anne exclaimed.

"That's not true. I have known him my whole life and have been waiting for him. He feels the same about me. I can't describe it, this is the real deal, and my happiness is finally being fulfilled."

Anne walked over and hugged Hazel. "We are truly happy for you."

"You know Hazel, Terrance got the name Tidy from being very, very neat," Rick said.

"He told all about his fixation, and I love it. We are going to set the date today for our travel plans."

"There never will be a money issue; Tidy is thrifty and inherited a small fortune from his parents." "Again we are so happy for you two." Rick said as he hugged her.

All of a sudden an old pickup truck pulled into the barnyard with horns a blasting. "What the hell is that?" Rick exclaimed.

Dar Moore jumped from the truck, and ran in the back door of the farm house. Completely out of breath "Where's Tony?" she yelled.

"Eric and he are still in bed, why?" Anne asked.

"I have to talk to him now!" and darted up the stairs.

"Tony, get up!"

Both Eric and Tony sat straight up in bed. "What's the matter?" Tony asked, still trying to understand the urgency.

"Put your pants on; you have to come with me right now."

"But I don't get it."

"You will. Hurry up. I'll be in the truck."

Tony put his pants and shirt on and just looked at Eric. "What the heck."

"Don't look at me; I hope you didn't do something real stupid last night," Eric said

"If I did, I sure can't remember it."

Tony walked through the kitchen and everyone at the table just stared.

He shrugged his shoulders. "I don't get it either."

MOM'S DINER

There weren't many people in the diner either. She counted only four farmers and Bill Sales from the funeral home sitting at the round table. "Did you boys have fun last night?" she asked.

"I think I did," Lester said. "Evelyn drove me home, and that pretty much sums it up. I do remember Billie getting the 4-H award and something about Johnny Cash and Elvis. I need some more coffee."

"Well, Tidy Tucker sure seemed to have a great time. He danced with some blonde, and the two were the last to leave the banquet." Mom said.

"I saw them also, and I didn't know Tidy knew how to dance. He's pretty good on his feet," Bill said with a grin.

Just then Tidy came in, "Here he comes," Marvin said.

"Hi, guys. Great party last night."

"It sure was for you. Who was the blonde that never left your side?" Mom asked.

"That's Hazel Henry. She's living with Rick and Anne Barr. She has only been here two weeks and used to live in New York with them. Did I tell you she's from Denmark?" Everyone shook their heads. "We are going on a picnic today, so Mom, will you pack me two nice lunches to go?"

"Sure, Tidy. How about fried chicken, potato salad and honeydew melon?"

"Sounds perfect."

Tidy left with the two lunches and never looked over at his prize trophy in Mom's window. Today the trophy was not on his mind and would never be again.

DARLENE'S 1984 FORD PICKUP TRUCK.

Dar started driving very fast and Tony just hung on. She pulled up to the limestone pit and told Tony to get out.

"I have only one question for you!" She yelled.

Tony just stood and looked, waiting for the question.

"Who is your father?"

"That's it? You want to know who my father is? His name is Anthony Becko, like mine" he said in complete bewilderment.

"My dad got a call from his lawyer this morning and the guy that was suing him; dropped the lawsuit, and not only that, the guy is sending my father a check for $1600.00 to cover the damages on his truck. There are no complaints, and my dad's even getting an apology from the guy doing the suing."

Tony just looked at Dar, "And?"

"My dad's attorney said a call to Cincinnati came from New York and that's all he knows."

"I don't know anything about this Dar, but I'm really happy for you."

"Did you call you're your dad and tell him about my mom and dad?"

"I mentioned it to him, but I also told him I have fallen for an Indiana farm girl, and I can't get her out of my mind," He said with a grin.

"You told me your father was in dry cleaning. You're probably right, but he must know some pretty good spot removers. That's all I can say."

"My father and I are close. I don't know what he really does, but he is a good dad, and I'm his only son. He wants the best for me and if that means Darlene Moore, he's in with both feet."

Dar came and put her arms around Tony. "My parents are going to Indianapolis this afternoon to sign off the lawsuit. I will be home alone, and I have been studying massage therapy; I want you to come over after 3:00 P.M., and I'll show a new technique," she said with a blushing grin.

"I'll be there at 3:00 P.M. sharp."

"This is one massage you won't forget."

Bald Hill Picnic Grounds

Tidy picked up Hazel in his 2008 Ford Ranger Truck which looked like it had just come off the showroom floor, and she noticed even the floor mats were waxed. They both felt a little awkward riding together making small talk. They had known each other less than twenty-four hours and the evening before, the talk was going to Denmark and Sweden together. Tidy pulled up to the picnic area and retrieved the large basket full of food.

"I have to admit; I didn't make the food, I had Mom put together the basket for us," Tidy said.

"It's all right, I'm just happy to be here with you." That was the comment to break the ice for them.

Tidy now felt comfortable and knew she still wanted to be with him.

"I've been kidded all my life for being too neat, but if it bothers you, I can try and be less organized."

"Terrance, I like neat, and I too am very orderly. One of my pet peeves is a dirty glass with spots."

"Me, too. That's at the top of my list."

"For not knowing each other for one full day, I'd say we're off to a great start," as she leaned over and kissed him on the cheek.

"I brought fried chicken, a salad, and a bottle of wine."

"I'll get the food out, if you open the wine for us."

Terrance wrestled with the cork and managed to get it open without incident. He pulled out the wine glasses and handed one to Hazel. She looked at it for spots, as did Tidy, they both started to laugh uncontrollably.

"Terrance, hand me your glass, and I'll wipe off the spots." She was still smiling.

Their lunch was great and after, they walked hand in hand to the top of Bald Hill.

"Hazel, I truly want to go to Denmark and Sweden with you. Can we go this fall for a couple of weeks? And I'm ok with separate rooms and will never pressure you into anything."

"You know, I'm forty-eight and you're sixty; I feel no pressure at all. I want to stay with you." She said blushing.

"I hoped you would say that. We've never been married before, and I want to start a new life with you, dirty glasses and all."

Hazel turned and kissed Tidy on his lips. The two felt a true connection, and they knew they would be the blunt of some slander and jokes, but that didn't matter. They felt that this was the soul mate that had eluded them all these years, and they kissed again.

Rick and Anne's Farm

Dar came flying up in the old truck, and Tony got out.

"Ok, what in the heck was so urgent for Dar to get us up this morning?" Eric asked.

"The lawsuit against her parents was dropped today, and she thinks my father had something to do with it. Maybe he did; I'm not sure, but I'm going to get a Darlene Moore massage at 3:00 today," He said with a smile.

"You lucky bastard! What if your dad didn't have a hand in it?"

"I'll wait till about 4:00 and tell her then. Can I borrow the truck?"

"Sure, but please don't tell me any details; I'm horny enough."

"I think I'll call my dad and see if there is some connection."

Eric walked back into the house to get some ice tea.

"Hi dad," Tony said. "I'm having a great time, and did you see me as Elvis last night? I sent mom and you the photos from my phone." "Yes, Eric, and I did a duet and some people even asked for my autograph. I'm not kidding. I told you about Dar, the girl I met here in Indiana; Dad, she's awesome! By the way did you call our cousins in Cincinnati on that lawsuit against her parents? The people dropped the charges and even sent an apology. You did know about that? Thanks, Dad, and I really do want mom and you to meet her. She is one beautiful cowgirl. Love you, and I'll talk to you soon."

Eric came out with two ice teas. "Did your dad know about this?"

"He told me our cousins in Cincinnati owed him a big favor and reassured him the matter would be taken care of. It sure was. My dad and mom loved our pictures from the banquet last night, but my sisters thought we looked like geeks."

"Apparently your sisters aren't as sophisticated and refined as I thought," Eric said. "They just don't have an eye for real talent, and here are the keys for the truck. Have fun, but I don't think that should be a problem."

Ann's Office, Gas City, Indiana

Anne thought she would stop by the office and make a couple of phone calls. Sunday is usually a good time to find people at home. She opened her computer, and there was a flashing memo to call Anita Adams right away.

"Hi, Anita, this is Anne."

"Hold on, I'll be right with you." It was almost a minute and she came back on. "Anne, Harvey's dead!"

"What? How can this be?" she said almost yelling.

"He fell in the shower yesterday morning and hit his head. I came last night to go to dinner with Harvey and found him in the shower. They are doing an autopsy this afternoon, but the medical examiner said it looked like a fall."

"Does anyone else have a key to his apartment?

"Not that I know of. We have been working on our marriage, and things seemed to be going well. Some nights I stay here with him."

"Did he mention anything about a case we were working on?"

"No, just that you had called, and he was helping you with a missing person."

"What can I do to help?"

"Nothing right now, but I will keep you informed because I know you two were close. There's only one thing that bothers me with all of this, but it's probably nothing."

"What?"

"I talked to him yesterday morning early, and he told me he had just taken a shower and was going to turn on the highlights of the baseball game. Why would he take another shower within two hours? That doesn't make sense?"

"It doesn't make sense to me either. Have the medical examiner look at the security tapes of who came into the apartment building that morning."

"Are you thinking someone did this to Harvey?"

"No, not at all, just curious," Anne said trying to hide her real feelings.

"I'll be in touch, and let you know about funeral services."

"I love you Anita, and we'll be praying for you. Goodbye."

After she hung up the phone, panic overcame her. Anne now knew something was really wrong, and she had to share this with the family when they all meet in Sissy's basement tomorrow. Why would anyone give a damn about a missing Boy Scout after seventy-three years? This doesn't make any sense at all. She now feared for her family and wasn't sure how to tell them without throwing everyone into total panic.

Darlene Moore's Farm

Tony pulled into Dar's barnyard and looked around for someone moving about. He only saw three horses with their heads hanging over the white fence by the house. He walked to the back door and knocked.

"Hello," he said.

"Come on in. I'll be right down!" Dar yelled from upstairs.

Tony liked the home; it was very modest, clean, and homey. His home in New York seemed sterile and uninviting compared to the little farm house. On the wall above the sink hung a drawing of Jesus holding a lamb.

Dar came into the kitchen and threw her arms around Tony's neck. "Ok, tell me; did your father have anything to do with the lawsuit?"

"He did, and he told me our cousins owed him some favor, and they followed through on their promise."

"They sure did. My parents started to cry when their attorney called this morning. He told my parents that he didn't know how anything like this could happen. He also told them they would have lost the farm. I'm going to do something for you; not because of what your father did, but just because I like you a lot. I was hoping this week my parents would go away so I could practice my massage techniques on you."

Tony got a big lump in his throat, and had a severe case of dry mouth. "What can I do?"

"That's just it; you do nothing, and I'll do everything for you," she said blushing.

He followed her upstairs into her bedroom. There were lots of pictures of horses and some blue ribbons hanging on her mirror.

"Take your clothes off down to your shorts, and lay on my bed. You don't have to be nervous, just relax."

He did, and laid on her bed face down. He could feel her straddle his waist as she applied some warm, lilac smelling oil. Her hands were gentle but firm as she moved her hands in circular movements. Boy did he like this! She told him she had taken classes for massage therapy and wanted to study sports medicine in college. She again thanked him for calling his father and following through with their cousins. Tony seemed to be in some form of a trance as she spoke quietly to him and would occasionally kiss his ear.

He could feel her gently pull his underwear down around his ankles and toss them onto the floor. Tony could only think if Heaven is half this good, he wanted to go. She quietly asked him to turn over, and he knew what she would see. He turned and looked up at Dar. She only had on a pair of pink silk panties and her breasts were fantastic. She was fairly large breasted, and her small brown nipples stood straight out. She reached down took his hands and placed them on her chest. "It's all right." She said in a whisper.

"Darlene Moore, you are unbelievable." Tony whispered back.

She put oil on his chest and slowly moved her hands up and down. She also put oil in Tony's hands so he could massage her chest. She nimbly removed her panties and threw them next to his underwear. She now put oil between his legs and hers and gently massaged his penis. She pressed her body on his and moved up and down with only the oil between them. He grabbed her buttocks and pulled her tightly as she continued to move. He never entered her but continued to slide up and down. That was it for Tony; he came as they moaned together. She continued to lay on top of Tony as he tried to collect his thoughts from the greatest experience of his life. He opened his eyes and she kissed him.

"Holy shit!" he said still whispering. "I've never experienced anything, I mean anything like that in my whole life."

"I really loved it too. I came the moment you did and it was great. I only have one question."

"What?"

"Do you think, I'll make a good massage therapist?"

Tony started to laugh. "You've got to be kidding. If you don't make at least a million dollars your first year, then that means you are living on a different planet. Gosh darn you, Darlene Moore; I'm in love with you, and I have never said those words to anyone in my life."

"Well, Tony Becko, I'm in love with you, but I've told that to at least twenty guys."

He flipped her over onto her back and stared into her eyes. "You are so full of shit."

SISSY'S BASEMENT

The Barr family was there. The meeting room Sissy set up was perfect. There was a chalk board, large bulletin board, two tables, and several chairs. Rick started the meeting with all the news about the Harris mansion in Evansville and the $1,000,000 endowment that went with it. He told of all the newspaper articles that Anne's intern found on line. Moses, Rahab, and Eric had no news to report. Mary Barr only reported that Gladys from her church thought Albert Harris was a homosexual because Gladys's brother Ernie told her once that Albert would watch the guys as they showered at the camp.

"Todd knows where Albert is because his imaginary friend NeeNee told him," Sissy said as the others laughed.

Anne stood and asked everyone in the room if they had shared any information or questioned people about Albert. They all looked around with blank stares.

"I haven't told a soul." Pamela Sue stated.

"Me neither," Eric said, "My friend Tony, from New York wanted to know why I was coming over to the beauty shop, and I just told him it was a family meeting."

Anne now looked serious. "I have something to tell you, and I hope this won't frighten you. Mr. Galey from the nursing home died five days ago after Tim and Rick talked to him. My twenty-eight year old intern died three days ago in New York after I talked with him, and now Harvey Adams, an investigator and former FBI agent died yesterday in his shower."

There was total silence. Everyone looked around the table for an answer or a comment.

"How could this be?" Tim asked. "Do you think there is a connection?"

"I don't know, but we better be darn sure we want to follow through with this. We should receive the DNA results from the Boy Scout hat tomorrow. I don't know what to tell you, but everyone is dying around us," Anne said with a sigh.

"This fun and games investigation has now taken on a new wrinkle," Mary Barr said.

"I don't want anything to happen to our family; I don't care how much money there is at stake." Rick said firmly.

"My only feeling is we should wait to see if there is any DNA connected to the hat." Tim said. "If there isn't, then maybe that's our sign to give it up."

"I'm with you. Let's meet three days from tonight, but don't mention anything about Albert to anyone." Pamela Sue said.

Just then Todd came running down the stairs, "I know where Albert is."

Sissy just laughed along with the others, "When we're ready to find him, we'll call you."

"Ok, Mom, but can we all go to gas station and get ice cream?

"Sure, Todd, they all said. "It will be a good break for us."

Anne and Rick's Farm

Dar dropped off Tony at the farm. Tony didn't want to get out of the truck as he looked over at Dar.

"You just did something to me that has never been done before." Tony said

"And what would that be, Mr. Becko?"

"Darlene Moore, you just stole my heart, and I've only known you for four days. I hate to admit; I have lost all control on my very soul, and I'm not comfortable with that."

"Tony, I can say the same thing. I have thought about you day and night since Eric and you came to Billie's farm that day. I don't like this either."

"I'm going back to New York in four days, and I want you to come and visit me before you start Purdue University. I'm going to NYU in three weeks, and we may not see each other for a long time."

"For some reason, I do think we will be connected for a long time and maybe forever. Does that sound crazy to you?"

"Believe it or not, it doesn't. I can't explain what has happened in the last four days, but I want it to last an eternity."

"I'm still a virgin, and I told Billie I would never let a man enter me until he became my husband. I still hold true to those beliefs, but dammit Tony, you make it real hard. I have never desired anyone as much as you."

"The weird thing is, I live in New York and have never been to the Midwest or have seen a real live horse. You have never been more than forty miles from Gas City and have never seen a skyscraper. Our lives are so different, but yet we have something that will not be separated by live styles or miles. I want to be your man. Does that sound absolutely foolish to you?"

"You are not a fool. I want you to take my virginity, and somewhere in the back of my mind, you will."

She leaned over and kissed Tony before he got out of her truck. "I want to see you tomorrow." Tony said.

"Well, I hope so. I'll pick you up around 10:00 A.M. and we can go to the limestone pits for a lunch and a swim."

"I didn't bring a swimsuit."

"Well, then, I may just have to forget mine," she said blushing slightly.

Tim and Pamela Sue's Farm

Tim pulled the truck up by the barn. Everyone piled out and walked into the kitchen.

"I'm not sure we should pursue Albert anymore." Pamela Sue said.

"I have the same feelings." Tim said in response.

Rahab said, "Come on you guys, what the heck can happen to a farm family living in Gas City, Indiana? No one knows we even exist."

"She's right; our family has never had an adventure or a quest in all the years we've been here. There is no way somebody will kill us for trying to find an eight-four year old man because he's probably been dead for years. We should start digging in the old farm yard and see if we can find bones," Moses said.

"Anne seemed concerned tonight." Pamela Sue said

"She should be, but one guy died at eighty-eight in the nursing home, one of a drug overdose and one in his shower. I don't see much of a mystery in this." Rahab said.

"Ok kids, we will keep looking, but if a red flag of any sort pops up, we're done."

"If it comes to that point, we should just ask Todd. He knows where Albert is." Moses said laughing.

Rick and Anne's Farm

Tony was sitting on the front porch with his feet on the banister as the Barr family pulled up. "Hey Tony, how was your day?" Eric asked.

"If I told you; I'd have to kill you." as the Barr family started to laugh.

"We're going to walk to my mom's farm in a few minutes and throw some steaks on her grill," Rick said.

Just then Tidy's truck pulled in to drop off Hazel. Rick walked over to Tidy and asked him to join the family for some steaks. Tidy looked at Hazel for some approval, and she nodded at Tidy with a big smile. The Barr Family, Tony, Tidy, and Hazel all walked down the dirt road to the Mary Barr farm. The big Barr family harvest table was all set for the dinner. Moses had already started the bon-fire, and Mary came out with a huge platter of T-bone steaks, corn, and ginger bread. Tim started grilling as the family sat and talked, but Albert Harris was not mentioned.

"Tony, I'm so glad you came to Indiana to be with our family. Eric has told us a lot about you, and now we finally get to meet the real Elvis. I'm just kidding; you guys were great at the banquet," Mary said.

"I've really enjoyed myself, but I have to admit, I didn't want to come to Gas City, Indiana. I'm not real sure why, but I thought you all were like the Hee Haw series, and I apologize. You've been wonderful and make me feel right at home. Everyone I've met has been honest, really don't care if their opinion goes with the flow, and aren't ashamed of their thoughts." as he remembered what Dar had told him.

"Come on over to the table; the food is coming off the fire right now," Tim said.

Pamela Sue said the blessing, and platters of streaks, corn, ginger bread, and beans were passed around and around. Sissy had to tell Todd he could only have two steaks. Everything was perfect, and Pamela Sue opened her third bottle of peach wine.

Tidy and Hazel were sitting very close together and couldn't quit touching or holding hands. "We have announcement to make," Hazel said. "Terrance and I are going to Denmark and Sweden in late September." as Tidy blushed.

"We're very happy for you two and we'll try and get by without your great cooking," Rick said.

"We're leaving now, and again thanks for a wonderful meal with your family." Tidy said as he led Hazel toward his truck. His truck slowly pulled out onto 550 E. and Mary stood.

"I know this is probably not the best time to say this but," as Mary hesitated for a minute. She really struggled with the next sentence. "The only reason I'm telling each one of you is because I care for you." She now had everyone's attention.

"What is it Mom?" Tim asked.

A gentle breeze now blew through the farm yard and the scent coming from the peach orchard gave Mary the peace she needed.

"Your father never knew what I am now going to tell you." Again a hesitation. Everyone was now leaning toward Mary.

"I was the nude girl in the famous painting by Calvert Wolf. I posed for him for over two months and no one ever knew, including my parents."

The shock hit the Barr family. "Mom why?" Rick asked.

"Calvert was a true gentleman. He treated me with the utmost respect and loved me in a special way."

"I think it's wonderful," Anne said, "but why tell us now?"

"There are two reasons. I looked over at Tidy and Hazel with love in their eyes, finding each other after decades of searching. I'm so happy for them. Such a love they now share as I did. The other reason is," another hesitation, "I had Calvert Wolf's son sixty-one years ago, and he just now found me after all these years. You kids have a brother living in Panama, and he's coming to see me in a week."

ANNE'S OFFICE, GAS CITY

Anne sat in the old barber chair and spun around and around. Her mind was now completely in the over load mode. Three people she knew had died within a week and a half, her mother-in-law just told the family she bore a son sixty-one years ago, and her son Eric is talking about marrying a girl he has only known for a couple of months. New York City and the high profile law office she worked in were nothing compared to Gas City, Indiana. She knew her plan of attack was to take on one of these issues at a time. Today she would receive the DNA results of the old Boy Scout hat and maybe some information on how Harvey Adams died. She had a security camera installed on Jim's Shoe Repair across the street from her office so no one would suspect she had her building wired. Jim didn't care and never asked why, so she sent him a pizza from the new shop down the street. He liked the pizza, so she followed up with a $25.00 gift certificate and now Jim was her new best friend.

"Hi, Honey," Rick said as he walked through her office door.

"Can you believe the bomb your mother dropped on us last night?"

"I haven't seen the nude painting in many years and thought maybe we could walk down State Street and check it out."

"I'd love to, but I'm waiting for the lab report on the hat that's due here any minute. Why don't you wait here and we'll go together in a few minutes. If you want I can cut your hair or give you a hand job." she said with a big grin.

"Now there's an offer I've never received from my barber."

"Hold that thought; my computer is just receiving the DNA report from New York. This could be a big break."

Anne's printer went right to work, and page upon page came spilling out. She counted forty-eight pages and stapled them together. She started to read and told Rick what it all meant.

"Rick, you can never tell anyone what this means. This DNA information must stay between the two of us, and if something would happen to either of us, then it can be made public," she said with a deep frown on her brow.

"You're scaring me a little."

"There is a place behind this mirror on the wall, and I am going to put it there. No one will ever find it."

Anne's cell phone ran, and she recognized the number.

"Hi Anne, this is Anita."

"How are you holding up?"

"It's been rough, but my sister Carol is here with me and her support has been wonderful. Harvey never wanted a funeral service, so we are going to have a cocktail party in his honor. I know this sounds nuts, but that's Harvey to a tee."

"When are you thinking?"

"Not until December because all my family can be here around the Christmas holidays. I would sure like to have Rick and you come out."

"We will be there. Did you hear anything from the medical examiner's office?"

"He called this morning and ruled it an accident. I told him my ex-husband had taken a shower not two hours before."

"What was his comment?"

"He basically said that accidents happen."

"Did you ask him to check and see who came into the building just before he died?"

"He told me that it wasn't necessary and to leave the investigation to him."

"I'll let you go, but please call when you set the date for Harvey's memorial."

"I will, and thanks for being his good friend."

"What did she say?" Rick asked.

"She said that the medical examiner ruled Harvey's death an accident. I don't buy it for a second. The examiner told her he wasn't going to check the tapes because it was an accident and to mind her own business."

"Should we try and get the tapes?"

"I don't know. The only thing the tapes would reveal is who came into the apartment building that day. There are over a hundred apartments in the building. I'll call the law office and see if they can send us a copy, but with strict orders never to say why."

"Close up, and we'll walk down to the museum. Why don't we stop and get a pizza from the new place down the block."

"It sounds good, but I'm sure it won't compare to Ray's in New York."

Mary's Farm

Mary now regretted telling the family about the picture and the son she put up for adoption sixty-one years ago. Mary took her small folding chair into the pear orchard and sat among the trees. Calvert Wolf was her first love, and she thoroughly enjoyed the time they spent together. She never felt embarrassed around him even though she was naked most of the time. They only made love once in the two months he painted her, but apparently it was enough.

She remembered the day like it was yesterday. He had just finished painting her and he was cleaning his brushes. She walked over to him and he slowly turn to see her; they were face to face. He ran his paint stained fingers through her hair and softly cupped her breasts. She was dying for this to happen. He took her by the hand and led her to the couch at the other end of the large parlor. She instinctively laid down and slightly parted her legs. He stood and undressed, never taking his eyes off her. She reached up and brought his penis to her mouth. She gently kissed and licked him. She had never done this to any boy in her seventeen years, but it came naturally for her. He brought his body on hers and when he entered, it hurt for just a moment. He placed his lips on hers, and she pushed her tongue in his mouth to the taste of cherry pipe tobacco. He came quickly and laid on her for a couple of minutes. She didn't have an orgasm, but the feeling of Calvert on top of her was magical. Even though he was forty two years older, she felt a strong bond to him.

When her parents found out she was pregnant, they sent her to Lexington, Kentucky to a Lutheran girls' school with a clinic attached. She never told her parents who the father was, and she refused to have an abortion. The pregnancy was easy, and she gave birth to an eight pound, six ounce boy. He had her blond hair but dark eyes like Calvert. After all these years, she now wondered if the boy was an artist in Panama and felt it was too bad that Calvert never knew he had an heir. Should she tell this sixty-one year old man who is father was? When she met him, she would know.

Calvert Wolf Museum, Gas City

Rick and Anne walked up the steps to the huge Victoria home that now housed an art museum. The lady at the desk took the $6.00 entrance fee and handed them a map. The foyer was massive with a large crystal chandelier hanging in the center. They viewed the rooms and noticed the luxury he lived in some sixty-one years ago, but it wasn't until they reached the parlor that their breath was taken from them. They slowly walked in as if they had entered something very holy. They almost felt they weren't worthy to be there. The twelve foot nude stood all alone, and seemed to pull the viewer into the painting itself.

Except for the guard sitting at the small desk in the corner, they felt they had just come into the presence of perfection. They couldn't speak; all they could do was stare. They looked around the room and noticed just where the artist and model were placed, and Rick wondered where his mother and Calvert had sex.

They started to walk out and the curator told them that the model was rumored to have been a local girl. They looked at each other as if they had the biggest secret in the whole world. They walked down the street toward Ann's office.

Rick finally spoke, "Shit!"

"Man, Rick, I never would have dreamed that a painting could have such an effect on me. I want to buy it."

"I don't think it's for sale, but I get what you mean."

"It still blows me away that your mom posed naked for a famous artist and had his child. I want to pick her brain and see how they interacted and touched."

"I can't go there. She's my mom."

"Just think, sixty years ago a seventeen year old Gas City girl took off her clothes and the artist created something that can't be described or explained. I've seen the picture before in a brochure of Gas City, but to see it face to face, there's no comparison. The painting almost brought me to tears."

"It totally pulled me in; my mother was beautiful," Rick said.

"I wonder how your half-brother ended up in Panama. He traveled from Gas City, Indiana, to a different continent, and now he's coming back to Indiana after sixty-one years."

Darlene Moore's Farm

Eric and Tony pulled up to the farm; Billie and Dar were just finishing brushing the horses. The girls looked over as the boys jumped from Eric's truck. The girls both threw their arms around the boys and kissed them on the lips.

"Come on over and sit with us," Dar said.

Eric and Tony sat on a bale of hay as the girls tied the horses up by the water troth. Tony had on blue jeans, cowboy boots, and a new plaid long sleeve shirt. Dar casually walked over to Tony and stared.

"You look really good today Tony, but there's just something missing."

Eric knew what was coming and moved a couple of feet away from Tony.

"What's that?" Tony asked

As soon as he finished his sentence, both girls threw horse manure on his shirt and pants. The only thing he could do was to look down at the damage.

"Welcome to Hoosier Land," Eric said laughing.

"I don't get it," Tony said.

"It's kind of rite of passage into the Indiana scene. I received my manure baptism at the county fair, and now we are brothers in a different way. Let's get the girls."

Billie and Dar heard the comment and took off running, laughing as they ran. Eric and Tony chased them into the corn field and lost them.

Through the tall corn the boys heard, "We knew you both were full of shit; now we know you're covered in it."

The boys went back to the corral and waited. A few minutes later the girls emerged from the corn.

"If you boys are nice to us, we may let you swim naked with us at the limestone pit." Dar said.

The boys looked at each other and knew they were not going to pass up an opportunity like this.

"We've just sprouted wings, how much more perfect can we be?" Eric said.

"Good, I'll pack some food and let's head to the pit," Billie said.

"Yeah, we're not sure how long this angel thing will last, but we're looking forward to you being real attentive to us," Billie said with a grin.

Rick and Anne's Farm

As Rick and Anne pulled in, the Yoder clan was loading up their buggies.

"We will finish in the morning, and if you find anything that isn't right, please tell us tomorrow. We have enjoyed working here, and

Eric and Tony are fun to be around. My wife would like to have all of you over for dinner next Friday, and I can show you what our lifestyle is like," Isaac Yoder said.

"You are wonderful carpenters, and we liked having you here," Anne said, "and we would love to come to your home."

"See you in the morning," as he slowly got into the old station wagon.

Rick and Anne walked into the old farm house; it seemed like they just stepped into a brand new home. The smell of the cedar and pine caught their nostrils like a fresh batch of popcorn. The Yoders' doubled the size of the kitchen and built on a glassed in breakfast nook. Their bedroom now was huge. A wall was knocked out, and a master bathroom was added. Anne also had a small deck added that overlooked the apple and peach orchards. She was beside herself with happiness. Rick too liked everything that was done, especially the small wine cellar in the old basement. Eric's room was finished, and he too had a small deck that opened to the barnyard below. The Ethan Allen Furniture truck was arriving in the morning with all new stuff, especially beds. Just about the only remembrance was the old plaque hanging in the living room that read "God Bless This Humble Home." They had to keep it as a reminder.

"Let's go for a walk in the orchard." as he took his wife's hand.

They walked for several minutes without saying a word.

"Rick, I'm not sure we should take Albert Harris any further."

"I know your concern, but let's wait until our family meeting tomorrow at Sissy's."

"This whole matter is keeping me awake at night, and I fear for Eric."

"My mind won't shut down either, and now since we've seen the painting of mom, I'm sure this won't help me to sleep any better. In three days my half-brother will be here, and I have no idea what to expect. I'm just hope this isn't a scam to trick mom into something she'll regret someday."

"Do you think we should contact the local sheriff and alert him?"

"No, definitely not; no one knows Mom gave birth to a boy sixty-one years ago, let alone posing naked at age seventeen. It this gets out, it will crush her spirit. Let's just see what happens in three days."

"Help me gather some peaches, and I'll make a batch of fresh peach daiquiris."

"Now that sounds like a winner," Rick said as he stooped to pick up the peaches.

Gas City Limestone Pit

Eric drove his grandfather's old pickup truck with Dar and Tony sitting on a bale of hay in the bed. It was a bumpy road, and Eric drove slowly. The abandoned pit had been closed since the early seventies. There was a sign that said "No Trespassing," but nobody had paid any attention to it for forty years. The water was crystal clear and very cold. No matter what the air temperature, the water never warmed up. The truck pulled to the south side of the pit, no one could see the truck or the kids from the road. Dar grabbed the picnic basket and blanket and spread the food out about ten yards from the water. They sat Indian style and ate chicken sandwiches and chips. Before they finished, they felt a little uncomfortable because of the statement by the girls. Eric had never seen Billie without clothes, and Tony felt funny around Dar even though he had received a massage two days before. The boys knew the ground rules and figured nothing would happen between them and the girls.

Dar stood and said, "I'm going in." and removed her blouse, jeans, and boots. She stood there as the three stared at her buffed body. Wearing only a bra and panties, she turned and dove in the water. "Wow! It's cold"

Billie stood and removed her blouse, jeans, and boots and looked down at the boys. Both boys were now in a trance. Billie wasn't wearing a bra and Eric's breath was pulled from his body. Her body was flawless and her breasts were firm with large pink nipples. "Come on boys," as she ran to the water.

Tony turned to Eric and they just looked like they had seen a ghost. Neither, Tony or Eric could utter a single word. They both stood and stripped to their underwear and turned toward the pit. Now they both had a big grin, and ran and dove into the icy water. The erections they were sporting were reduced to normal as soon as they hit the water.

"Holy shit!" Tony hollered. "Where'S the ice cubes?"

Eric swam over to Billie, barely able to move his numb arms and legs. She put her arms around his neck, and he felt her warm breasts press against his chest. He now felt invigorated. She guided his hands to her breast and he began to stroke them gently. This was his first encounter with her body. He had never seen her breasts, let alone touch them.

"I'm not trying to punish you or lead you on; I want to feel you close to me."

"I'm not minding this a bit. You have the most beautiful body I've ever seen."

She kissed him again and nibbled at his ear as he touched her gently.

Tony was touching Dar, as he removed her panties and bra. He slowly put his fingers between her legs, and she let out a gasp. Eric and Billie were far enough away that neither couple knew or cared what the other was doing. Now Dar was touching Tony, and he came back to life as she stroked him.

The touching lasted several minutes until Billie's teeth started chattering. Billie swam to the shore and hurriedly grabbed a blanket. Dar was right behind her. The boys were mesmerized as the naked cherubs left the icy water. Eric looked at Tony and grinned.

"We better get out before it falls off. We might need these someday," Eric said with a laugh.

The four sat with blankets around themselves. Billie's lips were blue and Tony's ears were a bright red. "Well, that was fun; what comes next?" Eric asked.

"For starters, we need to finish the chicken and have a couple of swigs of Gas City Soda Pop," Dar said.

They talked about their hopes, dreams, and someday starting families. The conversation lasted for two hours, but Eric and Tony couldn't erase the naked pictures from their brains. They got dressed, decided to go into town, get ice cream, and see if the boys could really tip over a sleeping cow at Mr. Shipey's farm. They all had fun and built up the trust and faith in each other, once again.

Sissy's Basement

The Barr family was sitting around the large table. Anne spoke first "Let me give you an update on where we are. Since three days ago we have received some information on Albert Harris. Yesterday I received the DNA report from the lab in New Jersey. My suspicions came true: there wasn't enough hair or skin traces to put together any conclusions. Even if we suspected someone and got a hair sample, it would prove inconclusive."

"Should we send it to another lab for a different opinion?" Moses asked

"It won't do any good. The lab I used in New Jersey is the best of the best."

"So that's it?, we are done with Albert Harris." Rahab asked.

"I don't know what to tell you, but unless we get another clue or we find some witness to the event, we're pretty much finished."

"What happened to the detective you hired?" Pamela Sue asked,

"I got a call yesterday from his ex-wife, and she said the medical examiner ruled his death as an accident. That case is now officially closed."

"So, I guess we're done now," Sissy said with great disappointment.

"Not necessarily so." Mary said. "After your dad died, I was throwing stuff out or just burning it. I came across some letters that your father saved from his father. The letters were all dated from

1937-1938 and came from Doc the old camp director. Doc mentioned of how Ray and he rescued AH from disaster. I never thought much about AH, but now it seems it was about Albert Harris."

"Mom, you knew all along that Albert Harris did exist. Why didn't you speak up when Dad would tell the scary stories around the campfire?"

"I promised your father I would never mention Albert to you kids. He told me there was evil and a supernatural power connected to his disappearance."

"What do you mean supernatural?" Rick asked

"I don't know. I just know your dad was told by his father to stay away from talk of Albert Harris. Your dad told me once that a curse followed Albert's disappearance."

"You mean to tell us that these deaths may be connected to the so called curse?" Tim asked

"I can't tell you that, but your father and your grandfather were frightened by something."

There was total silence as each looked at the other. Then Mary said, "Doc had a nephew living in Tampa and your father would talk to him on occasion."

"What did Dad want with him?" Tim asked

"I don't know, but I do have an old address and phone number for the nephew."

"I'd say we're back in business!" Rahab yelled.

"My guess is this nephew would have to be in his eighties," Anne said. "I'm willing to see if he is still alive and make a road trip to Tampa."

"Now we're talking!" Moses exclaimed.

"Listen everyone; this is a long shot at best. Rick and I will check this out after our long lost half-brother comes from Panama. We still better not say anything to anyone about Albert; I have bad vibes about this. I don't know what a curse entails, but Rick's dad and grandfather were scared of something."

TIM AND PAMELA SUE'S FARM

Moses and Rahab talked all the way home. They were energized and ready for another adventure.

"I don't like the words curse or supernatural," Pamela Sue stated as they walked into the kitchen.

"Oh, mom, get over it." Rahab said.

"Everyone just sit down for a minute. I'll bring out some cherry pie and ice cream."

She served Tim, Moses, and Rahab pie and ice cream and sat staring at her family.

"What's on your mind, Honey?" Tim asked.

"I knew you father and grandfather very well. They were honest hardworking men who weren't afraid of anything. If something about Albert really got to them, then it was a serious issue. I feel like Anne; there is much more to this missing Boy Scout story than what meets the eye."

"What do you propose, Honey?" Tim asked.

"I think we should drop the whole matter. Let Albert Harris rest in peace or continue to live his life without intrusion."

"Oh, mom, get over it. I've lived in Gas City my whole life and have never had an adventure or challenge like this." Moses said.

"Your mother might be right; I never knew your grandfather or great grandfather to be fearful of anything."

"Ok, Dad I'll back off if Rick and Anne don't find anything from Doc's nephew. I just want one more chance to solve a seventy-three year old mystery. I also want some more pie," Moses said.

MOM'S DINER

As Bill Sales walked in, Tidy Tucker was standing telling some sort of story. Bill took his seat and grabbed a slice of toast from Tidy's plate. "We're leaving on September 14th and will fly into Copenhagen. We will be there for four days and take the train to Holstebro and

Skagen. Then we take a boat to Stockholm and Sigtuna which is the oldest city in Sweden."

The guys could tell Tidy was just a little enthused. Bill knew the answer but asked, "Are you going by yourself?"

Tidy blushed, "No, I'm going with Hazel."

Mom heard the conversation and came to the table. "We're so happy for you two."

"I thought my life had been fulfilled when I won the best tractor at the fair this year," he turned to look at the trophy in Mom's window, "but what has happened to me cannot be explained. I've never had a girlfriend because my parents needed me at the farm. I've never traveled, seen anything but cornfields, and wasn't sure where Denmark was located until I got out the world map. Now I'm going to Denmark and eat something different than steaks and potatoes. Hazel told me I'd love the food."

"Wow, Tidy, when you make a move; you really make a move," Lester said. "Don't forget to get a passport."

"Oh my gosh! I never thought of that." What do I do?"

"Just take your driver's license to Indianapolis, and they'll crank one off in a hurry." "It only takes a few days." Bill said.

"Be sure and wear clean underwear because the examiner puts his finger up your butt," Lester said with a laugh.

With that statement, Mom hit Lester on the back of the head with a menu. "Just leave him alone."

"Sorry Mom."

"Send postcards to the diner, and I'll have Chris put them up for all of us to see," Mom said.

"Will do, and you can take the trophy out of the widow if you want. I'm ok with that."

ANNE'S OFFICE IN GAS CITY

Anne walked in carrying a large cup of coffee and a slice of pizza. The new pizza place was advertising breakfast pizza so, she thought, what the hell. She opened her computer and stared at the blank screen. Her first email was from her office in New York. The managing law partner, Stephen, left a message. Her office went to retrieve the old Boy Scout Hat, and the lab said it was missing. Stephen was very angry and wanted an explanation for the loss, but they couldn't come up with an answer.

This is just one more roadblock in the investigation. She never heard of the lab losing anything for all the years she used them. A feeling of uneasiness came upon her again, but at least the pizza was good. She set to work to find a Jonathon Roth in Tampa, Florida. The address Mary gave her came up blank. The phone also had been disconnected. She did a title search on Jonathon's old property and found it had been sold two years prior to a Mable Ellison. She called Mable.

"Hello, is this Mable Ellison?"

"Yes, it is," the older women said.

"I'm looking for Jonathon Roth that used to live there."

"What do you want with John?" she asked

"My name is Anne Barr, and I live in Gas City, Indiana. I'm trying…"and was cut off.

"John and I know your family. I'm John's sister, and he used to call Richard Barr occasionally. My brother is in a nursing home here in Tampa and is failing quickly."

"I just wanted to find out if he had information on his Uncle Doc and his connection with Albert Harris."

"Albert Harris is a name you should forget."

"It seems everyone is telling me the same thing."

"Heed the warnings; Albert Harris will bring nothing but misery for you and your family."

"But I," and the phone went dead. Anne tried to call back and no one answered.

Anne Googled Tampa Nursing Homes, and there seemed to be more nursing homes than homes in Tampa. She emailed the list over to Moses and Rahab to let them call and find Jonathon Roth. She told the kids not to give out their names or locations for any reason.

Pamela Sue walked in to check out Anne's office. "I like it," she said, "but I'm really concerned about this Albert matter."

"I am too. I just found out that Doc's nephew is still alive, living in a Tampa nursing home. If I can find out where he is, I'm going to leave first thing in the morning to talk to him. His sister told me he was failing quickly."

"Will you be back by Thursday? Rick and Tim's brother will be here sometime early afternoon."

"I don't think this trip will take more than a few hours. Do you want to go? I can use a companion and Tampa should nice this time of year."

"I'd love to go. I just have to let Rahab be the chief cook and bottle washer for a couple of days," Pamela Sue said with a smile.

"I'll book a flight for early in the morning from Indianapolis to Tampa. If we can't locate Jonathon, then I'll cancel."

"I've never been to Florida. I hope we find him," Pamela Sue said with great excitement.

Rick and Anne's Farm

Eric and Tony had their feet propped up on the porch banister surveying the barn and apple orchard. Alongside the boys were Dick and Jane, but neither was interested in catching any mice today. Hazel came out with a big pitcher of lemonade and cookies.

"Just think boys, three weeks and Copenhagen, here I come."

"Are you sure you want to go? Look around at the beautiful mountains and seas right here in Indiana," Eric said with a smile.

"Are you boys on something?" she said laughing as she entered the house.

"Eric I have to go back to New York in three days, and I don't want to."

"Tell your dad you are going to marry a farm girl and become the mayor of Gas City."

"Very funny. I'm enrolled at NYU, and my dad would kill me if I backed out of this."

"Why don't you ask Dar to come to New York over Christmas break? She would love to meet your family."

"I'm going to ask her tonight. She's taking me to a drive-in movie. "What is that?"

"I've never done it, but you park your car and watch a movie through the windshield. My dad calls it the passion pit."

"I think I'm going to like this."

Mary Barr Farm

When Mary got up, she tried to decide what to wear. After all, she is seeing her son again, some sixty-one years later. She opened her jewelry box and took out the unicorn necklace she held for the painting Calvert did of her. It had not been around her neck for the past sixty-one years. Today was definitely going to be the day to wear it. She put on a light blue summer dress and simple white sandals. Food didn't sound good today, but she forced down some cereal with bananas. She was to call Rick, Tim, and Pamela Sue when he arrived. She just couldn't think of what she would say. She rehearsed several lines, but none seemed appropriate for the occasion.

She looked out the window and noticed a large dust cloud coming down the country road. Two very large black busses pulled up into the barnyard. The busses stopped but no one got out. She wasn't sure if she should go out and meet them or stay inside. Two more black cars pulled around the busses and eight Spanish looking men in suits got out. Four of the men had automatic weapons and the other four walked behind the barn, house and shed. The men with the guns stood completely still and surveyed the farm like they were going to put a bid on it. Several minutes passed, and no one seemed to make a move. One of the busses pulled closer to the house, and the door opened. Six men walked out and joined the four with the rifles.

Mary walked out the back door, but wasn't sure which one was her son. Just then at the top of the bus stairs she noticed a tall blond man wearing dark pants and a white dress shirt. They both smiled at the same time. She knew this was her son, and he knew this was his mother. He ran to her, and she to him. He hugged tightly and kissed her on the cheek.

"Mama," he said.

"Son, I'm so glad to see you."

"Come into the bus," he said in broken English.

She entered and the inside was like a palace. "Mama, these are your two grandsons, Miguel and Carlos, and this is my wife Maria."

She could see both boys took after their father. They were tall and light skinned, and Carlos had blondish hair. She studied her son, Rodolfo, and could see Calvert in his eyes. Sixty-one years she said to herself; sixty-one years; it just can't be.

"Mama, can we talk in private?"

"Sure, do you want to come into the house?"

"I would, but can I ask you; did I ever live here?

"No son, I will tell you of your father and how you were taken from me."

SISSY'S BEAUTY SHOP

Rick and Tim stopped in to pick up Sissy to go to their mother's and meet this so called half-brother. They got on 600 E., and there was a utility truck blocking the road.

"What's up?' Rick yelled.

"We have a power line down and the road is closed."

"We need to get to my mom's farm just down the road!" Tim yelled.

"Can't do it! There are hot wires all over and it's going to be closed for a while."

Tim turned the truck around and headed for his farm. Tim parked the truck, and the three siblings got out.

"Let's walk to Mom's farm; it's only half a mile from here," Rick said.

They walked about a quarter of a mile and there was another utility truck parked in the middle of the road. "You can't go through here," The worker said in a commanding voice.

"Our mother lives just down the road," Sissy said.

"I'm sorry, but we have live wires on the road. You'll have to go back."

"Our mother is expecting us; we are to meet a relative from South America." Rick said

A Hispanic man came from behind the truck and asked, "Who are you?"

"We are the Barrs and need to get to our mother's farm." Tim said sternly.

"I need to see some sort of identification."

They produced a driver's license, and the Hispanic man spoke something into his cell phone.

"Sorry about the inconvenience; you go on."

They each had a puzzled look as they walked toward the farm.

"What was that all about?" Sissy asked.

"I don't know, but we are going to find out shortly," Rick said as four men approached them from three different angles carrying automatic weapons.

ANNE'S OFFICE, GAS CITY

Anne received an email from Rahab. She told Anne she had located Jonathon Roth at the Crestview Nursing and Rehabilitation Center in Tampa. Anne knew those kids could find him. Anne immediately called Pamela Sue and told her she would be picked up at 9:00 A.M. to fly to Tampa. Pamela Sue was so excited; she forgot to pack underwear.

Anne sat in the barber chair and spun around and around. What do you ask an eighty plus year old about something that happened over seventy years to an uncle? As she sat and stared at the ceiling, she noticed a little triangular box attached to her ceiling fan. She stood on the chair and knew exactly what it was. A microphone had been placed there in the last two weeks. She walked into her back office and again, there was another microphone. Anne panicked and ran to the mirror where the DNA results were hidden. The packet was still there but she needed a new hiding place. What the hell was going on? She asked herself. Anne became fearful and knew she couldn't tell anyone of this. All of sudden Anne thought of a guy she could trust, and nobody knows of him. She sent him to prison, but kept in touch with him over the last few years. He was an undercover agent and got caught taking money from the bad guys. This man was fearless and under the radar. He would be perfect, but wasn't sure he would work for her since she was the one who helped prosecute him.

Anne called Rick to see how things were going with his half-brother. Rick quickly hung up after telling her he couldn't talk.

Mary's Kitchen

Mary and Rodolfo sat across from each other and studied the other. She stood and gave him a piece of cherry pie that had just come out of the oven.

"Where do we start?" she asked

"We both must have a thousand questions for the other, so let's take turns. I'll start, but if you don't want to answer a question, just say so. Please call me Rudy."

"Fair enough, and please call me Dommy. I will answer all your questions."

"Is my father still alive?"

"No, he died before you were born. He was my first love, and I was only seventeen."

"How did you find me after sixty-one years?"

"My mother, or should I say my adopted mother, died two months ago, and she left me a letter. In the letter she told me of how I was adopted from Lexington, Kentucky. I never knew anything about this until months ago. I don't look Panamanian, as you can tell. My blonde hair set me apart from all my family."

"Who was my father?"

Mary now hesitated. "This may be difficult for you. I just told my two sons and daughter last week that I had a child sixty-one years ago. I think I threw them into shock. I've had this secret for all these years and no one, not even my parents knew of this. My parents sent me away when I became pregnant, but everyone in town thought I went to spend some time with my Aunt Clara."

"Do you not want to tell me?"

"I really do want you to know your father. His name is Calvert Wolf."

"The Calvert Wolf?"

"Yes. He was fifty-eight when I became pregnant. We had only made love one time, and I was still a virgin. He painted me, and I fell in love with him. I adored the pregnancy, and I held you the five days before you were so called adopted."

Rudy started to tear up. "My father is one of the best known artists of his time. I love his work."

Mary started to cry, "I wanted to keep you, but the Lutheran home took you one night when I was asleep."

"In my mother's letter, she mentioned that my father had come to Lexington, Kentucky, to buy race horses. This had always been his passion. My mother got something in her eye, and they took her to the clinic next to the Lutheran Home. Her letter told of how she fell in love with a blonde baby boy, and somehow she took me back to Panama. My parents couldn't have children, and I was accepted into my father's family. My parents were very wealthy, and my grandfather was the president of Panama."

"That's strange; I remember the clinic talking about an aristocratic woman from South America coming into there for an eye problem. I never dreamed you were taken to Panama."

"All these years my mother would never talk of where I came from or any of the circumstances. I wonder if she knew my real father was Calvert Wolf?"

"She didn't. I kept your father deep in my heart until five days ago. I had to tell my other children that someone was coming to claim me as his mother. Nobody knew that Calvert and I were anything to each other."

"I so needed to hear these words. I look different than all the Panamanians, and I just wanted closure."

"I know this sounds strange, but I've always wondered what happened to my son. When I nursed you, I felt such a bond to my baby boy. I still remember how you smelled and your tiny feet and hands. I knew when I saw you on the steps of the bus, you were my son. I think I could have picked you out of a hundred men."

Rudy came over and put his arms around her as they both cried. He kissed his mother's neck as he sobbed; he felt such satisfaction and love for this farm woman from Gas City.

"I love you mama."

"I love you too, son. Do you want some more pie?"

"I sure would, and how about some more ice cream?"

MARY'S BARNYARD

Rick, Tim, and Sissy sat in the second black bus. They were offered food and drinks as they watched all the screens showing the farm and surrounding roads. Two people sat at monitors and talked in Spanish. The other four people wanted to know if there was anything they wanted.

Tim said quietly, "Who is our brother?"

"I don't have a clue, but he must have something going." Rick said

Suddenly the bus door opened and a tall, dark skinned woman came in. "You may go into the house now if you choose."

"What if we didn't choose?" Sissy said in a whisper.

The three walked into the old kitchen. Their mother was seated and a blonde handsome man stood and put out his hand. "I'm Rudy."

"Oh my gosh!, you're Rodolfo Varela!" Rick exclaimed.

"I am. I apologize for keeping you in the bus. My security demands it. I have no say in my traveling or safekeeping."

"Do you know him?" Tim asked.

"He is the finance director for all of Latin America. I think you were the "Time Magazine Man of the Year" a few years ago."

"I was. You've done your homework."

"Wasn't your family instrumental in getting the Panama Canal built and financed?"

"My family actually owned most of the land where the canal was placed."

"How did you become our half-brother and end up in South America?" Sissy asked.

"Our mother will tell you all the details. I came here in total secrecy because I don't want my political enemies to find out I came from Kentucky. It wouldn't be safe for you or me."

"You've met every U.S. president in the last forty years and most heads of state," Rick said.

"I do get around. I want us all to have a dinner tonight. The bus is equipped to feed us, and the servants are setting up as we speak. You can meet my wife and sons over dinner. They all speak perfect English, and both were educated in the United States. My wife's English is a little rusty, but I think this will be an amazing reunion."

"That sounds wonderful," Sissy said

"I have only one request. I need to take my mother in town to the Calvert Wolf Museum. My people have already called for a private opening, so we should be back soon. Please go to the first bus and enjoy some Panamanian snacks. Oh, by the way, please bring some of your pie and ice-cream for our meal. My boys have never experienced anything like this before."

Calvert Wolf Museum, Gas City, Indiana

The large bus and two black sedans pulled up in front of the old Victorian House. Rudy told his mother to wait until the security people give them the sign.

"Rudy, I haven't been here since your father died. He painted me and during the last session, he fell over in front of the canvas. I ran away. I didn't know what to do; ran down the alley to my home and called the fire department. That was sixty years ago. I have not been here since."

"Are you going to be all right with this?" Rudy asked.

"Yes, I will. You are going to be introduced to your father. I'm excited for you."

"I feel funny, too. I have now found my mother and father within one day as he began to cry. Please hold my hand tight; I don't know what to expect."

The security men opened the door, and the two walked hand in hand up the stairs.

"Welcome," the curator said. "Here is a map that will guide you through each room. Well, hi Mary. Is this a friend of the family?"

"It is," She said with a slight grin.

Mary's memories were bombarding her left and right. She was so glad to be holding her son's powerful hand. Each room had paintings of Calvert's, but Mary knew what was coming up. The parlor was just around the next corner.

Tim and Pamela Sue's Farm

Anne pulled into the barnyard and walked into the kitchen.

"Pamela Sue?"

"I'll be right down."

Anne noticed the small worn suitcase sitting by the back door.

"I'm so glad you got an earlier flight. I want to see Tampa at night," Pamela Sue said

"You look nice."

"I put on my good summer dress and new sandals I wore to the 4-H banquet." Pamela Sue said with pride.

"I have reservations at the Tampa Yacht Club tonight. It's beautiful, and we can watch the boats come in and out of the harbor."

"I can't wait. This detective business is kind of fun. I would love to do this, but Tim and the kids wouldn't have a clue how to manage. I guess Albert Harris might be my only case, but I'll do my best to help. Hold on one second; I have to put a patch on Tim's overalls," as Anne grinned with approval.

Calvert Wolf Museum, Gas City, Indiana

Mary and Rudy walked into the large parlor still holding hands. Mary tightened her grip as she looked at the painting. Rudy just stood and gazed. It was just as she remembered it, and even the small book where she would pick up the necklace was exactly as it was sixty years later.

"Mama it's beautiful! You were beautiful!" He exclaimed

"Your father was just going to start on my face when he died."

The two both started to cry again. He put his arms around his mother and held her tight. She loved the embrace of her sixty-one year old son. This moment was a dream come true for both of them. They sat on the small couch together and looked at the painting with tears streaming down their faces.

Mary reached behind her neck and unfastened the unicorn necklace. She handed it to Rudy.

"This is yours."

He rose and walked over to the painting and looked closely at the necklace the nude was holding. It was the same. He turned and walked to his mother and knelt down in front of her.

"This is the greatest gift I have ever received. I've had presidents, kings, queens, and dictators give me lavish presents, but this...," and he started to weep.

She stroked her son's thick blonde hair and kissed his bent head.

"You have been the best gift any mother could have been given. My baby boy is has come home to meet his father. He would have been so proud of you," as she whiped her eyes with a handkerchief.

She looked down at her world renowned son crying with his head in her lap. His mother continued to stroke his hair and gently comb it back with her fingers. She now realized that this was the missing piece in her life. She felt totally satisfied and now could die a happy woman. This five day old son had just filled the empty hole she had been carrying all these years.

"Thank you God," she whispered, "I don't deserve this."

Rudy looked straight into her eyes and whispered, "I don't deserve this either, thank you Mama."

Tampa International Airport

Anne and Pamela Sue went to the baggage claim. They walked out and a limousine was waiting for them. "I can't wait to tell Tim I rode in an airplane and limo all on the same day."

They arrived at the Tampa Garden Hotel, and the valet came immediately to take their bags.

"I like someone carrying my bag. This is another new experience for me."

Their room overlooked the harbor and the twinkling lights on the boats. Pamela Sue plopped on her bed and stared at the ceiling.

"You know Anne; I really like you as a sister-in-law. I never had a sister, and for you to move from New York City to Gas City, I have to give you a lot of credit. Our town hasn't much to offer, but the people have taken to you like you're one of us."

"Thanks for saying that. Tim and you have made the move so much easier. Now let's go the Harbor Grand Restaurant and have a great meal."

The restaurant was open air, and their table looked directly onto the harbor. Pamela Sue tried oysters on the half shell and grilled swordfish. Anne ordered a bottle of champagne and a "grasshopper" after dinner. Pamela Sue was having the time of her life, and ordered "Sex on the Beach" from the drink menu just because she liked the name.

Mary Barr Farm

Mother and son held hands as they left the museum. They got into the black bus and headed back to her farm.

"I hope it was all right for just the two of us to go today. I didn't mean to offend your other children or my family either. It had to be just us."

"It was perfect. I swore I would never set foot in the house again, but with you it was absolutely the best. I didn't think it appropriate to tell you that you were conceived on the small couch we sat on to view the painting."

"You mean my father and you made love in front of his masterpiece?"

"Yes, but it wasn't intentional. It just happened," She said with a small grin.

"Mama, I'm very, very wealthy. Is there anything you desire?"

"Son, you just gave me the greatest gift in the world. For me just to know you're alive and introduce you to your father; that's the best. I'm the wealthiest woman in the world; what more could I want?"

The large bus pulled next to the other bus, and Mary and Rudy started for the door. He pulled her back. "I may never get to say this again; I love you." He embraced her, and they both began to cry again.

The other bus was loaded with food and there was laughter coming from inside.

"Come on in," Sissy said. "We've just met our nephews. Did you realize, our blood is the same?"

"I know it Sissy," Mary said, "We've all been invited to Panama, the whole family. I think we should go this winter and see a different culture and country."

The meal was fantastic. The maids and butlers wore fine silk dresses and suits. Rudy's sons played soccer and lacrosse for Princeton and Georgetown Universities, respectfully. The Barr family shared with the Varela family and vice versa. There was a knock on the door, and a tall dark Hispanic man said something to Rudy in a stern voice.

"We have to go," Rudy said, "I'll look forward to seeing each one of you and your children in Panama. Just let me know when you want to visit, and my secretary will make all the arrangements. I just need a moment of our mother's time."

The two walked out of the bus into the small farm kitchen.

"I know I'm going to repeat myself, but you have given a peace that I have never experienced before. All these years, my father and mother would never speak of my birth parents or place of my birth. I've had this gnawing in my soul for as long as I can remember. I don't know if I will ever see you again, but rest assured I now have you in my heart."

"My son, you have filled my void also. All these years and no word from my five-day-old baby. I carried this secret of your father and the painting for sixty years. I just wanted to scream and tell the world, but that is all behind me. I have another secret for you. I haven't told my children or anyone for that matter, she hesitated. I have an inoperable brain tumor. I found out last month, but I'm in complete peace with this."

"Let me find the best doctors in the world for you."

"Thank you but I want to go and see Calvert and Richard again. I have a strong faith."

"Mama, if there is anything..."

She interrupted, "No, you have given me everything."

They hugged tightly, and she kissed him on his tear streaked cheek.

"Rudy, it's really ok; now go and be with your family. I won't come out to the bus."

"Bye, Mama."

"Bye, son."

The busses and black sedans pulled out of the barnyard. Rick, Tim, and Sissy came into the kitchen.

"Mom, so what did he say?" Sissy said

"You know, my brain is on overload right now. Let me fix a big breakfast for you in the morning and I will fill you in on everything."

"Fair enough they said, get some sleep tonight."

"Oh, I'll have a wonderful sleep tonight. Goodnight kids."

"Goodnight, Mom," as she turned off the porch light.

CRESTVIEW NURSING AND REHABILITATION CENTER, TAMPA, FLORIDA

Anne and Pamela Sue had a great breakfast. This was Pamela Sue's first experience with pickled herring. She liked it along with a mimosa. She just couldn't get over having champagne for breakfast. The driver dropped them at the main entrance, and the nursing home seemed pleasant and clean.

"Just follow my lead," Anne said.

They walked to the receptionist and asked to see Jonathon Roth.

"What's the nature of your visit? He's not allowed to have visitors."

"We are with the Hillsborough County Medicaid Office. We'll also need his chart," as she produced a photo identification badge.

"Sorry about the questions, but his sister gave strict instructions that he is not to have any visitors."

"That's all right, rules are rules."

She handed the chart to Anne and pointed to his room. They walked down the hall and knocked on his door. There was no answer; they slowly pushed the door open. An elderly man was looking out the window and mumbling to himself.

"Mr. Roth?" Anne asked, "Mr. Roth?" she said louder.

He slowly turned his wheelchair around to face them.

"Hi, ladies," he said, "and how are you Carol?" he asked Sissy.

Anne whispered "Go with it."

"I'm just fine, Jonathon." Sissy said.

"You haven't been around to see me for a while."

"No, I've been busy."

"How are the kids?" he asked

"They're just fine," as Sissy looked at Anne.

"You ask the questions," Anne whispered as she handed Sissy the notebook.

"Say, have you heard from Albert Harris lately?"

"No, I haven't, but I think Doc has."

"Is Albert still alive?

"Of course he is. Doc helped him escape the camp."

"Who else knows Albert escaped?"

"You know, just Doc and Ray."

"Who's Ray?"

"We can't talk about him."

"Why not?"

"He's very, very, old, but his magic is still powerful."

Anne could see this wasn't going anywhere. She asked, "Have you talked to Mr. Barr recently?"

"No, he got mad, and won't speak to me now."

"Why won't he call?"

"Because of Todd."

"Todd who?"

"Todd who likes cowboys."

They were startled. Why would Todd's name come up with an eighty-four year old man? None of this makes any sense Anne thought.

"Have you talked to Todd?" Sissy asked

"No Carol, but Ray has."

"Do you have a picture of Albert?" Anne asked

"No. All my pictures were burned by the priest. I'm getting tired; I need to go to bed. Goodbye Carol."

"One more question," Anne said. "How can we reach Ray?"

"Stay away from Ray; you have no idea what you're asking," as he turned his chair back toward the window.

"Goodbye, Mr. Roth."

Anne thumbed through his chart. It showed he had slight dementia and shingles. He certainly seemed confused or was he? They turned the chart back to the receptionist and walked out the front door.

"What do you think?" Sissy asked.

"Not sure. I think we need to talk to Todd about Ray."

"What will that prove?

"Probably nothing, but it's worth a shot. How about some whale watching?"

"Oh yeah! I'm ready."

Mom's Diner

Mom came over to her table of farmers and the funeral director, Bill. "Did you guys see those big black busses come through town yesterday?"

"Yes, it was probably a tour group because I saw one parked at the museum," Bill said.

"When I was closing up yesterday I saw it too, but there were two well-dressed men carrying rifles." Mom said.

"Rifles? Come on, Mom, you must have dreamt that," Lester said.

"No, I'm not kidding. They even had Elm Street blocked with two black Cadillac Sedans."

"Who in the heck would block Elm Street for a tour bus?" Tidy asked

"I'm telling you; it wasn't a tour bus. I'm going to call Marsha Morris from the museum."

"Mom, it's only 5:45 A.M." Lester said

"She needs to get up sometime."

Mom came back to the table after about fifteen minutes. She pulled up a chair. Chris, the cook, and Jenny, the waitress, also sat down.

"Ok, this is what Marsha told me," with every eye and ear intently fixed upon Mom. "Someone called for a private tour of the museum, but she didn't know who it was. All she knew was the woman had a foreign accent. The two black Cadillac's arrived first, and some men walked around the museum. Two of them had guns. See I told you."

"Ok, already, finish the story!" Lester said in haste.

"Well, Marsha said the door opened, Mary Barr and a tall blonde man got out."

"What tall man? Was it Tim?" Bill asked.

"No, she had never seen him before. One of the men stayed next to Marsha in the office as Mary and this guy walked around."

"What else?" Chris asked.

"That's all Marsha knew. She did say the man that was with her, gave the museum a $10,000 check."

"Wow! We got to call Mary. This is one great story," Jenny said.

"I'll bet she's in trouble with the IRS," Marvin said.

"You guys just finish your breakfasts. Until we hear it from the horse's mouth, it's just going to be rumors, and you know, our little town frowns on rumors," Mom said with a laugh.

Faith Baptist Church

It was early, but Pastor's Roger and Ken were there hauling tables to the parking lot. Today was the day for the annual rummage sale. They no more would set the table up, and a lady started arranging her prize possessions in some sort of order.

"Roger, how many tables are we bringing out?"

"All of them, my advice to you; when we get done, don't stick around. This place is a mad house, and the women will push you down."

"Yeah right."

"I'm not kidding. Last year the volunteer fire department performed CPR on two women, and Bill Herald got four stitches in his leg."

"Thanks for the advice; let's hurry and get our part finished."

Bernice Henry came running up to the pastors. "As soon as you boys finish; we need help with unloading some trunks; I know Mabel is bringing over a freezer."

They just looked at each other and wondered if this was in their employment contract. Probably not, but they knew God would be watching along with each lady in their church, but they were much more afraid of the women.

MARY BARR FARM

Eric and Tony walked down the road to Dommy's farm with Rick at a safe distance.

"You got in late last night," Eric said "How was the drive-in movie?"

"I've never watched a movie through a car windshield before; quite an experience."

"Is it really a passion pit?"

"You be the judge. Dar drove her truck and we parked toward the back. Anyone under twenty, parks in the back. The old people park close for the concession stand and bathrooms. Dar put an old speaker in the driver's window and got out a bunch of food. We had just started eating and several kids opened my door, gave us beer, and took some food. I put my arm around her, and started to kiss her and the door opened again, and more snacks arrived. Every time I tried to kiss her someone would open my door. Dar told me to get out so we could visit other cars and trucks. We walked all over except where there was a bra hanging on the car antenna."

"What's that about?

"I guess if you can get your girlfriend's bra off, you hang it outside as a trophy of accomplishment and privacy. Dar wouldn't let me go to the cars and trucks with their banners hanging out."

"When did you hang her bra out?

"Very funny! I did get her bra off but it went immediately into her purse. There was no way that was going to happen; I couldn't have done it if she asked. I guess I'm turning into some old fashioned guy."

"Next thing is you'll be parking in the front by the restrooms."

"I'm not that old fashioned," Tony said with a grin.

They walked into Dommy's kitchen, and Eric could see a pile of pancakes waiting for them.

"Oh boy, pancakes!" they both said.

"Sit down. You're the first to arrive."

"My dad isn't too far behind," Eric said.

Within minutes, Tim, Moses, Rahab, Sissy, Todd, and Rick arrived. She loved to cook for her family; this was her gift. She cooked, they ate. Platters of pancakes and bacon were passed around and around.

"Are you all underfed?" Mary asked with a laugh.

"We are making up for the starving children in India" Tim said.

"What's the news from Anne and Pamela Sue?" Mary asked.

"Anne texted me this morning, and they'll be back early evening. They've had a good time, but told me to tell Tim she wants champagne for breakfast from now on."

"What in the hell did Anne do to my poor wife?" "Champagne?"

"Get used to it buddy", Rick said as he slapped his brother on his back. This is only the beginning."

Mary shared her story of Rudy and the trip to the museum. There were a lot of personal details she left out, especially of her cancer. She stressed to her family about the secrecy of the painting and Rudy. She told them if anyone should ask, just to say he was a nephew from her mother's side visiting from Mexico.

Rick and Anne's Farm

Anne dropped Pamela Sue off at her farm, and they exchanged a long hug.

"You were wonderful to take me with you," Pamela Sue said.

"I had a great time. You're not afraid to try new things and never once did you complain. I'd like to travel with you again."

"Really? I'm in for any kind of a trip; you know where to find me," as she headed for the farm house.

Anne drove home. Hazel and Tidy were sitting on the porch with the two cats.

"Welcome home," Hazel said, "There's some left over pot roast in the oven if you like."

"Thanks, but I'm full. Where's Rick?"

"He's in the barn, but you should knock first."

Anne walked over to the large door and knocked loudly.

"Who's there?" Rick asked.

"It's me."

"Hold on for one second."

He opened the door, looked around and let her in.

"What's going on? She asked

"Check this out," as he pulled a cover off a car parked inside.

"Wow!" was her reaction.

"This is the 1969 Chevy Camaro Z28 that Eric I found in the barn. The Evans Body Shop delivered it today, and Eric hasn't seen it yet."

"What a beauty! Do you have any idea what's it worth?"

"Jim Anderson offered me $50,000."

"Are you going to sell it?"

"No, I'm giving it to Eric. I know you think I'm crazy, but I've neglected my son for seventeen years and I want both of us to enjoy it together."

Anne started to cry. "You know he'll never forget this. You haven't given him anything his whole life, especially your love."

"I realize that I can't make up for the last seventeen, but these next years, I'll try and love him as best as I can."

"I feel you will Rick. As soon as he sees it, can we take it out for a spin?"

"I would love to take my best girl out for a drive. We can cat the drag downtown like I used to in high school, but it's only three blocks long," he said with a smile.

"Come on in Rick, I want to tell you about Jonathon Roth. Maybe you can help me piece this puzzle together."

"Let me put the cover on, and I'll be right in."

SISSY'S BEAUTY SHOP

Once again the Barr family gathered in the basement of the shop. Anne stood and shared what she and Pamela Sue found out from Jonathon Roth.

"Pamela Sue asked most of the questions because he called her Carol and seemed comfortable to talk to her. He wasn't much help. He talked of Doc and Ray helping Albert escape. He also mentioned Todd."

"Todd who?" Moses asked.

"Our Todd." Pamela Sue said.

"Why would he mention my son?" Sissy asked. "He went to Disney once and that's about it."

"Jonathon said he knew about Ray."

"He doesn't know any Rays," Sissy said.

"Have him come down. We'll ask him, if that's ok."

"Sure, why not," Sissy said.

Todd walked into the basement room and immediately sat down. "Hi," Todd said.

"Todd, do you know a person called Ray?" Anne asked

He hesitated for a full minute. "I know who Roy Rogers is, and his horse's name is Trigger."

"No, Honey, have you ever met Ray? Sissy asked

"I don't know Ray; let's get some ice cream."

"Todd, think real hard; do you know the name Ray?" Tim asked.

"Maybe NeeNee knows Ray."

"Thanks, Honey, we'll be up in a minute and go get ice cream," his mother said.

"Ok, everyone, unless we come up with something soon, we better shut our little investigation down." Anne said.

"Let's give it two more weeks and then call it quits. We have school starting, and corn picking is coming up." Moses said.

"Fair enough. Two weeks from tonight, we'll meet here and have one last meeting. Anne said. Let's keep in touch, but don't talk about Albert unless you know who they are."

"Come on you, guys!, let's get ice cream!" Todd yelled down the stairs.

Rick And Anne's Farm

Rick and Anne pulled in the farm yard and parked the truck by the barn.

"I'll get Eric, and tell him you need him in the barn."

"Perfect, but don't give anything away."

Eric walked to the old barn. "What do you want, Dad?"

"I need help with the plow. Just take the cover off; I'll help you put it away."

Eric walked over and threw the cover off. He was completely speechless.

"Dad!" he shouted.

"Awesome, right?"

"It came out perfect. Can I take Billie for a ride?"

"Of course you can. Be careful there's a bunch of power under that hood."

Eric embraced his father with all he was worth. He jumped behind the wheel and fired it up. It rumbled and roared.

Eric rolled down the window, gave his father the thumbs up and down the road he flew. Anne came out of the house and put her arm around Rick.

"I saw the thumbs up. You just took your son to a new level with that gesture. Come on in; we're all alone and I'm scared. I think I might need you to come up stairs; Albert could be hiding in our bedroom, and I might want to take off my clothes."

"I think you're right; Albert hasn't been found so I better escort you to the bedroom. That old guy might be hiding under our bed; we've never looked there."

FAITH BAPTIST CHURCH

Pastor's Roger and Ken finished putting away the last table from the parking lot. Their arms, legs, and backs were aching. The two hour task they started at 6:30 A.M. became a ten hour, back-breaking loading and unloading job. They walked into Roger's office and closed and locked the door. The air conditioning and overstuffed chairs were a happy ending to a long day. Roger took his shoes off and massaged his tired feet for a couple of minutes. Ken took off his shoes and put his stocking feet up on Roger's desk. Roger got up and pulled out his ring of keys. Ken smiled because he knew what this meant. Behind the old filing cabinet was an apartment size refrigerator.

"The usual?" Roger asked.

"Why not."

Roger unlocked the frig; produced two ice cold beers and two shot glasses. He opened the beers and poured two shots of Tequila.

"Here's to a very successful rummage sale," as took his shot and chased it with a beer.

"How much did the ladies make?"

"Doesn't matter; what does matter is we both survived the onslaught of women and carrying two tons of rummage."

"Here, here," Ken said as he downed his beer.

"For the life of me, why would any woman pay $6.00 for someone else's used electric toothbrush?"

"That's not as bad as the $30.00 dozen of used wigs that smelled like urine and one had gum stuck to the sides."

They both laughed uncontrollably and took another shot and beer.

"Do you think God will use the money to further the kingdom?" Ken asked smiling sarcastically.

"Yes, but he'll probably set the wig and toothbrush money aside for a special purpose," as Roger started laughing again.

Dar's Farm

Tony, Dar, and Billie loved Eric's car. The four of them went to Evansville to show off a little to the city folks. They certainly did receive the looks. They pulled into Dar's driveway and jumped out.

"You know, Billie, tonight would be a great night for a snipe hunt."

"You're right Dar, there's a full moon shinning which will make it easier to spot them."

"What's a snipe?" Tony asked.

"Haven't you boys ever seen a snipe before?" Billie asked.

They both shook their heads. "Is it like a kind of mushroom?" Eric asked.

"Oh no; it's a small furry animal like a gopher."

"They're easy to catch; Billie and I will bet you that we can catch more than you boys."

"You're on!" Tony yelled.

The girls gave Eric and Tony a gunnysack, two rocks, and instructions how to catch a snipe. The girls told them it was easy. All they had to do was make a smooching sound and hold the sack close to the ground.

If the kissing sounds didn't work right away, they could bang the two rocks together along with the smooching. Dar told them not to come back to the farm unless they had three snipes. The boys understood the rules, and took off running for the woods to get a good spot.

"That went easier than I thought," Dar said laughing as she pulled out two lawn chairs, handed Billie an ice tea and sat down. Within five minutes they could hear the smooching and rock banging. They started to uncontrollably laugh.

Two hours later the boys came back, hot, sweaty, and covered in mosquito bites.

"How'd it go?" Billie asked.

"Not so good. We didn't even see a snipe and Eric lost one of the rocks."

"We didn't do well either; we saw several but couldn't get them in the bag." Dar said.

"We're going home. I'm hot, dirty and hungry, but we'll pick you girls up for the picnic tomorrow about 11:00 A.M." Eric said.

"Sounds good. We'll be ready."

When the boys got home, they were dragging. Eric put the car in the barn, and the boys headed for the kitchen.

"What did you guys do tonight?" Hazel asked.

"Oh, we went a snipe hunt, and we're famished." Eric said

"Sit down; I'll warm up some the Italian beef for you boys. Snipe hunt, heh?"

"Yep. The girls didn't catch any either."

"Did the girls look hot and sweaty?"

"No, they were sitting in lawn chairs when we came back." Tony said

"Did it ever cross your minds, that just maybe there weren't any snipes, period?"

"What are you saying?

"Boys, there is no such thing as a snipe. You two have been taken! It's the oldest trick around."

They just looked at each other.

"No shit! Eric, we have been all over the woods making kissing sounds and banging rocks."

"When we get done eating, we have to do one better. If it takes all night, we need to come up with a doosie for the girls."

Hazel placed two big plates of Italian beef in front of them and started making the kissing sound.

"Ok, Hazel, you've made your point."

Mom's Diner

"I'll have the special." Marvin said.

"Anyone else?" Mom asked. Nine more hands went up. "Well, Mary told me the busses were for a nephew or cousin on her mother's side from Mexico. She said he had some sort of government job. That's the reason for the bodyguards."

"That makes more sense than her being in trouble with the IRS," Bill said.

Lester said, "I'll bet if you're involved in the Mexican Government, they probably automatically give you a bodyguard."

All the guys nodded their heads. Next week starts the corn and bean picking, so Mom knew there wouldn't be many guys around the table for the next two weeks. Bill Sales told the men he was seeing Polly Taylor. They were all happy for Bill, but Lester reminded Bill that Polly had a fetish for shoes. Her first husband left her because he told Lester there was no more room in the house for her shoes. Bill thanked him for the heads up, but thought to himself, how many shoes can one woman own?

Anne's Gas City Office

Anne got in early to try and piece something together on Albert Harris. Every road was a dead-end now. She opened up her cell phone, stepped outside, and called Brooklyn for Jimmy Keys.

"Hi, Jimmy, this is Anne Barr"...just then he answered.

"I certainly wasn't expecting a social call from you."

"This isn't a social call, and frankly I'm surprised you answered."

"I've been out of jail for eight months. I have no intention of going back."

"I don't want you to either. I want you to look into a death of a friend of mine in New York. If you are interested, I will send all the particulars in an email. The job pays well."

"I need work. The only offer I've received was to go back into the theft ring."

"This is nothing like that. The man that died was a friend, and the medical examiner ruled it an accident. I don't believe it for a second."

"I'll send you the dates, times and names ASAP. There is a lobby security camera but no one feels it necessary to check it. The death was supposedly accidental."

"I'll do it. I have someone very close that works in the medical examiner's office, so this might be a piece of cake."

"Just a warning-be careful. There is something very strange about his death and all the events that have happened."

"You don't need to worry about me. I've been to Hell and back; even Satan is my bud."

"Keep in touch."

"I'm on it as we speak."

Jim from the shoe repair came over to ask for free legal advice. He wanted to know if Bev Thomas could sue for medical expenses when her heel came off a pair of shoes he repaired. She gave Jim a bill for the emergency room. Anne told him she would look into the matter.

SISSY'S BEAUTY SHOP

Anne pulled up to the little yellow house. She sat in the car for a couple of minutes contemplating Albert Harris. She thought maybe by being alone with all the articles and notes in Sissy's basement, there'd be something she missed.

"Hi, Sissy," as Anne walked through the door, "I need to get something in the basement."

Anne noticed a lady in the dryer and one getting a cut.

"The door's open, and Todd is up here watching a western. If you need something, I can come down in a few minutes."

"I should be good."

Anne opened her computer and set her briefcase on the long table. Anne kicked off her sandals, propped her feet up, and stared at the wall covered with notes and newspaper articles. Even though things were arranged in order from beginning to end, it still didn't seem to make any sense. Albert's birth certificate was smack dab in the middle of the wall. She wondered why his parents kept the house intact and funded the upkeep all these years expecting his return, unless they knew he was alive. Her eyes scanned every piece of paper on the wall. One little piece of paper caught her eye. It was half covered by a large newspaper article, but the corner stuck out because of the color.

She took the paper off the wall and examined in closely. The paper itself was old and was written with an old fountain ink pen. The writing was cursive, flowing, and beautiful. Anne had never noticed this little piece before. She couldn't understand how this got there or was related to anything. The note had a man's name and address on it. She put it in her briefcase, shook her head, and headed up the stairs.

"What did you find?" Sissy asked.

Anne looked around; all the ladies had left and Todd was still engrossed in his show. "Nothing."

"I just ordered a pizza for Todd and me; want to stay?"

"Sure. Why not."

The pizza arrived, Sissy, Todd, and Anne went out back on the picnic table to eat.

"I found a little piece of paper pinned to the wall but for the life of me, I have no idea how it got there or even what it means."

"Let me see," Sissy said.

Anne reached in the briefcase and handed the paper to Sissy.

"Hum, I don't remember it either."

"NeeNee wrote that," Todd said.

"How do you know?" Anne asked.

"He told me. You never asked for help from NeeNee, so he wrote this down."

"Who is this?"

"I told you guys; this is Albert Harris and where he lives"

Sissy and Anne were stunned as they looked at the old frail piece of paper again.

BILLIE'S FARM

The boys pulled up in Eric's grandfather's truck. Hazel had packed a great lunch for the four of them. The boys acted like nothing had happened the day before, and they weren't going to bring up the snipe hunt unless the girls did. The boys knew where the picnic grounds and limestone pit was located. The boys and girls spread out the large blanket and folding chairs by an old willow tree. Dar and Tony sensed some tense feelings between them because Tony was leaving for New York in the morning.

Billie's phone rang. "What? What?" Billie screamed.

"What is it?" Dar asked seeing the tension on Billie's face.

"That's Lucy from 4-H. Her boyfriend Teddy called her and told he was going to kill himself over their breakup."

"Aw, he'll get over it." Tony said

"No, he apparently sounded desperate. They have been going together for five years. He told her his life wasn't worth living anymore, and he was going to the pit to end it."

"That's where we are, right?" Eric asked.

"Yes!" Dar screamed back.

"I heard someone talking over by that grove of willows trees." Tony said

The four jumped up and ran over a small ridge.

"Oh my God!" Billie shrieked, "There he is!"

The four looked at a large willow with a man hanging there.

"You girls stay here; Tony let's cut him down, and see if he is still alive."

They took off running as fast as they could go. The girls saw him cut down, and the boys were working on him.

"Is he alive?" Dar screamed.

The boys walked back slowly shaking their heads.

"He's gone," Eric said in a somber voice "We found this note attached to his pocket."

By now the girls were hysterical. Between the sobs and wailing, Dar opened the note.

It read, "I couldn't go on living, knowing that I couldn't catch a snipe."

It took it a few seconds for the girls to get it. The boys had already started to walk quickly away.

"You assholes!", as the girls chased them all over the picnic area with the boys making smooching sounds.

RICK AND ANNE'S FARM

Anne arrived home as Hazel and Tidy were leaving for a concert in Gas City. Rick was in the barn throwing away old boards and rusted metal. Anne came in, sat on a bale of hay, and stared at her handsome husband.

"Hi, Honey." The comment startled him

"Didn't see you come. Where have you been?"

"I went to Sissy's basement to look at the wall of articles and try to get an idea where all this might go, besides the garbage. I found a very interesting piece of paper half hidden on the wall. It has a man's name and address on it. The paper is very old, almost like parchment, and the writing is bold and beautiful. Sissy and I were looking at it, and Todd interrupted us and told us this guy was Albert Harris. His imaginary friend NeeNee wrote it for us and put it on the wall."

"That Todd sure has an active mind," Rick said with a laugh.

"You are going to think I'm crazy, but I called my office, had them look into this guy, and he does exist. His age even matches up with Albert's age by only three days."

"Don't tell me. Could this be Albert?"

"This is a real long shot. I've haven't been back to my office for a while because it's bugged."

"Why haven't you said something?"

"I didn't want to alarm any of the family. I've been making all phone calls from the phone booth in town. I called an old acquaintance for some help. He's going to physically meet this mysterious man and report back. Nobody knows of my contact, and I can't tell you his name yet. I warned him of danger, but he can handle himself."

"Where does this so called Albert live?"

"Alexandria, Virginia, I think we better not mention this to anyone in the family until we hear back from my source."

"What does Albert do.? "Is he retired?"

"Rick, he's a Catholic priest; not just a priest, but the highest ranking Catholic Cardinal in the US. This guy is powerful!"

MOM'S DINER

Today was slow, even the cook Chris and his wife Jenny sat at a table. Mom sat with them and watched the door for more customers. All six guys from the large, round table got up and poured coffee for the three employees.

"What are you guys up to?" Mom asked.

"Why do we have to be up to something when we want to wait on you three?" Marvin said.

"Because this not your normal routine."

"We do love you guys, and with all the grief we give you sometimes, it makes us feel bad. When Chris doesn't burn my hash browns just the way I like it, I send it back." Marvin said.

"That's not grief; that's just you guys," Chris said with a smile.

"Most of our wives aren't up at 5:30 A.M., so we descend upon you for our breakfast and advice for the day. We all do feel like family. Thanks for putting up with a bunch of old farmers, funeral directors, and insurance agents."

Mom started to tear up. "Damn you guys."

"Don't get too emotional; we won't do dishes or clean the toilets," Lester said.

"Speaking of that, Lester you have an anniversary on the tenth. Nancy would love something from Judee's Dress Shop, and I would suggest dark blue."

"Yes, Mom, and thanks," Lester said.

DAR'S FARM

It was only 7:00 A.M. as Tony pulled Eric's old truck into the barnyard. Tony was leaving at 10:00 A.M., and he had to tell Dar he loved her. It wouldn't come easy. He had rehearsed his speech off and on all night. Eric finally told him to just say what his heart told him.

"Hi, Tony," as Dar came out the back door.

"Hey, Dar," His stomach was feeling pretty weird.

"Come on in; I want you to meet my parents."

He came in the back door and her parents were sitting at the small kitchen table.

"Mom, Dad, this is Tony."

They both got up and embraced him like their own son.

"Please sit." Barb Moore said.

"Thank you."

"We need to thank you. We're not sure how your dad or his cousin in Cincinnati did what they did, but thank you. The law suit has hung over our heads, like a dark cloud, for the last six months. Our attorney told us to pray for a miracle, and then you showed up."

"My dad is definitely not miracle worker, but we do have many friends and family."

"We were on the brink of losing our farm and everything we worked so hard to get. We would like to do something for your father."

"You know, he loves sweet corn. I'll take some back for him if you like."

"We just picked some fresh, and we'll send a smoked ham also."

"He would like that."

They got up from the table, hugged him again, and scurried off to pack a nice gift.

Dar took Tony's hand and walked out in back of the barn.

"My parents are in love with you even though you could be a mass murderer."

"I am a killer. Could you ever fall in love with a guy like that?"

"You've already stabbed me in the heart. Tony Becko, why have you come from New York City to raise havoc with Dar Moore?"

"I can't answer that. I just know we will be together again. How in the hell can some farm girl from Gas City, Indiana, bewitch me like you have?"

"Tony, just give me one small kiss and go. I think it will be best."

He kissed her warm sweet mouth and turned toward the truck. On the seat was a box of corn and a huge smoked ham. He looked back but didn't see her as he pulled out on the county road. This was a strange goodbye for two people in love. Just then a dark black horse raced up to his driver's window. She blew him a kiss and took off her tee shirt.

"I love you, Tony Becko." and rode off into a field.

What a great sendoff! The mental picture of bare breasts bouncing as she rode her horse along the fence would be burned into his mind forever.

Anne's Office Gas City

Anne and Rick had rehearsed their speeches many times before entering the small office.

"You know, Rick, we've come to an end in the search for Albert."

"You're right. We have no clues, the trail has ended, and he's probably dead by now." Rick said.

"Let's close my office and the whole investigation."

"We have the office for three more months, but our pursuit of Albert has ended."

"Let's go to Mom's Diner, and I'll buy you a big breakfast."

"Sounds good," as they left the office.

They walked arm in arm down Elm Street. "Do you think the people that have been listening will buy the story?"

"I don't know, but I have some more information from my source in New York. After breakfast let's go to Sissy's and compare some new facts we now have." Anne said.

Eric's Farm

Tony came back with the old truck and a box full of goodies for his father.

"How'd it go at Dar's?" Eric asked.

"Good. We are both deeply connected to each other."

"In other words, you're pussy whipped." Eric said with a smile.

"If you want to put it that way, yes, I'm in love with her and her with me. I can't describe it or put it on paper, but we are crazy about each other. I know we're both young, but dammit, Eric, I don't think I can live without her."

"I feel the same about Billie. Why do you think I moved from New York City to Southern Indiana; it wasn't for fresh air. We have a bond that will never be broken, no matter where we end up. From the moment she pushed me to the ground, put a knife to my throat, and kissed me, I knew my life would never be the same."

"I asked Dar to come to New York over Christmas break. Maybe you could bring Billie and make it a foursome."

"That sounds fun. We could take them to Broadway and Times Square. I think this might be your ride; we don't have many limos pull into the farmyard."

"See you soon, Eric."

"Back at ya, Tony."

"Thank you so much for inviting me to Gas City. This trip has been a life changer for me; you are a good friend."

They hugged as the driver loaded the trunk with luggage and Indiana food.

"I'll keep an eye on Dar for you"

"I wouldn't expect anything different." "Thanks pal."

SISSY'S BEAUTY SHOP

Rick and Anne finished a big country breakfast at Mom's and waddled down the street to Sissy's.

"Morning, Sissy," they both said. "We need to go down to the basement for a few minutes."

"Go ahead; I'm expecting an appointment any minute now. If you need something, just yell."

They walked down the stairs, put a pot of coffee on and stared at the wall covered with paper.

"What more information do you have?" Rick asked.

"My source in New York texted me with some additional information. He got a copy of the surveillance video the day Harvey Adams died in his shower. He counted four hundred sixty-three people going through the lobby. He narrowed it down to a two hour window. There wasn't much to see except for two instances. You'll love this. One was a Catholic Priest, and the other was two men dressed in cleaning uniforms. He looked up the cleaning service name on the uniform, and it didn't match a single name in New York. They also were carrying briefcases."

"Wow! Do you think this Catholic connection could possibly exist?"

"I don't know. He also faxed me a copy of the Catholic cardinal's birth certificate; it showed he was born three days after Albert, but he was born in St. Augustine, Florida. As far as we know the cardinal never lived close to Indiana."

"Another dead end."

"Not necessarily. I have a plan to get an interview with the cardinal in Virginia. I think we can pull this off. My source is making us fake ID's, and we should get those in a few days. We better not tell anyone in the family what we are planning to do."

"You're right, but it does seem strange to go on a hunch from a yellowed piece of parchment paper stuck to our wall, supposedly written by an imaginary person."

"I know what you're saying; we are totally crazy, but I have a strong feeling about this one."

"Anne, I just hope we aren't taking on the whole Catholic Church."

"Me too; I haven't been to confession in twenty years."

Isaac Yoder Farm

Rick, Anne, Eric, and Hazel traveled five miles to the Yoder Farm for a dinner. The question all around the house was, what do you wear to an Amish dinner? They all decided simple was the best. They pulled up to the farm and Isaac, Sarah, their six sons and three daughters came to the truck to greet them. The Yoder farm was neat and clean; there was no clutter of any kind. They all walked into the modest home.

"Please, sit on the porch until the women have the meal prepared. We are so glad to have you in our humble home," Jacob said as he stroked his long grey beard.

"We are very happy for the invitation to your home. Anne and I can't get over what a fine job you did on our house."

"We are happy you are pleased. Our family feels a calling from God to do what we do. We never question what God has planned for us each day."

Anne noticed there were no pictures hanging on the walls, but a colorful calendar hanging in each room, including the porch. There was no carpeting, televisions, radios, computers or anything with electricity involved. She had a very pleasant feeling in their home.

"Dinner is being served," Esther, the oldest daughter, announced.

They went into the large dining room with eighteen chairs around the long table. Isaac pointed to the chairs where the four would sit. The boys all sat and put their hands in their laps. Even the two year old copied his older brothers. Sarah and the three daughters came out with platters of pork, potatoes, green beans and squash. Everything was handed to Isaac and he passed the platters to his left where the Barr Family and Hazel were seated. After each plate was filled, Jacob bowed his head.

"Thank you God for this bounty. We are not worthy to eat the scraps that fall to the floor, but acknowledge that we are your sons and daughters. Bless this food in the precious name of Jesus."

The young boys ate immediately like this could be the last meal. Conversations were flying all around the table. It was such a simple life, but it must have been rewarding to know their hard work and lack of worldly goods pleased God, Hazel thought.

"We so enjoyed Eric and his friend Tony being around your home, and we can't forget Hazel for bring us water and lemonade when we really needed it," Jacob said with a smile.

"I know this may sound crass, but how do you do all this with no electricity or motorized equipment?" Rick asked.

Mr. Yoder started to laugh. "I've been asked this question many times in my life. My answer is God provides for each and every task we do. We are completely debt free. We never pay for anything unless we have the money to do it. I don't know if you are familiar with any scriptures in the Bible, but it says "God feeds the sparrows and clothes the flowers of the field. He even knows when a sparrow falls to the ground;" that makes us very important in God's eyes. He watches over us each moment of our lives. We don't need much; he provides."

It was starting to get dark as the meal ended; the girls got up to light the kerosene lanterns. The glow through the home gave it a soft mellow texture. The meal finished with warm pecan pie. They walked out to their truck with the Yoder family following. Each child again shook their hands in order of age. Even the two year old knew exactly when to extend his small arm.

"It's been a blessing to have you in our home. Please know our family prays for your family each day," Isaac said as he extended his hand.

"We appreciate that, and thanks for a wonderful meal and fellowship." Rick said

As they drove off, the Yoder family stood completely still until the Barr truck reached the county road.

"I really enjoyed myself," Hazel said

"I did too, and I guess we really don't need all the stuff we possess," Anne said.

Rick laughed, "When we get home I'm going to turn the power off to the house."

At that they all started to punch Rick and laugh.

Trip to Alexandria, Virginia

Rick's truck was loaded for the trip out East. Anne had packed several changes of clothing not knowing what to expect when they arrived. On the trip out, they would formulate a plan of attack. They had fake ID's, forged letters of their names with intent, and a cross supposedly from the 16th century blessed by an ancient Roman Catholic Pope they purchased on the internet. They both knew this could be a dangerous trip or a complete farce. They were prepared for both.

"This will be our last attempt at finding Albert," Rick said.

"I know. We are going completely out on a limb with this trip."

"Our only evidence is the note from Todd's imaginary friend written on parchment paper."

"This is crazy, but I got some real vibes on this one," Anne said with a smile.

"I hated to lie to our family, but this secret must stay with us for now until we know for sure what we're up against."

"Eric seemed curious about our supposed trip to North Carolina, but I told him we would be back in a week and take he and Billie to dinner at Hugo's Frog Bar in Evansville."

"I've never met an Archbishop or Cardinal before, but we do have an appointment to see Archbishop Grey on Thursday. Michael Grey has been written up in many national magazines on his stance of same sex marriages. Billy Graham and he have been to the White House more times than George Washington. Msgr. Grey played football at Notre Dame and has written over sixty books on faith. I just hope this meeting goes well, and in the back of my mind I don't want him to be Albert Harris."

"Me neither, Rick; I just want this to be the final curtain call."

Rick and Anne's Farm

Eric, Billie, Dick, and Jane all sat on the big, newly remodeled porch. Dick was sound asleep next to Eric, but Jane, next to Billie, was listening to some rustling in the grass. This could be a mouse.

"I already miss Tony, and Dar is beside herself."

"I miss Tony, too; we've been best friends since third grade."

"Is his dad really in the Mafia?" Billie asked with wide eyes.

"I'm pretty sure, but even Tony isn't positive. His dad goes to work each day and comes home at 6:00 P.M. to have dinner with the family. I'm not sure who said this dad was in dry cleaning but it seems to work when Tony's asked."

"Do they live in a nice home?"

"Not a home-a mansion. They have an armed guard with a dog stationed at the main gate of their home."

"Apparently dry cleaning is a dangerous business," Billie said with a laugh.

"Well, Tony's one phone call to his father took care of the problem with Dar's parents. That has to tell us something."

"Dar is totally in love with Tony, not because of what he did for her family, but from her heart. She would be in love with him even if he lived on the street."

"What about me?" Eric asked with pouting lips.

"If you lived on the street, I would let you stay in our barn with Star Fire my favorite horse. I might even bring you some leftovers from our evening meal."

"That's what I like about Billie; such great compassion for the underdog."

"Come here you goofball; I need some sugar."

"Let's go for a walk in the pear orchard. I might find some fruit I want to squeeze."

"You're funny, Eric Barr; the only thing you might be squeezing will be your own ass," as she gave him a warm, wet, soft kiss on his lips.

"Billie Magic, you're a piece of work," and took her hand for the walk.

Jane decided to go also; they might scare up a mouse or chipmunk, but Dick never opened an eye.

Tidy Tucker's Farm

Tidy and Hazel sat on the small porch drinking lemonade. They hadn't talked much since Hazel's wonderful Danish inspired dinner.

"I got my passport today," Tidy said with excitement.

"Great! You should probably get a credit card for the trip."

"Hazel, are you a little scared?"

"I am, Terrance; I have never been with a man, let alone traveled to a foreign country with him. Why do you ask?"

"I'm afraid too. I don't want to be a disappointment to you."

"That's the reason you're afraid?"

"Yes."

"Terrance, I thought you were afraid of traveling and being on an airplane. I didn't know you were concerned about my emotions. I can tell you right now, we are going to have the best trip that has ever been taken. Terrance, you are my heartbeat; Denmark will be fabulous because I am traveling with my soul mate. I can't wait to show you the little mermaid in the harbor."

"Hazel, I will have a good time. I've never been out of the state of Indiana except for a couple of trips to Kentucky. I'm pumped and excited about traveling with the most beautiful Danish girl in the world."

"You sure know how to complement a girl."

"Don't consider it a compliment; it's the truth, Hazel."

She reached over and held his hand.

"Darn you, Terrance Tucker; where in the heck have you been hiding all these years?"

THE CATHOLIC ARCHBISHOP'S CHURCH, ALEXANDRIA, VIRGINIA

Rick and Anne arrived about 4:00 P.M; The Washington, D.C., Beltway was bumper to bumper. They checked into Lincoln Arms Hotel; it wasn't very nice but definitely under the radar of curious eyes. The room was clean and within walking distance of the major attractions Washington had to offer. They had a nice dinner and took a cab to the Cardinal's church where he was serving.

"This is one big church," Rick said with a smile.

"Let's go in. The sign says mass at 7:00 PM. Just maybe Archbishop Grey will be there."

They walked in as the Mass began. There were only about thirty people attending but the church had seats for well over a thousand. The gold, paintings, and statues were magnificent. They had both had been to the Sistine Chapel, and this church was right up there in beauty. The priest doing the Mass was about twenty-five and seemed a little nervous. They only stayed for a few minutes, walked to the back of the church, picked up a brochure, and walked outside.

"Look Rick, here's a picture of Cardinal Grey."

They both looked intently at the picture of the eighty-three year old Archbishop, hoping to see Albert Harris in his face. The last picture of Albert was when he was nine years old. It listed all he had done for the Catholic Church, and it was extensive. They hailed a cab and were dropped off in front of the Lincoln Memorial. As they stepped from the cab, their breath seemed to be taken from them. The lights on the statue of Abraham Lincoln had just come on, and they stood in awe. They both had seen Lincoln before, but for some reason they were mesmerized. He seemed to be looking down at them with some sort of approval. They sat on the steps and poured over the brochure.

Anne spoke, "It says here, he is an Archbishop and Cardinal. His diocese has jurisdiction over all the U.S. Military branches, and is highest ranking Catholic official in the United States. The College of Cardinals and he elect the Pope each time and he has a home in Rome. The Cardinals are in charge of the day to day running of the church, and the word Pope means Papa in Latin."

"If Abraham Lincoln wasn't sitting directly behind us, I would just give this whole thing up." Rick said

"I too felt some inspiring power when we stepped from the cab. Rick, we have to follow through even though we could be taking on a very powerful person."

"We do. You're right. Let's go back to the hotel and rehearse again."

SALES AND SON FUNERAL HOME

Bill and Wyatt finished sweeping the funeral home and locking the doors. Bill loosened his tie and patted Wyatt on the back.

"You did a great job tonight with the Bailey Family. They were having a tough time, but you stepped up to the plate. I can't teach you to be compassionate; it has to come from your heart. When you hugged Mrs. Bailey, I could tell it wasn't just a kind gesture but heartfelt. She knew it too. If you still want to work here with me, I would feel honored."

"Dad, I have watched you all my life; you are a man of integrity and honesty, and I hope I can fill the big shoes you have set before me."

He hugged Wyatt with all he was worth.

"You just paid me the highest compliment I've ever received," as Bill began to tear up.

"Does that mean I can have the car tomorrow night to take Susie to a concert in Evansville?"

"Yes, Wyatt, but you can also be a pain in the butt," Bill said with a smile.

Bill went upstairs, changed into jeans and a Chicago Cubs jersey, and told the kids he was walking down to Polly Taylor's house to sit on her porch. They just rolled their eyes.

"Hi, Polly," as Bill walked around back.

"Hi, Bill, come on in."

Polly had a bottle of wine and some snacks waiting for him

"Tough day today?" Polly asked.

"No, not too bad, but Wyatt gave me a huge compliment, and I'm still reeling from that. I was thinking, would you like to go to Mackinaw Island in Michigan with me this fall? I understand the colors are breathtaking. I also know the town will talk about us, but I've been alone for seven years. I want to travel; I don't want to go by myself."

"Bill, I'd love to go. My kids live far away, and I don't care what people say; I've never been to upper Michigan, and I have a sister that lives in Irons, Michigan. Maybe we can stop and see her new home on the way up. She lives on a small lake."

"Let's go next month," Bill said.

"I have time coming from the state highway, and I'll let them know Monday."

"Great." He hoped this was a good move because he was still thinking about what Lester had told him about her shoe fetish. Bill thought, if she brings more than twenty-five pair of shoes or sandals, this relationship may not work.

Alexandria, Virginia

Rick and Anne took a cab because they didn't want their license plate checked. The home was immense; it was brick and appeared to be very old. The cab dropped them and they walked the long winding brick walkway to the home. They were met by a security guard and a mean looking dog.

"What's your nature?"

"We have an appointment to see the Archbishop. Our names are Homer and Betty Grant; we are here with the Catholic Digest for an interview."

"Go on in, and the receptionist will give you directions," as he looked at his clipboard.

The massive oak door opened automatically. They stepped into a huge entranceway decorated with gold and silver objects. It looked like something from a movie set.

"Step here, please," the young priest said.

"We are Homer and Betty Grant."

"I know who you are; I need to see some identification," he said sharply.

They produced the fake ID's and photos for the man. He looked at them very carefully and asked for the letters of reference. Anne reached into her briefcase and handed him a file. He again read every word and would occasionally look up at them.

"Go into the room on your right; someone will be in shortly." He said abruptly.

Rick and Anne went into the large room and sat on two chairs facing each other. They knew not to speak because their words would probably be recorded. The large door opened; two different priests walked in and stood next to each of them.

The older priest said, "You only have thirty minutes for your interview. You may not take any recording devises or cameras in. Leave your cell phones here on the desk along with the briefcase. You must remove your shoes, and we are going to give you a full body scan in the next room. If you are not comfortable with the rules, the interview will not take place."

"We are fine with the rules." Anne remarked

"Then step through that door and leave your things here. You may take pens and two pads of paper."

They walked through another oak door into a smaller room with electric gadgets everywhere. There were two different priests standing as they came into the room. An electric wand was passed over them as they stood without shoes. They walked over to the scanner and stepped in; apparently it was ok because they were asked to sit. Rick thought there is more security here than at most airports in the world.

An older priest stepped in. "The Archbishop will see you now."

He led them down the long hall to two very large oak double doors. A priest was sitting next to the doors. "They may go in now."

The young priest nodded and rose. Rick noticed he was carrying a gun half concealed under his robe.

The electronic doors slowly opened; they looked, and at the end of the very long room sat an elderly gentleman behind a massive desk. Rick took Anne's sweaty hand as they slowly walked to the two overstuffed chairs positioned in front of his desk.

MARY BARR FARM

Mary became dizzy and had to sit down. Her doctor said this would happen and progress into migraine headaches and blurred vision. Today wasn't a good day. Her eyesight was failing which made her afraid to drive. The tumor was slow growing but now was pushing on vital nerves and blood vessels. He told her she wouldn't live to see Christmas-only three months away. She called Mabel from the diner.

"Mom, this is Mary."

"How are you feeling, Mary?" Mom asked with concern in her voice.

"Not too good today. I just wanted to ask if you received my papers on making you my medical power of attorney."

"I got the paper work yesterday. Mary, you have to tell your kids."

"I can't yet; they will make a fuss, send me to Mayo Clinic, and hang all over me. I can trust you not to say anything and carry out my wishes as specified."

"Of course I'll do this for you, but the kids should know."

"I don't want to be kept alive under any circumstances. I have a date with two fine gentlemen that have gone before me. I loved them both, so when I get to heaven, I'll have to choose which one will be first," she said with a chuckle in her voice.

"I'll make you a deal. I open the restaurant at 5:00 A.M. every day. You have to call me by 5:15, or I will come to the house or send the volunteer fire department."

"It's a deal. I knew I could rely on you to be in my corner. I just can't trust my kids to follow through with my demands. They mean well, but are too close to the situation."

"Stop down to the diner this week, and we'll have coffee in the back."

"Love to. Bye."

Albert Harris

Archbishop Michael Grey came from behind the desk and shook their hands. He was wearing khaki pants and a golf shirt. Rick and Anne were surprised to see the highest ranking Catholic official in the U.S. so casual. He was spry; he sat on the edge of his desk and removed his glasses.

"You two don't have to be nervous; this is just an interview for the magazine right?"

"Yes," Anne said, we want to talk to you about some stances you've stated in the Catholic Digest."

"Your editor James Keene and I went to Notre Dame together. How is he?

"He's fine and sends his regards." Rick said

"How are Rick and Anne Barr?" the Cardinal asked.

"Pardon?" Anne asked.

"I know who you are. James Keene never worked for the magazine; he was executed five years ago in Texas for murder. What do you want from me?"

"We believe you to be Albert Harris."

"Who is Albert Harris, and what proof do you have I'm that person?"

Anne reached into the small notebook she was allowed to bring in and handed him the little yellowed parchment paper with his name on it.

"Shit! You've got to be kidding!" as he jumped to his feet.

He bolted the large oak door and walked quickly to his desk.

"I don't want to be disturbed under any circumstances!" he yelled on the phone.

"Where did you get this note?" he yelled again

"We also have DNA proof."

"Shut up!" He yelled, "I asked, where did the note come from?"

Rick saw the archbishop's eyes were red and completely fixated on the small piece of paper.

"First we need an answer; are you Albert Harris?" Anne asked meekly.

"I am Albert Harris, but his information will never leave this room."

Anne clicked her pen to write on her tablet.

"No need for that; the papers will be taken as you leave the room. I now will speak to you frankly and expect feedback. I will give you one hour; at 2:00 P.M. I have a meeting that demands my immediate presence."

"The note came from my mentally challenged nephew's imaginary friend," Rick said with a laugh.

"What's his name?"

"He calls him NeeNee."

"Did he ever refer to him as Ray?"

"Not that we know of."

"His imaginary friend was also my friend. I called him Ray, but his full name is Rayneelandersonne, and he saved my life. How did you come by the note?"

"It was pinned on a bulletin board in the basement of a beauty shop in Gas City."

"Damn, he's still there!" the Archbishop said, "I have spent hundreds of thousands of dollars trying to find him. Apparently you haven't met Ray or NeeNee; is that right?"

"We never knew him to be real." Anne said

"Oh, he's real all right!"

"Who is he?"

"He's a magical elf. I don't expect you to believe me, but it is true. He comes to people in need, especially the ones that believe in him."

"Why have you never wanted to be Albert Harris?"

"I'm going to give you the short version. What I'm about to tell you, no one except Ray and a priest know. For the last seventy-four years, I have been Michael Grey."

Tim and Pamela Sue's Farm

"I don't think your mom looks well," Pamela Sue said

"Why do you say that?"

"She nodded off in church and didn't want to go to the Farm Bureau Ladies Auxiliary dinner on Friday; that's not like your mom."

"She could be just tired."

"No, it's more than that, as if she was just giving up. I have beef stew on the stove; I'll call her to come to dinner. She loves my beef stew."

Fifty minutes later Mary, Tim, Pamela Sue, Moses and Rahab were sitting around the table.

"Mom, are you feeling well?" Tim asked.

"Why would you think that? Of course I'm fine."

"Pamela Sue noticed you sleeping in church and not going to the auxiliary dinner."

"I guess a little tired. Moses sleeps through church every week, so I guess I'm in good company," she said with a smile and reached across the table for a Moses fist pump.

"Ok mom, but if you need anything, we are all here to help."

"Thanks kids and you can start helping by passing the stew," she said with a slight grin.

Albert's Confession

The Archbishop had now pulled up a stuffed chair across from Rick and Anne and crossed his legs.

"I was sent to camp at nine and was looking for some relief. My parents were from Evansville and had lots of money and influence. I was an only child and completely spoiled. My dad's brother, Charlie lived with us for two years. From the day he moved in I was raped or molested almost every day. I tried to tell my parents, but they laughed it off. Mind you this was from 1935-1937. There were no agencies or anyone to hear my pleas; it just went on and on." He reached inside his pants and retrieved a handkerchief.

"What happened at the camp?" Anne asked.

"I loved the camp director, Doc. He took me under his wing and became a father figure to me. We had a new scout come into our cabin; he had it in for me. He pushed me down, spat on me, and made me the blunt of every joke. I just ran away. I ran into the woods after campfire; I thought about killing myself. Then Ray showed up. Can you imagine at nine wandering around in the dark and then meeting a three foot elf that took you to his small cabin the woods. We talked all night, and I told him everything about my uncle and the other scout."

"What did you do, and how did you end up here?"

"When I awoke the next day, it was late afternoon. I thought maybe everything was a dream, except the tiny cabin had miniature furniture, almost like a doll house. I went back to the camp at early evening; there were police cars and fire trucks everywhere. They were on a man hunt for me. I hid in the camp kitchen until dark. Every so often I would get food from the refrigerator. I quietly snuck back to our cabin and softly tapped on the window screen where my nemesis slept. I whispered to him and he came out. I told him I had found treasure by the pond, and he followed me wading into the shallow water. I hit him with a rock and held him under water until there was no movement. I looked up, and Doc was standing next to the shore. He smiled and motioned me to go. I ran into the woods not knowing where the small cabin was. Ray met me, and we walked together to the cabin, but his time the same cabin was next to a small stream. He told me it was a magical cabin and could be moved anywhere in the world."

The cardinal poured himself a glass of water from a beautiful cut glass pitcher on his desk. He offered one to his guests, but Rick and Anne refused.

"This story is really hard for me to understand, especially the elf," Anne said.

"I'm not asking you to believe me; I'm just telling you my gut story. Rayneelandersonne is originally from Norway and has a sister living around London. I don't know if he is considered an elf, fairy, troll, or leprechaun; these are just words we have associated with a type of people."

"We know you have a birth certificate from St. Augustine, Florida; how did that happen?"

"Ray took me to a family in Mill Creek, Indiana. He knew they were childless and desired a family. He wrote a note explaining my situation and that I could never go back to my own parents. They took me in with such love, like I had never seen. My new father, Michael Grey, took me and my new mom, Greta, to St. Augustine where he had grown up. His family was very wealthy, so a new birth certificate in 1937 was easy to obtain. My new parents were devout Catholics, and since my first Catholic mass, I felt at home. God had a place and a purpose for me, and I felt truly loved. This is how I'm here."

"Did you ever want to see your birth parents again?"

"I did want to, but my new family and the church fulfilled my every desire. I went back to Evansville to my mom's funeral, and at fifty-eight no one was the wiser. I even attended your father's burial five months ago."

"My father?"

"Yes, and it rained at the cemetery."

"Did you have people killed to protect your identity?" Anne asked sternly

"There are a group of priests assigned to me to take care of any need I have. It's a secret society that has protected Cardinals for hundreds of years. I never authorized any killings, but they knew I must be sheltered in every aspect of my life. If you ever tried to repeat this story, they will come after you. There is no place to hide from their power."

"Why have you been looking for Ray all this time?"

"I had dreamed of becoming Pope someday, and Ray could have made it possible with his magic and miracles. I could have healed people and performed wonders that would have ushered me in as Pope. I'm too old now; I can't become Pope at eighty-three."

"Even if we told this story; no one would believe it." Anne said

"If you can find Ray or NeeNee, like your nephew calls him; they would believe you."

"How old is Ray?" Rick asked.

"He told me he was taken from his family in Norway around 1670 and brought to America."

"What? You mean he's over three hundred fifty years old?"

"That's what he told me. His grandfather and father traveled with the Vikings as good luck charms and visionaries."

"No one will ever believe any of this. I'm having my own doubts," Rick said.

"It's almost 2:00 P.M. and I have to go. I only ask three favors from you as he reached into his desk. I have made an exit strategy for myself. On this first small piece of paper I have written the name of a man that died twenty years ago. If you want to pursue the reward for Albert Harris; his name is written here with his place of burial. His DNA is all over my old room in the Evansville mansion and will match Albert Harris. If you desire; this will give you the new Albert. I had my old hat destroyed by the lab in New York. My DNA will not match anything. This is your way out. Also, if you pursue me as Albert Harris; you and your family will be destroyed."

"Secondly, please give this note to Ray for me. You won't understand it, but he will; this is very important. He must receive this note. Thirdly, give this note to my son. No one knows I fathered him including him. He needs to know who his father and mother are. He will inherit a fortune from my estate. I just hope he won't resent me. Rick, put these notes in your socks or if found they will be taken from you."

"We will do what you want, but why don't you make peace with all this?"

"I have made peace with God, not by going to confession and admitting the murders, infidelities, lies, and deceptions, but on my knees: just between God and Albert Harris."

He sat behind his desk and smiled at Rick and Anne with a calmness they hadn't seen for the last hour. They never saw it coming; the gun went off with a loud bang. They jump completely out of their seats and noticed the blood and brain matter spattered all over the red velvet curtains behind his desk. They both panicked as hands were ponding loudly on the large oak door. Rick quickly put the notes in the bottom of his socks; unbolted the door, and stood aside. Eight priests ran into the room to the desk. The young priest with the gun grabbed Rick's arm and escorted them to the room with the scanner.

"Sit!" he commanded "We'll be back in a minute."

Rick and Anne sat across from each other in complete bewilderment; their ears still ringing from the blast. The door hurriedly opened a man dressed in a dark blue suit stood looking at them.

"What the hell happened?" he shouted.

"We were interviewing the Archbishop for our magazine, and he pulled out a gun with no warning." Rick said hastily.

"What did you say to him?"

"Nothing, and by the way, who are you?" Anne asked

"I'm the medical examiner for the District of Columbia. Michael was a personal friend of mine. You two had to provoke him."

"We said nothing; just listened to his opinions on many different subjects," Anne said nervously.

"Why then were there no notes taken. Your notepads are completely empty and you have no recorders."

"He asked us just to listen and observe," Rick said.

"This doesn't make any sense to me. Did he mention to you about any illnesses he has?

"No not at all. I told you we were here to listen and ask questions."

Two priests came in and stated they would have to go through the body scans again. The medical examiner told them to collect their shoes, personal effects, and purse in the next room. They were sternly told not to mention any of this to anyone, including their own families. They both were still under investigation; charges could still be brought against them if any information should leak out.

GETTING OUT OF DC

They left the building and hailed a cab. Rick started to say something and Anne stopped him in mid-sentence. They arrived at the hotel; their door was wide open with clothes and bedding strewn all over. Rick went to get the manager and noticed his truck door ajar.

He looked in, and the seats had been torn open. The manager's only comment was to the fact, this wasn't a good neighborhood, and they wouldn't be getting back the security deposit. They quickly got into the truck and headed west.

They got out of Washington and found a car dealership just off the expressway. With a little haggling, and a credit card, they were now driving a new Dodge pickup.

"Rick, we have to go back into Washington for a short time."

"You got to be crazy."

"I know what I'm doing; here's the address of the pizza place."

"Pizza! Why in the hell do you want a pizza now? I'm a bundle of nerves."

"It won't take long; then I will explain."

They pulled up to Big Jim's Pizza.

"I'll be right out." She said

Five minutes later she came out carrying two large pizzas.

"Will you please tell me what that was all about?"

She laid the first box on the seat behind her and the second box she opened to Rick's amazement. It had a small disc and chip taped to the inside.

"At least I know this truck isn't bugged. We can talk freely," She said.

"Freely about what?" "My mind doesn't comprehend anything right now."

"This pizza box contains the complete confession of Albert Harris, with photos. I hired this ex con to tape the whole thing from his service truck parked outside the Archbishop's home. It's all here."

"Where did the photos come from?"

"All I had to do was click my pen, and it not only took his picture, but transmitted the conversation to the van out front. The pizza place was setup before because I knew our room would be turned upside down."

"Why didn't you tell about this before?"

"I thought if something would happen to one of us, the other would be contacted by my source."

"We have a big decision to make. We can expose Albert Harris and possibly be killed for telling the truth, or we can use this other name in my sock and claim all the money with the mansion."

"Rick, I don't know about you, but I'm hungry, and the second box has cheese and sausage" Anne said with a smile.

NOT QUITE THE END

PART THREE CONNECTING THE DOTS

PART THREE

Rick and Anne's Farm Gas City, Indiana

Rick and Anne were glued to the television and internet. Five days prior they witnessed the highest ranking Catholic official in the U.S. blow his brains all over the curtains in his office, and yet not a thing was posted in the news. They went online to get the Washington Post Newspaper, hoping something would be mentioned.

"I don't get it," Rick said.

"Why wouldn't there be any news about the Cardinal's suicide?" as she gave Rick a blank stare.

"You know, Anne, there may be a conspiracy involved; we were rushed out his office like a herd of cattle."

Eric was at Billie's farm. Hazel was at Tidy's farm, and Rick and Anne sat with Dick and Jane watching the evening news. A news flash appeared across the bottom of the screen. It stated, *"Cardinal Michael Grey passed away suddenly today from a massive heart attack. He was taken to Mercy Hospital in Washington, D.C., but he couldn't be revived. More news to follow at 10:00 P.M."*

"Heart attack? You got to be kidding!" Anne said.

"So that's how they're going to play it. I'll bet we've been erased from our interview and meeting with the Archbishop; no one will ever know we went to Washington, and I'll even bet the hotel has no record of us."

"Rick, we could come forward with our secret information, but we better make sure all our ducks are in a perfect row. The info is hidden in our loving place; no one must ever know where it is."

"I have to stay up for the news tonight. If you need to go to bed, I'll fill you in when you get up."

"Oh no, I'm going to be up and analyze every statement they make to the press. I want the Washington D.C. Medical Examiner to state publically what happened to the Archbishop."

"You know it's going to be some snow job because he told us himself; he was a good friend of Cardinal Grey. I'll bet we are only a handful of people that really know what happened, and we are the only people who witnessed his death."

Rick went to the kitchen and made a batch of popcorn, and they were now ready for the big show to start. As he began the news report, the newscaster flashed a photo of Cardinal Grey. He reported that the Archbishop had been in good health and read Mass at a small church in Italy two weeks prior to visiting the Pope. A video flashed on the screen interviewing his personal doctor.

"Holy crap!" Rick shouted, "He was the guy that interrogated us posing as the medical examiner."

"You're right. I did wonder how the District of Columbia Medical Examiner could get to the Archbishop's home in fifteen minutes, and we never did ask for any identification."

The news went on to say how saddened our country was, loosing such a fine moral and civic leader. Next the president gave his condolences and mentioned the two were best friends.

"Best friends? You know if we come forward, we'll also take on the U.S. Government."

"Great!" as Rick turned off the television. "We are literally sitting on a powder keg of information."

Mom's Diner 5:15 AM

Mom looked at the diner clock and realized Mary Barr hadn't called like she promised. Mary had been faithful to call each morning to check in ever since Mom gave her an ultimatum.

"Darn her!" Mom said to herself. "I'll wait ten more minutes."

The diner was filling up with the farmers and Gas City early birds.

"Chris, Jenny, can you run the restaurant for a little bit? I have an errand to run."

"Sure, Mom," Chris said, "and we are running low on toilet paper in the women's room."

"I'll get some on my way back."

Mom didn't expect anything unusual as she drove to Mary's house. Mary's brain tumor was slow growing, and the doctor told her she probably had months to live. Mom pulled into the farm yard and did notice Mary hadn't put her laundry out to dry.

"Mary, Mary, it's Mom," as she walked through the kitchen door.

The house seemed quiet and peaceful as Mom walked into the living room. Mary was sitting in her old recliner.

"Why didn't you call me? And do you want me to fix you some breakfast?"

Mary had her eyes closed, and Mom touched her gently. She now knew; Mary had died in her chair with needle work in her hands.

"Oh, Mary," Mom sighed.

Mom called Tim and Pamela Sue; they were in complete shock. She then called Dr. Ben, and he told her he would stop over after he finished his toast and cereal. Mom sat opposite Mary and stared at the peaceful look and position of her friend. She heard a pickup truck come racing into the barnyard, and then running feet.

"What happened?" Tim shouted as he bent next to her chair.

"She must have gone peacefully in her sleep last night," Mom reassured him.

"We don't understand," Pamela Sue cried out, "she's never been sick a day in her life."

"That's not completely true," Mom said in a whisper.

"What do you mean?" Tim asked as he sobbed.

"Here comes Dr. Ben; he can explain everything."

Dr. Ben was an old country doctor. He still made house calls, and occasionally would give someone's pet a shot or bandage a horse's ankle. He nodded to everyone as he came into the living room.

"Gosh darn you, Mary; I'm going to miss you and especially your southern fried chicken smothered in that fantastic gravy," as he kissed her on the forehead.

"Ben, what's this all about?" Tim asked.

"Your mother had an inoperable brain tumor, but I had to promise never to tell anyone of her illness."

"How long has she had this?" Pamela Sue questioned.

"About six months. It was slow growing, and we thought she would make it well past Christmas."

"Mom, how come you're here?" Tim asked.

"She told me never to tell anyone because I had her medical power of attorney so no medical heroics would take place. She thought Rick, Sissy or you would make her go to a hospital and extend her life. You know your mother; that's not her style. No fuss. No muss."

Just then Sissy and Todd came in the room. Sissy threw herself on her mother's lap and wept. Rick and Anne stepped in the room and stared at their peaceful mother sitting in her old chair. Tim embraced Rick and Anne as he continued to cry. Rick now was weeping softly. Dr. Ben told them he was so sorry for their loss and would call Bill and Wyatt at the funeral home when he left. They all nodded in agreement.

"How could this happen?" Sissy said as she wiped her eyes.

Tim explained to them about her tumor and that no one except Dr. Ben and Mom knew.

"Not exactly." Mom said, "She told me last week about telling a relative from South America. Mary also told me about having a date in heaven with the two men she loved; your father and another guy whose name was not mentioned. I wanted to tell you, but she wouldn't hear of it. Your mother called me every morning at 5:15 A.M., and if I didn't get the call, I was supposed to come here or call the volunteer fire department. I'm so happy to have come out here this morning. She left a large envelope for you kids, but its back at the diner. I'll dig it out later today."

"I can't believe we've lost both our parents in less than a year," Sissy said.

"I'm going back to the diner; if you need anything, just call." Mom hugged everyone in the home and kissed Mary on top of her head.

"Can we get something to eat?" Todd yelled "I'm hungry, and my mom didn't feed me yet."

They all chuckled as Rick said, "You know; Todd always seems to put everything in perspective. Pamela Sue, can you and fix us something while we wait for the funeral home guys?"

"Sure, why not; just don't ask for her famous pancakes. I'll never master that."

SALES AND SON FUNERAL HOME

Bill and Wyatt placed Mary Barr on the embalming table and immediately began to wash the body with a disinfectant soap. Bill started to cry.

"What's the matter, Dad?"

"Mary and I have been friends for many years, and after your mother died, Mary brought us dinners and cleaned our house every Saturday for a year. She wouldn't take a penny for it and told me to give a discount on her funeral. She truly had a servant's heart, if she saw a need in anyone."

"What time is the Barr Family coming in?"

"They'll be here at 1:00 P.M. with her clothes and jewelry. Wyatt, be sure and put on a pot of coffee for them."

1:00 P.M. came quickly for Bill and Wyatt as their front door opened, and the complete Barr Family walked in. Wyatt took them to the arrangement office and offered coffee. Bill came in and hugged each one except Todd; he was playing some video game on his device.

"Again, I'm so sorry for your loss, but as you know she had everything arranged right down to the finest detail." Bill said with a soft smile.

"She did?" Sissy asked. "I didn't know anything about this." as the whole table shook their heads in disbelief.

"Right after your dad died, she made an appointment and came in."

"Can we see the paper?" Rick asked

"I made additional copies, so look it over if we need any changes."

"It looks like the arrangements are similar to our dad's funeral." Tim said.

"I think she wanted the same service at the Faith Baptist Church," Bill remarked.

"I see your Dommy wants you to sing at her funeral," Pamela Sue said as she looked at Rahab.

"I'll do it, but it's going to be tough. What does she want me to sing?"

"Somewhere Over The Rainbow."

Rahab laughed "I'm just happy it wasn't "Stairway To Heaven"

"We should probably head over to the diner to pick up the packet that mom left us. Our mom might have put more information about the funeral or wishes. Thanks Bill; you've a great friend to our family for many years," Tim said.

"I should be thanking you for sharing your mom and dad with our whole community. Call me if you have questions; I'll run the obituary in tomorrow's paper with the funeral on Saturday at 11:00 A.M."

ALEXANDRIA, VIRGINIA

The preparations for the public wake and funeral mass for Archbishop Cardinal Michael Allen Grey had been finalized by the Catholic Church. His body was to be laid out at the Capital Building in Washington D.C. for two days, then flown to Rome for a Mass in St. Peter's Church, with burial to follow in the tombs under the church reserved for high ranking church officials. The wake and funeral were to be televised from beginning to end. If ever Rick and Anne Barr were to make a move and expose the Cardinal as Albert Harris, they now would have to make their play. In a few days the possibility of pulling this off would be minimal. They also had to bury Rick's mom and stand by his brother and sister through her funeral.

"What do we do?" Rick asked his wife.

"Maybe we should let Albert Harris be buried in Rome and forget the whole thing."

"My only dilemma is that Albert Harris or Michael Grey literally got away with murder."

"I know honey; we are the only people that can prove and expose the truth. If we do this, we will be pursued and probably killed by the cardinal's guard. Our whole family will be at risk, and we will take on the President of the United States. This is no small task. I feel sick to my stomach."

"I have a connection at the New York Times; I could call him and give just a taste of this information. Maybe he could publish this without using names."

"The Cardinal's entourage would certainly know. Maybe we should talk to Todd and find out about his friend NeeNee. The cardinal was certainly energized when the name was mentioned, and we do have a note to give to him anyway."

"If this NeeNee does exist, this story will blow the cardinal's confession out of the water. Just think, we discover a magical elf and tell the world a supernatural being is living in Gas City, Indiana. Every person living on the planet would come to us."

"Rick, wise up! We need to take care of our own business first."

SISSY'S BEAUTY SHOP

Rick, Anne, Eric, Tim, Pamela Sue, Moses, Rahab and Sissy gathered in Sissy's basement to take down the wall of Albert Harris information. Todd was up stairs watching a western.

"We'll, I guess this is the end of Albert Harris," Tim said.

"Yeah, we followed every lead that we had. He probably died many years ago," Rick said.

"Darn, I wanted the money and the fame for finding him."

"Son, we can't have everything we wish for. We have plenty to do around the farm," Pamela Sue said in a mellow tone.

"I know, but to find him would be the pot at the end of the rainbow."

"I have the packet that Mom at the diner gave me, and each one of us has a sealed letter from our mother and grandmother." Tim said.

He opened the large envelope and handed everyone their letter.

"Check this out," Rahab exclaimed. "The letters are sealed with a wax seal on the back. Cool."

"I know," Sissy said, "let's gather around a bonfire at Mom's farm and share what our mother wrote to each of us."

"I think that would be fun, but let's wait until the funeral is over and we can have a last meal so to speak. The funeral is Saturday; let's have our fire at 8:00 P.M. Saturday night." Tim shared.

"Let's do it!"

Every article and remembrance of Albert Harris was removed from the wall. Moses told the family he would like to keep it, just in case something would break in the investigation or new evidence would surface. They all agreed, but in their hearts they knew Albert Harris was done. As everyone was leaving; Rick and Anne asked Sissy if they could talk to Todd for a minute. She told them that would be great because she needed to run to the Dollar Store for Tupperware snack containers.

Todd was still watching his movie when Rick and Anne came up the stairs.

"Todd, will you pause the movie for a minute? We have a couple of questions to ask you?" Anne asked.

Even though Todd had seen the movie at least thirty times, he gave them a disgusted look and paused the movie.

"Do you see NeeNee very often?"

"Yup."

"When do you see him?"

"All the time."

"Could we meet him sometime for ourselves? We don't mean to harm him but just to talk to him."

"He doesn't like big people, but I can ask him."

"Tell him we have a letter for him from Albert Harris."

"I'll tell him, but he is isn't here now; he had a friend die."

"Do you know the friend's name?"

"No."

"Tell him we saw Albert Harris and thank him for giving us his name."

"I'll tell him. Can I watch my movie now?" Todd said in a huff.

"Sure, let us know about NeeNee." Todd just nodded his head as the movie resumed.

Rick and Anne walked to the car shaking their heads.

"Are we nuts?" Anne said. "We just asked a mentally handicapped man about a magical elf."

"This seems way too weird, but we have to follow through. Don't forget, the only way we found Albert Harris was a note written on parchment paper by this so called elf. Even the cardinal was shocked that NeeNee, or Ray as he called him, was still alive. There has to be something here, but I'm not sure we'll ever connect the dots on this one," Rick said with a laugh.

Mom's Diner

It was 5:15 A.M., and the diner was half full. The guys sitting at the round table were speaking loudly for such an early hour.

"She did not," Marvin said.

"She did too. I heard it from a very reliable source," Lester said.

Mom came to the table with a pot of hot coffee.

"What in the heck are you guys so vocal about this morning?"

"Lester told us Mary Barr committed suicide because she couldn't live without her husband."

"I know for a fact she didn't; I was the one that found her. She had an inoperable brain tumor that was kept secret. She just wanted to go with dignity, not stuck in a hospital hooked up to a machine."

"That's what I want, too," Marvin said.

"She just looked so healthy and even helped all day on the church rummage sale three weeks ago," Lester said

"Mary was a tough woman; she worked alongside Richard Sr. her whole married life." Mom said. "Here comes Bill; he can give us details of the service."

"Morning, guys." as Bill sat next to Willy and took a piece of his toast and a slice of bacon.

"What's up with Mary's funeral?" Mom asked.

"It's going to be like her husband's service, with visitation on Friday from 4-8:00 P.M. and a funeral at 11:00 A.M. Saturday at the Faith Baptist Church. She requested donations to The Lutheran Girls Home in Lexington, Kentucky."

"Why there? She wasn't Lutheran," Tidy asked.

"Don't ask me; she had it all written out with explicit instructions. I'm counting on you guys to be pall bearers again. If any of you can't, let me know ASAP."

"You can count on us," Marvin said.

"By the way, Bill, we were talking before you arrived about a certain lady," Harold said.

"What certain lady? What are you guys talking about?"

The table now was quiet.

"We heard you're seeing Polly Taylor, and you've planned a trip to Northern Michigan with her," Marvin said

"You Bozos are worse than the girls from Sissy's shop."

"Well?" the guys said.

"We're just friends; that's all."

"Are you or are you not going to Upper Michigan with her?"

"You boys won't let it go, will you?"

In unison they said, "No."

"Yes, we are going to take a week and see the fall colors."

"What else will you see?" Marvin asked with a laugh.

"That's what I like about you guys: always worried about my well-being."

"Her ex-husband told Otto at the hardware store she had big boobs and a shoe fetish." Lester said.

"I'll tell you what; if you don't badger me with more questions, when I return I'll report in on both the subjects you brought up."

All the guys nodded and thought that's a fair compromise; the conversation then returned back to the funeral arrangements for Mary Barr.

Sissy's Beauty Shop

Sissy gave Todd a movie about dinosaurs, and he couldn't wait to watch it. She didn't have a hair appointment until 2:00 P.M., so this would give her an hour to read the note her mother left her.

"Todd, I'm going out back to the picnic table to read something; call me when Mrs. Abbott comes in. Todd?" she yelled.

"Ok, ok. I'm trying to watch the monster movie."

She knew this would keep him occupied for a long time. He told her he wanted to learn about dinosaurs because he was tired of cowboys and horses. He got a picture book about prehistoric animals from his friend NeeNee, and Todd was enchanted. Sissy didn't have any idea where the book came from, but it sure wasn't from a magical elf.

The midmorning sun was warm on her back as she sat looking at the sealed letter carefully lying on the picnic table. Her yard was small but nicely landscaped. Her dark, blue lilac bush was in full bloom and the smell was now drifting toward her. With trembling hands, she carefully broke the wax seal on the back of the envelope. Sissy really didn't know what she would read but knew this was from her mother's heart.

Dear Sissy,

When you are reading this, I will be gone. Please don't cry but just read what I have to say. This won't be easy for me in some parts, but I need to clear the air with you. I love you more than you can ever imagine. Your brothers were tough on you, but rest assured they would have given their lives for you. Many a time some high school guys would talk about you or want to date you; your brothers put a stop to any boy they felt had bad intensions.

I always felt close to you as a mother, and it seems like yesterday I was in the delivery room with Todd and you. You have been such a good mom to your son; I know he can be a handful, but you've made many sacrifices for his well-being. Your father has set up a trust for Todd, and I'm going to add to it from my estate. No matter what happens to you, be rest assured Todd will get the best care. You've worked very hard at the beauty shop so I'm going to leave you enough money to completely remodel Sarah's Charm and Chatter if you wish.

This part is difficult for me. I know your father molested you, and Todd is his son. I was aware of his sneaking out of our bedroom at night and going to your room. I would cry myself to sleep many a night. I was so afraid to lose a husband and maybe a daughter if I spoke up. I'm so sorry, honey. After Todd was born, your father confessed to me and promised it would never happen again. It didn't. Not only did your father repent to me, but he got down on his knees and asked God for forgiveness. I do believe your father has been forgiven. I hope somewhere in your heart you too can forgive him. Honey, don't carry this nightmare anymore. Todd is a fine young man and a blessing to our whole family. When you go to bed tonight, try not to double lock your bedroom door. I think this will help.

All my love,

Mom

Sissy cried and cried. If only her mother would have shared her feelings sooner. Todd came running out the back door.

"Mom, Mrs. Abbott is here; I think she may want some auburn tint."

"Ok, Honey, I'll be right in, and go ahead and get some tint from the basement."

SALES AND SON FUNERAL HOME

The Barr Family including Billie came into the large front doors of the funeral home. Bill and Wyatt were both standing in the lobby with matching navy blue suits. Bill hugged every family member and said, "Sorry." Pamela Sue had a large basket of food for the family lounge and proceeded to arrange everything as it should be.

"You guys can help yourselves if you wish," as Pamela Sue looked at Bill and Wyatt.

"Thank you. We might. Are you ready to see your mom?"

"We are." Rick said and grabbed Anne's hand.

Wyatt opened the large oak doors to the chapel, and it seemed like just yesterday, they had walked in here holding their mother's arms; now they were here to see their mother holding each other up. The flowers and their smell were overpowering. It was quiet as they walked to the casket except for Todd's humming a verse from "YMCA". The casket was a beautiful off white covered in red and white roses. They all knew she would be pleased.

"Well, mom, you kept our family together all these years; we'll try and do the same," Tim said as he extended his long powerful arms to embrace as many family members as he could reach.

"You're right, Tim; the Barr's must pull together and be strong," Sissy said between the sobs.

Billie touched Eric's arm, and led him out the back door of the funeral home.

"This is where it all started for us," as she looked at the patch of grass where Eric was thrown down.

"Oh I remember quite well; you had a large Bowie knife then."

She reached under her denim jacket and flashed the same large knife.

"I never leave home without this," she said laughingly.

"You know, Billie, you haven't changed a bit since I met you."

"Oh, yes I have. I've fallen in love with a snobbish, self-righteous New York punk."

"Do I know him?" Eric asked.

"I think you do, but some of that New York cockiness has faded. He's really a nice guy now. It has to be the training he received from some beautiful, bright Midwestern girl."

"I should throw you on the ground now."

"Just try it big boy, and we'll see what happens." she said with a cute smile.

"We better go back in; my family will think we're up to something evil."

She kissed him softly on the lips and again her charms and smell enchanted him beyond his greatest expectation. As with their father, so many people came to pay their respects. Rick's old prom date was there but this time she looked pretty good. Anne did notice she had on two different sandals, maybe the new style for Gas City. It was almost 9:00 P.M., the last of the friends were just leaving. The Barr family flopped down on the couches as Bill Sales told them about the funeral tomorrow.

"You all need to be at the church by 9:00 A.M. Pastor Roger wants to have a prayer with the family before the service starts. I understand Rahab is going to sing and Ken, the worship leader, will be there to practice with you. We are not going to have Hugh play the bagpipe at the cemetery; he was absolutely horrible for your dad's funeral. I hope that's ok."

"By all means; please don't have Hugh even close to the cemetery," Rick said with a laugh.

"Do you have any questions?" Bill asked

"Are we allowed to put something in her casket before we leave for the cemetery?" Pamela Sue asked.

"After everyone steps out, do whatever you feel that will give the closure you need. Try and get some rest; it will be a long day for you tomorrow."

"Good night, Bill and Wyatt. See you in the morning at the church," Sissy said as she stepped out the front door. She was going straight home to reread the letter.

TIM AND PAMELA SUE'S FARM

With what little strength they had left, they slowly walked into the house.

"Does anyone want some food?" Pamela Sue asked.

"Mom, you got to be kidding. All the food we had at the funeral home almost made me sick," Rahab said with a repulsed look on her face.

"I'll have some pie!" Moses shouted

"Me, too." Tim echoed.

"You guys disgust me." Rahab yelled as she walked up the back stairs.

"Got to keep our strength up," Moses said with a smile.

Tim wasn't tired enough to go to bed, so he walked out to the barn and looked at the letter his mom wrote to him. He sat on a bale of hay and looked at the unopened envelope for ten minutes. He knew where Moses hid the bottle of Gas City Soda Pop and put the jug to his lips. Whoa! he thought. That's a drink! He set the jug next to him and broke the wax seal on the envelope.

Dear Tim,

If you are reading this, then I'm with your father. I'll tell him "Hi" for you. You worked your whole life with your father, and he told me he could always count on you. He also knew your passion was the farm, and I am leaving it to you. Rick and Anne will understand; your sweat and hard work is displayed all over our farm. Enjoy it, son.

I know that your father wasn't the man he appeared to be around his friends and civic leaders. He hurt Sissy, but you were the shoulder she needed and the father figure that held her when she was violated. Thank you, son. I've known about his dishonoring your sister, and I shared this with her in the letter I wrote to her. Please forgive me Tim, I thought I was going to lose the whole family. Your father did repent and ask God for forgiveness, and I really feel your dad meant every word.

You're a fine son and father to your children. Pamela Sue adores you; please treat her with tenderness when she needs your affection. You truly are a man of integrity.

Love, Mom

Tim took another swig from the jug and began to cry. Pamela Sue looked through the small barn door and saw Tim holding the letter and weeping. She quietly closed the door, and as she walked back to the house she said, "God, please keep your hand on him tonight."

Rick and Anne's Farm

When they arrived home, all sat on the porch, and Anne broke out Pamela Sue's homemade blackberry wine. They took off their shoes and propped their feet on the porch railing.

"Thanks, Billie, for being with our family tonight," Anne said as she handed her a small glass.

"You're welcome, I enjoy your family very much. Mary taught me how to cross stitch and quilt and I especially loved her sense of humor."

"We'll all miss her. One thing about my mother, what you saw, is what you got. She was so honest. I don't know if we will ever move back to New York, but the last few months with her were delightful. I came back here to heal and find myself, but what I discovered was how much I missed my family. Billie, you are one of our family."

Dick and Jane jumped to their feet and looked toward the barn.

"What is it guys?" Eric asked.

Just then a coyote walked about twenty-five yards past them toward the apple orchard. Dick and Jane were ready if it came to that, but they just settled back down and were fast asleep in a matter of seconds.

"Billie, I talked to your dad, and the three of us are coming for parents' weekend at IU in October. I know Eric and you will be fine at school, but we are only a phone call away," Anne said.

"Thank you for the offer; I hope to be a great lawyer like you someday."

"I don't think great would describe me, but thanks for the compliment. Come on, Rick, let's go to bed; we have a long day tomorrow," as he followed her inside.

"My parents really like you. My old girlfriend in New York was so hated by my parents; they even offered me money to stay away from her."

"How much would they pay you to stay away from me?" she said with a smile.

"If I ever left you, they would disown me and probably adopt you. Come here, Beverly Magic," as Eric patted his leg.

She snuggled up to him and kissed his neck. Her smell of lilac and blackberry wine was about to send him into orbit. She put her tongue in his ear and whispered "Eric, do you carry a flashlight?"

"Very funny," as his breathing increased.

She gently pulled down his zipper and stroked him softly. He moaned and she continued to kiss his neck.

"Are you doing what I think you're doing?"

She never said a word but put her tongue in his mouth. She continued the movement of her hand as he reached under her dress and touched her cotton panties. She moaned also and her breathing became heavy. It didn't take long for him to explode as she held tightly onto his penis.

"Damn," He said just above a whisper.

"What do you think big boy; was that a stress reliever or what?"

"This truly was a first for us. I'm going to mark it on my calendar." Eric said still reeling from a fantastic orgasm.

"What will you write?"

"Not sure, but probably something to the effect that I just came back from the center of the sun. I better run you home; we all need our sleep for tomorrow."

Anne heard the old truck start up and knew Eric was taking Billie home. Rick was snoring away so she came back downstairs and sat on the porch with Dick and Jane. She set her glass of wine on the banister, stretched her arms high in the air, and put her bare feet up on the railing. Anne wasn't wearing underwear, and the cool breeze felt wonderful as it blew gently up her nightgown. She looked at her letter with the wax seal on it and smiled. She took a long drink of wine and opened the letter.

Dear Anne,

Thank you for taking the time to read my letter. I'm not on this earth, but as I penned this letter to you, I'm picturing you with a glass of wine and your tall, chiseled body reading this with a smile. You have been such a blessing to me since Rick and you came to live here. All my friends look up to you for strength and free legal advice; I do apologize for them. You are so strong and make every woman envy your virtues.

Rick reminds me so much of Eric. I know Eric has been a challenge to you both, but Rick was my challenge. If the crowd went left, he went right. Bullheaded! Oh my gosh, yes! He set goals, and you've come along side to help him fulfill his dreams. Thank you from a mother's heart, my first born child will always be special to me, and now you have the task to love and respect him as it should be.

I wish you the best. I know it has to be difficult coming from New York City to Gas City but you are up for the task or maybe I should say trial; it sounds more legal. Hang in there! I love you and watch out for my boy.

All my love,

Mom

Anne started to cry quietly. Mary was as strong a woman as she was, even stronger. She'll miss her mother-in-law, and will take good care of Rick; this she promised.

"Come on, cats, let's go in and find you some chicken treats."

Dick and Jane certainly remembered the word "treats". They jumped up and followed Anne into the kitchen.

Mom's Diner 5:00 AM Saturday

Today was the big funeral for Mary Barr. The guys all knew not to expect Bill Sales today; at least their toast and bacon would be safe from his greedy fingers.

"Are all you guys going to Mary's funeral?" Mom asked as she poured hot coffee into their cups

Everyone nodded and ordered the special: two pork chops, fried potatoes, and coffee with a small cup of pork gravy on the side, in case they might want to douse their potatoes. Lester ordered a fruit plate.

"What? A fruit plate!" Marvin yelled.

"Yeah, Betty thinks I'm getting too fat, and my cholesterol is climbing."

"You'll need your strength today carrying Mary's casket at the cemetery." Otto said

"You're right, Mom, I'll have the special, but if Betty should ask, just tell her I ordered the fruit plate."

"You did order the fruit plate; you just changed your mind," Marvin said with a grin.

"I love the way you guys think."

Mom and Jenny came back to the round table loaded with food. "I'm closing the diner for the funeral and will reopen at 4:00 PM. You boys better look good at the church today."

"For as good as we can be; we'll do our best to make you proud, Mom." Lester said

"I heard Rahab is singing for her grandmother's funeral. She has such a sweet voice." Mom said.

Marvin remarked "I just loved her in "The Music Man", do you think she'll sing "Seventy-six Trombones?"

"You goof ball; this is a funeral, not a musical production," Lester said and all the boys started laughing uncontrollably.

He started to blush, "I really do like that song."

FAITH BAPTIST CHURCH

Bill and Wyatt were all set for Mary's funeral. The flowers were arranged throughout the church and altar, with the casket down front by the pulpit. Pastor Ken was practicing some hymns, and Rahab just finished "Over The Rainbow."

"You have a nice voice," Pastor Ken said, "Would you like to join the church choir?"

"I'm really committed to my school musical and the marching band."

"The door will always be open if you change your mind. We really could use some young blood in the choir."

Pastor Roger came out from his study and surveyed the church and flowers. He knew this was going to be a tough funeral for him; he liked Mary a lot.

"Ken, are you and the choir ready for today?"

"We're all set. I'm going to put Rahab's solo just after your message. The ladies are ready for a large crowd when the meal is served after the cemetery. You better announce the ladies' restroom isn't working, and they'll need to use the men's."

"Great, that announcement will surely be popular. I think I'll call Marvin Sacks; he has a port-a-potty business, and maybe he could bring one over for the men to use. The guys don't care where they go, and this way the ladies can fix up the men's room with some flowers and pictures before we get back. I could even put some flowers in the urinal, so it won't look so bad."

"Roger, chill out. You're going to have the big one if you don't calm down. It's just a bathroom; you're not asking the ladies to pee in front of the congregation," he said with a laugh.

"You just don't get it. I'm calling Marvin ASAP; you just worry about the music."

The Barr's came in, and sat in the front row by the casket. They didn't say much but the three people that had read her letter, were replaying her words.

Rahab walked outside and sat on the church steps. She opened her letter from Dommy.

Dearest Rahab,

You have been such an inspiration to me. You seem tough on the outside but soft like melted marshmallows on the inside. I used that comparison because we burned many a marshmallow together on an open fire. You are so talented and can do anything your mind thinks up. I especially love your voice, and I know it is a lot of pressure on you, but I do hope you sing at my funeral. I didn't ask any of the other grandchildren to do anything because you are so special. The song I selected is a little out of the ordinary, but I know you'll do a great job.

I hope and pray you do something with your voice. I have left you $20,000.00 to further your studies in voice. It's a tough business, and the competition is like a pack of wild dogs, but you have a God-given talent, so please don't let it go to waste. I don't want to you wake up some day and say I should have. Like the ad says "Just Do It."

Dommy will always be with you. Be of good cheer and love always.

Your loving Dommy

Rahab started to cry, and she was going to give her grandmother the best voice she could muster. She jumped into the car and drove home to get her ukulele. No organ today; just her voice and the instrument.

MOM'S DINER

Mom closed the diner and walked slowly toward the Baptist Church. This funeral was going to be tough for Mom; she loved Mary and everything she stood for. Stormy Hay met her, a block from the church. She was sitting with her three little children on the lawn of Christi's Nail Emporium that had closed three years prior.

"Hi, Mom," Stormy said

"Hi, Stormy. What are you guys doing?"

"Oh, Larry got picked up last night for drunk and disorderly. We are just walking around looking at the pretty flowers that Christi planted years ago."

"You know, I have some hot dogs back at the diner, and I need to cook them up. You kids interested?"

"Oh yeah! We're hungry," they all said in unison; even the two-year-old knew about hot dogs.

"I even have some chocolate ice cream just wanting for someone to sample."

They jumped to their feet and followed Mom down the street. Stormy put her hand in Mom's as she started to cry.

"Thank you so much; you have just saved our lives"

"I have a strong feeling Mary would want me to do this rather than go to a funeral. I can go to funerals anytime, but to spend time with your children; this is priceless."

The little boys were throwing sticks and running a head of Mom and Stormy. Sammy, the oldest, picked up a stick and used it like a sword; swishing and cutting up his make believe monsters, as he ran ahead. Mom remembered many a time her son would do the same. Those are precious memories, but he died at age twenty-one, nonetheless, he was still her little boy.

Faith Baptist Church

The church was packed. Pastor Ken played soft hymns as the people were being seated by Bill and Wyatt. The choir came out and stood as Pastor Roger came out and nodded to the choir to be seated. His favorite redhead was seated on his left next to the stairs. She gave him a subtle wink and sat down. Pastor Roger was getting ready to stand but there seemed to be a commotion in the back. Roger strained his neck but couldn't see anything. All of a sudden four men in black suits walked toward the front of the church. Each man was at least 6'9'' and was dark complexioned. They got to the front of the church, parted, and there stood their half-brother, Rudy.

"Sorry about the grand entrance, but my security have strict orders."

They all hugged Rudy and welcomed him to the church.

"We'll talk after the funeral; thank you for emailing me about Mama," he said in a whisper.

Pastor Roger couldn't help staring at the four mountains standing no more than three feet from the new arrival.

"Mary was a woman of God," he said. "I know of no other woman that can stand shoulder to shoulder with her. Her requests were simple for this service. She told me not to say much and sit down", as everyone chuckled. "I'm going to read a poem she gave to me when her husband died. We don't know the author, but this really sums up her life.

"I'm Free"

Don't grieve for me, for now I'm free;
I followed the path God laid for me.
I took His hand when I heard Him call;
I turned my back and left it all.

I could not stay another day,
To laugh, to love, to work or play.
Tasks left undone must stay that way;
I found that place at the close of day.

If my parting has left a void,
Then fill it with remembered joy.
A friendship shared, a laugh, a kiss;
Ah yes, these things, I too will miss.

Be not burdened with times of sorrow;
I wish you the sunshine of tomorrow.
My life's been full, I savored much;
Good friends, good times, a loved one's touch.

Perhaps my time seemed all too brief;
Don't lengthen it now with undue grief.
Lift up your heart and share with me;
God wanted me now; He set me free.

Pastor Roger sat down for a minute to compose himself. There wasn't a dry eye in the church. The choir rose and sang "How Great

Thou Art." The small boxes of tissues were passed down each row and back again.

"Mary gave our little town everything, and she gave you children and grandchildren even more. Thank you for sharing her with us. Our lives have been enriched by her examples and our hearts have been touched by an angel. She requested Rahab to sing a song for us." as he sat down.

"You're probably expecting a religious hymn, but that's not my grandmother's style. She wanted me to sing "Somewhere Over the Rainbow", and I decided this morning I would play my ukulele and sing the version a Hawaiian man recorded before he died. This won't be easy, but for my Dommy, I'll get through this song."

Her voice was beautiful; even the choir director started to weep. Rahab was dressed in a long denim skirt, red 4-H blouse, and worn brown cowboy boots but if one closed their eyes, all they would hear, was an angel dressed in pure white clothes singing at the feet of Jesus. Her voice came from everywhere and nowhere. Each person in the congregation felt they had just experienced something incredible. When she finished, the people stood and quietly applauded. Then it turned into loud clapping and whistles. Tim stepped out from his pew and threw his large arms around his daughter. As they walked back to their pew, the clapping continued until Pastor Roger stood and held up his hands.

"Did I do ok, Dad?"

"Oh, Honey, there is no word in the English language that can describe what you just did. Dommy would be so pleased."

Pastor Roger wiped his eyes, blew his nose, and took a long drink of water.

"I have a few more things to say about Mary, but the words can't begin to compete to what we just heard. I'm going to close in prayer, and we'll have Bill and Wyatt escort you by the casket as we prepare to go the cemetery."

Pastor Roger closed with a short prayer, and stood by the casket.

People filed by the casket and most touched Rahab's hand as they passed by her pew. The church was empty except for the Barr family and four big bodyguards.

"Remember when Mary placed a pair of needle nose pliers in Richard's hand?" Well, I have something for her." Pamela Sue reached into her large purse and pulled out Mary's favorite spatula and gently placed in her hands. "There now. That is what it should be. I'll bet at least 10,000 pancakes were flipped with that thing."

Everyone smiled and knew that had to be buried with her. Everyone kissed her forehead or patted her hands, except for Todd.

"Bye, Dommy, see you again," and he put a small plastic cowboy and horse next to the spatula.

Everyone knew Todd was right and walked out the church.

Rudy and his bodyguards stood quietly and looked at her.

"Goodbye, Mama. Thank you for being my real mom and letting me back in after sixty years." Rodolfo leaned forward and kissed her forehead.

Outside the church was Rudy's big, black, iron-plated security bus. Rudy had words with his security advisor and walked over to where Rick had his truck parked.

"I want to ride to the cemetery with you."

"Of course you can." Rick said.

"I told my security official that the kids can ride in the bus if they want. He asked them, and they thought this will be neat."

Anne climbed in the back seat of the truck and Rudy sat up front with Rick.

"Are you going to stay here long?" Anne asked.

"No, I have to go to Rome for Cardinal Grey's Mass and burial. I have to leave right after the burial for Mama."

"Did you know the cardinal?" Rick asked.

"Not well but I had met him several times. I was asked to attend the funeral on behalf of Panama and the South American Financial Union."

"I know you won't repeat this, but I have a question for you. What if I had evidence that could prove Cardinal Grey wasn't who he said he was?"

"What do you mean?"

"Cardinal Grey had his name changed and is really someone else."

"That statement would rock the Catholic Church!" "As your brother, don't do it. You have no idea what consequences there could be."

"He did some evil things along the way."

"We all did. There's talk about requesting sainthood for the cardinal. Do you know what that means? He's untouchable. You better let God deal with Michael Grey or whoever he is."

MOM'S DINER

"Thank you Mom. You have always taken care of us but this is beyond your call of duty." Stormy said.

"You're welcome. I will never have grandchildren, so I look on you and your kids as my own. I know you have a tough time raising the children almost by yourself, but you have been a good mom. You keep them clean and never complain to others about the short comings of your husband."

"Larry is a good man but never seems to get a break. He's tried lots of jobs but always gets in trouble with the manager. I know he drinks too much, but I still love him and will do whatever he asks of me."

"Most women would have divorced him many years ago."

"I know that, but they don't know the real Larry Hay. His childhood was horrible and his father beat him on a regular basis. Larry stood up for his mother once, and his father tied him up and beat him with a fishing rod for three days."

"You know Stormy; I think your kids might need some more chocolate ice cream. I just got my tax check back and I'll just blow it on something stupid. I want you to have it."

"I can't take it."

"You will take it for me. I want my almost grandchildren to have a few things they need. I won't hear otherwise."

Mom handed her a check for $2315.00.

"Oh my! I thought it was for like $50.00."

"It doesn't matter the amount; you use it for expenses and the kids."

Stormy started to cry and threw her arms around Mom's neck.

"The way I look at it, Uncle Sam owed it to me, so I'm just sharing his wealth."

Oak Grove Cemetery

The hearse led the sixty plus cars to Mary's burial space, and just like Richard's funeral, it started raining lightly. As soon as Rudy got out of Rick's truck, the four bodyguards were practically on top of him. The grandchildren came from the big bus and were all smiles.

"Dad, wait till I tell you what we saw in the bus," Moses said to his father.

"Not now son; wait till the funeral is over."

Pastor Roger had a prayer and sprinkled sand on Mary's closed casket.

"Don't forget about the luncheon back in the church basement," Roger announced.

Everyone got back in their cars and headed to the church for one big home cooked meal. Just the Barr family remained at the grave. They looked at their father's plot with some red dye still clinging to the grass.

Rudy walked over to where his father's monument was. It was by far the biggest memorial in Oak Grove Cemetery.

CALVERT BENJAMIN WOLF

1874-1950

ONE OF THE GREATEST PAINTERS TO EVER PICK UP A BRUSH

Rodolfo looked at the large headstone and then looked thirty yards to the east at his mother's grave. She was only seventeen when Calvert died, but as she shared with Rudy, she loved him and always would. His father and mother were again united and now Rudy had the closure he needed. He released an enormous sigh.

"I have to go. I don't know if I ever will be back, but you are my flesh; if there is anything you need, call. Please come to Panama and visit. Our country is beautiful and much warmer in February. You have my invitation and for some strange reason, I think we will see each other again."

Rodolfo hugged the family and tearfully ascended the stairs of the bus. They all waved as the monster pulled out onto County Road 600 E.

"Come on everybody," Todd yelled. "I'm hungry."

They all smiled and slowly pulled out of the rain-soaked cemetery.

Faith Baptist Church Parking Lot

Moses came up from the basement feeling like he was going to explode. He belched and farted twice before sitting on the handicap bench in front of the church. He opened Dommy's wax sealed letter.

Dearest Moses,

You are my handsome, blonde, over eating grandson, and I love you to pieces. Every time I look at you, I see your father looking back at me. Your head is on straight, and I know someday you'll run the Barr Farm; it's in your blood. Never one time did I ask you to do something that you didn't follow through for me. I still remember the time you and I helped birth the colt in our barn. It was so cold, and the mare was trying to deliver breech. It took hours, and you held the small colt in your arms all night. That little guy grew up to win a blue ribbon for you at the nationals.

I don't know if you are going to college; it wasn't for your dad. Whatever you decide will be the right decision, so I'm leaving you all the horses and cattle. This should give you a good start on your own farming projects. Be kind to people, and remember to love your neighbor as yourself.

Your loving Dommy

P.S. I gave the pancake recipe to your mother; there is still time to break your grandfather's pancake record. I know you can do it.

Moses just hung his head and reached in his coat for a cigarette. He didn't want anyone to think he was getting emotional, so when Pastor Ken asked him if he was ok, he told him he had allergies.

Pastor Roger's Home

Boy, was he tired! The funeral for Mary just about killed him. His emotional attachment and her faith in God was so hard to convey to the congregation; he felt he let them down. He cut the eulogy down because he just didn't have it in himself. Rahab's song kept replaying in his mind; he threw his Bible on the nightstand and kicked off his shoes. He could hear his wife Libby working in the kitchen downstairs and walked down to get a beer.

"I took the kids to Erin's birthday party, and remind me to pick them up at 7:00 P.M. You did a nice service today for Mary; I don't think there was a dry eye in the church. I could tell you were struggling to hold it together but it went well. Who were those big guys that escorted the other guy to the front row?"

"They told me; he was a cousin from Mexico, and he flew in just for Mary's funeral. Did you think he was handsome?"

"He was very good looking but not compared to you."

"Why are you still wearing your choir robe?"

"The sash around the middle was frayed so I brought it home to cut the small tassels off. I have a surprise for you."

"Is it a good one?"

"Oh, I think you'll like it," as she opened her robe.

"Wow!" he exclaimed

"Told ya."

Libby had shaved her pubic hair into a small patch and colored it the same color as her bright red hair.

"What do you think of my little landing strip?"

"It's awesome! Should I check my flight plans?

"No need for that; if your plane is fueled and ready for flight, that's all I need to know," she said with a large smile.

She removed the purple sash and dropped her robe on the kitchen floor. The only thing she had on were a pair of red pumps, and two matching patches of bright red hair. She removed his pants, underwear, and socks. Now all he had on was his white shirt and blue tie.

"Sit." She commanded and led him to the small stuffed chair in the corner of the kitchen.

"Are you sure about the kitchen?"

"I'm going to prove to you that I know my way around the galley."

She rapped the sash around his arms and middle and tied him to the chair. She knelt before him and gently parted his legs. She kissed him on the lips and put her hands between his legs.

"If you even think about escaping this horrible torture I'm about to inflict on you; I'll make you walk the plank."

"Yes Blackbeard, or maybe I should Redbeard." He said with a chuckle.

She tied a tight knot for a red headed choir member, because he couldn't move his arms.

She lowered her head and began to kiss and lick between his legs. He moaned and whimpered like a little child. She now sucked slowly, and she knew he was close to an orgasm so she straddled him in the chair. She controlled all the movement, and up and down she went; she loved being in charge. She grabbed his hair and threw his head back and screamed. He tried to kiss her but she still held his hair and continued to run the show.

Mrs. Hilton, their neighbor and church member, heard the screams, since she was headed across the back yard to return the Tupperware container from the funeral dinner. One look through the screen door told her to quietly back up and bring the potato salad later.

Their orgasms were incredible. She walked over to the sink and filled a glass with water.

"Do you want some?"

"I would, but could you please untie me; I'm starting to get a cramp in my arm."

"What do you think sailor?" "You going to be in town long?"

"Libby, what in the heck has gotten into you?"

"I'm madly in love with you, but now I want to learn how to show it." Our married life has been on your terms and our sex life was a scheduled event." "No more!"

"Well, every time I see you wear the robe and sash, I'm going to have flashbacks."

"Yeah, but good flashbacks," she said with a smile.

CALVERT WOLF MUSEUM

Eric and Billie left the church basement and walked hand in hand down two blocks to the museum.

"Do you want to go in?" Billie asked.

"Naw, I want to sit outside and read my grandmother's letter, and I'm happy you're here to share it with me."

They sat in the side yard of the museum, and Billie put her arm around Eric as he broke the wax seal.

My Dearest Eric,

I bet you never thought you'd be reading a letter from a dead lady, but here it goes. We've only known each other for a few months, but what a great time we've had, and the late evenings eating pie and ice cream around my little kitchen table. All the stories, thoughts, and dreams we shared together-they were the best. I love all my grandchildren, but when you showed up; my heart found a special place for Eric Barr. We have a bond that will never be broken, neither here nor the next world. I know you won't settle down here because there is a big world for you to explore.

Billie Magic is the best thing that ever happened to you, and I can tell, she is the love of your life and always will be. Eric looked over at Billie and smiled. *You two have something that many couples search their whole lives for, and some never do find that special love. Hang on to her, or I'll come back and haunt you. Billie is a strong- willed girl; I like that in her, so don't squelch that fire. Give her plenty of space.*

I'm leaving you grandpa's truck, the old shotgun, and my favorite cat, Johnny Cakes. He'll get along with Dick and Jane just fine. When you see Billie, tell her I'm leaving her my grandmother's cameo broach and my wedding and engagement rings. She is such a dear.

I have to be going now; I have a harp lesson in fifteen minutes.

All my love,

Dommy

"Wow!" Billie said, "She is one cool lady."

Eric started to cry quietly. "Damn, I'll miss that woman."

"Me, too"

Tim and Pamela Sue's Farm

Pamela Sue changed out of her nice dress and put on jeans and a tee shirt,

"I have to run out back for minute!" she yelled to Tim and the kids as they watched a show about people hoarding stuff. They never said a word, so Pamela Sue walked out the kitchen door clutching her letter from Mary. Pamela Sue went directly into the corn field mumbling to herself. The corn was so high she disappeared in a matter of seconds and sat down. The rustling sound of the corn made it sound like small waves on a tranquil beach. She took a deep breath and opened her letter.

Dear Pamela Sue,

For the last twenty-four years we saw each other almost every day; I'll miss that even if I'm hanging out with God. You are the most amazing woman I've ever met, and I know a lot of people. Your life growing up was tough, but you arose above all the negative circumstances and have excelled. Your

husband and children absolutely adore you, and I watch as Tim looks at you; there is still an enormous love in his eyes. You have made the family. You are the best cook I've ever seen, and the reason I know that is that I used to be the best.

You two work so hard at the farm; I'm giving you an unlimited timeshare to anywhere in the world. February is a good time to leave the farm, so think about taking a month to wherever you choose. Please don't let Tim take you to a farm convention; the timeshare is yours. Tim and you enjoy, so go for it girl. This timeshare is for the next ten years, so start planning, and if you find some place special; send me a post card.

Thank you for loving my son and sharing his bed.

Love, Mary

PS Sissy and you divide up my jewelry, but I want you to take the ring Calvert gave to me the first day I posed. It's special.

Rick and Anne's Farm

Rick and Anne were watching the funeral mass for Cardinal Michael Grey, and they both shook their heads. It was midday in Rome. The special showed the crowds and the massive St. Peter's Church also filled to capacity.

"Rudy is right; we need to let this one go. Albert Harris will be judged by someone way more powerful and perfect than we are," Rick said, "but it does seem strange that the casket we are looking at holds a body of a completely different person than everyone is praising and praying over. I just realized that the person in that casket was a Boy Scout who lived not more than a quarter of mile from here."

"We need to follow through with the notes he gave us. We did promise him," Anne said. "All we have to do is find his son in Florida, dig up the fake Albert Harris, collect almost $1,000,000, and give the third note to a magical elf; I see no problem here, do you?"

"Piece of cake, and I thought we had something difficult to do," Rick said with a laugh.

"What do we do with his taped confession and the photo of his brains all over the wall?" Anne asked.

"No one knows we have this, but for some reason I think we should keep it a place safe."

"Rick, it's more powerful that a barrel of nitroglycerin. We better guard it carefully; this piece of evidence will prove fatal in anyone's hands."

"Ok, we both know where it is right now; let' keep it there."

"I'm going to have a glass of wine and sit on the porch; do you want to join me?"

"I will in a few minutes; I have to get something from mom's house," Rick said as he walked off the porch.

He walked down the dark road looking at the stars and the brilliant full moon. The crickets were really serenading tonight, and occasionally a bull frog would chime in. He got to his mom's farm, walked in the dark, lonesome kitchen, and retrieved her letter he had been carrying for several days. Now was the time and the place to read it.

Dear Ricky,

I bet you waited a little while to read this; I know you so well. You were my first born by your father and the first I held to my breast. You have a special place cut deep in my soul, and it's huge. When you left Indiana and went to New York; I knew in my heart you wouldn't be back. I know you're here now and have bought a farm close to me and your brother, but Honey, your heart is still in New York. Now that I'm gone, Anne and you should go back. Eric will be right behind you after Billie and he have decided where they will land. You have my permission to take back all the virtues and simplicity from Gas City; we have plenty to spare. Just because you live in a town with millions of people that doesn't mean you can't carve out a nice simple nest for Anne and you. Put things in perspective son. Your family and you have been a blessing to me, but it's time to move on. New York is calling.

I'm leaving you your great grandfather's gold watch and diamond ring; your father treasured these more than anything he owned. Your dad would only wear these on a special occasion. Then they would go back into the brown leather box, because your great grandfather wore these to Abraham Lincoln's first inauguration in Washington D.C. In the small box, you'll find a cuff link that fell off of Lincoln's shirt that day. Supposedly your great grandfather picked it up, and Lincoln told him to keep it. We have an old picture of Lincoln shaking hands missing the cuff link. Pretty cool, heh?

Anne and you have grown so close together, and I see the love you share. You know, it just doesn't happen in Indiana; you can take that along with you also.

Love you, Ricky,

Mom

His mother was so right he thought, and he loved Indiana but this was not his heartbeat. True, Anne and he grew very close in Indiana and they even had their first sex here in over five years. He hoped to keep the fire burning even though the two of them would be bombarded by the city. He would have to tell Anne his feelings but was sure she felt the same. He looked around the empty kitchen and the spark was gone. No wonderful smells, no humming from his mother, no laughter and no mom. He turned off the light and locked the door; he would never set foot in there again. Never!

SALES AND SON FUNERAL HOME

Bill finished packing his suitcase, sat on the end of his bed, and looked on his dresser at the picture of Ellie. She had been gone seven years this past May, and now he was going on a road trip with another woman. He mentioned the trip to his children, and they seemed disinterested, but were they? For the last seven years, four months and three days, Bill lit the candle next to her picture. It certainly didn't bring her back, but this ritual helped him sleep, but tonight he wouldn't be here, and he just couldn't bring himself to take her picture on the trip.

"Goodbye Ellie; I'll be back in a week."

He picked up his suitcase and walked into the family room where Wyatt and Susan we sitting.

"I'm going now. Mrs. Carlson will look in on you, and Bill Krege will help with funerals. Wyatt, Bill isn't busy at his funeral home and will be here in thirty minutes if you call him."

"I know Dad; you've told this same story at least ten times. Just go and have a good time."

He hugged his children and started to say, "Do you think that…"

"Just go Dad; we know you love mom, get out of Gas City."

He smiled and said, "You guys are the best."

He drove to Polly's house, and she was sitting on the back porch.

"Hi, Polly; ready for a road trip?"

"I sure am; my suitcases are in the living room."

He had been warned; now he wondered how many shoes can one pack in a suitcase? Because she had two.

They got in the car and he turned the radio to the oldies station.

"I love the oldies." she said with a smile.

He looked over and nodded; she did have big boobs, and the sweater she wore gave every indication the guys were right.

SISSY'S BEAUTY SHOP

Sissy just finished Helen DeNaut's hair, and she looked stunning. At eighty she was a class act and all the younger women in town envied her. Helen was well read and the best bridge player in the county.

"Thanks, Sissy. I'm so sorry about losing both your parents in the same year." Helen said.

"I'll miss them that's for sure, and I'll see you next Thursday."

"Todd, come up here, please."

"Ok, Mom." as he ran up the basement stairs.

"You've never opened your letter from Dommy."

"Give it to me," he said.

He jumped into a styling chair. He ripped it open and a $100.00 fell out.

"Wow! He yelled, Mom, read it to me."

Dear Todd,

Your Dommy loves you. I'm giving you some money to take your mom and cousins to get ice cream. You can pick any flavor you want and even bring some back for NeeNee. I loved to cook for you because you ate everything I made and, you told me thanks at least a hundred times. I appreciate your love for my food.

Be a good boy for your mom and eat all the ice cream you want.

Love, Dommy

Sissy started to cry.

"Mom stop it. I have all the money in the world to buy ice cream. Let's go and pick up Eric, Moses, and Rahab. I want a double chocolate surprise. Come on."

BILLIE'S FARM

Eric and Billie sat on a bale of hay and Dar drove in.

'Hi, guys."

"Hi, Dar, come on over and sit: we are having some soda pop," Billie said with a smile.

Dar sat and tipped the jug for a swig.

"What do you hear from Tony?" Billie asked

"He emailed today. His father is real sick, and his uncles want him to meet with the Becko Family."

"About what?"

"He didn't say, but hinted that he might be taking over his father's business."

"I thought he was going to college next week. Will he still go?"

"He didn't know; Tony will call me Friday and let me about the meeting."

"Eric and I have our dorm assignments but it seems we are at opposite ends of the IU campus."

"You two won't let that small distance bother you. I leave for Purdue next week also and I have a roommate from Wisconsin-probably a cheese head. I went to the Dells once, got so sick on a roller coaster and spent the next two days in bed. That's my only memory of Wisconsin."

"If she's a Packer fan, be careful; I guess they're crazy," Eric said with a smile.

"Why don't you two come to Purdue when we play IU and we can hang out?"

"Sounds good but we'll be wearing red and white."

"I wouldn't expect anything different."

Eric's cell phone rang.

"Yes, yes, Ok. What time? Sure, why not." And hung up the phone

"Who was that?" Billie asked.

"That was my Aunt Sissy; she wants us to meet at the ice cream shop. Todd is treating all of us to ice cream, and we are supposed to go now," Eric said laughing.

"Come on, Dar, let's go and see why Todd is buying."

The three jumped into Eric's old truck and headed to town.

Rick and Anne's Farm

The farm seemed quiet because Eric was gone to Billie's, and Hazel and Tidy were in Copenhagen. They were blown away thinking Tidy Tucker, who had never left Lincoln County in sixty years, was now in Europe. He had never been on an airplane, left the country, had a girlfriend, and never slept in the same room with a woman except his mother. All these transformations happened in less than two months; talk about a one-eighty.

"What note should we tackle first?" Anne asked.

"I think we should try and find the fake Albert Harris or Cardinal Grey's son first. The hardest will be finding the elf; don't you think?"

"Unless the elf just walks in the door, you're probably right."

"The name and last address we have show him living close to Orlando. Let's leave Monday and look for him. If we do find him, we need to let the cardinal's lawyer know because apparently this guy is heir to a fortune. Are we going to tell him he is Albert's or Michael's son?"

"That's a good question; I guess we should just play it by ear, but my inclination is to tell him his father is Cardinal Michael Grey. No one knows he really is Albert except us and some of the cardinal's guards."

"Yes, we better stick to the cardinal's name for his and our sake."

"It's a nice night; do you want to go to the drive in movie in Union Mills?" Rick asked

"What's playing?"

"Does it matter? We'll be making out anyway."

"Very funny." "If you really want to make out, let's stay home."

"Yeah but I heard Eric and Tony talk about the drive in; if you score with the girl, you hang her bra on the car antenna."

"Is that what this all about? Do you want to hang my bra on your car?"

"I guess not."

"I hope not, too; you're forty-four years old and if you want to show off my bra to a bunch of sixteen year olds, then maybe you should find another date."

"Sorry I brought it up," as he hung his head.

"That's Ok. I was thinking about putting my panties on the antenna," she said laughing.

"I love you, Anne Barr; you sure keep life interesting."

"Let's go; I just hope they're not playing a monster or slasher movie."

SISSY'S BEAUTY SHOP

Sissy and Todd arrived back home, and Todd was on a high from all the ice cream, two sugar cookies, and a small bag of M and M's he consumed. He looked in his pocket and still had $74.60 left; this was a fortune to Todd. He could do the math well enough to know this money would bring him back to the ice cream shop any time he wanted.

"You better save some of the money Dommy gave you," Sissy said

"I know mom; I'll put it in my old jelly jar."

"Good idea, but what are you going to do with the small cup of vanilla ice cream you brought home?"

"I told you; I'm giving it to NeeNee." And down the basement he went.

Sissy knew Todd would eat the ice cream as soon as he was out her sight. This was going to be a big night for Sissy; tonight she wasn't going to double lock her bedroom door. She wasn't going to lock it at all. Sissy also decided not to get her pistol out of the closet either. Sissy had double locked her door every night for over twenty-five years, and she was frightened tonight.

"Todd, I'm going to bed. Come up soon."

"I will, Mom. Goodnight."

She quietly closed her bedroom door and slipped under the covers, and when her eyes closed, the vision of her father coming through the door wasn't there. Her ears were also attentive for any strange sounds; there were none. Maybe this will work, she thought, as her eyes became heavy.

"NeeNee, I'm going to bed" Todd said, "and I hoped you liked the vanilla flavor."

"It was good; you know it's my favorite. Goodnight Todd."

Indiana University Campus, Bloomington, Indiana

Rick and Anne were exhausted having carried at least ten loads of Eric's stuff up three flights of dormitory stairs. Eric was finally settled in, his roommate was from New Jersey, and they seemed to really hit it off. Eric was a New York Ranger fan and Allen was a New Jersey Devil fan; this little competition would be good for the both of them.

"Goodbye son," they both said. "we'll see you in two weeks for parent's weekend. Call if you need something."

"I will and thanks for everything."

They got into the truck and started heading to Indianapolis to catch a flight to Orlando.

"What's the matter?" Rick asked

"Nothing," she said between sobs.

"Could it be just maybe you'll miss Eric a little?"

"Maybe a little," and she was crying now.

They drove for over an hour and she got her composure back.

"I have to tell you something." Rick said with conviction

"You look awfully serious."

"I want to move back to New York. I came here for healing, and I'm finally at peace."

"What was this healing you needed? You promised to tell me sometime."

"When we had Tim and his family out this summer, he told me something that devastated me. My father was a pedophile and raped our sister consistently when we were growing up. I never saw it coming; I must have been so into myself. I never realized anything was wrong and wasn't there to protect my sister." He started to tear up.

"Rick, you can't blame yourself; you were only a teenager."

"Doesn't matter; I adored my father and all those wonderful things they said at his funeral make me sick."

"Have you talked to Sissy about this?"

"I have, and she is doing pretty well. That is the reason she never appeared at my dad's funeral or visitation; she just couldn't do it."

"Remember when I told you it was strange that she never asked about his funeral? Now it makes sense."

"That's not the worst of it; Todd is my father's son."

"What? You can't be serious!"

"I know this is so bizarre; I'm still in denial."

"Poor Sissy. She is one strong woman to endure that and raise Todd in such a loving manner. No wonder you had to leave New York; I really thought it was me." Now Anne was crying.

"It wasn't you at all; I had to come back to find something I could physically hang on to. I bought a farm, and Eric and you followed. I loved that about you."

"I want to go back to New York with you. I do miss the action and hype. Plus, I'm wanting to run for a federal judgeship."

"It's time then. Eric is settled in, and Billie will keep him grounded. Just think we might have grandbabies someday."

"A year ago I thought Eric would end up in prison, or dead on a New York City street, but now I have great hope in that kid."

"Me, too. Here's the airport, I'll drop you off and park the car."

Plymouth, Florida

Rick and Anne landed in Orlando, Florida, and they were just about the only parents without children under the age of ten. Even the airport carrousel was loaded with strollers and stuffed animals. They rented a car and headed to Plymouth, Florida. On the map Plymouth looked like a suburb of Orlando. The only way to find Cardinal's Grey son was a name, address, and the mention of a distinguishing birthmark. They looked on the internet and Orlando had twenty-three Jack Rosenbaums, and Plymouth had two. The address didn't match anything with that name, and they knew this was going to be a challenge. The Jack they wanted may be dead or living in Fargo, North Dakota, but hey also had a good idea about how old Jack would be. If Cardinal Grey was eighty-three and fathered Jack at about twenty, then the man they wanted would be about sixty-three.

Anne came up with the idea they should pose as random sweepstakes judges and carry $500.00 cash in an envelope because everyone wants money. She had official photo badges made and Rick carried a clipboard with all the Jack Rosenbaums on it. The very first house they stopped at in Plymouth, they were told Jack was at his junior high football practice.

When they got back to their hotel, exhaustion was all they knew. They covered twelve Jacks, and it ran the gambit of: he's in school, he's dead, he's in jail, and he had a sex change. They both thought they never should have promised Albert Harris a thing. Their deck overlooked Disney, and in the distance they watched the fireworks with a scotch and water and a margarita in their hands. Tomorrow would be another adventure if they could stand it.

MOM'S DINER 5:15 AM

The Gas City High School Football Jamboree was Friday night, and every guy around the table had an opinion of who the quarterback should be. The team had dismal record of 2-12 last year, but the hopes were high this year because most of the seniors were back. Several of the men favored Donnie Organ, and the rest were for Al Brauer. Donnie was tall, lean, and a homegrown boy and Al was a transfer from Minneapolis. His father was the new Lutheran Pastor, so they didn't know much about father or son. Al was built like an Army tank, and he just plain looked mean.

"Has anyone heard from Bill and Polly?" Lester asked.

"No, and don't you remember, that Bill was going to tell us about the trip when got back?" Marvin said

"I just thought maybe one of you guys would have gotten a post card saying she had big boobs."

"Lester, you're a jerk! Do you really think Bill would send a card like that?"

"I would," Lester came back with.

"Yeah, but you've also been married four times."

"Good point. Ok then, has anyone heard from Tidy and Hazel in Copenhagen?" Lester asked again.

"I have," Mom said. I got a card yesterday, and it said they were having a great time and that Tidy really enjoyed the airplane ride. He stated that from the air the cities appeared like little dots of oil on his driveway."

"I bet Tidy gets married when he comes home," Leroy said

"It wouldn't surprise me; I've never seen him so happy," Mom said with a smile.

ORLANDO, FLORIDA

Again Rick and Anne were still looking for the cardinal's son, and they were down to three names on their list.

"After the next three names, I want to go home." Rick said.

"Me, too. I think we will have fulfilled our promise to Albert."

They stopped at the Baptist Mission House in the center of Orlando, Florida. The neighborhood was deplorable, a far cry from the beauty and glitz of Disney. In front of the old yellow cement building was a group of men sitting looking for trouble.

Rick said, "I better go in and check this place out; why don't you lock the car, and I'll be out shortly."

"I want to go in. I feel safer around you."

They walked in the old rusty metal door wearing their official sweepstakes badges and carrying the clipboard. There was a desk in one corner and about forty to fifty guys playing table games and reading. The smell wasn't good, like dirty feet in July.

"Is Jack Rosenbaum here?" Rick asked.

"He's on the phone, but he won't be happy to see you!" The old man said as he rose.

Rick and Anne looked at each other in bewilderment.

"You can come back now."

They entered the tiny office and sat in the only two chairs in front of the beat-up old desk. There were pictures all over the walls, but they didn't recognize a single person. The door behind the desk opened and a slender, white-haired man entered. His eyes sparkled, and he was clutching three small envelopes.

"I have most of it," the gentleman said as he sat on the edge of his desk.

"What do you mean?" Anne asked

"The money, you know the mortgage and the food service deposit. We are short again, but I assure you, I will have the balance in two months. I've sold my house and the closing is in November."

"We are not here for that. We are here to see Jack Rosenbaum regarding a contest," Rick said proudly.

"I'm not that man. I've never entered a contest in my life."

"No, you didn't have to. We are here to give you $500.00 if you answer a couple of questions," Anne said.

"Sorry, I'm not him."

"It looks as though you could use $500.00 for your feeding center."

"What I really need are your prayers. My wife and I have beaten down time and time again, but this go around has put us in peril. We are about to lose it all. I still love God, and I know this is just a test, so if you don't mind I would love a prayer from you two," and he bowed his head.

Rick and Anne were completely taken off guard. Rick looked at Anne with huge eyes. She acknowledged his fear but coxed him with her eyes. Rick bowed his head.

"Dear God, watch over this place and keep giving this man hope. Amen." Rick said.

"See that's what I needed. God bless you two." He shook their hands and left through the small door behind the desk.

They walked out the front door to the car.

"Rick, not a bad prayer."

"What was I supposed to do? I saw the way you looked at me to make a move, so I just followed your lead."

Rick started the car, and said "Two more Jacks and we go home."

"Rick, this guy isn't the Jack Rosenbaum, but he can use the money. Why don't we just give him the $500.00 and go home. What will it hurt?"

"Yeah, I'll be right out."

Rick walked back in the building, but the old guy wasn't sitting at the reception desk. Rick walked past the desk to the inner office to place the money in the room. He laid the envelope on the desk and heard voices behind the door where the white haired man disappeared. Rick knocked but no one responded; he quietly opened the door and there kneeling next to an older woman was the man. He never turned around, but Rick instantly recognized the birthmark on the man's upper bicep of his out stretched arm.

"You are Jack Rosenbaum, and I have great news for you," as the two turned to face Rick.

New York City Anthony Becko Home

Tony sat in an overstuffed chair next to his father's bed. His father was sleeping a lot, and Tony felt compelled to sit with him. Tony's mom and sisters kept coming in bringing him coffee and encouraging him to get some rest. He had a meeting with his uncles two days prior, and he wasn't sure what to make of it. They kept saying his father was head of the family, and it now was his turn to step up to the plate. He hoped his father would tell him what this meant and just what would be expected of him. He was supposed to start college this week, but that had been put on hold for now. Tony texted Dar several times but told her he didn't know much. He said if his father's condition changed, he would let her know.

It was 2:00 A.M., and his father called his name.

"I'm here, Dad." Tony said.

"I'm dying son, and I want you to take care of your mother and sisters."

"Of course I will, but you're not dying."

"Just listen for a minute; I want you to take over my business. You'll have to learn the ins and outs from your uncles, and they are receptive to this. They know my feelings and will watch over you. Hand me my white pair of dress shoes from the closet."

Tony took the old scuffed shoes to his father. His dad pulled the lining out of the left shoe, and there was a flat key taped to the inside. He handed the key to Tony.

"Never let this out of your sight. This simple key can unlock the downfall of many powerful men and women. The box is located in the basement of Renaldo's Restaurant on 83rd Street. No one knows it's there except you and me. If trouble arises or you are ever prosecuted for anything, go to the box. It makes you almost untouchable."

"But Dad."

"Don't say anything; just come closer so I can kiss you."

Baptist Mission House

Rick brought Anne back into the mission. Rick, Anne, Jack Rosenbaum, and the woman he was praying with all sat in the small inner office.

"Honey, this is Jack Rosenbaum."

"Who are you people for real?"

"My name is Rick Barr and this is my wife, Anne. We have been trying to find you because a promise we made to your father."

"My father? Do you know him?"

"We have met him." Anne said.

"This is my wife, Irene, and will you tell me about this quest you've taken?"

"It is a long story, and we'll try to keep it brief."

"Tell me this first; how did you know I was Jack Rosenbaum?"

"By the birthmark your father described."

"It is unusual; Irene thinks it looks like a parrot but most people call it a bird of paradise."

"Your father gave us an address in Plymouth, Florida, and that's where we started," Anne said.

"We used to live there, but God called us here. We live just down the block, or at least did; our house was repossessed so we now live in the back of this building."

"What exactly do you do here?" Rick asked.

"We feed and house over two hundred and twenty men and women. Just because we live in Orlando, it isn't all about Mickey and Donald. There are some very poor people here and we feed them with food and the Gospel of Jesus. Irene and I have the same calling; this has been our ministry for the last thirty one years."

Irene said as she started to cry, "Jack told me you prayed over him and our ministry. Thank you from the bottom of my heart."

Jack handed her a handkerchief and ran his fingers through his thick white hair. Irene crossed her legs and Anne noticed her shoes were completely worn through. Irene wore no makeup, but her complexion was flawless and her white hair was the exact color of her husbands. She handed the cloth back to her husband and took his hand.

"Your father was Cardinal Michael Grey."

"You mean the priest that just died? I watched some of his funeral in Rome and the Pope did his Mass."

"That's him."

"Why are you telling me now?"

"Anne and I saw him just before he died, and his request was for us to contact you, but we aren't sure who your mother was." Rick said

"My mother found me about five years ago. She died last year in a Colorado nursing home with her daughter by her side. Irene and I met her, and she told me someday my father would reveal himself to me. She would not tell me who he was, and now it seems kind of funny to find out my father was in the ministry also."

"Your father has left you a fortune. From what we understand, he was a multimillionaire, and now it's all yours."

Jack started laughing uncontrollably. "It's not mine. It's God's. Remember when I asked you to pray for me?

"Yes."

"You specifically prayed for this building and to give me hope. I could tell you were not a praying man, and I'm sorry for putting you on the spot, but look what happened. You should pray more often; I don't think I've ever seen a prayer answered in less than five minutes." And again he began to laugh.

Rick and Anne both teared up. "We can't think of a better place for the cardinal's money to go."

"You have the terminology wrong; it isn't the cardinal's money, its God's. There is nothing I need or want on this earth, but God brought you here to help hundreds and hundreds of people. When we stand in judgment before our Father in heaven, the four of us will be united again."

"Jack, we are only the messengers; this isn't our money," Rick said.

"You could have told my father you would find me and never bothered, but you took time to honor his wishes. That says a lot about your characters."

"We were down to two Jack Rosenbaums, and we honestly were ready to go home, but for some reason we both felt compelled to bring the $500.00 back to you for your mission."

"Compelled? No! It was God that put the desire to help in your hearts. Never underestimate the Creator of the Universe," as he smiled at them.

Rick and Anne were now crying and sniffling.

"I have only one request for you two; would you oblige me?"

"Sure," they both said.

"Stay for dinner. The people will be arriving in less than two hours, and I want to introduce you as angels of compassion."

"We would love to stay," Anne said whiping her eyes.

"Ok then, but first I need help peeling twenty five pounds of potatoes; you two put us behind schedule," he said with a laugh.

POLLY TAYLOR'S HOME, GAS CITY, INDIANA

Bill and Polly pulled into her driveway at 4:30 P.M. Bill helped her unload her two large suitcases and carried them in the house for her.

"Bill, I had the best time of my life. The colors in Michigan were spectacular and no photograph in the world could capture their beauty. You were a gentleman and I would like to see you again."

"Polly, I haven't been alone with a woman for over seven years, since Ellie died. I forgot just how much fun companionship can be. You were absolutely fantastic. I want to see you again and again and again."

He put his arms around her, and they kissed.

"Bill, I know how people here talk; the rumor is I have a horrible fetish for shoes and big breasts. I do like shoes, but my ex-husband loves to embellish the story for the guys at the hardware store. The second thing is that you saw them, and you can be the judge on their size," as she laughed.

They both started laughing and kissed again.

"It was funny when I picked you up; I thought the second suitcase was filled with shoes, and I didn't know you could get all that fishing gear in one container. You are one good fisherman!"

"Bill Sales, you are amazing."

"Polly Taylor, you are fantastic, and I love the size."

RUMELY GARDENS HOTEL, ORLANDO, FLORIDA

Rick and Anne sat on their deck and again watched the Disney fireworks from a safe distance.

"I thought maybe we could go to the Magic Kingdom, but what we did tonight was the best." Rick said.

"I've never peeled a potato in my life, let alone about twenty pounds. It was fun. There were a lot of smelly people at the mission, but I never noticed after about ten minutes. One man named Guy asked me if I was married, and I did hesitate a little with my answer," she said with a smile.

"Funny you should mention Guy; Jack told me he used to work for NASA, and after his family was killed in a house fire; he just took to the streets. Think how many stories those people must carry with them."

"Jack Rosenbaum is the humblest man I've ever met. I am so glad we followed through with Cardinal Grey's request. Did you have any inclination to tell him his father was really Albert Harris?"

"Not at all," Rick said. After we met Irene and Jack, the whole matter of hidden identity didn't seem to matter."

"I felt the same way. Albert's money will help generations of people."

"When we get back home, let's follow through with Albert's other wishes."

"Are we really going to dig up a man that is supposed to be Albert and collect $1,000,000? We aren't sure if this so-called Albert is buried or alive." Rick said

"This part doesn't bother me about Albert. The real challenge will be finding this imaginary magical elf. Albert told us he spent a ton of money and many years, but with no avail. What makes you think we can do better?"

"This sounds nuts, but Todd is our key to NeeNee. We have no other way to turn, so how can we convince Todd to introduce us?"

"Have you been listening to yourself?" you just asked, "how can we talk a mentally challenged twenty-five year old man into meeting an imaginary fairy."

"Sound crazy?"

"More than crazy; we are insane even talking about this," Anne said with smirk.

Anthony Becko, Sr. Home, New York City

Tony, his mother and two sisters stood staring at the lifeless body of Anthony "Rolls Royce" Becko.

"Your father was a good man and a wonderful provider for his family," Marie Becko said.

"I feel bad not really knowing my dad like I should have," Tony said.

"Your father also could have met you halfway, but that wasn't his style. He truly loved you, just couldn't express it."

"What do we do we do now?" Tony asked.

"I called your Uncle Paulie; he should be here soon, and he will take care of all the arrangements."

Tony went to his bedroom feeling little emotion. The dead man in the next room was just a corpse to him because his father never once gave Tony a hint of approval. Tony thought if Dar and he got married; he would love his children unconditionally and would strive to be a part of their lives. He picked up his cell phone and called Dar.

"Hi, Dar, my dad died just a few minutes ago. Thanks, but I don't need anything right now. I know you just arrived at Purdue, and I don't expect you to come to the funeral. After this is over, I'll fly out for a football weekend, if that's ok. Sure, sure, I will, and I love you too."

Tony's Uncle Paulie walked into his bedroom and sat on the edge of Tony's bed.

"Your father was a good brother and the toughest of us all. When our dad died, Anthony went to work in the sewers to support Mom and the three of us, and worked real hard. Along the way he met some people connected to city hall, started his own sewer business, and eventually received all the city contracts. The sewer business is long gone, but his connections are still very strong. He wants you to take over our family businesses, and Jimmie and I will help guide you. In two years, you will be my boss." Paulie said with a smile.

"I'm enrolled at New York University and should start classes now."

"Forget school. The education you now will receive will open your eyes to a whole new adventure. We will teach you things that most people never knew existed. It's going to be a rollercoaster ride to say the least, but the family has confidence in you to run it like Anthony."

"When do we start?"

"Right now. I called our tailor, and he'll be here in an hour. You need ten suits, three tuxedos, three sport coats, shirts, shoes, socks, ties, and your own personal handgun. He will bring them all over and by tonight you will be transformed into a leader."

"When do I start my education?"

"It already has; just watch and listen."

MOM'S DINER 5:30 A.M..

The diner was nearly full, and Chris was scrambling to keep up with the orders. The special of the day was three eggs any way, corned beef hash, choice of toast, slice of melon and coffee. Today was the day everyone wanted the special because Chris was running low on the corn beef hash. The farmers' round table was completely full because Bill and Tidy were both back from their trips with their gals.

"Well, well," Lester said "the world travelers are back."

Everyone turned to Bill and Tidy for some great stories about their trips.

Marvin asked, "So, Tidy, how was Denmark?"

"It was wonderful. I had pickled herring and smoked salmon every day for breakfast."

Mom was pouring coffee around the table "Well don't expect me to add that to the menu," she said with a wink.

The guys all laughed and Tidy told of Denmark and Sweden with such great enthusiasm. At one point Tidy got so animated, Clarence told him to slow down and drink some coffee. Hazel knew Danish and Swedish, so he explained they both felt like natives and Tidy knew they weren't getting ripped off. After a good fifteen minutes of talking and smiling, Tidy announced Hazel and he were getting married. The guys all knew that Tidy had waited his whole life for someone like Hazel. Tidy even told the table that Hazel was almost as neat as he. This really floored the guys. As neat as Tidy...wow!

All attention now turned toward Bill, with a grin on each man's face.

Bill told of his trip to Northern Michigan and how beautiful the trees were, with perfect weather. He told them that Polly was a great fisherman, and that she caught her limit each day. Everyone knew Lester would ask the big question.

"So, what about her shoes and the boobs?"

The table was extremely quiet now. Bill took a slow sip of coffee and grabbed another piece of wheat toast from Marvin's plate. The suspense was killing the guys.

"Like I said, she caught her limit." With that, the whole table broke out in a loud laughter.

"Good answer," Mom said as she poured another round of coffee.

Tim and Pamela Sue's Farm

Tim came in for lunch after riding the tractor since 4:30 A.M.. He was hot and dirty.

"I sure miss the kids when they're not around." Tim said

"Me, too. Moses would be next to you in the field and Rahab would be helping me in the kitchen and with household chores. By the way, Rahab's play is in three weeks; we should probably get tickets soon."

"I have to go in town to pick up feed, and can swing by the high school. Should I get tickets for Rick and Sissy?

"For sure, Rick was really impressed with her voice at the last musical. It will seem strange not having your mother sitting with us. She was so proud of Rahab."

"If Moses gets home from school before I get back, have him haul the grain to the elevator. I loaded the truck this morning. Now, what's for lunch?"

"I only have prime rib sandwiches and potato salad."

"Only? Honey, you keep me so filled with great food, you are the best."

"Tim, if something would happen to you, I wouldn't want to live a single day."

"Do you have a vision? Am I going to make it to tomorrow?" He said with a laugh.

"Seriously, Tim, I truly love and respect you," as she leaned down and kissed his sweaty forehead.

He reached around and patted her chubby bottom.

"Want to fool around?"

"Timothy Paul Barr, you go and get that seed," she said with a smile. "There'll be time for that later. My vision says, you'll live a long time. Now get out of here."

Rick and Anne's Farm

Rick and Anne arrived home to find Dick, Jane and, Johnny Cakes all sleeping on the front porch. Mary was right; Johnny, Eric's inherited cat, became a perfect fit with the family. Dick and Jane were a little apprehensive at first, but now they were best buddies. Hazel was working in the kitchen singing to a country song on the radio.

"You seem happy." Anne said. "Tell us about Denmark and Tidy."

"I was hoping you would ask; I've fixed a great dinner for the three of us, and I'll give you all the details."

Rick and Anne took their suitcases up stairs to unpack. Anne thought how strange it will be to go back to New York and live in their huge house. This house was so homey, especially after she remolded it to her liking. The two of them didn't need much in Indiana, and whatever they decided to wear to any Gas City function was perfect. Rick put on a pair of shorts and Anne dressed in jeans and a tee shirt. They came downstairs to play with the cats, and eat. Hazel had set the dining room table with candles and fresh flowers from the garden.

"Sit." She told them. "I want to wait on you tonight."

Hazel was right; the diner consisted of prime rib beef cooked on the grill, roasted new potatoes, fresh green beans, and chocolate pie.

"Tells us." Rick said

"Our trip was amazing. The weather in Denmark and Sweden was perfect, and Tidy is a wonderful person to travel with. He loved everything I suggested, tasted foods he couldn't pronounce, and complimented me over and over for being such a great tour guide."

"Are you two going to travel again?" Anne asked.

"Better than that; Tidy asked me to become his wife, and I accepted. I'm moving out tomorrow so this is kind of a last meal together. I wanted to make it special."

"We are so happy for you," as Rick and Anne hugged her tightly.

"You both have been so kind to me; I will never forget your generosity. You two took me in back in New York because I had no place to go; I feel you are my family."

"We are family, Hazel. You helped raise Eric, and he has turned into a fine young man. Thanks again," Anne said.

Hazel flashed her ring across the table.

"We bought it together in Copenhagen, and he let me pick it out. It is styled like the Danish Queen's ring, so now I feel like royalty."

"Rick and I are moving back to New York; we both feel the calling to return. We are so happy that you will be living close to Eric just in case he has a need."

"Oh, I'll check up on him all right, and between Billie and me, his needs will be taken care of," She said with a laugh.

"Tim and I will help you move to Tidy's when you have your things together."

"I'm already packed, but let's wait until morning. I want to sit on the porch with you two one more night."

"Great! I'll break out the champagne. This calls for a celebration."

ROSELLI'S RESTAURANT, NEW YORK CITY

The basement banquet room was packed with big Italian men in suits. The long table was filled with all sorts of pasta dishes, breads, and bottles and bottles of red wine. When the meal was almost completed, Tony's Uncle Paulie rose to his feet.

"This is Anthony's son, Tony; we are going to teach him family matters so he can lead us. Anthony was adamant about this, and we promised our brother it would come to be. Tony is a sharp, loyal, kid and we want you all to give him the same respect as his father."

"What about the deal in Queens and the hit in Flatbush?" someone yelled.

"All in due time, gentlemen. We are going to take this slow so just be patient for a little while."

All the men stood and held their wine glasses toward Tony. "We are behind you."

Tony was overwhelmed by the meeting and still didn't really get exactly what was going to happen.

"We have decided that Maria Franco should be Tony's wife."

An Old Italian man stood and in broken English said "A match made in heaven; this would unite the Franco Family with us." Every man stood again and held their wine glasses toward Tony. "Salute!" they yelled.

Tony just smiled, and thought to himself; they don't do arranged marriages anymore. That ended fifty years ago. As Tony drank down his wine, he couldn't help thinking that these guys are a hoot.

GAS CITY HIGH SCHOOL

Tim loaded his pickup truck with the feed, and thought he would swing by the high school and get tickets for Rahab's play. Tim walked into the school with no recognition of when he went to Gas City High School. After they consolidated with Union Mills and Mill

Creek Schools, they built a new building. School would be letting out soon so Tim lingered a little to see Rahab, a sophomore and Moses a senior. The halls were a mass of kids after the bell rang. He saw neither one so he returned to his truck. Tim looked over in the student parking lot and noticed a large circle of kids yelling. Tim saw no teachers so he got out of his truck and walked over to the mass of kids. There in the middle was a small young man lying on the ground holding his nose; his books scattered all over the ground. Standing over the kid was Homer Drew, the fullback for the football team. Homer was a mountain of a kid; he stood 6'4'' and probably weighed 280 pounds. Homer was taunting the kid to get up. Just then Moses stepped in the circle and picked up the kids' books and held them tight to his chest. He walked straight up to Homer and stood inches from him.

"I'm a nerd too; when do I get pushed down?"

"I have no beef with you Moses," Homer said.

"Oh, but you do. See I'm bookworm too, and I want some of what you're giving out."

"Moses, just get out of here."

Moses gently laid the books on the ground and again put his 6'2'' frame and face right up to Drew.

Moses said, "I see it two ways; either you hit me now as hard as you can, or you help this guy to his feet and say you're sorry."

The crowd was yelling for Drew not to back down. Drew had a tough decision to make in a hurry.

"If I get in a fight with you, I'll be late for football practice." Drew said boldly.

He stooped down and helped the kid to his feet and said in a, whisper, "Sorry man."

The football players backed up Drew up by saying, "Come on, we have practice." And they all walked away in a tight group.

"Thanks, Moses." the young boy said.

"Think nothing of it; he probably would have mopped the parking lot up with me anyway." Moses said with a laugh.

Tim slipped away in the crowd back to his truck and wept. He was so proud, and he knew between Pamela Sue and he, Moses turned out ok.

Rick and Anne's Farm

Rick and Anne woke up when Dick, Jane, and Johnny Cakes all jumped on the bed for their breakfast.

"Come on, you guys; it's only 5:30 A.M.. Give us another hour," Rick said.

The cats would have none of that. They started scratching the covers and meowing loudly.

Anne said, "I'll feed them but keep the bed warm, I'll be back."

Anne walked downstairs, and it seemed so strange not to have Hazel in the house. Her presence was a welcome sight each morning when the family got up.

Anne got back in bed.

"I called my parents yesterday and told them we were moving back to New York."

"What was their reaction?"

"They want to come out here and see where we've made our home for the last six months. I think they can come next week."

"It will be nice to have them here. They can stay in Eric's room and we can take them to Mom's for some fine dining," Rick said laughing.

"When my father finds out you can get a two pork chop breakfast for $3.99, he'll be in pig heaven."

"Why don't we take a drive today to Mt. Washington and try and find the grave of Albert Harris. This could end up being a $1,000,000 trip. I have a funny feeling about digging up a man that is supposed to be Albert Harris when we saw Albert Harris blow his brains out."

"I know what you're saying. The real Albert planned every last detail for him to remain Cardinal Michael Grey and be buried in Rome. Maybe we'll have a better idea when we get to the cemetery."

Rick slowly put his hand between Anne's legs and stroked her gently. Anne responded with a moan and reached over and stroked Rick. Just then all three cats jumped on the bed and wanted to play. They were jumping, scratching, and wrestling on the bed. They started to laugh and knew this love making session was going nowhere.

"Maybe later?" Rick asked

"Maybe."

BECKO HOME, NEW YORK CITY

Tony came home from the dinner. His uncles dropped him off, and he flopped down on the couch.

"How was the dinner?" His mother asked.

"It was fine, but I didn't completely understand the meaning of it."

"This was kind of a coming out party, you might say, that your uncles put together. They wanted to introduce you to the family."

"I got that part, but what about the mention of me being the head of our businesses? I wasn't sure what they meant and what kind of businesses are they talking about?"

"Your Uncle Paulie will have to explain about the business, but being in charge is what your uncles are training you for."

"They even had a toast to me and my future bride." Tony laughed

"It's not a laughing matter; they have picked out your wife, and you'll be married on your eighteenth birthday in less than three months."

"How can they do that? I haven't even met her and besides, I'm in love with Darlene Moore back in Gas City."

"You better put Darlene out of your mind right now; the family won't hear of it."

"You can't be serious. I can choose to marry anyone I want."

"No, you can't. I was chosen to marry your father and we lasted almost forty years."

"I don't want to just last in a marriage; I want to love a woman for her."

"You will learn to love her; Maria is a nice girl, and the Franco Family is top notch."

"I don't think I can go through with this. I don't want to be trained in anything; I just want to live my own life as I see fit."

"Tony, you will do this for the family. You have been handpicked, and if you don't, your sisters and me will put out on the street."

"On the street, come on."

"You don't understand loyalty son. You have to do this for everyone."

"Mom, I want to think about this before I decide anything."

"There is nothing to think about; you will take over the family. Now get ready. We need to be at the church in two hours for your father's wake."

TIM AND PAMELA SUE'S FARM

The Barr family finished with Pamela Sue's extraordinary meal.

"Great dinner, Honey. Are you related to Betty Crocker?" Tim said with a smile. "By the way I got tickets today for Rahab's play."

"This play really sucks, Rahab said. The plot is stupid and my leading man is a dork."

"What's the play about?" Pamela Sue asked.

"Oh, it's about two doctors; husband and wife that had their first date at a small town bowling alley. He plays the piano, and she plays a harp at the bowling alley. One of my parts is dressing up like the ten pin. Stupid!"

Moses starts to laugh, "This may be a new Broadway hit."

"Shut up!"

"Well, Honey, it sounds interesting; what's the name?"

"*Nine Down-One To Go*" I hope you don't come."

Moses said, with a smile, "Oh, we'll be there all right, I'm going to tape the whole thing."

"You are such a jerk. Why don't you tell Mom and Dad about the fight you got into at high school today?"

"You fought today?" Pamela Sue asked.

"No, it never came to that, but I was ready."

Tim wanted to jump up and tell the family that Moses was a hero, but he'd save his comments for just Moses.

"I'm going up stairs and rehearse my stupid lines and song."

"Honey, you'll do just fine," as Pamela Sue put her arm around her daughter.

"Yeah, right!"

Tim and Moses went out to the barn to finish the evening chores.

"Son, I saw you today in the parking lot. You saved a kid's honor and forced down a bully. I'm very proud of you."

"You were there?"

"I stopped to get the play tickets and noticed the crowd."

"Did you see the size of Drew? Whoa!"

"No one probably ever stood up to him like that. It took guts, son."

"You got guts enough to play a little basketball?" You know I'm the best."

"Moses, I take back everything nice I said about you; now give me the ball. You're going to get a whipping," Rick said laughing.

"In your dreams, old man."

MT. WASHINGTON, KENTUCKY

The three hour drive from Gas City wasn't bad. Rick and Anne went through many a small town on their way, and Mt. Washington was also tiny. The downtown was quaint and not well inhabited, but their goal was the Mt. Washington Memorial Cemetery. They stopped at the only gas and convenience store in town. The sixteen year old kid pointed to his left and said, "Three miles."

Rick drove over three miles, but Anne spotted it on a small hill. The cemetery sign was held up by two old rusty wires, and it appeared they might break at any moment. They parked the car and walked to the small shed but there was no one around. The sign read *See Jacobs Funeral Home For Info.*

"Since we're here; we might as well try and find the grave. It can't be too difficult; this is a small cemetery." Rick said

"What's his name?"

"We're looking for August Dsendew. Why don't we walk row by row and stay close together."

They walked, and walked but found nothing close to August. Just as they were heading to the car Anne yelled.

"I found him."

The grave was completely covered over with grass and the marker had his name and date of death. It was in bad shape. Rick pushed the grass back and took a picture with his cell phone.

"Well, whoever is buried here; we now have a photo of his grave. Let's go into town and find Jacobs Funeral Home; maybe they can shed some light on this guy."

Rick drove the three mile trip back into town and found the funeral home one block from the store. They pulled up, and a guy was pulling weeds in the back.

"Excuse me; do you know who owns the funeral home?" Anne asked

He looked up and said "Yes."

They waited for more response but received none.

"Is there someone in the funeral home that can help us?" Anne asked again

"No." he said

This guessing game was going nowhere.

Rick said sternly, "We need to talk to a funeral director."

"Why didn't you say so? How can I help you; I'm Mr. Jacobs."

"We need some information about a burial you had eighteen years ago."

"Sure, come on in; just let me wash my hands."

They walked behind Mr. Jacobs into the drab, dark office.

"Now what do you need?"

There was an August Dsendew that passed away eighteen years ago, and we are wondering if you have any information on him?

"Are you two family?"

"No but we might have information that he isn't really August Dsendew."

Mr. Jacobs pulled out an old leather bound book and looked in the index.

"There he is. Oh yeah, I remember now. He was a drifter found dead along the road just outside of town. My notes said he had $1,928.00 and a name in his pockets."

"Did the police do an autopsy or send his finger prints to the FBI."

Mr. Jacobs started to giggle which turned into a laughing spree.

"You guys are great, plus you watch way too much TV. The sheriff probably finger printed him and the $1,928.00 was used for his funeral. End of story for Mt. Washington."

"Can we get a death certificate and police report?"

"Yes, but not today; the health department is closed until 9:00 A.M. tomorrow."

"Is there a motel close by?"

"Depends if forty miles means close by to you. Tell you what; my cousin Coco lives across the street and she'll put you up for the night. Her son finally got married and he had a little apartment above their garage. Sounds bad, but it's nice."

"We don't want to put her out."

"Ha, she'll love to have you. I'll call her and tell her you're coming over."

"Thank you for being so nice." Anne said

"I have to; I'm also the county sheriff and my wife runs the health department." He said with a grin.

SISSY'S BEAUTY SHOP

It was almost 7:00 P.M., and Sissy was exhausted. Penelope Ransom and her entire wedding party had been there since 3:00 P.M. The girls went through countless bottles of champagne, and they were just getting started. The limo arrived as she finished the hair on Sandy Ransom, Penelope's first cousin.

"Come on, girls, the night is young, and we need to party." Penelope yelled.

"Sissy, can we take Todd with us?" Sandy asked.

"No, he needs to go to bed soon."

"Mom!"

Sissy looked at her twenty-five year old son sitting in the empty beauty chair. She knew he would never marry and loved having him home. Todd had two glasses of champagne and was now the life of the beauty shop. He was not her baby; loved being around the pretty girls, and they continued to beg.

"Sure, why not. You guys have a great time."

Todd jumped to his feet and hugged Sissy with all he was worth.

"Thanks, Mom, you're the best." Seven beautiful girls and Todd ran out the door to the waiting limo.

Sissy sat back in her styling chair and smiled. She thought she should probably be sad, but wasn't. Her son was going out on his first date, and already she was wondering if he'd be late. Now she started to laugh; if there is ice cream involved, Todd will be in heaven. Sissy wasn't locking her bedroom door anymore, and there was now a peace in her home. She occasionally would recall the image of her father on top of her, but it seldom came.

Sissy walked outside to reread the letter her mother left her. There was so much comfort in her mother's words, and she cherished the piece of paper. She heard a noise coming from the basement and stood at the top of the stairs.

"Anyone down there?"

There was no sound-probably one of those ground squirrels had gotten in she thought.

MT. WASHINGTON, KENTUCKY

Coco was a wonderful hostess. Rick and Anne arose to find a hot pot of coffee and fresh baked blueberry muffins on the table. The food was arranged beautifully on a wicker tray with fresh picked flowers in a vase. Rick carried the tray to their bed.

"This is better than a B and B; she made us breakfast in bed," Anne said.

"We need to pay her," Rick said.

"Let's ask Mr. Jacobs what would be fitting?"

They showered, dressed, and walked down the stairs from above the garage. Coco was sitting in a chair by the side door.

"Did you sleep well?" she asked

"Great sleep, and thanks for the breakfast"

"No, no, that wasn't breakfast; I have breakfast in the kitchen for you. Come on in."

Coco's house was modest, but she had flair for the eccentric. Coco wore a flowered hat, pink print dress, and high heels. Her arms were loaded with bracelets and her fingers with rings. The house was stuffed with glassware and statues, something out of a designer magazine.

"My parents named me Coco after Coco Chanel, and I've been to Paris six times. Oh, I love France! Have you two been there?"

"Yes, and we also love it." Anne said.

Coco passed around a plate of croissants and French jellies. She had little poached eggs and slices of imported cheeses.

"I love to entertain, so please eat up."

They finished the wonderful breakfast but she would not accept a penny. They told her over and over that she was a wonderful hostess.

They walked across the street to the funeral home, and Mr. Jacobs was again pulling weeds in the back.

"I got a kid to help but he's never here when I need him. Why don't I walk you down the street to the health department. The records should be ready. I told my wife to get the stuff together."

"Your cousin, Coco, was great. Can we get her something because she wouldn't take any money?" Anne asked

"Did she overdue the French thing a little?"

"No, she was very nice."

"I don't know where you two live but send her a box of French chocolates. She absolutely adores them."

"We will and thank you for calling her for us. Will she be going back to France again?"

"Again?" He laughed. "She's never been out of the state of Kentucky, but in her mind, Paris is her second home. A little kooky but she has a big heart."

The small, dusty health department had two employees and they guessed which one was Mr. Jacob's wife because he kissed her on the lips.

"Got your papers right here. That will be $8.00." She said

Rick asked, "If we want to dig up Mr. Dsendew, how can we do that?"

"Since there are no relatives; you need to send a form to the Kentucky Attorney General and request permission. It takes about sixty days; then you'll need to get grave diggers to open his grave, and that runs about $1000.00. It really isn't too involved. What is your interest in the drifter?"

"Oh, he might be a long lost relative." Anne said as she looked at Rick.

"Thank you for your help; be sure and tell Coco we enjoyed her hospitality. One more question; why is the town called Mt. Washington?" Rick asked.

Mr. Jacobs started to laugh, "As you leave town look to your left and you'll see a small hill; supposedly George Washington stood there. Why he would come here is beyond me; maybe he got lost."

Sissy's Beauty shop

I was almost 2:00 A.M. when Sissy heard the limo and the laughter in her driveway. Should she greet Todd at the door or ignore him and see if he comes to her room? She opted for the later. The door banged open and Todd made a bee line to her bedroom. Sissy pretended to be sound asleep.

"Mom, Mom I'm home!" He yelled

"So you are." as she sat up in bed.

"I went dancing and saw some girl's boobies!" he yelled again.

"Tell me all about it."

"We rode in this long black car, and we had some strange drinks with umbrellas in them and then we drank these little drinks all at once. It was fun!"

"You drank shots?"

"Yeah, that's the name."

"When did you see boobies?"

"This nice place we went to had dancers, and a girl took off her shirt."

"Did you like that?" she asked

"I sure did Mom!" "This is the best night of my life. I danced with a whole bunch of girls, and they really liked me. I even did a thing called the limbo."

"Todd, you are amazing. I thought you would come home feeling upset."

"I am a little dizzy. I'm going to bed now, and I'll tell NeeNee about it tomorrow. Goodnight, Mom; I love you."

"I love you, too."

Sissy sat back in her bed and smiled. Her son had a great time, and the girls watched over him. Maybe it's time for Todd to get out more and experience life. Her baby boy was really a man now, especially since he experienced his first set of boobies. She just laughed and wondered what his dance techniques were like. Her prayer tonight would be thanking God for watching over her only son.

"Thanks, God, you had a son, too."

RICK AND ANNE'S FARM

Rick and Anne got home and put their clothes in the laundry. They now had an agreement with Rahab to clean their house and cook dinner three nights a week. It was a perfect arrangement, and Rahab made good money.

"Your dad told us he has tickets to your play this weekend. We're excited."

"I'm glad someone is; this play is awful. The playwright is some new LA jerk that thinks he has a selected insight on the Midwest. What an asshole!"

"Your mom said the music is beautiful," Anne said.

"My mom would say fingernails on a chalkboard would be beautiful if her daughter was involved. Please don't come."

"We really want to. Anne's parents will be here from New York and we want to bring them."

"Oh great!, New York critics," Rahab said with a laugh.

"What's the play about?"

"It takes place in a small town bowling alley where two people have their first date, and they become doctors. They come back and entertain the bowlers. What a bunch of crap!"

"It's a musical?"

"If you call it that. The only redeeming song I sing is about a bowler who falls in love with a one-armed girl."

"Sounds different."

"You have no idea. I fixed you a pot roast with potatoes in the crock pot and there is asparagus in the oven. I'll see you tomorrow and reconsider not coming to the play."

They laughed and sat down to eat in the solarium. Anne heard a car horn blaring.

"Who in the heck is that?"

She looked out, and her parents were unloading their car in the barnyard.

Anne yelled "You drove?"

"Yes. Your father wanted to see if he could still do it. It was a wild trip, but here we are."

Anne ran out and hugged them, with Rick following close behind to be the bag handler.

"We thought you were arriving in Indianapolis, and I was to pick you up at the airport tomorrow morning," Rick said

"Change of plans my boy. I wanted to see the Midwest first hand, not from 35,000 feet." Bob Miller came back with.

"Well, welcome to Indiana. We are just sitting down to dinner, come on in and share."

"We're starving. That sounds good."

The four sat around the table with three cats looking up, hoping for some clumsy person to drop some food to the floor.

"Honey your house is beautiful. Your dad and I expected an old beat up farm house."

"It was, Mom; before we started this place was a pit. We had Amish builders complete the house, and we now are friends with the whole Yoder clan."

"This pot roast is fabulous! Anne, you've become a wonderful cook," her father remarked.

"I didn't do this; our niece comes over three days a week and fixes our dinner."

"Anne has become a good cook in her own right. She picks fresh from our own garden and our meat comes from my brother's butchering shed right down the road."

"The Barr Family is having a cookout on Friday after a high school play. This is what we do in Gas City."

"Sounds like fun. Last week your father and I went to the Met, and we got to go backstage and meet the opera singers. It was unbelievable!"

"My niece has the lead, so if you want to meet her and go backstage, I can score you some tickets." Rick said laughing out loud.

"May I have another piece of pot roast?" her father asked. This is great, and I can't wait to meet this young lady."

"What's the play about?"

"We understand it takes place in a small town bowling alley."

"Humm, this may not be on quite the same level as the Met." Bob Miller said with a smile

MOM'S DINER EARLY FRIDAY MORNING

Mom was as busy as a bee. Ever since the guys painted her diner, put up a new sign, and added new checkered tablecloths, her business had been good. Today the large round table was in a twit, and mom went over to shut the guys up.

"Keep it down; I do have other customers besides you hayseeds."

Marvin said, "Ok then answer a question for us. The Indiana Farm Bureau has the annual feather party to raise money for the less fortunate at Thanksgiving. We have to come up with a theme and money raiser. Last year we had a turkey flying contest; the year before, guess the turkey's weigh; year before that was catching a turkey blindfolded. This year it was suggested we have a turkey race down Main Street or killing a turkey the fastest using only your bare hands."

"You guys can't be serious. Nobody wants to watch a turkey being strangled."

"I would," Lester said.

"Me, too," Ralph replied.

"Let me rephrase that; no normal person wants to watch a turkey die."

"So you think a race down Main Street would be good?" Marvin asked.

"Oh no, don't put my name on that one. You guys are on your own. Remember about five years ago you guys spray painted the turkeys for a beauty contest, and they all died from being painted?"

"Oh yeah." Lester said.

"Why don't you just have a raffle for a turkey dinner with all the trimmings? I'll even donate ten dinners for your raffle."

"That sounds good," they all chanted.

"At least this way we don't have to see turkeys being tortured or killed."

"Mom, you're the best," Marvin said.

She just walked away from the table shaking her head.

Rick and Anne's Farm

Bob and Marge Miller awoke feeling wonderful. Marge looked at the foot of the bed; all three cats were fast asleep and were such a tight ball, you couldn't tell where one cat started or ended. Marge and Bob walked downstairs to the smell of fresh brewed coffee.

Anne said, "Put on your tennis shoes; we're walking to breakfast today."

"How far are we going, Honey?"

"Just a quarter mile down the dirt road to Tim and Pamela Sue's farm. Pamela Sue noticed your car in the barnyard and invited us down to breakfast. She just finished curing a ham, and is one amazing cook; you won't be disappointed. You can meet Rahab before her play tonight; she's also a sweetheart," Anne said.

"Sounds good; let's go," Bob said.

The four walked slowly, but for both her parents being in their early eighties, they did well. As they approached the farm, the smell of cows, pigs, and horses caught their noses. Her parents never said a word.

Rick and Anne didn't bother to knock; they just walked in. The kitchen was large and Pamela Sue had her back to them tending to something on the stove. She turned with a large smile.

"I'm Pamela Sue, and this is my house. Welcome."

Instantly Bob and Marge fell in love with her. She put a loaf of warm fresh-baked bread on the table and invited them to sit. Pamela Sue pointed out the homemade jams, jellies, and apple butter for the bread. She then pulled from the skillet three large slices of cured ham and a pan of fried potatoes. Bob and Marge looked at each other like they were dreaming. Tim came in from the barn and introduced himself and sat at the head of the kitchen table. He reached his long arms to hold the hand of Marge, and the others followed for the blessing. Marge's hand was completely engulfed in Tim's large powerful hand. They fell in love with him also. Platters of food were being passed, and Pamela Sue was pouring coffee and warm apple cider.

Anne asked "Where's Rahab? We want to introduce my parents."

"She left early this morning for one last practice before the play tonight. She really doesn't like the play."

"Does she have the jitters?" Marge asked

"No, it's the play, and her leading man doesn't know his lines or the songs."

"This is the best breakfast I've ever eaten, and trust me; I've had many a breakfast in the past eighty-two years," Bob said with a smile.

"Thank you. When you leave, I'll send some cured and smoked hams with you."

"That would be fantastic. Your kitchen is so inviting."

"We spend a lot of time in here," Tim said "This is our meeting room."

"I have some fresh picked berries and melon for desert, if you like?"

"You're trying to kill me. When can you move to New York and open a restaurant? People will be lined up for blocks," Bob said.

"We visited New York and, it was great, but I have a mission to feed and respect the man at end of the table."

Tim looked up and smiled.

BECKO HOME NEW YORK CITY

This was to be Tony's fourth day of traveling with his uncles through New York. The first three days were spent meeting guys and collecting money. His uncles told him that it was for rent, but they didn't own the buildings. Tony carried a laptop with all the accounts registered by name. It seemed tedious to Tony, and he wondered why they couldn't send someone else to collect money. He was told it will happen in due time, but first he needed to meet the guys he would be working with. Today they pulled in front of a large building, and a doorman came out to greet them.

"This is Anthony's boy, Tony," Paulie said.

"I'll be seeing a lot of you," as he held the large door for them.

They took a private elevator to the sixteenth floor and got out. The lobby area was all glass and marble from the turn of the century.

"This is Tony," Paulie said to the receptionist. "We are meeting in his office, so call Willard."

Down a long hall was a large oak door. Paulie opened it to reveal a huge desk, sink, and oak bar that rapped around the far wall. The huge window behind the desk looked out on Central Park.

"This is where you will come each day. Your father sat in that chair for the last forty one years and served the family faithfully. We know you will do the same."

The receptionist knocked quietly, and then stepped in. She was about mid-thirties and beautiful. Her skirt was way above her knees and the dress was so tight, Tony noticed she wasn't wearing underwear.

"Can I get anyone a drink?" she offered.

Both his uncles ordered Bloody Marys, and Tony asked for a Mountain Dew.

Another knock at the door, and a frail older man entered.

"I'm Willard Duer, and I'm here to help you."

"We're going to leave you two. We'll be back at 5:00 P.M. for dinner."

Tony took off his sport coat and sat behind the desk. Willard opened his laptop and sat back for a minute.

"Tony, this going to seem Greek to you, but I will help you make heads and tails of the businesses. I've worked for you dad for over thirty years, and we had a good relationship. I hope we can continue the bond. You may ask me anything, and I will never tell of our conversation. I'm not your father, but I'm going to act like it. You're my boy now and can trust me."

"Ok, my first question is; do I have to marry Maria Franco?"

Willard laughed "You do. It will be a merger of families, so to speak, and everyone is counting on it."

"But I haven't even met her yet and I'm to be married in three months."

"Soon enough you will, but a word of advice, don't touch her. We can fix you up with anyone you wish, Playboy Bunnies, prostitutes, or even your receptionist. Do not touch Maria until you're married. This little information may save your life."

"I appreciate it, but is Maria nice looking?

"I'm seventy years old, and from my stand point she's a knock out. Let's get down to business; you have much to learn."

GAS CITY CONSOLIDATED HIGH SCHOOL

The parking lot was nearly full when Rick, Anne and her parents arrived. Anne told her mother she was way overdressed for the play, but she insisted on wearing a cocktail dress, high heels, and a lot of jewelry. Tim and Pamela Sue were in the first row and had saved seats for the family. As they started to sit Pamela Sue remarked, that she was so nervous; four trips to the bathroom, and she was beginning to get the urge again.

"This play is well attended," Marge said.

"In another fifteen minutes people will be standing in the back and aisles," Tim said.

The high school band started to play, and the lights began to dim. The curtains opened to an enormous bowling alley with ten very large pins centered in the middle of the stage. As the music played there was singing, but no singers were present; all of sudden the bowling pins began to turn, and each one was a student. Rahab was the first pin. She was wearing white tights, and her face was white with a red ring around her neck. The music resembled some soft rock from the 70's. Her voice was far superior compared to the rest. The play continued, and there were many costume changes. There was a fifteen minute intermission, and everyone stood.

Bob and Marge stood and looked at Pamela Sue.

"I have to tell you," Bob said, "your daughter's voice is spectacular, and I'm not just saying that. Marge and I belong to many musical guilds and we support the arts heavily, so I know what I'm talking about."

"He's right; with some training, she'll go far. We have many connections in New York, and after the play we would like to talk to Tim, Rahab, and you. She could finish her high school in New York attending a private music school."

Pamela Sue looked over at Tim as the lights began to dim. This was a lot to take in watching a mediocre musical at best.

The play ended on a high note. The two lovers went to medical school but continued to return to the bowling alley and play the piano and harp for the patrons. Everyone rose, but the Barr's, Marge and Bob remained seated. The auditorium was almost empty when Rahab came out from back stage. Tim and Pamela Sue hugged, kissed, and praised her.

"We have good news for you," Pamela Sue said.

"What, I haven't been expelled, or you haven't disowned me?"

They all arrived at Tim and Pamela Sue's. The fire and food was already going. Moses left the play right away to get things ready. The big harvest table was set with candles, gourds, and small pumpkins. Everyone sat down, and Tim tended the fire and the meat. Rahab went in the house to take a quick shower and cry a little. Tim came to the table with a huge platter of sliced prime rib, potatoes wedges, and sweet corn.

"Shall we wait for Rahab?" Tim asked.

Todd yelled "No, let's eat!"

"He's right. She'll be out in a minute." Pamela Sue remarked.

They held hands and Tim prayed for the food and his daughter.

"Amen," They all said.

Again Bob and Marge were blown away by the food.

"This prime rib is awesome; how did you do this?" Marge asked.

Pamela Sue's mind was on Rahab but she said "Well, we start with the best fresh meat you can get; then I soak the prime rib in French onion soup, and slow cook it for five hours. We throw it on the fire, slow cook it, and here it is."

Bob said, "We really feel welcome here. Thank you."

"The way I see it, we're all family," Tim said as he stabbed another slice of meat.

Rahab finally came out and sat at the table.

"Honey, what would you like?"

"A gun."

"It was an entertaining play; we all enjoyed it," Rick said.

Even Moses knew he better not open his mouth about the play. He was dying to tease her, but if he did, his life would be shortened by several years.

"Anne's parents loved your voice, and they want to talk to you about going to New York and attending a private music school."

She looked down the table and both Bob and Marge were nodding their heads. Rahab sat up straight and asked for some prime rib.

"Really?"

"Your voice is unbelievable, and with some training, you can write your own ticket," Bob said.

After dinner they sat around the campfire and talked. It was a beautiful fall evening, and the crickets were in full concert tonight. Pamela Sue passed around her home made blackberry wine, and Tim brought out a bucket of his favorite local beer. Todd was anxious to get home to watch a movie on dinosaurs, but first he had to tell the family he saw a girl's boobies. This comment brought the house down, and everyone laughed but Sissy. The others were also getting tired, and everyone started to leave. Marge told Rahab they would talk about her coming to New York in the next couple of days.

Tim and Pamela Sue went up to bed, and as Tim was almost asleep, she asked "Can we give her up?"

"We aren't sending her to the moon."

"That's not what I asked; can we let her spend these precious years away from us?"

"Let's talk to Rahab tomorrow; I can't keep my eyes open."

Pamela Sue kissed Tim, and walked down stairs to sit on the porch and process this offer. She stepped on the porch, and Rahab was sitting on the swing, curled up in a blanket.

"Mom, can we talk?"

Rick And Anne's Farm

Anne's parents talked all the way home.

"Your brother and sister-in-law are wonderful people. Are you two sure you want to move back to New York?" Marge asked.

"Mom, Rick and I do have some doubts, but we're not challenged enough. I want to run for judge and Rick needs to take the business to another level. We love it, but it's hard to live here."

"I understand, Honey, but from our perspective, this place is heaven. Dad and I talked about staying here each summer and coming back to New York when the weather starts to get nasty. Our summer home in upstate New York is filled with nice people, but they are a bunch of snobs, and everyone talks about what they will wear and the newest fashions. I guess here, you can be and do what you want."

"That's true, but we have our own gossip group. Tomorrow we'll go to the beauty shop, and Rick can take Dad to the diner for breakfast; your eyes will be opened."

"Maybe so, but for right now, can we sit on the porch and have some wine?"

"Of course, Mom; I'll have Rick fix a batch of Indiana popcorn smothered in butter, and we can watch for a coyote to run through the yard."

The four went on the porch, took off their shoes, and put their feet on the railing. The three cats didn't want to be left out, so they came out to be a part of the group. It wasn't five minutes and all three cats sat straight up, and looked toward the barn.

"Watch, Mom."

Just then a coyote and three pups ran no more than ten feet from the porch. The mom just glanced over and gave a look like she wasn't too concerned who was sitting there.

"Wow! That Coyote was big," Bob remarked.

"Wait till you see the male; you can tell he's been in many a fight and he won't be too far behind the brood," Rick said.

They talked, ate popcorn, and watched the shooting stars until their eyes became heavy; the four adults and three cats went inside to bed.

MOM'S DINER

It was nearly 6:00 A.M., Rick and his father-in-law walked in. They walked toward a booth, but the guys started yelling for them to sit at the round table.

"This is my father-in-law, Bob, from New York."

"Hey, Bob," they all yelled.

All fourteen guys introduced themselves with a first name, and even Terrence told Bob his name was Tidy.

Bob ordered the special, which consisted of two pork chops, fried potatoes, toast and coffee for $3.99. Bob already loved this place. The conversation resumed about Butch Garwood and his foot.

"He looks bad," Lester said.

"The doctor warned him about the diabetes, but he lived the life style he chose. They took his left leg just below the knee."

"Why don't we go to his farm on Friday and pick beans for him?" Marvin said. "I think we can get it done by 5:00 P.M."

Mom brought the food over. "I think it's great you can help Butch. He has the three grandchildren they're raising, and he'd do the same for you guys."

Ralph said, "I have some money that's not getting any return; I'll put in the first $500.00."

They all nodded in agreement, and Tidy did the math. They figured to give the family $7500.00 on Friday.

Bob Miller spoke up, "I'll match the $7500."

All the guys looked down the table at Bob.

"Thanks, Bob, Marvin said. What's cool is you've never met him."

"If you guys vouch for him, he must be good."

Sissy's Beauty Shop

Anne and her mother had breakfast with Pamela Sue and brought fresh cinnamon rolls to Sissy and Todd. They pulled up to the little yellow house, and Anne carried the picnic basket Pamela Sue had arranged. The closed sign was still on the door, but they just walked in.

"Sissy?" Anne called.

"I'll be right up; Todd is helping me arrange my supplies."

Anne set the basket on the kitchen table, and the two sat down and waited.

"What brings you by?" Sissy asked

"Pamela Sue packed a basket of cinnamon rolls and fresh fruit for Todd and you because she knew we were coming to town."

"Thank you, but let's take it outside on the picnic table. Todd, come on up; we have cinnamon rolls."

Todd ran up the stairs, grabbed two rolls, and back down the basement he flew.

"Why is he in such a hurry?" Anne asked.

"Oh he's putting a 3D dinosaur puzzle together, and he's nearly done."

"Do you have time to trim my hair?" Marge asked

"Sure, my first appointment isn't until 10:00 A.M., I have time to do a perm if you like."

"Why not, the boys went to the diner and then they were going to the Yoder Farm. Bob is fascinated by the Amish."

Marge sat in the styling chair, and Anne picked up a magazine.

"Bob and I liked the play last night."

"It certainly was different. Rahab made the play with her voice and acting."

"She sure did, I hope she will consider coming to New York."

"Mom, you have to remember; this is a huge choice for a fifteen year old girl that's never been anywhere."

"I know, Honey, but your father and I see a big career in that girl."

Just then Shari B came in for her weekly trim and rinse.

"Hi, Sissy. Hi Anne," Shari said.

"This is my mother, Marge, from New York."

"Nice to meet you. I saw you at the play last night sitting in the front row, so I knew you had to be family."

Marge moved to the other chair to let her hair dry, and Shari sat in the large beauty chair.

"Did you girls hear about Libby's bush?" Shari B said with a big grin on her face.

"What are you talking about?" Sissy asked.

"Libby had her bush dyed red"

"Which bush?"

"You know, her bush, her pubic hair."

"Oh, My! Well I didn't do it." Sissy said.

"No, she did it herself for Roger."

"She also has a small yellow butterfly tattoo by her red bush."

"Get out of here." Anne said, "Where did you hear that?"

"Their daughter Emily told my daughter, Ellen, at a sleep over last night."

"Whoa! Now there's some gossip that is hot off the press."

"I wonder if Roger likes it?" Sissy asked.

"Apparently, because their neighbor, Bea Hilton, saw them having sex in the kitchen on a chair," Shari said with a grin.

"Wow! I think the shop is beginning to heat up a little," Sissy said laughing.

"Who are Roger and Libby?" Marge asked.

"Oh, he's our minister and wife."

"Man! And I thought my beauty shop in New York had some good stories."

Tony's Office New York City

It had been a week and Tony got an eye and head full of knowledge. His uncle Paulie was a tough guy, and wanted Tony to get up to speed quicker. Tony poured over his laptop; the numbers were staggering. He counted eighty-six employees on the payroll, but he hadn't met more than three. There was no job description for a single one. He knew at age seventeen, eighty-six employees were a lot, but who were they? Tony picked up the phone and told his secretary to call Willard.

Fifteen minutes later Tony's phone rang and his secretary announced Willard was here.

"Send him in please."

Tony liked playing the power boss. All he had to do was ask, and someone would bring him anything he desired. He couldn't wait to call Eric at IU and tell him what was happening. Tony had access to any sporting event, rock concert, or club in the city, and not to just get in, but front row.

"Good morning, Mr. Becko." Willard said

"Ok, no more Mr. Becko; call me Tony."

"Sure, now what did you want?"

"I've been looking at the payroll, and who are all these people we pay?"

"I can go over each name if you wish or just give you an idea what they do."

"That's all I want."

"The majority of people are family in one way or another. Some own flower shops, gas stations, towing services, livery and limo businesses, funeral homes, and New York City employees. The other people are contract workers, and we keep them on the payroll. When their services are needed, we just call."

"What kind of services?"

"Attorneys, bodyguards, and hit men."

"Hit men, really?"

"Yes, but it's not like Al Capone with machine guns or mob hits; it's when someone gets in our way and won't move. Sometimes people just disappear."

"Could I have someone disappear?"

"Sure, but keep in mind, whatever decision you make has its consequences. Never make a rash decision; always think it through carefully. Your father was the best when it came to that, but your Uncle Paulie tends to jump before looking. Keep that comment between us."

"I also noticed these same people we pay; pay us. How does that work?"

"Your family is very tight, and for example, your cousin Alex who runs twenty-six flower shops may need for you to order $20,000.00 of flowers, and on paper you do. You pay him for the banquet flowers, and he will pay $20,000.00 to your towing company for towing cars and trucks. Again, all on paper. The towing company will arrange for a $20,000.00 funeral from your cousin Vince. Do you kind of see now?"

"I'm beginning to get the picture."

"Good news for you. Next Saturday you will meet your future wife at the Franco Family cookout. Maria is anxious to meet you also. This party is huge, and every major player in New York will be there: Politicians, movie stars, sports figures, a U.S. Supreme Court Justice, and the Vice President of the United States. Even with all these people there; every eye will be on Maria and you. We have some staff coming to guide and coach you through this dinner."

"What am I supposed to do?"

"Walk through the crowd like your shit doesn't stink, and you'll be fine," he said laughing out loud.

Rick and Anne's Farm

Anne and her mother pulled into the barnyard, and all three cats were asleep on the porch.

"Honey, I get what you were saying about people talking. Even in New York, I've never heard anything close to a minister's wife coloring her bush and having sex in the kitchen."

"I guess the cool thing is that even though you might talk about people, they would still lay down their lives for you or come running if there was any problem. The people here are real, and I'm so glad Dad and you got to experience our little town."

Marge started to cry "You two are the happiest I've ever seen you. Just five months ago you were going to leave Rick, and now you're madly in love with him."

"We are happy, and the return to New York will be a challenge, but we have a new perspective on our lives together."

"Honey, the lady at the beauty shop, why do you call her Shari B?"

"Her maiden name was Bailey, she married Rick Barns, they divorced. She married Jimmy Baxter, they divorced. She married Dave Birchfield, they divorced and she is now married to Billy Brooks. See why it's Shari B?"

"Oh" her mother said with a smile.

Just then Rick and Bob pulled in the barn yarn. The two guys exited the truck laughing out loud.

Marge said, "You boys seem amused."

"We had a great time; the guys at the diner are a hoot," Bob said. "I'm going to help pick beans for a guy who lost his foot, and I've never seen a bean except at Whole Foods. This may be fun. Marvin told me I can drive either the picker or his tractor."

"You boys and your toys," Anne said with a smile.

Bob continued, "I met the Yoder Family and they are remarkable. No electricity, no cars, no phones, no televisions, no radios, but a faith in God like I've never seen. Mr. Yoder prayed over Rick and me for safety and discerning decisions. I have some ideas I want to share with you all tonight after dinner, and maybe we can have a bonfire."

"Sure, Dad, right after dinner."

SALES AND SON FUNERAL HOME

Susan was washing the dishes from the great meal she had just fixed for Wyatt and her dad. Bill went downstairs to the funeral home office to do bookwork. He opened his locked desk, and gently retrieved a fancy ring box. He opened the box, and there was a one carat diamond engagement ring staring back at him. He was going to propose to Polly Taylor, but first he had to ask his children if they would approve. He rehearsed the speech at least ten times before he walked upstairs while they were watching television.

"Will you turn the television off for just a minute; I have an announcement to make to you two."

His hands were sweaty and he felt really uncomfortable. Bill fidgeted for a minute, and for the life of him, he couldn't remember how the speech began.

"Dad, what?" Wyatt asked.

"You know your mother has been gone for over seven years, and, and, I've been thinking."

He paused and tried to regroup his thoughts

"What are you trying to say?" Susan asked.

"Well, I've put a lot of thought on how to tell you something."

"Come on, Dad, what? Just let it out."

"I'm going to ask Polly to marry me."

The two kids started laughing uncontrollably. It took about three minutes for Wyatt to say something.

"That's it?" That's all you have to say?"

"Yes, why?"

"Because we thought you were going to tell us you had cancer and would be joining Mom in heaven." Wyatt laughed.

Susan smiled, "Dad, we think it's great. We like Polly, and you've been alone too long."

"Really?" Bill said.

"Dad, grow up. You shouldn't be alone, and everyone in town talks about her big boobs," Susan said.

They all laughed now.

"I thought maybe you would think I wasn't being faithful to your mother's memory."

"Mom would want this for you. Until she became so depressed, she adored and wanted you to be happy," Susan said with a tear in her eye. The two kids hugged their father, and turned the television back on. Bill walked downstairs in disbelief. That was easy. Now he was going to Polly's house to get her verdict.

RICK AND ANNE'S FARM

Pamela Sue brought over a large pot of beef stew, cornbread, and a cherry pie because she made too much for her family. That suited Rick and family perfectly. Rick started a bonfire, and the four of them sat around and talked.

"Your mother and I have been talking. When you two move back to New York, we don't want you to sell the farm. If it's a money thing, I'll buy it from you. The last few days for us have been fantastic; we like your town, your friends, your family, and even the cats. Mom and I feel at peace here; does that make sense to you?"

"Dad, we get it. We have found the same thing ourselves."

"Honey, we want to stay on when you move back. Your dad feels needed here and the people respect him for who is, not what they can get out of him. Aurora Corporation is doing well but your father is worn out with the day to day decisions."

"It's not money. You can live here forever; this now is your home also," Anne said.

"We are so happy you've taken to Gas City like we have, and the guys at the diner today think you're super."

"Mom, what are you going to do with all your help? Are you going to let Andre, your chef, go?"

"We've decided to pay them until they can find other work. Our driver and gardeners should be fine, but Andre is another story. He is so particular and anal about everything; I just don't know about him."

"Well, Pamela Sue will keep an eye on you, and she hasn't a judgmental bone in her body. She might even cook meals for you."

"We would pay her well," Marge said.

"She won't take a dime, but if you buy a steer from Moses when the fair is on, that will clear any obligation you feel you have."

"How about some smores?"

"What's that?" Marge asked

"Two graham crackers with a toasted marshmallow and a slice of chocolate between them."

"Sounds good; bring um on," they both said.

POLLY TAYLOR'S HOME

Bill kept playing with ring box the three blocks to Polly's house. His first speech went well with the kids, and he hoped there would be a repeat. Polly was sitting on her back porch, and Bill walked through the screen door. He bent down and kissed her.

"How's my favorite fisherman?" he asked

"Great, and by the way, I have the fish all cleaned and packed for you to take home."

"Awesome, and I have the pictures printed off, but I forgot to bring them."

"Bill that was the best trip I've ever been on. I still can't get over the beauty in the trees and the sunsets off Lake Michigan."

"Me, too."

"I'm having a vodka and cranberry; would you like one?"

"Sure, sounds good."

They both sat back, and Bill was ready for the speech.

"Polly, I need to ask you something. I had the best time, and you are a wonderful, gentle lady. I've been alone for over seven years, and I don't want that anymore. Will you be my wife?"

Polly started to cry. "Bill Sales, you are a great guy, but I can't marry you now. I thought you might ask me sometime, so I prepared a speech of my own. My last marriage was horrible. My ex-husband was abusive both physically and mentally. Nothing I ever did was quite right, and I cried myself to sleep each night for ten years. The wounds are deep; real deep. I need to heal for a while and find Polly Taylor again. She's way down in my soul and I need to reconnect with her. I love you, Bill Sales, but until I mend; I can't be the wife I want to be for you. It's kind of like a rain check at the ball park; the game is delayed, but not over. Please continue to come over and see me, and maybe we can take another trip, but now isn't the time for me to become Mrs. William Sales."

Bill started to tear up. "Polly, I had no idea."

"My ex talks a good talk, but it's all about him. He used to beat me with a catcher's mitt so there wouldn't any bruises. My nightmares are real life. I'm sorry to unload on you, but you needed to know why I made this decision."

"Polly I completely understand. I want to continue to see you and we'll have fun together. When the time is right, we'll both know."

"That's the reason I love you; kindness is your middle name," she said with a smile.

"After I hock the ring; how about Vegas?"

"Keep the ring, and Vegas sounds great."

SISSY'S BEAUTY SHOP

It was getting late, and Sissy had just finished cleaning the brushes and combs when she heard Todd scream and run around the basement.

"Todd, are you ok?" Sissy yelled down the basement.

"Yeah, Mom."

"Well, what in the heck are you doing?"

"NeeNee took my dinosaur magazine and wouldn't give it back."

"Todd come up here; I need to talk to you about something important."

"Can we get ice cream after?"

"All right, but please come up now."

Todd came up the stairs and sat in the styling chair.

"Todd, you're twenty-five years old, and you had a good time the other night with the girls."

"I sure did. I got to see…

"I know, Todd," she interrupted, "you shouldn't talk about boobies for a while. I want you to go out more and be with other people. Sunday night the church is having a young adult outing at Cougar Park and I think you'd have fun."

"What do they do?"

"They're having games, a camp fire, and probably ice cream or something like that."

"I'll go."

"And Todd, maybe you can forget about NeeNee for a while. There are some great things to do outside this house."

"I still want to be friends with NeeNee."

"You can dear, but maybe not so often. He isn't real anyway."

"He is, too!"

"Todd, we've been through this a hundred times: then why can't I see him?"

"He doesn't want grown up people around."

"You have blamed NeeNee for things that happen around here for years. You can't keep making up an imaginary friend."

"Mom, he's real!"

"Prove it then!"

Todd got up from the chair and walked to the basement stairway.

"NeeNee, Mom doesn't believe; show her."

All of sudden the house began to shake. Everything started to fall off the shelves, and chairs were moved from the violent movements. Dishes fell off the sink, and the light above the kitchen table was swinging back and forth. Sissy's hairspray, tint, and brushes fell to the floor.

"Ok, Todd enough!" Sissy screamed.

"All right, NeeNee." Todd yelled down the basement stairs and the shaking quit immediately.

Sissy sat in the styling chair and stared at Todd. She couldn't form any words to communicate with her son. How did Todd pull that off? She thought. Random earthquake, gas line explosion, what?

Before she could utter a word, Todd said, "You promised ice cream. Let's go."

ANNE'S OFFICE GAS CITY

The lease was about up, so Rick and Anne started to pack up what little they had.

"Look, Rick, all the hidden cameras and microphones are gone. I bet they came when we were in Virginia."

Rick put all the papers and notes in a cardboard box. On Anne's back desk was a small envelope addressed to Anne.

"Honey, I found something."

She opened the letter and it read.

Thank you for staying out of our business. Please call the number below when you find this."

"Should we follow through or let it be?" Anne asked.

"At this point, it can't hurt to call."

Anne called the number from her cellphone, and the other end picked it up, but there was silence for a few seconds.

"Thank you for calling, Mrs. Barr. Your husband and you made a wise choice in not pursuing any further."

"We felt pressured not to."

"Everything went well for our friend's wishes. It couldn't have been better."

"It's really comforting to know Albert Harris is buried in Rome," Anne said sarcastically.

"We have found our friend's son, and he will be richly rewarded, thanks to you."

"You had us followed?"

"Like I said before, Thank you." and the phone went dead.

"Those bastards! They just think we are nobodies and can push us around."

"Anne, settle down; we decided to let Albert rest and not go there."

"I know, but he literally got away with murder."

On the trip back to the farm, Rick could tell Anne was fuming.

"If you decide to do something stupid; you have to let me know."

"I'll be all right; maybe we should dig up August Dsendew and collect the money. Screw them! Wait a minute; I knew something was strange."

Anne got out her laptop and started to type away.

"I knew it. Albert Harris was born in August on a Wednesday, and he had $1928.00 on him. Get it?

"No, what are you talking about?"

"Albert Harris was born in August and if you spell Wednesday backward it comes to Dsendew without the a and the y. He didn't want to be too obvious. Plus he was born in 1928.

"That son of a gun!" Rick said." Still playing the game after his death."

"Rick, let's dig him up and give the poor guy a decent burial."

"And collect the money?"

"Duh, yeah."

SISSY'S BEAUTY SHOP

Todd was back to watching westerns again; dinosaurs had lost their appeal. Sissy was cleaning up the shop from the earthquake that hit

Gas City, but it didn't hit the town. As soon as the building quit shaking, she called three neighbors around her and they felt nothing. Sissy was scared. NeeNee couldn't be real she thought. She had to talk to someone with a level head and weren't going to send her to the insane asylum. She decided to call Rick and Anne. They told her they were in town and be right over.

"Hi, Sissy," as they walked through the door of the shop.

"Come out back for a minute; I need to talk to you."

Rick and Anne sat at the picnic table and looked at Sissy.

"I don't where to start. Todd's friend NeeNee has been a part of our family for twenty-one years. Todd still believes in him and spends a lot of time in the basement with NeeNee. I want Todd to get out more and experience life, like he did with the bachelorette party, so I told him to forget about NeeNee for a while and consider going out, like the church's young adult fellowship. He was all right with that, but didn't want to give up his relationship with NeeNee. I got mad and told him that NeeNee wasn't real, and to get over him. He insisted, so I told him to prove it. He yelled down the basement stairs and the house began to shake violently, I mean like an earthquake. It was awful. I told him to stop; he yelled down the basement stairs, and it quit immediately. Now, am I crazy or was that a just a fluke?"

"Wow, what about the neighbors?"

"I called each one and nobody felt a thing."

Rick asked, "If I ask Todd for the same thing, do you think he would be ok with that?"

"I don't know. Why don't we ask Todd to come out, and maybe he can ask NeeNee to do it again."

"Sissy, I think you should be the one to ask." Anne said.

"I will, but I hope he doesn't get upset."

Todd was watching television and Sissy called him to come outside. Todd reluctantly came out.

"Todd, I want ask you a question, and be very honest with me. Last night when I asked for you to prove NeeNee was real, what did he do?"

"He shook the house."

"I know the house did shake, but how did he do it?"

"He can do a lot of things."

Rick asked, "Like what?"

"Oh, he can be invisible, heal people, move his house when he wants to, see the future, and stuff like that."

"Have you seen him do these things?"

"Sure, he lets me do all kind of things."

"Why can't we see him?" Anne asked

"Because he doesn't want you to, but he wants to talk to Uncle Rick."

"Why me?"

"I don't know, he just told me the other day."

"When can I meet him?"

"Soon he will let me know."

"Does he know me?"

"He knows all of you."

"Can I meet him now?"

"No, he isn't here, he went on a trip."

"Where did he go?"

"I don't know, but his friend Michael died and he's a little sad."

"Michael who?"

"I don't know; can I watch my movie now?"

"Sure, Honey, as Todd ran into the house. What do you two think?"

"I'm not sure, but if I have a chance to meet NeeNee, I'll be here in a flash."

Tony's Office New York City

Tony felt guilty for not calling or texting Eric or Dar. Since he arrived back in New York, his life had been a whirlwind after his father died, and he didn't have anything to say to Dar that would make any sense to her. How could he tell her he was getting married in three months to a girl he's never met? Tony's first thought was to never make contact with Dar again, but as a friend, he had to tell her the truth. Eric was going to be madder than mad. Tony also wanted Eric to stand up with him at the wedding, but he knew Eric, and this probably wouldn't fly.

"Mr. Becko?" His secretary said over the desk phone.

"Yes."

"Your coaches are back; do you want me to send them in?"

"Give me ten minutes then show them in."

This will be his third session with his social coaches. So far he learned about shaking hands, sitting, standing, laughing and touching. It seemed simple to Tony, but his coaches were emphatic about his meeting the Franco family and especially Maria. Today they were going to show him pictures of the guests that would be at the Franco Home; then tomorrow he was going to be quizzed on all he learned.

The door opened "Mr. Becko, we're back."

Tony noticed all three coaches carrying large portfolios, and he knew this was going to be a long day.

RICK AND ANNE'S FARM

"Did you notice what Todd said?" Rick asked Anne.

"You mean that NeeNee was sad because his friend Michael died."

"Yes, could this be the same Michael as in the Cardinal Michael Grey?"

"It crossed my mind also, and do you think Sissy was telling the truth about the house shaking?"

"There'd be no reason for her not to tell the truth; she's the one that called us over to the shop."

Anne's parents pulled into the barnyard driving Eric's old pickup truck.

"Where have you two been?" Anne asked

"Your father took me to meet the Yoder's. What a nice family, and all those children the mother home schools. They sent two fresh baked pies, rhubarb and cherry, home with us."

"Rick, tomorrow's the day for picking beans, I can't wait." Bob Miller said

"Dad, I haven't seen you this excited in years."

"Well, the Yoder's told us they would be there also and two other Amish families will bring us lunch. I've never worked much with my hands, so I'm venturing out in unexplored territory."

"Dad, just be careful; you're not thirty anymore."

"Sounds crazy, but Gas City has made me feel thirty. I started a multimillion dollar business, but I've never felt so needed and accepted. I know; let's go in town and see if the convenience store has any new ice cream flavors."

"Honey, maybe he'll give you a balloon or a piece of penny candy if you're nice," Marge said laughing out loud.

"Very funny!"

JAMES AND MARIANNE FRANCO SUMMER HOME, ALEXANDRIA BAY, NY

Tony, his mother, and two sisters were picked up by a stretch limo and two black sedans followed them. Tony was apprehensive to say the least. We was going to meet his future bride with about four hundred people watching. Tony felt it was like a reality show with the cameras following his every move. At least his social coaches thought he did a good job, but they also reminded him not to touch Maria. He made a funny comment about jumping her bones, and all three coaches gasped. Tony had to find Willard because he was rock solid and knew everyone there. For being seventy years old, Willard had become a good friend, and Tony could talk freely without repercussions.

"Tony, don't worry about your sisters and me. We'll be just fine at the party," his mother said.

"Mom, I've memorized about two hundred photographs; all I have to do is to put a name with each. You probably won't even see me the entire party."

"Tony, I hope your future wife is real ugly," his twelve year old sister chirped.

"You know, Becky, you better be nice to me. I'll be supporting our family shortly and new clothes for you could be out of the picture." He said laughing.

The cars pulled up to boat dock, and the driver opened the door. There were six guys in suits and they demanded to see the invitation. They all nodded and motioned for Tony's family to get on the ferry. The boat pulled away from the dock and a young, pretty woman came around with a tray of cocktails and sodas.

"Where are we going?" Tony asked.

The young woman told them the family owns an island up the river and boat is the only way to get there. She went on to say the house is a mansion, and there is even a horse track on the other side of the island. The ferry pulled up to the dock, and off in the distance they saw an enormous house perched upon a hill. There were several young men in tuxedos driving golf carts to the home. The closer they got, he could music and laughter. Tony got a big lump in his throat like a cat with hairball that just wouldn't come up. The cart stopped in front of a large lavender awning, and Tony immediately recognized Maria's parents, Sal and Pepper Franco. Maria's parents shook their hands and greeted them with a welcome. Tony stared at them thinking these people will be my new in-laws in less than two months. Strange he thought.

"Son, this will be your summer home also," Sal said beaming.

Sal was a tough-looking man with piercing black eyes and Pepper was a sweet, charming woman probably at least fifteen years his junior. There was a man off to Sal's right about seven feet tall and had a large scar running down his face below his chin. Tony thought if he decided to touch Maria, this would be the guy to correct the situation. Most people were dressed in cocktail dresses and sport coats; Tony fit right in thanks to the coaches. He mingled and saw his uncle Paulie hanging all over a way younger woman. Tony spotted Willard and made a bee line toward him.

"Hey, Willard nice party."

"Tony, you look great, and so does your future wife."

"Where is she?"

"She heard you arrived and went into the house to powder her nose."

"Should I go in and find her"

"No, definitely not. Let her make an entrance and come to you."

"Damn it, Willard; how much longer?"

"Keep your pants kid; let me introduce you to the Vice President and the Chief Justice of the Supreme Court."

TIM AND PAMELA SUE'S FARM

Rahab was pacing back and forth, and then went out to the barn. Pamela Sue observed her daughter and thought a good chat might help.

"What's the matter, Honey?"

"Mom, what shall I do? I have a chance to go to New York and study at a private music school or stay in Gas City and graduate with my class. I feel safe here; I'm surrounded by friends and family, but I'm also thinking this may be my only opportunity to study music."

"You have to follow your heart."

"Easy for you to say; you grew up here and will probably die here."

"Number one, I had no offers to do anything like you. I was forced to help raise my two younger siblings; I didn't have much choice. I worked in the fields for hours, then went to our grandmother's house and cooked the evening meals. At the end of a week, I literally didn't have enough money to buy a candy bar."

"But mom, are you happy now?"

"I'm the most joyful woman on the planet. I have a husband that adores me and the two best kids in Lincoln County; what more could I possibly want?"

"I love it here, too, but I'm going to be a little fish in a big, big ocean of other musical kids."

"Anne's parents really think you have talent and your dad me too."

"I know. I guess I don't want to wake up someday at age forty living in Gas City and say "I wonder if."

"Your grandmother left you money for your education, and Anne's parents will also help. Is this the big opportunity that happens once in a life time? I can't answer that for you; your father and I want you to make the decision, and we'll stand behind whatever it is."

"I love that you two support me, but I have only a couple of weeks to decide. I just wish I could get a sign or something big would happen to help me make up my mind."

"It might, Honey; keep believing. There's a true answer just around the corner."

"Mom, I had a dream last night that I left and never came back. In my dream; I tried to come back but something prevented me, and I woke up frustrated and sad. Mom, I was really scared."

"I don't put much stock in dreams. I think the Good Lord has a purpose and a direction for each one of us."

"I feel that way too but I wish God would just step in and tell me what was to happen."

"I'll pray for you, Honey. Some door will either open or close; just trust."

"Thanks, Mom, I'm running over to Sissy's and get my hair highlighted."

FRANCO SUMMER HOME...THE MEETING

Tony wasn't nervous meeting the Vice President of The United States, but he was scared shitless on his first encounter with Maria, his future wife. The next sixty years of his life was getting ready to walk out the front door at any moment. Tony not only thought about her looks but was she just a plain, spoiled bitch? If there was a rock big enough, he would crawl under it in a heartbeat. The door opened, and Tony looked at three young ladies; which one was to be Mrs. Anthony Charles Becko, Jr.? They were all pretty, and Tony spotted the one, far to the right; she looked Italian and had an air of confidence about her. Her jet black hair gave her a regal look and she walked down the stairs like her shit didn't stink. The three walked up to Tony and the dark haired girl lead the procession.

"You're Tony Becko?" she asked.

Trying to get the hairball out of his throat he said, "Yes."

"You're not too bad to look at."

Tony thought this isn't how he expected to meet her but he would play along.

"Well, then, let me introduce you to my sister Maria."

The other young lady stepped to her left and, there stood his wife. She was shy, unassuming, with light brown hair, almost blonde. She was wearing a pink cocktail dress that came just above her knees, flats, and a beautiful pink tea rose in her hair. All his coaching went down the drain; he couldn't speak.

"Can I show you the house?" Maria asked.

"Sure."

The two walked up the stairs back into the house, not saying a word as three hundred plus people stared.

"The house is beautiful."

"Thanks. It was built in the late 1800's, and our family has owned since 1941."

Each room she showed him was better than the last. The furnishings were all period style.

They came down the front staircase and knew if they opened the front door, the three hundred gawkers would begin their ritual.

"Let's slip out the back, and I'll get a golf cart."

They walked through the kitchen, and there was a golf cart for the waiters, sitting, waiting to be taken. She jumped behind the wheel and off they went through the wooded forest.

"Great idea; I felt we were under the microscope."

"We are, and I felt like two ants getting ready to be burned in the direct sunlight."

They both laughed and the cart took them far from the party. She drove past a lot of men in suits and toting guns. She told Tony because the Vice President was there, the whole island was surrounded by security and secret service. She took him to a secluded boat launch covered in bushes and trees.

"This is about as far away I can get without being spotted."

"Nice spot. Do you come here often?"

"No, my sister and I found this place last year, and it's very peaceful."

"I hope I can talk frankly with you. I have much to say, and I'm not sure where to begin."

"Tony, I too have a lot to talk to you about, and I hope we can honest and upfront with each other."

Tony looked into her green eyes and didn't see much Italian coming out. Her features were delicate and fine and spoke in quiet tones.

"Are you Italian?" he asked.

"My father is, but my mother was Irish and I took after her. She died ten years ago, and Pepper is my step mother. We get along all right, but she knows I'm my father's favorite. You saw my step sisters come out of the house with me, and I apologize for the charades. It was my sister's idea."

"To be truthful, I hoped of the three it would be you," Tony said blushing.

"I know where our lives are headed, and I'll be the best I can, but I'm in love with another guy."

Tony started to laugh "I'm also in love with another, but not a guy," as they both laughed out loud.

"I talked to my father about our marriage, and he won't let me even mention anyone but you. I'm afraid our destiny has been made for us."

"I feel the same way. My Uncle Paulie runs the family affairs and won't hear of anyone but Maria Franco. This may sound crazy, but I want to date you, and get to know you before the marriage."

"I'd like that. I will try and be the wife you expect but I want you to meet me half way."

"Maria, I'll try. Can I kiss you?"

"Of course you can; we are to be married in less than two months."

Tony leaned over and kissed her full on her mouth. Her lips were soft and inviting, but it just wasn't the same as Darlene Moore. Her kisses made his feet tingle, and the passion just wasn't there with Maria. Maria kissed him back, and she too felt it was just a kiss. Neither one remarked, and Maria started the golf cart to get back to the party.

Butch Garwood's Farm Gas City

It had been a long day for the guys that showed up to pick Butch's beans and corn. The Yoder Family women provided a fried chicken lunch with all the trimmings, and their buggies were loaded for the trip home. Rick's father-in-law was filthy dirty, and his shirt was soaked with sweat, but he couldn't help grinning. He got to drive the corn picker and start the auger to put the corn in silo. Bob Miller just found his fountain of youth.

Wendy, Butch's wife, brought him out to watch the guys finish up. Butch was trying not to cry so every guy kind of looked the other way when he spoke.

"I knew I had good friends. I knew I had people I could count on, and I knew God would provide, but you guys."

That was all he could get out. Every man walked past him and hugged him sitting in the wheelchair with his amputated leg extended. Wendy ran into the house to get her purse to pay them something and the men smiled, shook their heads, and handed her $15,000.000 cash.

"Damn you guys!" she yelled between her sobs.

Rick and Bob got into their truck to head home.

"You really have something here. I've been in the corporate world my entire life and have never experienced anything like this," as he began to tear up.

"You know, Dad; Anne and I have experienced this also. The people here would give you the shirt off their backs even if you didn't ask for it. Let's go home and see what the gals have fixed, sit on the porch with the three cats, and watch the moon come up over the pear orchard."

"I'm all for that. You know even your mother-in-law is starting to cook again. When we were first married, she could cook up a storm. We've had a French chief for thirty years and to tell you the truth, she can out cook him, hands down."

"When Anne and I move back to New York, I'll miss this place. Gas City saved our marriage, our son and my relationship with my family."

"Rick, you truly are my son," and reached over to touch Rick's sweaty arm.

SISSY'S BEAUTY SHOP

Sissy was just finishing Mrs. Condon when Todd ran up the basement stairs.

"Mom, NeeNee has something for Rahab."

"Ok, Honey, I'll be down in a minute."

"I heard Todd went to Penelope's bachelorette party at Christos with seven girls," Mrs. Condon said with a smile.

"Oh yeah, apparently he was the life of the party."

"Ricky, my cousin, the bartender, told me Todd stood up to a guy that was being obnoxious to one of the girls. The guy was drunk and Todd pushed him off the girl before the bouncer got to them."

"Really? I hadn't heard that."

"He told me Todd became an instant hero, and everyone was buying him shots and dancing with him. My daughter Angie was in the wedding party and she wants to invite Todd to her party. Is it all right?"

"My Todd has surely been a surprise to me lately. If Todd wants to, why not?"

"I'll let Angie know when I get home. The girls love Todd."

Mrs. Condon walked out the door and Sissy sat in her styling chair and grinned.

"Ok, Todd, what's so important?" she yelled down the stairs.

"NeeNee gave me something for Rahab."

"What is it?"

"I don't know NeeNee has it wrapped."

"Rahab will be here in fifteen minutes for coloring, and I'll let her know."

Sissy sat down in her styling chair and looked out the window that faced Main Street. Her son was becoming popular, and he knew right from wrong. She loved it. Evansville has a large group home where each person living there is responsible for themselves. Maybe now would the time for Todd to live around other young people, and be accountable. Sissy saw Rahab pull up in her truck, and wondered if Rahab was moving to New York or staying in Gas City.

Franco Summer Home

The party was beginning to wind down, and Tony and Maria were definitely the center of attraction. Maria ran into the house for something, and Willard came up to Tony.

"Well?"

"She's nice, and we had a great talk."

"Are you two still going through with the wedding?"

"Willard, do I have a choice?"

"No, you sure don't, but the talk at the party is you two make a beautiful couple."

"What's your take?"

"The jury is still out on that decision, and I hope love will enter in, or the rest of your life will be miserable. Maria is motioning you to come in the house. Good luck kid."

Tony walked in. His mother, Maria, and her parents were sitting around the large dining room table.

"Sit down, son." Mr. Franco said.

Tony sat next to Maria and waited.

"You two make a nice couple, and we are happy to have you in our family. As I was telling your mother, all the preparations for the wedding have been completed. The wedding will be just before Christmas at St. Joseph's Church in Brooklyn with the reception at my country club. If you kids would like to pick out some music for dancing, just tell the wedding planner, Amada Bowman. Do you have questions?"

"What about our honeymoon?"

"All taken care of my boy. My brother owns a resort in the Dominican Republic; it's beautiful."

"What about the ring?"

"Again all done, I'll have it to you in a week."

Tony looked over at Maria as she raised her eyebrows. Tony reached over and took her hand to reassure Maria; they can get through this. A young lady stepped forward, introduced herself as Amanda and told the kids they would be getting a packet in the mail shortly with all the wedding details.

"Tony and I would like to see the plans as soon as possible, in case we might want to make a few minor changes." Maria said in a soft voice.

"There will be no changes!" Amanda said sternly. "Just pick out some music."

SISSY'S BEAUTY SHOP

Rahab and Sissy had a long talk about New York and life in general. Rahab really liked the blonde highlights in her hair; she felt it made her look older. Sissy told Rahab that Todd had something for her and was down the basement. She walked downstairs and yelled for Todd.

"I'm in the little room."

Rahab knocked on the closed door and Todd immediately opened it for her.

"What do you want, Todd?"

"NeeNee has something to give you for New York."

"Oh, that's nice. What is it?"

"I don't know he wrapped it for you."

The paper was like old parchment paper tied together with really old string. Rahab sat next to Todd and opened it. She was amazed; it was a little cross carved from one single piece of a tree branch, and it was connected to an old piece of string or twine.

"This is nice. Where did you get it?"

"I told you, this is from NeeNee."

In the bottom of the old paper was a note that read *Wear this for protection in New York.*

Rahab untied the string and retied it around her neck. She felt something very strange happening to her. Her face became flush and dizziness came over her. She sat back down touched the little wooden cross again.

"Where did NeeNee get this?"

"He told me he made from a Buckeye tree. You are never to take it off in New York."

"I'm not sure I'm even going to New York."

"NeeNee said you are, and you'll live on Stockholm Street in Brooklyn."

"Todd, how did you remember this?"

"Look, it's on the board"

Sure enough, Stockholm Street, Brooklyn, New York was written on the chalk board they had used for the Albert Harris notes. She took the necklace off, and her dizziness immediately stopped. She told herself there had to be a good explanation for this.

"Todd tell NeeNee thank you for me."

"Sure will."

Rahab came up the basement stairs clutching the little cross.

"What did Todd give you?" Sissy asked.

"This", and put out her hand to show Sissy.

"It looks very rustic; where did Todd get it?"

"He said it was from NeeNee," as Rahab started to laugh.

"You probably shouldn't laugh; wait until I tell you about how NeeNee shook my house like an earthquake."

INDIANA UNIVERSITY BLOOMINGTON, INDIANA

Eric and Billie were so busy; they didn't have much time for a social life. They had only one freshman class together but still emailed and talked almost every day. The days were crisp and the Maple Trees were in full color as they walked between classes.

"I got an email from Tony today. Guess what; he's getting married in less than two months."

"You boys are sure creative in your stories."

"I'm not kidding. His father died, and the family has arranged for his marriage to an Italian girl."

"People don't do that."

"I'm going to try and call him and get the scoop. It's another Italian family, and they feel it's good for everyone involved. He just met her yesterday."

"Has he told Dar? She'll be devastated."

"He didn't say; I'm assuming he will be upfront with her. He wants me to stand up for him, and you're invited too. The wedding is December 21st. We'll be on Christmas break."

"Eric, I'm not going. I don't think it would be right. Dar is my best friend."

"He also said he was taking over the family business."

"Does that mean dry cleaning?"

"I'm not sure, but I think it entails a little more than that."

"Dar is coming here when we play Purdue, and maybe we can console her or just get drunk."

"As soon as I hear back from Tony, I'll let you know."

Mom's Diner 5:20 A.M.

At this time of year most of the farmers eat quickly and head to the fields for picking crops. It had been a good year for Lincoln County, Indiana. They got rain when they needed it and plenty of sunshine in between. Rick and his father-in-law, Bob, had just ordered the special when Wendy Garwood brought her husband in his wheelchair. She wheeled right up to the round table and told him she would be back in a little while.

"I just had to come and say thank you again for helping pick and store all my crops" Butch said. There is nothing I can say or do, to ever make up for your kindness. As you all know Wendy and I are raising our three little grandchildren while their mom's in jail. Our daughter has made some really bad choices along the way."

"Butch, you've been a part of our group since day one, and we could never let you down," Lester said.

"Wendy and I are using the money for my medical bills and our grandchildren."

"The guy that really enjoyed helping is sitting next to Rick," Marvin said as he looked at Bob Miller. "This guy is almost eighty, and he drove the corn picker straight as an arrow. We now want Bob to help us too."

"For never seeing a tractor or corn picker except in a photo book; Bob Miller was an inspiration to us all," Tidy said with a smile.

Bob responded, "Thank you for letting an old man do something for someone else."

They all raised their coffee cups to Bob and said, "Here's to the old man" and everyone started laughing as Mom and Jenny came with an arm load of breakfast specials. Today were biscuits smothered in chicken gravy, and for an additional $ .75 you could get a slice of country-cured ham, and not one guy could pass up that deal.

TONY'S OFFICE NEW YORK CITY

Tony was still reeling from the Franco party and meeting his future wife. Tony told his secretary to let Willard in as soon as he arrived. Tony's first order of business was to call or email Dar about his marriage. He dreaded that. Maybe Willard would have some ideas on composing a letter. His secretary buzzed him and told Tony Willard wouldn't be here for at least an hour. His secretary knocked softly and walked in his office holding a Mountain Dew, Tony's favorite.

"You seem a little stressed out today, Sir."

"I am. I need to compose a Dear John letter, and I don't know where to start."

"I can help. When your father was troubled I had a remedy."

She walked behind Tony's desk and pulled up her already short skirt and knelt in front of Tony as he sat in the large leather chair. She put her hands between his legs and started to unzip his pants.

"What are you doing?" Tony shouted.

"I just thought this would be a stress reliever for you. Your dad loved it."

"Get out!"

She jumped to her feet, adjusted her skirt, and left the office.

Tony was really stressed now. He couldn't bear the fact that her mouth had been around his father's dick. He almost felt sick.

Willard arrived, and was ushered in to Tony's office.

"I want her fired!" Tony yelled to Willard before he found a seat.

"Why? She has been with the business for eight years."

"I don't have to give a reason; I just want her gone today."

"Ok, Tony, and I have someone else in mind if you don't care?"

"I want the change to take place now!"

"Done, but besides that, what did you think of Maria?"

"She's very nice and we had a chance to talk in private. We're both on the same page and willing to bend to all the Franco wedding plans."

"Good. The talk at the party was all positive, and the Franco's seem to like you."

"What do you have for me today?"

"Well, Tony, I want to talk about your enemies."

"My what?"

"You've met most of your family, but along with that, you have people who don't like you. These foes are the same that hated your father and wanted him dead."

"People want me dead?"

"Yes, and some are your family"

"Do I have to memorize their names and faces?"

"Not all of them. Many live in other parts of the country, and you'll never have contact with them. You'll receive invitations to many meetings, and dinners, but we will coach you to which ones you will decline."

"It seems strange that people want me dead, and I'm only seventeen. I just got out of high school, and now I have to watch my back."

"You will. We also have plenty of loyal people that will help you. We will never put you in harm's way, and if one of these people tell you to leave, you leave, no questions."

"Got it. Now let's look at my adversaries," he said with a smile, "and don't forget to take care of my secretary on your way out."

Tim and Pamela Sue's Farm

Rahab came in the house; her mother was busy finishing up canning vegetables.

"Your hair looks nice, Honey; I like the blonde streaks."

"Sissy always does a nice job, and we talked about everything."

"Did she ask about New York?

"Yeah, and I've decided to go. I'm really scared, and I'll miss you so much. On the way home I looked down on the truck seat and saw a little wooden cross that Todd gave me, and something came over me. This opportunity will never come again, and I have to give it a try."

Pamela Sue started weeping and through her arms around her daughter.

"You'll do fine."

"I know, Mom, but I've never been anywhere without Dad or you."

"We are only a phone call away, and Uncle Rick and Anne are moving back."

Rahab showed the little cross to her mother, and asked her to put it on. Pamela Sue tied the old string around her neck and looked at Rahab."

"Mom, do you feel dizzy?"

"No, why?"

"No reason. I'm going to my bedroom and email my application to the music school. I'll know by tomorrow if I get accepted."

"Don't forget to put Robert and Marge Miller as references; they apparently have a lot of pull."

Rahab went upstairs and sat at her computer. Just for the heck of it, she tied the little cross around her neck again. Instantly she became dizzy. She took it off immediately and laid it next to her bed. She picked up the phone and called the beauty shop.

"Hi, Sissy, it's Rahab. Can I talk to Todd?"

"Hi, Rahab." Todd yelled over the phone.

"Todd, I need to ask you something. Every time I put on the cross that NeeNee made me, I get dizzy."

"I told you Rahab; it's only for New York," And hung up.

She started to laugh. He did indeed tell her that, but what's with the lightheadedness? She filled out the application on line and sent it to the school. Next she scrolled down to see student activities, and housing. She read because of such a late application, the only housing was the alternant student housing building on Stockholm Street in Brooklyn.

"Holy shit!" she yelled out loud. "Who in the hell is this NeeNee?"

BAPTIST MISSION HOUSE ORLANDO, FLORIDA

Rev. Jack and Irene Rosenbaum where just finishing putting away the morning breakfast dishes for the three hundred and twelve men, women, and children they just fed; when a tall, nicely-dressed man stepped in.

"Can you direct me to Rev. Rosenbaum?"

"You're looking at him," Jack responded.

"I need to talk to you privately."

"Sure. Come on back to my office."

Jack had to clear the desk and chair for the two to sit. It was mostly bills, and threating letters from creditors.

"My name is Grant Hofer, and I represent the estate of the late Cardinal Michael Grey. I have some paper work for you to sign. Would you like to have your attorney present?"

Jack laughed, "My attorney? That's a good one; I can't even afford stationery or stamps."

"The Cardinal names you the primary beneficiary of his estate. All I need is your signature, and I have a certified check for you."

"Sure, where do I sign?"

Jack signed at least fifteen times, and Grant closed his briefcase. "Thank you, Pastor, for being so cooperative, sometimes I run into some belligerent people. Here's the check."

Jack looked at the check and started to laugh and laugh. He laughed so hard he fell off the chair onto the floor. Irene heard him and came running in.

"What's the matter?" she shouted.

"Remember how we prayed to get $125,000.00 to pay all the mission bills?"

"Yes."

"Look," as he handed her the check.

She started to laugh. Grant Hofer felt a little uncomfortable and didn't know what to say or do as he looked at the Rev. still on the floor. Finally Jack got back into his seat.

"You know, Mr. Hofer, I never expected this. He looked again at the check. Do you know what $23,812,432.15 will do?" There are people here in Orlando that haven't lived in a real home for years and years, haven't eaten except for here, and can't clothe, or send their children to school. Whoever Cardinal Grey was to me has been a blessing."

"I have given hundreds of checks to many, many people, but this one's been special," as Grant Hofer started to tear up.

"Tell you what Mr. Hofer; why don't you stay and help us cook and serve dinner tonight, and tomorrow morning we can go to the bank together. You can show me how to open an account to pay my bills. I'll pay you any amount you want."

"I can do better than that. I have a vacation coming up, and I will stay a week and get all your finances lined up. And about pay, I was thinking maybe $1.00 an hour. Does that sound fair?"

Jack handed him a tissue and rubbed his chin.

"I think that's a good price, but I need you to peel potatoes right away," he said smiling.

"I'm your man; I used to be a cook in the Navy, so I need no formal training," as he hugged Jack and Irene and continued to cry and laugh at the same time.

Rick and Anne's Farm

Rick and Anne were sitting on the porch with the three cats. Anne's parents went to The Seniors in Action dinner at the Faith Baptist Church. They had become regular members and volunteered for the church food pantry. Gas City was now their new home even though they sometimes missed the New York Opera. The phone rang, and Anne picked up the portable next to her.

"Hello, sure hold on Todd," and handed the phone to Rick.

"Ok, Ok, sure, Ok," Rick repeated.

"What was that all about?"

"Todd said NeeNee wants to meet with me at 9:00 A.M. tomorrow at the beauty shop. This is it. Either NeeNee is fictitious, or he is real and has lived in Gas City for ninety years."

"Don't forget Rick, you have the note from the cardinal for him."

"I know. I looked at it, and it's in some strange language that makes no sense."

"We promised Albert, and this will finally end our obligations to Albert Harris. We should decide if we are going to gig up August and prove he is the real Albert."

"We know for sure that August Dsendew is not Albert; we saw Albert blow his brains out."

"I know, Honey, but $1,000,000.00 is a lot of money."

"I feel funny taking the money."

"Me, too, but $1,000,000.00 Rick, by the way, if NeeNee is real, what are you going to ask him?"

"I don't know; what do you say or ask a three-hundred year old elf?"

"Rick, chances are you are going to sit in Todd's basement and wait for nothing. Todd will come up with some excuse as in the past."

"I feel the same way. Why don't you come in town with me and wait with Sissy. We can go to the diner for breakfast after this so called encounter."

"I will, and besides I could use a wash and trim."

FAITH BAPTIST CHURCH BASEMENT

Pastor Roger opened with a prayer, and the seniors got up for the buffet line. The senior group was an active part of the church and community. They numbered about sixty, and several people didn't belong to the church; some were members of the Hawkins Church and Trinity Lutheran Church. They enjoyed their time together, making trips to Evansville for plays or to Indianapolis for a Colts game. Bob and Marge Miller also enjoyed their company, and were invited to join a square dance club. They had never square danced before but jumped at the opportunity to learn. Today the Miller's ate at long banquet tables covered in newsprint for table covers and ate with plastic knives, forks, and spoons. They had a private table at the Café Amor in Manhattan but they enjoyed this meal even more.

Pastor Roger spoke, "Ok, everybody I want to announce that we are having a Bible study on the book of John and you are all invited. We'll have a light dinner at 5:00 P.M. and end by 7:00 P.M. so it won't be dark by the time you get home. Also Pastor Ken is planning a bus trip to Clarksville to their wine and cheese facility to watch how they make their products."

Someone yelled, "Do we get free wine tasting?"

"Yes Roy, that's what I understand. But I know none of you will take part because most of you are Baptists. Right?" Roger said winking at the group.

"Yeah, right, Pastor," Roy yelled again, "and I will keep an eye on the group for you."

"I knew I could count on you for chaperoning," he said now laughing, "oh by the way, I need to tell you about a young girl in our church who is pregnant and needs some assistance because she wants to keep the baby."

"It's Megan Wilson," Mrs. Fry said.

"I never said the name."

"You didn't have to Pastor; we all talked about it before you arrived, and the situation is all taken care of."

"I swear you guys, if you all decided to build the Brooklyn Bridge here in Gas City, I think you could do it and probably in half the time the New Yorkers took."

They all collectively laughed and headed toward the dessert table.

SISSY'S BEAUTY SHOP

Rick and Anne arrived at the shop. It was only 8:30 A.M, but Rick wanted to be on time or even early because he wasn't sure how this NeeNee meeting was to be. For some reason Rick was nervous. Over the years he had met with bank presidents, CEO's of many different corporations, and a host of US Senators, but today was different. How could an imaginary elf live all these years and never be detected? Why should he be nervous, he thought, NeeNee doesn't even exist.

"Hi, Sissy," they both said "We are here for..."

"I know why, and I'm very curious about the results. All these years I've lived with NeeNee stories told by Todd, and now maybe I can put my mind at ease. Todd is down the basement and will come up when he is ready. While we're waiting, I have coffee on in the kitchen, and I can wash and trim you, Anne, if you want."

"I do want my hair done and thanks."

Rick walked into the kitchen and retrieved two steaming cups of coffee.

Sissy said, "I noticed how your parents really like Gas City."

"Oh, my gosh, yes! They went to a seniors group last night and have joined a square dance club. My mother is cooking again, and Pamela Sue comes over to help her. I have never seen my parents so happy."

"Well, all the gals that come in absolutely rave about your mother. She got an invitation to Bea's baby shower on Saturday, and I didn't," Sissy said with a smile.

Todd ran up the stairs, "Uncle Rick, NeeNee wants to see you now."

Rick laid his coffee cup down, and walked down the stairs as Anne and Sissy stared at him. Todd led him into the large room they had used for the Albert Harris investigation. There were six chairs around the table and two tall stools in the corner. Rick sat at the table and looked at Todd.

"What happens next?" Rick asked

"Be patient, Uncle Rick, he will be here in a moment. NeeNee wants me to turn off the lights until his eyes get use to the light."

"Ok, but how long do I wait?"

"You don't; he's in the room now." And Todd turned off the light, closed the door and left.

Rick sat incomplete darkness, but there was a strange powerful odor in the room resembling fresh burned pine needles. His senses were sharpened by the odor.

From the opposite side of the room came a voice. "I'm glad you could meet me," it said.

Rick's head started spinning. Was this a cruel joke that everyone was in on, or was this voice real? The voice was soft with a slight Swedish accent but not old sounding. It was a male voice and had a funny calming effect on Rick. Rick never saw anyone come into the room before Todd killed the lights so Rick reached over and flipped the lights back on.

"Damn!" Rick hollered.

Tim and Pamela Sue's Farm

They had just finished loading the truck for the trip to New York, and no one said much. It seemed to be solemn parting. Tim and Pamela Sue were going to drive Rahab to New York and get her settled in. She had been selected right away at the New York Music Academy, and they were sure Anne's parents had a hand in it. They would see her at Christmas but it seemed a long way off. Moses would finish the picking while they were gone, and he didn't know what to say to his sister. They had shared much, and he had been her protector all through school. Now he wouldn't be there. He was not going to let himself cry.

"Bye, Sis, he said, I'll watch your goats, and you watch your back." He threw his powerful arms around her and practically hugged her to death.

"I'll miss you, Moses," as she started to cry.

He turned and headed toward the barn. As soon as they pulled out, he began to weep, but he knew nobody saw him except the barn cats and her goats.

She looked out the back truck window and knew she would never see the farm again. She tried to take a mental photograph to store in her mind, but it just wouldn't stay.

Sissy's Basement

Rick sat for a moment trying to collect his thoughts. When he turned on the lights, there was nobody in the room. He got up and walked over to where the voice seemed to come from. There were no speakers or NeeNee, unless he was invisible. He started to open the door to leave, but the voice told him to stay and turn the light off. Rick sat and flipped the lights off.

"Just give me a minute," the voice said.

Rick sat and wondered what the heck was going on. The room still smelled like pine needles and voice was extremely calming.

The desk lamp flipped on, and Rick was looking at a miniature man. Not a midget or a dwarf, but a very small man. Instantly Rick knew he was in the presence of something extraordinary. The man had bleached blonde hair parted in the middle, and his skin appeared to be translucent. His features were delicate, but yet rugged, and he had very few wrinkles, except around his eyes. His eyes were a deep blue like the ocean just off shore, and he was smiling. He wore a green wool poncho, dark brown cotton pants, and small leather boots. He continued to smile at Rick as Rick studied the little man with all his might. The small man had an aura about him that screamed with a mighty power. He crossed his short legs putting his hands on the knees sitting on the tall stool.

"We finally meet, Richard. I will let you ask questions, but I have a favor to ask you first. This is the only reason I'm revealing myself to you."

"I'll do everything in power to help."

"That's the reason I selected you. You get things done, and I have a need."

Rick noticed he had six fingers on each hand but no thumbs; other than that he appeared to be very small man maybe about two feet tall. His appearance pulled Rick in, and he had a million questions.

"My name is Rayneelandersonne, but you've heard me called NeeNee and Ray. I have been called many names over the past two hundred and eight-six years. Yes, I'm that old."

"Can I ask one question before you go on?"

"Sure."

"Did you know Albert Harris?"

"I did, and I saved his life. He made some bad choices along the way. When he was nine, he was destined to die, until I came into the picture."

"I have a note from him for you."

"Save it for now; when you leave, I'll read it."

"How can I help?"

"Have you ever heard of Stavanger, Norway?"

"No."

"I have to get there within thirty days. My only sister is dying, and I have to be by her side. I have all the details planned out, and this is where you come in. I need for you to drive me to New York, where I will board a cruise ship that will take me to Norway. I also will need a traveling companion and it can be someone in your family."

"Why don't you fly; you can be there in hours."

"I won't go into details, but I can't travel on an airplane. The ship leaves next week so we need to hurry."

"I can do this for you. Anne and I are moving back to New York, so we'll make the trip sooner."

"I knew I could count on you, and please be discrete on what you tell about me. I have many people looking to capture me for my powers. If I'm caught, I will be imprisoned the rest of my life."

"I will tell no one except my wife."

"Let's leave next Tuesday, and we can meet again for the final details."

"All this time we thought Todd was making you up."

"Benjamin Franklin thought the same thing," he said with a slight grin.

All of a sudden the desk lamp went out and the room was empty. How was Rick going to tell Anne they were going to help a miniature man get back to Norway, as he came up the basement stairs?

Anne and Sissy were sitting wide eyed as Rick walked into the beauty shop from the basement.

"Well?" Anne asked.

"Well what?"

"How was the meeting with NeeNee?" Sissy asked immediately.

"He wasn't there. I sat in the empty room and waited but he never appeared, but if Todd calls again; please let me know."

"Ok," Sissy said with disgust.

Rick and Anne got into the truck and headed for home.

"I'm really sorry, Rick; I guess I hoped he would be real."

"Anne, he is real!" Rick exclaimed, "And he wants us to do him a favor. I'll explain it all before we get home."

Anne's jaw dropped as she turned toward Rick and intently waited for his words.

TONY AND MARIA

Tony took Maria to a Nets game, and he knew she was completely bored. Center court seats and a body guard to boot. He was loving the life style, and thoughts of Dar were far less frequent now. Thoughts of Gas City were almost nonexistent. Tony couldn't help looking at Maria, thinking for the rest of his life this person will be next to him. He had no desire to sleep with her and this bothered him a lot. Where was the passion? Where was the yearning to screw her? Where was the love? He felt like her brother, not her lover.

Maria looked over at Tony as he jumped to his feet to cheer a three pointer by the Nets. She hated sports but didn't mind being with Tony when he would call. Her passion was horses and she knew Tony could care less about animals. She felt if they continued to date the next three weeks, before the wedding, maybe then there would be something that triggered their mutual admiration. The only decision for the wedding they had to make was the music, and they were at complete opposite opinions.

RICK AND ANNE'S FARM

"Man, Rick, how are we going to be able to go to Norway and take NeeNee?"

"I had a thought. He has the trip booked and paid for, so why don't we see if Sissy would like to go. He has a three bedroom suite on the boat. All she has to do is bring him meals and get him off the boat unnoticed. Tim and Pamela Sue can watch Todd for two weeks."

"Great idea! Sissy would probably like to be on a cruise ship with all the goodies that go with it."

"I have to meet NeeNee on Friday to work out the details. I can't wait for you to meet him; there is something extraordinary about him and you sense a gentle power within him. It's hard to describe."

"I want to go with you on Friday if you think its ok."

"He won't mind. I just couldn't say anything to Sissy about him until the right moment."

"We need to get packed if we're leaving on Tuesday, and don't forget we are going to parent's weekend at IU on Saturday when they play Purdue."

"I haven't been back to an IU Football game in over twenty years; it's going to seem strange."

"Will you show me your fraternity house and where you made out with all the girls?"

"All what girls? I waited my entire life you Anne Miller?"

"Yeah, right."

ELKHORN, IOWA

The six hour trip from Gas City seemed to fly by. Libby Shepard noticed the small town hadn't changed much, and the memories were so vivid in her memory. Her sister Osa still lived there and worked for the Danish Museum. She called her sister and told her she was coming for a couple of days. Libby pulled into the small drive next to the blue frame home. Osa came out to greet her sister she hadn't seen for three years.

"My gosh!" Osa exclaimed. "What did you do to your hair?"

"I changed the color just a little," as she laughed.

"I almost didn't recognize you when the car door opened."

"I've even talked four other women in our church to go red, and now we are known as the Red Rocket Bowling Team."

"Well, come on in; I can't wait to hear the story."

Libby put her bag in the spare bedroom and joined Osa in the living room.

"My main reason to come here was to see Dad."

"You've got to be kidding. I'll bet it's at least ten years, maybe more."

"Eleven to be exact. I never once sent him a card or called because he wounded me terribly."

"Libby, he wounded Mom and me also," as Osa began to tear up.

"I have to confront my demon before I die. It took red hair and a brand new look at life to get to this point. I have been a pastor's wife for the last twenty-three years and that's it. Nothing else, period. Roger is a fine man, but he treated me as a lesser being. Not any more kid. My beautician made a huge mistake on my hair color, but it turned into my biggest blessing. Roger now loves me for myself. Our sex life is great, and all the women in the church look up to me and ask for advice. It's awesome!"

"What are you going to say to Dad?"

"I haven't rehearsed a single word, but I know they'll come when I see him."

"I had to put him in an assisted living home just up the road. He criticized everything we ever did or said and he is still that way with the staff. They can't stand him. Our mom was a saint to take all that abuse for thirty-two years."

"I think she would have lived much longer, but her spirit was broken," Libby said with a sigh, "do you see dad often?"

"I go on his birthday or Christmas, but that's it. Last Christmas I walked in, and he told me I was fat and no wonder I could never get a man. I wish he would just die."

"Go with me tomorrow. We can both put this curse behind us."

"I don't know. I physically get sick when I walk into his room."

"We'll go hand in hand and take on the enemy."

"I'll see, but tell me about Roger and the kids."

"For starters, I've also colored my bush red and got a tattoo by my vagina."

"Holy cow! What has come over you?" Osa said laughing out loud.

Sissy's Beauty Shop

Todd had called, and Rick and Anne arrived for their meeting with NeeNee.

"Sissy, I have to admit something to you." Rick said

"Is this some kind of confession?"

"No, but a few days ago when I came to meet NeeNee, he is real. I had a talk with him, and he needs our help. He is going back to New York with Anne and me and take a boat to Norway to see his dying sister. The catch is we want you to go with him to Norway and be his traveling companion."

"I knew he was real. Our house shook so violently, I could barely stand. Nothing close to a volcano could do that. Why do you want me to go?"

"It will be a beautiful trip, and you can get to know Todd's best friend for the last twenty-two years. Todd can stay with Tim and Pamela Sue until you get back."

"I'll do it! This might be my way of seeing the world other than through the beauty shop windows."

"Anne and I are going down the basement to see if it's ok. We'll be right up."

Rick and Anne walked down the stairs and sat in the small room and waited. Anne was beside herself; she couldn't quit fidgeting. The air was filled with the strong aroma of pine needles and wood. The room went completely dark and then the desk light came on; he was sitting on the tall stool smiling at them.

"I'm sorry, Anne, for my grand entrance, but I need darkness momentarily."

Anne was completely captivated by his appearance, and demeanor. She could feel a power like she had never experienced before, almost like meeting an angel for the first time. Neither Rick nor Anne could utter a word.

"Thank you for helping me, and I think Sissy would make a fine traveling partner. I heard your conversation a few minutes ago."

"We will come by and pick you up on Tuesday morning; do you much luggage?" Rick asked

"I haven't any luggage, just a shoulder bag."

"Can I ask you some questions now?"

"Let's save our talk for the trip to New York."

"Answer me this; you mentioned Benjamin Franklin's doubt of your existence. How was that?"

"Briefly, Mr. Franklin had an illegitimate son, William. I bonded with him as a young boy and when Willy shared me as an imaginary friend, Mr. Franklin just laughed."

"I can't wait for our trip," Anne said.

"I'm looking forward to seeing my sister again. It's been one hundred and two years."

MOM'S DINER

Most of the crops were picked, and the farmers seemed relieved. The prices weren't very good this year, but the guys that planted tomatoes did very well.

"Who's going to the Harvest Dance on Saturday?" Lester asked

"We sure know Tidy and Hazel will be there. They never miss a dance or any function for that matter," Marvin said laughing.

"Bill, are Polly and you going?"

"We're going, and then we have another trip planned to Las Vegas for the National Funeral Directors Convention."

Marvin started to laugh, "I can just image what the new caskets will look like. Do the models change like cars?"

"Very funny Marvin, and yes some styles do change."

The table was now filled with laughter. "Sorry, Bill, the rest of us look at seed corn and fertilizer catalogs, so this seems completely foreign," Albert said.

"Tell you what; if I find a casket for ignorant farmers, I'll have one shipped and you can all come over and look at it."

"If it comes with a bar, count me in," Marvin said grinning.

RESTVIEW ASSISTED LIVING, ELKHORN, IOWA.

Libby and Osa pulled into the parking lot and stared at each other.

"We can do this," Libby said.

The two walked down the long hall toward their father's room. There he was in all his glory watching a daytime game show.

He glanced up, then back to the TV. "You two look like hookers," he said sarcastically.

"We love you too, Dad." Libby said.

She then walked over, unplugged the television, and took his walker to the other side of the room.

"Hey!" he yelled.

"Just shut up and listen." Libby was now regaining her confidence and stood in front of his large stuffed chair.

Osa stood off to Libby's right with her large blue eyes fixed on her father.

"You are the most evil man I've ever met. Even Judas took thirty pieces of silver for his betrayal, but you did it for free. You are charged with murder for killing three lovely women who adored you and bent to your every wish. We obeyed you and at one time even looked up to you. Those days are long gone. You gave our dog Buster more attention than the three of us combined, and now you are confined to your cell for life."

He barely looked up and Libby could see his eyes were dim, without much light. She began to pity him a little but she needed to finish.

"You robbed our mother from any dignity she might have had, and turned all the household attention to you. Our mother loved you and never one time did she ever tell Osa and me a single negative thing about you."

"She's right, Dad," Osa uttered in a quiet whisper.

He looked at each of his daughters and smiled "Like I said, hookers." "Now plug in the television and get your asses out of here!"

Libby's face turned red. She pushed the television off its stand as it crashed to the floor, and grabbed her sister's hand.

"Let's leave him to solitary confinement," and the two walked out.

He stood and shuffled to his walker. He took the walker with wheels and walked to the recreation room which had a view of the parking lot. He sat down and watched as his daughters got into Libby's car. He pushed the walker over, wept out loud and continued to weep until the car was well out of sight.

Osa looked over at Libby and said, "You know, I'm going to color my hair a bright red and just maybe I'll get a tattoo."

The two laughed all the way back to Osa's house and knew they would never come back to see their father again. Both had the peace they had longed for many, many years.

RICK AND ANNE'S FARM

Rick and Anne arrived home after their encounter with NeeNee, and they were still blown away.

"Honey, I have a million questions for NeeNee, and I know you have at least that many."

"I do, but when you see him face to face, there is something that takes your thoughts away. I mean come on, Benjamin Franklin's son? Wow!"

"I know; he was here when our country was formed."

"This sounds crazy, but I want to make love to you one more time in our bed. After Tuesday, the bed will become your parents."

"It's not crazy. I want you also, but I need to be on top."

"You can be in any position you want, but let's hope your parents don't walk in on us." He said with a laugh.

***

Tuesday came quickly, and the truck was loaded. Rick and Anne said goodbye to her parents and wished them luck living in Gas City.

"We don't need luck to live here; we just want our new friends to keep us busy," Marge said.

They drove to the beauty shop, and Sissy's bag was sitting on the steps.

"Where's NeeNee?" Rick asked

"I don't know. I haven't seen him but Todd and he had a long talk yesterday. Todd seems a little down, but Tim picked him up and told him he could drive the tractor. This will the longest time I've been away from Todd but I know Tim and Pamela Sue will keep him busy."

Rick loaded her bag and went down the basement. No NeeNee or even a trace. His truck horn started blaring, and Rick ran to the truck.

As soon as he opened the driver's side door, he got a strong whiff of pine needles and wood.

"I'm in the back seat and ready for the trip," NeeNee said.

Rick looked in the back but saw no one. He went back into the beauty shop and told them NeeNee was ready. When he got into the truck NeeNee was fastened in holding on to his little shoulder bag. Sissy sat next to NeeNee and couldn't quit staring.

"It's all right," NeeNee said in a soft voice, "I get this a lot."

"NeeNee, thank you for watching over Todd for me," Sissy said.

"I enjoyed his company, and he's a very intelligent young man. I told him that he needs to move to a group home and find a nice companion."

"What was his reaction?"

"He is in full agreement and when you get home, I think Todd will be ready to go out on his own."

Sissy started to cry. "I only want the best for him," she said between the sobs.

"I know."

Anne turned to face NeeNee, "Ok, who are you?"

"I come from a long line of special people. I was born in Norway and was captured by the English and brought to this country in 1712 just before the American Revolution. My captor was a rich Englishman, and he owned a huge tobacco plantation. He used for me for healing people, and interpreting the Native America languages. Many people did die from diseases, and I was briefly captured by the Indians. Our line has been imprisoned for generations and our powers have been used for thousands of years. I can't afford to be caught, or I'll never see my sister again."

"What kind of powers do you possess?" Rick asked.

"We can heal, move place to place undetected, become invisible for short periods of time, predict the future on a limited basis, and we have knowledge of every language that is spoken."

"Could you predict the winning lottery numbers?"

"I could give you every number every single week; that takes no effort. This why people want to capture us. If I could tell every person what would happen in their near future; don't you think everyone would want to know?"

"I see your point."

"Albert Harris spent millions trying to find me and came very close many times. With his power and me by his side, he could have been the Pope and one of the most powerful men in history."

"Will you come back to the U.S.?"

"No, I want to live out my life in Norway and be with my sister."

"Do you have any other family living?"

"I have a nephew in Sweden, and I want to connect with him. He is my sister's only child and he told about my sister. I knew what I had to do."

"Why don't you just turn invisible and travel?" Sissy asked.

"I can't stay that way for long, and I have limitations that could render me helpless. I truly need your help, and if I hadn't of trusted you, I would have taken your lives."

"You can do that?"

"I have the power to stop your heart by the very thought, but I won't. I will give you a number to reach me; if you ever have a problem, call me."

"If I want to win Powerball, I'll call." Rick said laughing.

"If that's your desire, you may call."

They traveled all night and most of the next day. NeeNee shared many stories of America's early history and stories that were told to him by his parents and grandparents of ancient history and even the building of the great pyramids. They were completely enthralled. Early the next morning NeeNee told Rick to pullover.

"Why?" Rick asked.

"Just wait."

Within a minute a truck slammed into a car on the other side of the median. The car was mangled, and the semi had overturned.

"I'll be right back," NeeNee said as the car door opened but they never saw him get out.

The police or ambulance had not arrived, but after twenty minutes there was a group of people around the wreck. The door opened and NeeNee got back in.

"What happened?" Anne asked.

"They needed my help."

"Is everyone ok?" Sissy asked.

"They are now. I had to help a four year old girl begin breathing again. When she turns twenty-three, her picture will be on the cover of Time Magazine," he said with a slight grin.

"Did you know of the accident in advance?"

"Yes, and that the little girl would be in grave danger."

The three just looked at NeeNee in total amazement. They all thought collectively, who is this guy? Really?

"How long can you stay invisible?" Rick asked.

"Depends; usually about thirty minutes."

They arrived at the New York Harbor and Sissy became nervous.

"I've never traveled overseas before."

"You have nothing to worry about; I will be next to you holding on to your arm. Just carry my bag and once on board, I'll become visible. Thank you for bringing me here; I had no one else to trust."

"You are welcome and I hope your reunion with your sister will be enjoyable," Anne said.

They hugged Sissy and NeeNee had already vanished. They got back into the truck and headed to their New York home, once again to begin a very hectic lifestyle.

THE END

Epilog Three To Five Years Later

Rahab met a drummer at music school; they dropped out after a year and traveled with a band. Her fourth time at heroin was too pure, and her heart stopped. She died at the age of seventeen and is buried in Oak Grove Cemetery close to her Dommy.

***

Tidy Tucker and Hazel got married. Their house is as neat as a pin, and they travel to Denmark three times a year.

***

Bill Sales and Polly got married and she secretly orders a lot of shoes on line.

***

Moses only attended Purdue University for a year, and, like his father, came home and married Jill Hawkins, the daughter of Chris and Jenny Hawkins from Mom's Diner. They had a baby girl and named her Rahab Sue and Pamela Sue was ecstatic. They live in Dommy's old farm house.

***

Rick was knifed at a subway stop in New York by two sixteen year olds over his cell phone. He, too, is buried at Oak Grove Cemetery in Gas City.

***

Anne became a full partner with her law firm, and is on the short list to become a Supreme Court Justice.

***

Tony and Maria got married but never loved each other, and the age of twenty three, was gunned down by his first cousin and is buried by his father. Dar attended his funeral.

***

NeeNee got to see his sister, and she is still alive, but both live in fear of being captured.

***

Anne's parents are still alive and live at Rick and Anne's farm, but Bob is getting very forgetful.

***

Eric and Billie got married, and live in Los Angeles. She is an international lawyer, and he is in international banking. They have no desire to have children.

***

Todd moved to a group home in Evansville, and has a girlfriend that will show him her boobies anytime he likes.

Sissy remolded her shop and has another beautician working with her, sharing the Gas City gossip.

***

Albert Harris's money continues to grow because no one has come forth to claim it.

***

THE END

CPSIA information can be obtained at www.ICGtesting.com
Printed in the USA
LVOW08s1025250115

424262LV00002B/546/P